THE
PERFECT HOST

Theodore Sturgeon (circa 1960).

THE PERFECT HOST

Volume V:
The Complete Stories of
Theodore Sturgeon

Edited by
Paul Williams

Foreword by
Larry McCaffery

North Atlantic Books
Berkeley, California

The Perfect Host

Published by
North Atlantic Books
P.O. Box 12327
Berkeley, California 94712

Cover art by Michael Dashow
Cover and book design by Paula Morrison

Printed in the United States of America

The Perfect Host is sponsored by the Society for the Study of Native Arts and Sciences, a nonprofit educational corporation whose goals are to develop an educational and crosscultural perspective linking various scientific, social, and artistic fields; to nurture a holistic view of arts, sciences, humanities, and healing; and to publish and distribute literature on the relationship of mind, body, and nature.

Library of Congress Cataloging-in-Publication Data

Sturgeon, Theodore
    The perfect host / Theodore Sturgeon : edited by Paul Williams : foreword by Larry McCaffery.
        p.   cm. — (The complete stories of Theodore Sturgeon. v. 5)
    ISBN 1-55643-360-3 (alk. paper)
        1. Fantastic fiction, American.   2. Science fiction, American.   I. Williams, Paul, 1948–   .   II. Title.   III. Series: Sturgeon, Theodore.   Short stories : v. 5.
PS3569.T875A6   1998 vol. 5
813'.54—dc21   98-20023
                                                                    CIP

1   2   3   4   5   6   7   8   9   /   04   03   02   01   00

EDITOR'S NOTE

THEODORE HAMILTON STURGEON was born February 26, 1918, and died May 8, 1985. This is the fifth of a series of volumes that will collect all of his short fiction of all types and all lengths shorter than a novel. The volumes and the stories within the volumes are organized chronologically by order of composition (insofar as it can be determined). This fifth volume contains stories written between late 1947 and early 1949. Two are being published here for the first time; and five others have never before appeared in a Sturgeon collection.

Preparation of each of these volumes would not be possible without the hard work and invaluable participation of Noël Sturgeon, Debbie Notkin, and our publishers, Lindy Hough and Richard Grossinger. I would also like to thank, for their significant assistance with this volume, Larry McCaffery, the Theodore Sturgeon Literary Trust, Marion Sturgeon, Jayne Williams, Dorothe Tunstall, Ralph Vicinanza, Dixon Chandler, Gordon Benson, Jr. and Phil Stephensen-Payne, Judith Merril, Tom Whitmore, William F Seabrook, Paula Morrison, Catherine Campaigne, T. V. Reed, Cindy Lee Berryhill, The Other Change of Hobbit Bookstore and all of you who have expressed your interest and support.

BOOKS BY THEODORE STURGEON

Without Sorcery (1948)
The Dreaming Jewels (1950)
More than Human (1953)
E Pluribus Unicorn (1953)
Caviar (1955)
A Way Home (1955)
The King and Four Queens (1956)
I, Libertine (1956)
A Touch of Strange (1958)
The Cosmic Rape (1958)
Aliens 4 (1959)
Venus Plus X (1960)
Beyond (1960)
Some of Your Blood (1961)
Voyage to the Bottom of the Sea (1961)
The Player on the Other Side (1963)
Sturgeon in Orbit (1964)
Starshine (1966)
The Rare Breed (1966)
Sturgeon is Alive and Well ... (1971)

The Worlds of Theodore Sturgeon (1972)
Sturgeon's West (with Don Ward) (1973)
Case and the Dreamer (1974)
Visions and Venturers (1978)
Maturity (1979)
The Stars Are the Styx (1979)
The Golden Helix (1979)
Alien Cargo (1984)
Godbody (1986)
A Touch of Sturgeon (1987)
The [Widget], the [Wadget], and Boff (1989)
Argyll (1993)
The Ultimate Egoist (1994)
Microcosmic God (1995)
Killdozer! (1996)
Star Trek, The Joy Machine (with James Gunn) (1996)
Thunder and Roses (1997)
The Perfect Host (1998)

CONTENTS

Foreword

by Larry McCaffery

I. Preliminary Remarks

"And now, though the idea behind the [Normalcy] program
was still the same ... a new idea was gaining weight daily—
to examine Irregulars always more meticulously, with a view,
perhaps to letting one live—one which might benefit all of
humanity by his very difference; one who might be a genius,
a great artist in some field.... It was the thin end of the wedge
for Homo superior, who would, by definition, be an Irregular."
—Theodore Sturgeon, "Prodigy" (1948)

INNOVATIVE ART THAT really matters—*Citizen Kane, Waiting for
Godot,* the music of Charlie Parker, John Cage, Bob Dylan and Jimi
Hendrix, Pynchon's *V.,* the short fictions of Borges, the collabora-
tions of Brecht and Weil, "The Waste Land," Picasso's *Guernica,* or
the works of Warhol and Pollock—always manages to alter funda-
mentally our notions of what a given genre can do. One of the sub-
sets of innovation that is especially attuned to postmodernism's spirit
of intertextuality, collaboration, and the dismantling of distinctions
between high art and popular culture has been the exploration by
"serious" artists of commercial genres. These sorts of artistic leaps
often have an especially broad impact precisely because the artist is
working with, and extending, codes, themes and motifs that a mass
audience is already familiar with. When an artist confounds our
expectations by exploring and extending the boundaries of a popular
genre—the way Dylan did with folk music in his pre-electric albums,

and as Sturgeon does with a variety of genres throughout this volume—the reverberations seem larger and more intimate simply because more people are in touch with (and hence can appreciate) the nature of the transformations involved.

II. A Saucer of Loneliness

Don't talk to me about the Fifties if all you're going to say are the predictable clichés about Eisenhower, prosperity, conservatism and drive-in movies. There was a lot more going on back then than tail fins, ICBMs, and McCarthyism. Like Ted Sturgeon.

The first time I encountered a work by Theodore Sturgeon was sometime in 1957. I was an eleven-year-old kid growing up in what seems, in retrospect, almost a parody of an alienating environment: living with two alcoholic parents in a hyper-repressive military community on Okinawa. And as with a lot of other alienated kids from that era, science fiction—together with rock 'n' roll—provided me with some of my first intimations about the existence of another, alternative world that was totally alien from the limited, limiting world I was living in, and yet utterly exhilarating, exotic, and alive. It was a world in which Robert Sheckley and Elvis Presley, Chuck Berry and Philip K. Dick, Jerry Lee Lewis and Ray Bradbury, Theodore Sturgeon and Little Richard were all equally important.

The writer who was most responsible for creating a bridge between me and that other, more sensuous, more exciting world of open-ended possibilities was Theodore Sturgeon. My introduction to Sturgeon's work wasn't through the usual sf magazines or books but through a chance conjunction of a radio and a tape recorder—a couple of those technological devices that were already transforming my world into something that FELT like the sf worlds I was just then reading about for the first time.[1] Of course, a lot of kids in those days had radios, but it was the tape recorder I had won one Saturday night at the Harbor View bingo game that really changed my life. This may not seem like much in today's age, where there's a Blockbuster Video store on every streetcorner and in which mechanical reproductions of all sorts are as commonplace as the common cold, but for an eleven-year-old kid to personally own a tape recorder in 1957 was a very big deal indeed. For one thing, having a tape recorder meant that I was now freed from having to save up enough money to purchase the latest tunes by Pat Boone, Chuck Berry, Jerry Lee Lewis, the Everly Brothers and Coasters, Patti Page, Dean Martin, Stan Freberg, and, above all, Elvis Presley. Elvis was especially important because my dad disapproved of Elvis so much that my playing "Heartbreak Hotel" on the living room's hi-fi set would frequently result in him taking me to the barber shop, where I would be relieved of all that unruly excess hair I kept trying (unsuccessfully) to coax into something resembling Elvis's magnificent ducktail.

The only thing more important to me in those days than being sure I had my tape recorder rolling on Saturday morning for the Top 50 radio broadcast was the ritual I observed each Thursday evening when I would slip under the covers with my radio to listen to (and record) the weekly science fiction broadcast *X Minus One*. And the first show I ever taped—one I would listen to again and again over the next few years—was "A Saucer of Loneliness" by Theodore Sturgeon.

What struck me then was how different that story seemed from all the others I was reading and listening to. Here was a story that was undeniably sf, but without any of the gadgets or alien invasions or technological extrapolations or other plot devices from that era. In today's terms, the story might be categorized as "psychological sf," but what seems most obvious is that the story is pure Sturgeon, a *love story* warmly and lyrically presented, subtly nuanced in its depiction of two people struggling to connect with other beings. Undeniably science fiction, it was also obviously a story that used its sf motifs as a means of metaphorizing a universal human condition.

III. The Professor's Teddy Bear

Twenty three years later, I finally met the man responsible for "A Saucer of Loneliness." Like other literary critics who wind up teaching and writing about science fiction, I had drifted away from the field in my late teens, and only rediscovered it when I decided in middle age to prepare a course (at San Diego State University) in contemporary science fiction. I encountered a number of pleasant surprises while doing background reading for this course, but nothing really prepared me for the shock and amazement I felt when I opened *More than Human* and read the first page. Not only did that opening passage remind me of a different passage—the opening to Benjy's section in Faulkner's *The Sound and the Fury*[2]— which had once jolted me out of my plans to pursue a career as a lawyer, but it immediately placed me back in contact with the Sturgeon stories that had so enthralled me as a young boy.

A few months later, when I discovered Sturgeon was living in San Diego, I gave him a call to see if I could entice him into visiting my class, even though I could only offer him a Mexican lunch by way of payment. Ted agreed, and in just a few weeks I was guiding Theodore Sturgeon—who in 1980 looked very much like an impish hippie, with a ponytail and bell-bottoms— to the front of a large lecture hall to answer questions from an overflow crowd of students. The q&a session that followed was one of the most memorable I've ever seen or heard. Ted quickly took control of the discussion and directed it to boldly go to realms where none of these kids had ever gone before. Mixing stories about his background and influences together with more specific anecdotes about the writing of *More than Human* that clarified some of the book's treatment of parapsychological union, Sturgeon was soon bringing to life a whole slew of issues concerning mankind's long-term potential, communication, music, sexual identity and so on. The real highlight of the class was an exchange between Ted and a gorgeous 20-year-old red-headed co-ed who somewhat timidly asked Sturgeon if he felt that *More than Human*'s notion of *homo gestalt* anticipated the experiments from the 1960s with communes, sexual experimentation, and so on. I'm not sure about the rest of the class, but I was certainly blown away when Ted proceeded to use this occasion to launch into an extended discussion, vividly illustrated by his own experiences, about marriage, jealousy, group sex, homosexuality, and his personal efforts at determining the ideal number of participants in a committed sexual relationship. My only regret about that afternoon is that I can't remember what that number was.

IV. *The Perfect Host:* Ted Sturgeon's *Sun Sessions*

The Perfect Host—the fifth installment in this grandly ambitious *Complete Stories of Theodore Sturgeon* series—is a revelation, a gift to be treasured, a mind-blower, a time machine, a stick of literary dynamite, an eye-opener. Or, to borrow an analogy from Sturgeon's own favorite resource of simile (music), it can probably best be compared to one of the more impressive of the recent "boxed set" compilations on compact disc. Like, say, *The Capitol Years: The Best of Frank Sinatra,* or *Charlie Parker: The Complete Savoy Sessions, The Perfect Host* provides enough of a representative sampling of Sturgeon's "greatest hits" (e.g., such classic Golden [Age] Oldies as "Unite and Conquer," "Prodigy," and the volume's title story) to give the uninitiated a good sense of what all the fuss was about way back when. And at the same time it offers a generous selection of alternate takes, rarities (notably several of Sturgeon's best forays into other forms of genre writing, such as his wonderfully-rendered cowpoke yarn "Scars" and his jazz-drenched tour de force crime story, "Die, Maestro, Die!"[3]), and previously unreleased cuts (including one of the volume's major finds, "Quietly," which appears to be an early warm-up for *More than Human*)—which altogether offer even the most knowledgeable Sturgeon fan the chance to gain a more complete picture of the author's influences and range, and an awareness of patterns of connection and influence that were not so evident in the stories' original formats (magazines, anthologies, radio dramatizations). Add to this Paul Williams's informative "liner notes," and some nifty new packaging, and it becomes obvious (to me) that *The Perfect Host* deserves to be considered one of the major literary events of the year. Actually, given the transformative impact that the stories from this period of Sturgeon's career had on the science fiction and fantasy genres, a more accurate comparison would be to boxed sets focused on Elvis Presley's *Sun Sessions* or Bob Dylan's *Highway 61 Revisited.*

V. Stranger in a Strange Land

As was the case with Presley's and Dylan's arrivals on the pop music scenes in their respective eras, it is difficult today to appreciate just how truly out of place—how truly "Irregular"—this totally cool-cat Sturgeon dude must have seemed while he was bebopping his way onto the center stage of the commercial sf and fantasy scenes during the late 1940s. It must have been a little as if this long-haired Italian painter named Michaelangelo had showed up as one of the illustrators for Disney back in the '30s. Indeed, Sturgeon's anti-intellectualism and mysticism, his fascination with sexual desire and other ecstatic states of human consciousness, his abhorrence for conformity (and frequent suggestion that science was not only potentially dangerous but one of the principal agents of conformity), his experiments with language and metaphor as a means of depicting the inner, irrational lives of characters, and his love of jazz—all these features indicate that the authors from this era with whom Sturgeon shared the deepest affinities were not genre writers of any sort but the Beats.

Of course, by the time Sturgeon was writing the stories included in this volume he was already recognized as one of the leading luminaries of science fiction's "Golden Age," a community of writers and a body of work that John Campbell had helped nurture as an influential magazine editor since 1937. But "Golden Age" or not, it's important to recall that this was still a fairly conservative commercial genre that Sturgeon was trying to earn his livelihood in in the late '40s. Yes, there were plenty of other talented writers around who found themselves forced to earn a living with the clichés and formula-methods of genre sf. And talented artists nearly always find ways to loosen the corset of genre expectations to give themselves enough room to move around in, personally and artistically, so that they can produce genre works that seem to them fresh and original.

On the other hand, as *The Perfect Host* demonstrates, truly *great* writers like Theodore Sturgeon are rarely content with merely loosening these restrictive norms; what they are often after are much more thoroughgoing reconfigurations that will permit them to break on through to an entirely new textual space—an alternate genre

xiv

world where they can set themselves and their readers down and begin exploring what they *really* want to write about. In this regard, one thinks of the way Dashiell Hammett recast the elements of the classical detective novel back in the late '20s to accommodate new themes and character types which contrasted starkly with those that had previously been central to the genre. The end result was the "Hard-boiled" novel, which portrayed a world in which chaos, mystery and depravity were no longer isolatable elements that could be identified, contained and eliminated via the careful application of ratiocination and logic but far more active agents permeating not merely all aspects of society, but the nature of truth and perception.

Interestingly enough, classic detective fiction shares a number of key assumptions with the science fiction field during the period when Sturgeon was writing the stories that appear in *The Perfect Host*. The most important commonality between these two genres was a faith in the power of men's minds, disciplined by logic and scientific method, to solve nature's riddles—and a consequent emphasis on characters and plot lines which embodied this faith. These norms—which had been originally championed by Campbell and had replaced the genre paradigms that had governed science fiction during the rise of the pulps in the 1930s— had helped channel the limitations of sf authors, enabling them to sacrifice a certain amount of wild imagining in order to attain a much greater degree of credibility and conviction in their work. The end result was sf which was more thoughtful and credible, which had better speculative development, and which was more effective as literature as well.

VI. More than Non-Human: Sturgeon Breaks on Through

However, even such undeniable advances within genre sf had a downside, especially for an author like Sturgeon, who was obviously unsuited by temperament to approach the craft of writing from any position requiring him to sacrifice *anything*, least of all wild imagination. Certainly the stories in *The Perfect Host* make it clear that Sturgeon had little interest in depicting the usual sort of science fiction characters (courageous, bold, self-restrained, dedicated to applying technology for the betterment of mankind).[4] or plot lines. These stories make it equally clear that by now Sturgeon had found a way to present some very radical topics indeed. These include a greater attention to semiology, philosophy, psychology and sexual desire, and a related set of concerns that would later be explored in his greatest work, *More than Human,* the postulated existence of being without ego, of a movement across the borders of a unified self, and of displacement of physical fusion onto a mental plane.

A different way to put this is that what one finds throughout these stories is a writer grappling mightily with a means of *humanizing* science fiction, often via the incorporation of stylistic features new to genre writing. Examples of Sturgeon's innovative approach to form here include his use of multiple points of view and the story-within-a-story device, stream of consciousness, poetic discontinuities and other methods of conveying the movement of the mind, and a whole host of metafictional devices.

Related to these metafictional impulses is a general foregrounding of authorial self-consciousness that wouldn't be common in sf until the late-Sixties "New Wave" work of Delany, LeGuin and others. While many of these stories are about "love" in the most obvious, romantic sense, it is equally apparent that nearly all of them are about Sturgeon's own love affair with language. Sturgeon was probably the first American sf author to bring language to the foreground of his work, not merely in the sense of unfolding his narratives within prose mannerisms that are lyrical and rely on assonance, alliteration and other poetic devices, but also in the sense of providing an ongoing (frequently hilarious) commentary on the limits of language even as they offer themselves as new possibilities of how words can function. This sort of reflexiveness and inquiry into the role of language and of the artist appears in a surprisingly large number of these selections.[5] Many of them describe individuals who are seeking a form of union and connection that will also preserve their individuality and sense of freedom. These questions, meanwhile, are frequently analogous to those of Sturgeon himself. Can he, the stories seem to be asking, find a stylistic and semiotic freedom that is not simply a meaningless cliché or incoherence? Can he find a form that will not trap him inside existing genre norms?[6] Can he construct a verbal, textual space where he will be free to examine those philosophical and psychological issues that prior sf (or crime, or fantasy, or western) spaces simply could not express?

One of the most obvious indications of Sturgeon's impulse to construct a verbal space that mediates between social space and the private, inner space of the story proper is the manner in which he chooses to constantly draw attention to his own linguistic performance. Consider the following passage, which appears near the outset of "The Hurkle Is a Happy Beast":

> "Lirht is either in a different universal plane or in another island galaxy. Perhaps these terms mean the same thing.... Now, on Lirht, in its greatest city, there was trouble, the nature of which does not matter to us, and a gwik named Hvov, whom you may immediately forget, blew up a building which was important for reasons we cannot understand... So on Lirht, while the decisions on the fate of the miserable Hvov were being formulated, gwik still fardled, funted, and fupped. The great central hewton still beat out its mighty pulse, and in the anams the corsons grew..."

This sort of playful, reflexive commentary is one of the many ways that Sturgeon demonstrates his resistance to, and liberation from, the conventions concerning how one should use words to present reality. This sort of foregrounding is reinforced by a more general self-consciousness about the strange and problematic relationship between words and things—and the problematical position of human beings, who participate in both[7]. The end result is that throughout nearly all the selections in *The Perfect Host* readers are compelled to submit to the turbulence, or share in the delight, of Sturgeon's mind working itself out in visibly verbal performances.

The obvious analogy would be jazz.

VII. CODA:
Literary Critic Announces Refutation to Sturgeon's Law

Borrego Springs, California. At a press conference today, postmodernist expert and cyberpunk promoter, Dr. Larry McCaffery announced results of recent tests he has been conducting to determine the accuracy of "Sturgeon's Law." First proposed by the late science fiction author Theodore Sturgeon in the mid-1950s, Sturgeon's Law essentially states, "Of course 90 percent of science fiction is crap, 90 percent of *everything* is crap." According to McCaffery, however, his own literary research indicates that while Sturgeon's Law is valid in the great majority of cases, there are important exceptions—specifically, Sturgeon's own stories. "After careful analysis of some 17 stories written by Sturgeon himself and collected into *The Perfect Host: Volume Five of the Complete Stories of Theodore Sturgeon,* I'm forced to conclude that Sturgeon's Law simply doesn't apply to Sturgeon's own stories." When pressed, McCaffery added that readers and critics could continue to apply Sturgeon's Law in the great majority of cases: "Careful measurements taken on a control group of non-Sturgeon stories consistently produced "crap-percentages" that were consistently in the 93 to 97 percent range; however, this percentage dropped drastically when applied to Sturgeon's own stories.

Asked if he could explain the remarkable disparity in crap-percentages, McCaffery cited a number of possible factors that might have contributed to his findings: "Empathy is undoubtedly one of the main factors. If you look at the main characters in the 17 stories I conducted my readings on, you'll find that, first of all, they're a marvelously motley crowd: you've got your usual sf types—scientists, military figures, and so on—but you've also got cowpokes, outcasts, musicians, murderers, misfits, kids, old people, idiots, geniuses, heroes, villains, and several different kinds of aliens. And yet somehow Sturgeon seemed to be able to empathize with them all, even with truly repellent figures like Fluke, the hipster jazz musician and murderer in 'Die, Maestro, Die!'"

Asked if the empathy factor might not be related to the well-known theme of 'Love' which Sturgeon himself had posited as being one of the commonalities present in all his stories, McCaffery agreed, but hastened to add, "There's no question that 'love' is one of the building blocks in all Sturgeon stories, but there's so many different kinds of love—so many "isotopes," as it were—that just noting its presence in his work doesn't really tell you much. It's like saying that carbon is one of the common features of human beings—that's true, but unless you know something about what that carbon is *combined with,* you aren't going to really know much about any given person. For instance, in the case of these particular 17 stories, my research was able to identify several different kinds of love—parental love ("Quietly," "Prodigy"), romantic love (for example, "The Martian and the Moron,""One Foot and the Grave" and "The Dark Goddess"), and of course sexual love (in "Scars," "The Music," "Till Death Do Us Join" and "Die, Maestro, Die!"). You could also say that Sturgeon 'loves' all his characters in the sense that he cares enough about them to produce some understanding of them— whereas in most crappy genre writing, the authors don't really (if you'll pardon the expression) *give a shit* about their characters, especially the bad guys. This doesn't mean he forgives them or sympathizes with them—just that he empathizes with them."

McCaffery also noted that Sturgeon's well-known stylistic virtuosity undoubtedly contriburted to the low level of crap detected in the stories he analyzed. "One of the things that my readings of these stories confirmed is that Sturgeon's stories nearly always exhibited a far greater attention to language—assonance, alliteration and other features of sound, patterns of symbol and metaphor, and so forth— than do the works in the control group."

By way of conclusion, McCaffery noted, "There's a lot of other tests that need to be done, and there will no doubt be other experiments that will contradict these findings. That's okay. Ted Sturgeon himself would have welcomed these sorts of contradictions and controversy. He always liked to keep things stirred up."

Larry McCaffery
April 1998

Foreword Notes

1. Sturgeon reminds us of how truly mind-altering radios seemed earlier in this century in several stories in *The Perfect Host*—most notably "The Martian and the Moron."

2. " 'And Faulkner—have you read any of Faulkner?' "—"The Martian and the Moron." Surely other readers and critics have noted the likely influence of Faulkner on Sturgeon's writing?

3. For what it's worth: in the humble opinion of the author of this Foreword, "Scars" and "Die, Maestro, Die!" are the two finest stories included in *The Perfect Host*.

4. To the contrary, Sturgeon's choice of characters in this volume's stories tends to run towards madmen, misfits, freaks, murderers, and other similar "abnormal" figures.

5. "The Martian and the Moron," "Unite and Conquer," "The Hurkle Is a Happy Beast," "Die, Maestro Die!", "The Perfect Host," "The Love of Heaven" and "Prodigy" are all stories that, at least on one level, can be read as allegories of the artist generally, and of the sf writer in particular.

6. "This sort of thing is strictly against the rules." —"The Perfect Host"

7. Cf.: "It isn't easy to to tell what happened next." from "One Foot and the Grave"; "It's sort of hard to describe." from Hulon, in "What Dead Men Tell"; "Damnit, it's hard to find words that make sense!" from "One Foot and the Grave"; "Please don't translate. It couldn't be phrased as well in English." from "The Martian and the Moron"; "There is no word for it." from "The Perfect Host."

Quietly

SHE WAS BORN in a house near a very old town, quietly. Her father was turning the pages of very old books, and thinking strange thoughts in the gloom of his study. Her mother lay silent and suffering, two flights above him. Her father was lost in his studies, but waiting for some sign, some faint sound of the borning. Her mother lay still by the light of a candle. The peak of her suffering came to her swiftly. Her eyes puckered deep, and they looked like the mouths of the burrows of animals scarring the face of a white limestone cliff. She stiffened, and, crushing the pillow beneath the taut arch of her nape, she bit her thin lips and she buried her nails in her palms. The breath whistled out of her delicate, quivering nostrils; and then she decided to draw no more, and in silence she trembled and died.

"You're a fool," said the doctor.

"Do your work," snapped the child's father.

The doctor went on with his work amongst the clutter and clabber of childbirth. The windows at dawn were at last showing lighter than their frames, but the light did not challenge the doctor's lamp. Rolled up and tumbled away, the bedclothes strayed off on the floor, full of hollows and shadows. Rolled away, useless and spent and inert, the body of the mother lay out of the lamplight, graying with the growing dawn.

The doctor, his supple hands saving the child, said, "My work is to heal and to cure, and to right what I can of the bungling of fools. But it is also to fight fools' work by speaking my mind. Why didn't you call me days ago? Why didn't you send her to the hospital?"

"She wouldn't have gone," said the father starkly.

The doctor glanced up at him. The father was flat, wide, tall, with a nose like an eave and sea-going eyes. "*You* couldn't have taken her? You could carry off six like her under your arm."

"She wouldn't have gone," repeated the father. "She'd have died."

"She did," said the doctor bluntly.

"Then she was bound to. I had her for a day or so more. In that time, with all she fought, she did not have to fight me as well."

The doctor wrapped up the child and put it in the waiting basket. "You loved her, didn't you?"

"That is not a doctor's question. Have you written out the things to be done and what the child will eat?"

"Yes."

"And the certificate for her?" He motioned toward the corpse. "And whatever papers are necessary for the child?"

"All those."

"You are paid."

"Too well, in money."

"Good. Now go. Do not come back here for anything, ever."

The doctor moved to a basin and washed his hands. "You'll send for me if I'm needed? Children sicken, you know."

"This one won't. I am not accustomed to failure and there will be none of it in my house. The child will not sicken."

The doctor packed his instruments, glanced around the room, and walked out. The father followed him to the door with that in his bearing which ensured the departure and was not polite. At the door the doctor turned suddenly, to stare up into the long controlled face, to look blatantly at the signs in it of the naked grief that was about to break there. "Have you no friends, man?"

"Friends!" spat the father. "There are friends about me as there is disease about you. No sickness will get the better of you if it is within your power. No friend will eat, and suck, and weaken me. Go back to your ingrown nails and your physics and your death-watches, and leave me to myself."

The doctor shrugged and left, blowing what seemed to be a taint out of his nostrils.

She was born quietly, and quietly she passed her childhood. Her father, when he thought about her silence in other terms than appreciation, thought her a mute. When she showed she was not, he felt no surprise.

The house was large and as alone as its master. The rooms and the stairs and the wide hallways were carpeted, wall to wall, with heavy gray rugs. The house was old and solid, its timbers pegged, its paneling and joinery screwed and glued and immovable. Inside the brassbound oaken slab of a door, a cushioned vestibule held a rack for shoes. Barefoot he glided about the house, and barefoot his daughter toddled until, early indeed, she learned his soundless stride.

He named her—Quietly. Quietly she grew.

She was not beautiful—not if mannequins and calendar girls are beautiful. Her face was her father's, but softened with womanliness and with something else. Her nose was his, but rounded. She had his far-horizoned gray eyes, but wide and wide-set. Her jaw was strong and planar, yet only a part of the clean complex curve of shoulder, neck and cheek. Her hair fell to her waist and was the color of black-iron heated until it just begins to glow its deepest red.

He taught her strangely. He brought her, in his teaching, not only the contents of his library, but the quintessence of his own astonishing experience. All that he said was simple—simple and quiet. He explained that often, saying,

"What is basic is simple. Complicated things are not basic, and are not important."

So everything she learned was simple. She learned about earning—that things could be had without being earned, but that without being earned, they could not be kept. She learned about fear—that it's not a shameful thing, nor a foolish one, since it is the essence of self-preservation; but that he who truly hides his fear is accepted as superior. She learned about giving—that to give is to get, but that to give too much is to take and to lose. She learned to define evil: that which is extreme. She learned to define good: that which is moderate. She learned, above all, to be alone. She learned to accept aloneness at any time—halfway through a meal, or on waking, or even in the midst of a lesson, for her father would sometimes leave a sentence unfinished and step out of the room, to be gone, sometimes, for days. There were occasions when there was no food in the house, or when there was food hidden. In these cases, she did without, or she went into the woods and made snares and caught small animals or collected berries and wild birds' eggs. The one inexcusable offense was to sit frightened and bleat her father's name. That happened once, and all her life she bore the scar of it, for he shouted at her. Her conditioning made her immune to the one thing that had taken her father by surprise—the dreadful fact that aloneness can come to any human being, without warning or justice.

"If you ever leave me," he said once, "you must find your own way."

"Why would I ever leave you?"

"Because you must. You will. For a year."

"You sometimes speak as if you knew the future, Father."

"I do," he responded immediately. "I do because I make my own."

"I'll never leave you," she said positively, and he smiled.

She hunted, but only to eat. She loved flowers, but never cut one. She ran and climbed, and in the warm days would leave the house naked and leap through the meadows to the woods which began at the top of the hill. She followed secret glades and deer-runs known only to her, to a secret pool, cold in the shade, but with its margins all but steaming at the end of three midday hours, when the sun vaulted over it on a thick pillar of light.

One August evening, after swimming and drying her clean brown body in the sun, she returned to the house by the orchard path, stopping for a while by her rabbit-hutches. When the lengthening shadows reminded her of the hour, and her healthy young appetite gave a sudden and hearty seconding, she skipped to the kitchen door.

It was locked.

She paused, a small frown flickering between her wide-set eyes, then shrugged. Small and unexpected changes in her environment were part of her father's way. "Nothing is 'always,' Quietly," he had often said. "Look, child. The spoon is in the drawer. It is there today. It was there yesterday and last year. So by all means say 'The spoon is in the drawer.' But when you say 'the spoon is *always* in the drawer,'

4

you are saying, partly, 'The spoon will be in the drawer tomorrow.' You can't know that!"

The kitchen door had always been unlocked until now. . . . She shrugged, and went round to the side door.

The side door and the front door and the wide doors over the cellar steps, and the bedroom windows which opened on the roof of the shed—they were all locked.

She went back to the kitchen door and stood looking at it. She was eighteen now, strong, well-balanced as she shifted her weight from one bare foot to the other, well-balanced as she thought.

She was hungry and naked. It was growing cool. She gazed without expression at the expressionless windows. A small breeze stroked her body, leaving a brief puckering of gooseflesh. She stepped to the door and tried it again. It never occurred to her to knock. If her father were inside at all, the chances were that he would be in the study or upstairs, to be called only by thunderous hammering—something unthinkable in that house. There could be no possibility that her father had locked the doors by mistake, for he was not a man who made mistakes.

Well, then, she must wait. She went to the shed, which was warm and dry, if nothing else. But—it was locked. So was the barn.

Then she knew.

"You must find your own way . . . you will leave. You must. For a year. . ." It had been that way when first she was left by herself in the house; when first lunch-time had come and she suddenly realized that he had made no effort to prepare it. Always there had been a warning beforehand, buried in a lesson, perhaps, or mentioned casually in conversation. And this was like him. She must leave, but she would not be sent away, with clothes and money and a starting-place somewhere.

She went into the garden and looked about her. The tomatoes were green, but edible. It would be a crime to take any of the baby ears of corn, but in this emergency . . . she shook her head stubbornly. Not the corn. Let it grow. It was not responsible for her plight. A rabbit, then.

She walked to the hutches. The rabbits tumbled towards her, wanting more food. She smiled at them. There had always been rabbits. Always ... suddenly it became clear to her that these rabbits were part of the place, as the corn was, as were the tomatoes. And she no longer had any part of it.

She nodded, looked briefly, bleakly, up at the house and strode away through the orchard. She did not look back for an hour, when she was on the mountain's shoulder. Then she paused.

The house was invisible now, and dark. So he had gone away. She wondered remotely if she hated him. She had never hated anything in her life. She missed him, however, as much as one can who has never attached any importance to the idea of loneliness.

Beyond the house, far beyond, the lights of the town drifted like crumbs in a cup of ink. She had had no compulsion to go to the town. She was not known there, but she knew that she resembled her father very strongly, and that she would be brought back to the house by well-meaning but uncomprehending strangers who would do what they could to upset her father's plans for her. She did not question those plans for a moment. Her father held a position in her cosmos outside such mutable abstracts. His law governed her as completely as did gravity.

The wind touched her again, colder now, and, as before, its breath brought her back to her immediate problem. She cast about her for a fallen tree, found one, and broke off a thick four-foot piece. She worked her way carefully into the darkening forest. A glance up through the trees told her that tonight, at least, she need not fear rain.

She chose a spot where two large trees grew close together, with a bed of moss at their roots. She gathered up dry leaves and piled them up over and beside the moss. Setting her club close to her hand, she lay down, pulled a mountain of leaves over her, and almost instantly lost her hunger in a deep sleep.

She woke before the sun was up, rested and ravenous. She stood up, shaking the leaves from her firm body, and immediately set about the business of breakfast. Retracing her steps of the night before,

6

she reached a meadow. She gathered clover heads and tender shoots of upland grass, and found, to her joy, the "walking" vine known as a Judas traveller. She uprooted about twenty feet of its tough, meandering stem and carefully stripped it until she had ten or twelve feet of flexible withe. This she took back into the woods, made a noose-snare by tying down a sapling so that when triggered, it would snap up and draw the noose tight. She put down the clover and shoots as bait, blocking them from behind so that they must be approached through the noose, and then went back to the meadow. She selected some round, smooth stones, and then stepped to a tree at the edge of the forest, put her back against the trunk, and stood there motionless.

The sun was up now. Great lazy clouds floated overhead, brindling the hills. She saw a woodchuck out on the meadow, and let it be. Hungry as she was, she did not consider its rank flesh worth the trouble of cutting it off from its nearby burrow. She waited patiently.

A movement caught her eye—something like a clump of grass moving within the field of grass. Moving very carefully, she set down her handful of stones. She raised her club up and back in her right hand, and with her left tossed a pebble to the side of the moving thing she had seen. As it fell, the surprised head of a grouse popped upward. Quietly's club, unerringly thrown to turn end over end in a horizontal plane, caught the bird solidly on its ruff. In a half-dozen great bounds she was on the stunned creature and had wrung its neck.

She carried it back into the woods toward the two trees where she had slept. On her way was the snare. The sapling was upright, and a fat cottontail hung kicking in the noose. It had caught him around the withers; he was very much alive and frightened. Quietly looked at him thoughtfully for a moment, then dropped her grouse and bent the sapling down, catching the rabbit deftly at the nape of the neck. She slackened the noose, smoothed the animal's rumpled fur, and let him go, smiling a little as his powder-puff quarters disappeared through the trees. She had the grouse, and no way to carry anything extra. In addition, she had perfect confidence in her ability to get more food when she wanted it.

From a basalt outcropping she got an edged stone. She stripped some dead reeds for the soft, dry pith inside, crumbled it, and pounded with the stone on the rock until she had a spark. Nursing it carefully with her breath, feeding it with more pith and then with leaves, she soon had a healthy little fire. She spitted the bird with a green stick, singed it, plucked it. Then, pinching out the soft underflesh, she cut it with her stone against the rock and cleaned the grouse. With two forked sticks she made a frame for the spit. She piled stones around her fire to shelter it and to concentrate the heat. Then she squatted beside it and, between turnings, occupied herself by patiently combing out her long heavy hair with her fingers, and braiding it tightly.

At last it was ready—or at least, ready enough for her clamoring appetite. She ate slowly, however, and she ate the whole bird. She took the neck-bones apart for the tiny succulent strips of muscle there, and she cracked the other bones and sucked out the marrow. Then she gathered up the remains, scooped out a hole, and buried them. She drew up a large chunk of root to the fire, to keep it fed for the next few hours, wiped her hands and mouth carefully on some grass, and with a green twig meticulously cleaned her teeth.

Then she stretched out in a bright patch of warm mid-morning sun and quietly, half somnolently, began to think.

She had nothing—no clothes, no shelter, no knife or axe or other tools. She did not question the fact that she must take care of herself completely for at least a year.

She was not worried, and she was certainly not frightened. Fear is a functional thing, and she was happy to yield to it when it had a function. Now it had none, so she was not afraid.

She rolled over and cupped her chin in her hands. Food? Well, hunting was good. She could snare or club what she needed, and if she had to go a day or two without, she could stand it. There would be nuts and berries throughout the fall, and eggs aplenty in the spring and early summer. There was plenty of ash to be fire-cured and shaped and trimmed with stone, so that she could make bows and arrows. She had killed deer before this way. Clothing? She wanted none, at least until the cold came. By then she should have enough pelts to keep her warm—fox and deer and skunk and possibly coon and beaver. There were caves in these parts; she could certainly find one. She could make rope from grasses for her snares, and possibly dig a pitfall or two. It would be hard, sometimes, but she would survive.

She lay still for a long while, her mind flickering over this detail and that. Gradually she let it go blank. *What is complicated is by definition not important.* This above all was her father's creed, and she had learned from babyhood that, after a time of preoccupation with details, it paid to leave them for a while to see what basic, if any, emerged from their framework.

It came, without effort on her part. It was a sudden realization that her father had not turned her out so that she could prove her woodcraft. That was past proving. Had he expected her to live off the land for a year, he could have judged her ability to do it years ago without this specific trial. No, he expected her to go farther.

She forced her thoughts to turn to the towns. The only one she had ever seen was the one near the house. She had never been there, but she had seen it from the mountainside. She remembered:

"Why are they all clustered together like sheep in the winter, Father?"

"Like botflies on carrion," he had answered. "They are built that way because they are used by folk who cannot bear to be by themselves."

"Why not?"

"Each of them seeks better company than he finds when he is alone. You'll see for yourself, one day."

Quietly sat up and looked at the trees around her, and listened for a moment to the whispering song of their high branches. She shut her eyes and remembered the pictures she had seen, of crowds pushing up narrow, dirty streets, of ill-kempt children and of fat, bald, sickly doctors whose duty it was to heal and to cure. She thought of the noble things: great curved dams and high buildings with their windows lit. So much that was wrong—so much that was not wrong but was simply inconsistent. And it would be noisy, noisy, noisy.

Why not live out her year here in the hills, with her fire-building and her hunting and her thoughts? It would not be so different; her father had said, "The same laws, the same forces, apply to men

everywhere as apply to beasts. Kill or be killed, fill your belly, reproduce your kind. The difference is only in the fact that men kill and
eat and reproduce beyond necessity, without regard to their basic
need."

That was it, then—that difference which he wanted her to see.
And why not let her accept the truth of it, without this?

She remembered again—years back. "Quietly, what would it feel
like if I hit you, hard, with my open hand?"

She had considered, carefully. "It would thump and it would
sting."

He had nodded, and then lashed out brutally and struck her. It
was one of the very few times when he had suddenly gathered her
up and held her close. She was stiff and silent for a long moment.
Then she trembled and hid her face in his shoulder, and cried without making a sound. He held her, rocking her a little, until she quieted, and then said, "Never forget this, child. You did not cry when
you answered my question. You could not; you had no reason to.
You did *not* know what it would feel like. Now you are crying. Imagination is a good thing, but it can only approximate experience. You
can only learn by doing. If ever you want to know what a thing is
like, do it, Quietly, do it."

Quietly rose and stepped to her fire to push the root-chunk further into the coals. She had a year, and the decision of what to do
with it was hers. Her father's wish was obviously that she live out
her year in the world—other people's world. She could follow his
wish, or not. If she did not, she would survive; by the same token,
she had no doubt of surviving if she did what he obviously wanted.
Survival was not the question, nor was it a matter of which she would
enjoy the most; for enjoyment had always been a substance to be
squeezed from events as they were lived, and she would enjoy what
she did, or not, only as her capacity for enjoyment changed, and not
as events dictated. The important consideration sprang from her
training. If, in any matter, she did what was expected of her, she was
rewarded by the food or the quiet or the freedom her action had
earned. If she did not do as her father wished, she took the consequences—not in punishment from him, but in the exact deprivation

that her lack warranted. If it were made possible for her to eat, and through her own choice she did not eat, then she went hungry. If, in the afternoon, she refused the privilege of a certain one of her father's books, that book was unavailable to her in the evening. To accede to her father's wishes was invariably to do the functional thing, to make the most of opportunity when it offered itself; and so rigorously did he control his environment—and hers—that there never had been an accident which proved this principle false.

To stay in the hills, or to go to the towns . . . she was free to choose. Purely by the placement of events, she knew which her father wished her to do. The fact that she did not want the opportunity to live among other people was unimportant. The fact that she may never have another opportunity if she did not take this one was important, vitally so.

She stared into the fire, felt its radiant heat, watched its pale sunlit flames. The living flame was the symbol of her competence here in the hills. Its vitality was the product of her own hands. She was its master.

Abruptly she bent, scattered it, kicked earth over its coals, turned the heavy, glowing chunk face downward in the ground and palmed earth around it. Then she marched off, leaving behind her, already forgotten, the dwindling smoke of her indecision.

By evening she had crossed the range through a high pass, and was descending the westward slope. Twice she had seen people, and both times she had kept herself hidden. She was determined to live with people, but she wished to choose her own point of entrance. The first she saw was a young man in what she considered a bewildering amount of clothing—rough shoes, heavy socks, breeches and a flannel shirt, and over all a knapsack and a bandolier. She gained on him, keeping to the rocks in the pass, and was about to call when he stopped, aimed his rifle at some movement on the hillside, and fired. The roar of the gun caught Quietly completely by surprise, and she dropped behind a boulder, rocking back and forth, with her hands over her ears. She had heard guns before, but never this close. She peered out after a moment; he was staring fixedly across the cut, with his gun resting on his left forearm. He raised it abruptly and fired twice more, waited, shrugged, and then trudged off. Quietly sat watching him in utter amazement and disgust. Far off on the hillside she could discern the jerky motions of a rock-squirrel kicking and kicking its life away. The man had hit it with his first bullet, and had fired again as it writhed there. It was wanton; it was useless. Quietly felt no particular pity for the animal; she was not a sentimentalist, and had a scale of values for the lower orders. What offended her was the waste of a life, of powder, even of skill—the skill of the man himself and that of the precision workers who had made his weapon. He had not wanted the creature for fur or flesh, but had as his only apparent desire an affirmation of the evident fact that he was bigger and stronger and more intelligent than a chipmunk. Enter civilization she would, but not in the company of this pervert.

Her second encounter was just over the crest of the mountain. There was a well-beaten trail following the ridge, and near the point at which she encountered it was a shelter made of logs, and roofed startlingly with asphalt shingle. There were neat piles of wood stacked beside it, and from it came the rhythmic sound of a voice—a light, full voice, chanting in a near-monotone. Quietly drew closer, stopped near the open window with one hand on the logs, and listened:

> *"One moment in Annihilation's Waste,*
> *One moment, of the Well of Life to taste—*
> *The Stars are setting and the Caravan*
> *Starts for the Dawn of Nothing—OH! make haste!"*

The "OH!" emerged as an explosive squeak. Quietly started and pursed her lips. What *was* this?

> *"How long, how long, in definite Pursuit*
> *Of This and That endeavor and dispute? . . .*

(and here the voice rang with something between a toll and a tinkle)

> *. . . Better be merry with the fruitful Grape*
> *Than sadder after none, or bitter, Fruit."*

Slowly, Quietly leaned to the window and with one eye peered inside.

A thin young man with a pot-belly, dressed in shorts which emphasized his bony knees, strode back and forth within the shelter, holding in front of him a battered book with a rococo cover done in gray and tarnished gold. His face was pink, his nose was peeling, and the backs of his legs were fish-belly white.

On the earthen floor by the far wall crouched a girl of about Quietly's age, with coarse hair, spectacles, bad teeth and an adoring expression. "Oh, Carstairs," she cooed, as the young man stopped to blow his nose on a khaki handkerchief, "You read gorgeously— just *gorgeously!* Anyone can tell—" and here her voice became a whisper—"that you've really *lived!*"

Quietly fled.

Three hours and ten miles later, Quietly walked the timberline tiredly, wondering whether to keep to the woods and kill something for her supper, or to go on until she found some suitable crevice between the scales of civilization into which she might crawl. She was hungry and she had come a long way. She skirted cornfields now, and buckwheat, and for a while she followed a fence which enclosed grazing land, though she saw no cattle. She judged that she had another two hours of light and an hour of dusk. If she were going to a make a snare, she would have to do it very soon.

Suddenly she stopped, head up, nostrils dilating. From the woods to the right she heard faint sounds of splashing and calling. A pleasant vision of cool water crossed her mind. She had found a spring about noon, and had been able to wet her face and arms in it and drink, but that had been hours ago. She turned toward the sounds.

She reached a creek about a quarter of a mile north, and followed it upstream a few hundred yards to its source, a small spring-fed lake surrounded by trees. Across the water was a shelving bank, on which were scattered towels and robes and clothing. Splashing about in the water were five girls, screaming and giggling and quite as naked as she. She sat down in the shadows between the trees to watch them.

She noticed with some surprise that their bodies were tanned except for patches of white around their breasts and hips. She nodded to herself. She had learned of the clothing convention, and was quite aware that it was of major importance among people "outside." This piebald tanning was a strong reminder to her of the fact that she must circumscribe her own behavior to this and many another taboo if she were to win acceptance among people.

She tried to remember if this taboo applied in a group of the same sex, and could not remember immediately. It obviously did not apply to the girls in the lake. Yet if she, an outsider, appeared among them, it might be regarded as a violation.

There was a violent spasm of coughing from the water. One of the girls was floundering near the middle of the pond, her breath coming raggedly. Immediately there was a commotion among the others.

"Bee! Bee-*triss!* Clara—look! Bee's drownding!"

There was a chorus of frightened exclamations. One of the girls said, "I'm going after her!"

"No!" cried another. "You can't swim well enough! You'll drown too!" and she laid restraining hands on the would-be rescuer, who half-heartedly fought her off. The other two climbed out of the water as if it were suddenly hot, and stood on the bank, where they could see better, wringing their hands.

"Oh-h!" moaned the one called Clara. "Miss O'Laughlin will kill us for this. We're not allowed to swim without suits!"

"She'll never know if we don't tell her," chattered one of the girls on the bank.

"She will too when they find Bee's body," said the other ghoulishly.

"We could say that only Bee—"

"Help! Help!" screamed the would-be savior.

"Help!" all the girls screamed, including the one who was drowning.

There are certain zones of indecency, Quietly was thinking, peculiar to certain lands and certain times. In certain tribes in Africa virgins must go naked until they marry, when custom demands that they don a narrow belt. In the Far East it has long been the custom to cover the faces of the women. In Bali the only woman who covers her breasts is the courtesan. The question is, would the effect of my saving this girl be cancelled by my indecency in their eyes?

It was a very complicated matter. She wished— Complicated? Unimportant, then. What was important? That she, Quietly, be accepted sooner or later. Was there anything more important here?

Yes, there was. A life was being lost uselessly. If saving it meant the disapproval of these people, she could get away from them and try again.

She slipped into the water, took a deep breath, found a rock under her feet and pushed off strongly. She swam fifty feet under water, with the breath trickling deliciously from her nostrils and tickling the dusty sides of her neck. She broke surface and trod water, getting her bearings. The drowning girl was not in sight. She glanced at the bank. The four girls were all out of the water now, clutching at each other in a noisy, hysterical ecstasy. She heard one of them say, "All this yelling ... have the whole countryside here in a minute ... where's my sunsuit?" Then, from the corner of her eye, she saw a disturbance in the water. She swung to it and sounded. She found bottom at about fourteen feet, according to the pain in her ears. She beat her way along it, until something thumped her on the shoulder. She rolled over and looked up, and in the dimness saw the doubled-up body of the girl Beatrice, with weakly flailing hands and round, terrified eyes.

Quietly got her feet under her and sprang upward, winding her hand in the girl's long hair as she shot past. They came to the surface together, the last of Quietly's wind whooshing out of her. She slipped her arm around the girl's neck, and with a thrust of her knee turned the half-unconscious creature over on her back. With Bee's chin in the crook of her arm, her shoulder holding Bee's head up, Quietly swam for shore with a powerful side-stroke.

"Look!" squeaked one of the girls.

"It's a *man!*" gasped Clara, and dived for her clothes.

"It is *not,*" said another, already in a brief sunsuit.

The four stood open-mouthed as Quietly found footing and

stepped up the bank, carrying Beatrice in her arms. Two of them splashed into the water to clutch and grab and weep. "Speak to me, Bee darling!" Quietly shouldered her way through them with such directness that the girl in the sunsuit sat forcibly in the water.

"Who's *she?*"

"She *pushed* me!"

Quietly swung her burden to the ground, turned the limp body over with her foot so that it was face-down, and knelt with one of her knees between the girl's lower thighs. She turned Bee's head to the right, separated the clenched teeth, pulled the tongue out, and then began a steady pressure and release on her floating ribs.

"Get a towel!"

"Chafe her wrists!"

"Where did *she* come from?"

"Is she dead?" asked Clara of Quietly. Quietly said nothing. She was counting to herself, to get the rhythm right.

"Miss O'Laughlin'll *murder* us!"

"Will you *look* at the calluses on her *feet!*"

"Bee's dead! Oh, oh, oh-h-h!"

"No she's not. She's upchucking."

Quietly slacked off until the weak spasm had paused, and then went on. A minute later Bee moaned and coughed. Quietly sat back on her haunches and waited. The breathing was irregular, but stronger. She rose and turned the girl over on her back. The four immediately clustered around, weeping, lifting Bee's head, rubbing her wrists, begging her to say something. Quietly could have walked off at that moment and it would never have been noticed. Instead she stood by, her face impassive, concealing a mingled amazement and amusement at this stupendous misdirection of nervous energy.

Bee was helped to a sitting position now, supported by the affectionate arms of her friends. She began to cry softly. Clara, for the moment deprived of anything to embrace by the importunities of the other three, rose and came to Quietly.

"Say," she said, "That was wonderful of you. I just don't know what we would've done without you, really I don't."

Quietly smiled. Clara asked, "Where did you come from? You seemed to come right up out of the bottom of the lake!"

Quietly hesitated. There was something she had been taught once about this kind of situation ... She remembered it now. Her father had been reading aloud; it was one of the eighteenth-century picaresque novels. At its involved climax, he put the book down and said,

"You see the amount of trouble a man can get into by talking too much, Quietly? Among men, the less you say, the better. Human beings have, among their other diseases, a crazy desire to explain things, each in his own way. If a man knows little about you, he will fill in the details to suit himself. If you tell him all the details, the chances are that he will not believe you. Let him, and all his brethren, draw his own conclusions about you, and neither confirm nor deny anything. Then he may compliment himself on his insight, and you may be assured of your privacy. The most fortunate humans are those who, by preoccupation or through illness, find themselves deaf and dumb."

All language has its labeling nuances, its idiom, its little signposts of accent and emphasis. Quietly knew that her progress among people would be faster if she could start at the level of her first associates. If to say little was good, to say nothing would be even better. So, in answer to Clara's questions, she simply smiled.

"What's the matter; can't you talk?"

Quietly shook her head.

"You can hear me all right, though."

Quietly nodded.

Clara left her standing there and went to the group around Beatrice. There was a rapid and exclamatory conference and some pointing and gaping.

The Music

Hospital . . .

They wouldn't let me go, even when the clatter of dishes and the meaningless talk and complaining annoyed me. They knew it annoyed me; they must have. Starch and boredom and the flat-white dead smell. They knew it. They knew I hated it, so every night was the same.

I could go out. Not really; not all the way out, to the places where people were not dressed in gray robes and long itchy flannel. But I could go outside where I could see the sky and smell the river smell and smoke a cigarette. If I closed the door tight and moved all the way over to the rail, and watched and smelled very carefully, sometimes I could forget the things inside the building and those inside me, too.

I liked the night. I lit my cigarette and I looked at the sky. Clotted, it was, and clean between clouds. The air was cold and warmed me, and down on the river a long golden ribbon was tied to a light on the other side, and lay across the water. My music came to me again, faintly, tuning up. I was very proud of my music because it was mine. It was a thing that belonged to me, and not to the hospital like the itchy flannel and the gray robe. The hospital had old red buildings and fences and a great many nurses who knew briskly of bedpans, but it had no music about it, anywhere, anywhere.

A light mist lay just above the ground because there were garbage cans in a battered row, and the mist was very clean and would not go among them. Entrance music played gently for the cat.

It was a black and white mangy cat. It padded out of the shadow into the clearing before the cans and stood with its head on one side, waving its tail. It was lean and moved like a beautiful thing.

Then there was the rat, the fat little brown bundle with its long

18

worm of a tail. The rat glided out from between the cans, froze, and dropped on its belly. The music fell in pitch to meet the rise in volume, and the cat tensed. There was a pain about me somewhere and I realized distantly that my fingernails were biting into my tongue. *My* rat, *my* cat, *my* music. The cat sprang, and the rat drew first blood and squealed and died out there in the open where it could see its own blood. The cat licked its wound and yowled and tore at the quivering thing. There was blood on the rat and on the cat and on my tongue.

I turned away, shaken and exultant, as the music repeated its death-motif in echo. She was coming out of the building. Inside she was Miss Starchy but now she was a brown bundle—a little fat brown bundle. I was lean and moved like a beautiful thing ... she smiled at me and turned to the steps. I was very happy and I moved along beside her, looking down at her soft throat. We went out into the mist together. In front of the cans she stopped and looked at me with her eyes very wide.

The cat watched curiously and then went on eating. We went on eating and listening to the music.

Unite and Conquer

THEY WERE DIGGING this drainage canal, and the timekeeper drove out to the end, where the big crane-dragline was working, and called the operator down to ask a lot of questions about a half-hour of over-time. Next thing you know, they were going round and round on the fill. The young superintendent saw that fight and yelled for them to cut it out. They ignored him. Not wanting to dirty his new breeches, the super swung up into the machine, loaded three yards of sand into bucket, hoisted it high, swung, and dumped it on the scrambling pair. The operator and the timekeeper floundered out from under, palmed sand out of their eyes and mouths, and with a concerted roar con-verged on the cab of the machine. They had the super out on the ground and were happily taking turns punching his head when a labor foreman happened by, and he and his men stopped the fuss.

The red-headed youngster put down the book. "It's true here, too," he told his brother. "I mean, what I was saying about almost all of Wells' best science fiction. In each case there's a miracle—a Martian invasion in 'War of the Worlds,' a biochemical in 'Food of the Gods,' and a new gaseous isotope in 'In the Days of the Comet.' And it ulti-mately makes all of mankind work together."

The brother was in college—had been for seven months—and was very wise. "That's right. He knew it would take a miracle. I think he forgot that when he began to write sociological stuff. As Dr. Pierce remarked, he sold his birthright for a pot of message."

"Excuse me," said the dark man called Rod. He rose and went to the back of the café and the line of phone booths, while the girl with the tilted nose and the red sandals stared fondly after him. The Blonde arrived.

"Ah," she mewed, "alone, I see. But of course." She sat down.

"I'm with Rod," said the girl with the sandals, adding primly, "He's phoning."

"Needed to talk to someone, no doubt," said the Blonde.

"Probably," said the other, smiling at her long fingers, "he needed to come back to earth."

The Blonde barely winced. "Oh well. I suppose he must amuse himself between his serious moments. He'll have one tomorrow night, you know. At the dance. Pity I won't see you there. Unless, of course, you come with someone else—"

"He's working tomorrow night!" blurted the girl with the sandals, off guard.

"You could call it that," said the Blonde placidly.

"Look, sunshine," said the other girl evenly, "why don't you stop kidding yourself? Rod isn't interested in you and your purely local color. He isn't even what you want. If you're looking for a soulmate, go find yourself a wolfhound."

"Darling," said the Blonde appreciatively, and with murder in her mascara. "You know, you might get him, at that. *If* you brush up on your cooking, and if he can keep his appetite by going blind—" She leaned forward suddenly. "Look there. Who *is* that floozy?"

They turned to the back of the café. The dark young man was holding both hands of a slender but curvesome girl with deep auburn hair. She was laughing coyly up at him.

"Fancy Pants," breathed the girl with the red sandals. She turned to the Blonde. "I know whereof I speak. Her clothesline is right under my window, and—"

"The little stinker," said the Blonde. She watched another pretty convulsion of merriment. "Clothesline, hm-m-m? Listen—I had a friend once who had a feud on with a biddy in the neighborhood. There something about a squirt gun and some ink—"

"Well, well," said the girl in the sandals. She thought a moment, watching Rod and the redhead. "Where could I get a squirt gun?"

"My kid brother has a water pistol. I got it for him for his birthday. Can you meet me here at seven o'clock?"

"I certainly can. I'll get the ink. Black ink. *India* ink!"

The Blonde rose. "Be sweet to him," she said swiftly, " so he won't guess who fixed Fancy Pants."

"I will. But not too sweet. The heel. Darling, you're wonderful—"

The Blonde winked and walked away. And at a nearby table, a gentleman who had been eavesdropping shamelessly stuffed a soft roll into an incipient roar of laughter, and then began to choke.

"Colonel Simmons," said the annunciator.

"Well, for pete's sake!" said Dr. Simmons. "Send him in. Send him right in! And—cancel that demonstration. No . . . don't cancel it. Postpone it."

"Until when, Doctor?"

"Until I get there."

"But—it's for the Army—"

"My brother's the Army, too!" snapped the physicist and switched off.

A knock. "Come in. Leroy, you dog!"

"Well, Muscles." The colonel half ran into the room, gripped the scientist by the upper arm, scanned his face up, back, and across. Their eyes were gray, the colonel's gray and narrow, the doctor's gray and wide. "It must've been—" they said in unison, and then laughed together.

"Eight years, anyway," said the colonel.

"All of that. Gosh, gosh." He shook his head. "You and your shiny buttons."

There was a silence. "Hardly know where to begin, what to say, h-m-m?" grinned the colonel. "What've you been doing lately?"

"Oh . . . you know. Applied physics."

"Hah!" snorted the colonel. "Question: Mr. Michaelangelo, what are you doing? Answer: Mixing pigments. Come on, now; what since you invented magnefilm?"

"Nothing much. Couple of things too unimportant to talk about, couple more too important to mention."

"Your old garrulous self, I see. Come on, Muscles. Security regulations don't apply here, and between us especially."

That's what you think, thought Dr. Simmons. "Of course not," he said. "What branch are you with now?"

"Publicly, the Air Corps," said the colonel, indicating his wings. "Actually, I'm on the Board of Strategy. This won't be the kind of war which can be fought with semipublic conferences and decisions after advisement in the General Staff. The Board operates practically underground, without any publicity, and without any delay."

"Board of Strategy, eh? I'd heard only vaguely . . . and I'm in a position to hear plenty. Well now. When you say no delay, what do you mean?"

"I mean this," said the colonel. He put his hands behind him on a high lab table and lifted himself up on it. He crossed his bright boots and swung them. "We have plans . . . look; you know how M-Day plans work, don't you?"

"Certainly. The personnel of draft boards is all chosen, the questionnaires are printed and almost entirely distributed, the leases and domains of examination centers are arranged for, and so on and on. When mobilization is called, everything starts operating without a hitch. You hope," he added with a grin. "Why?"

"The Board operates the same way," said his brother. "But where Selective Service has only one big problem to arrange for in detail we have—" he shrugged. "Name your figure. We have planned what to do if, for example, Russia attacks us, if we attack Russia, if France attacks Brazil, or if Finland takes a swing at Iraq. What's funny?"

"I was thinking of the legend about the emperor who tried to grant the reward asked for by a certain hero, who had stipulated simply that he be given some wheat, the amount to be determined by a hypothetical chessboard, putting one grain on the first square, two on the second, four on the third, eight on the fourth, and so on . . . anyway, it wound up with an amount equal to a couple of years' world supply, and with the empire and all its resources in the hands of our hero. Your plans are like that. I mean, if one of the possibilities you mention should occur, but if you should lose the third battle instead of winning it as scheduled, why, you'll have a whole new set of plans to make. And this applies to every one of your original master plans."

"Oh, don't misunderstand me. I don't mean that each plan is as detailed as the M-Day deal. Lord, no. The plans are policies of action, rather than blueprints. They stay within the bounds of statistical probability, though we push those bounds outward as far as possible. I've mentioned possible enemies, and possible combatants aside from enemies. There are also plans covering combinations and permutations of alliance. Anything is possible after such precedent, for example, as the situation in the Second War, when our close ally Russia was at peace with our worst enemy." He laughed. "If that happened in human instead of international terms, with my closest friend lunching daily with a man who was openly trying to kill me, we'd call it fantastic. Maybe it is," he said cheerfully, "but it's most engrossing."

"You rather enjoy it, don't you?"

"I have never had such fascinating work in all my life."

"I didn't mean strategy, soldier-boy. I meant war."

"War? I s'pose it is. Now another thing the Board is doing . . . wait a minute. Muscles! You're not still the dewy-eyed idealist you used to be—brotherhood of mankind, and all that, are you?"

"I invented the sonic disruptor, didn't I?" *You probably think that answers your question,* he thought bitterly.

"So you did. A very healthy development in you and in the noble art of warfare. Nicest little side arm in history. Busts a man all up inside without breaking the skin. So little mess."

Healthy! Dr. Simmons stared at his brother, who was looking into his cigarette case. *Healthy! And I developed the disruptor to focus ultrasonic vibrations under the skin, to homogenize cancerous tissue. I never dreamed they'd . . . ah, neither did Nobel.* "Go on about the Board," he said.

"What was I . . . oh yes. Not only have we planned the obvious things—political situations, international crises, campaigns and alliances, but we are keeping a very close watch on technology. The War Department has, at long last, abandoned the policy of fighting this war with the last war's weapons. Remember how Hitler astonished the world with the elementary stunt of organizing liaison between his tanks and his dive bombers? Remember the difficulties they had in promoting the bazooka to replace the mortar in jungle warfare? And how the War Department refused to back the Wright Brothers? There'll be no more of that."

"You mean we're preparing to use the latest in everything? Really use it?"

"That's right. Atomic energy and jet propulsion we know about. Then there's biological warfare, both disease and crop-hormone techniques. But it doesn't stop there. As a matter of fact, those things, and other proven developments, account for only a small part of our plans. We have the go-ahead on supplies, weapons, equipment, and techniques which haven't even been developed yet. Some haven't even been invented yet!"

Dr. Simmons whistled, "Like what?"

The colonel smiled, rolled his eyes up thoughtfully. "Like impenetrable force fields, mass multipliers—that's a cute hypothesis, Muscles. Increase the effective mass of a substance, and the results could be interesting. Particularly if it were radioactive. Antigravity. Telepath scrambles, which throw interrupting frequencies in and around thought waves, if thoughts *are* waves ... we've considered practically every gadget and gimmick in every story and article in every science-fiction magazine published in the last thirty years, and have planned what to do in case it suddenly pops up."

Ignoring all the utopian, philosophical, sociological stories, of course, thought Dr. Simmons. He said, "So your visit here isn't purely social?"

"Gosh no. I'm with the observation group which came here to see your Spy-Eye in action. What is it, anyhow? And how did it get the cute soapsuds name?"

Dr. Simmons smiled. "One of the armchair boys in the front office used to work in an advertising agency. The device is a 'Self-Propelled Information Interceptor'—SPII—which, once it touched that huckster brain, became 'Spy-Eye.' As to just what it is, you'll see that for yourself if you attend the demonstration, which starts as soon as we've finished talking."

"You mean you postponed it until I was through with you?"

"That's right." *I thought you'd like that,* he thought, watching the pleased grin on his brother's face. "Tell me something, Leroy. All these plans . . . are we at war?"

"Are we . . . well, no. You know that."

"But these preparations. All they lack is a timetable." He squinted quizzically. "By golly, I believe you have that, too."

"We have plenty," the colonel sidestepped, winking.

"Choose sides yet? What's the line-up?"

"I won't tell you that. No, I'm not worried about security, it's just that I might be wrong. Things move so fast these days. I'll tell you one thing, though. We already have our neutral ground."

"Oh yes, of course—like Switzerland and Sweden. I've always wondered what exact powers kept them neutral."

"Well, if you're going to fight a war, you've got to have some way to exchange prisoners and have meetings with various interested parties, and so on—"

"Yep. And it used to come in pretty handy for certain manufacturers."

The colonel eyed him. "Are you sure you're off that lion-and-lamb kick?"

Dr. Simmons grimaced. "I think the Spy-Eye can answer that adequately."

The colonel slipped off his perch. "Yes, let's get to it," he said eagerly.

They went to the door. "By the way," said Dr. Simmons, "just what have you picked out for your neutral ground?"

"Japan," said the colonel.

"Nice of 'em to agree to anything so close to home."

"Nice of 'em? Don't be silly! It's the only way they can be sure it won't be fortified."

"Oh," said his brother. They went out.

The demonstration went off without a hitch, and afterward the six Army observers and the plant technicians repaired to the projection room for Dr. Simmons' summation.

He talked steadily and tiredly, and his thoughts talked on at the same time. As he reeled off specifications and characteristics, his mind rambled along, sometimes following the spoken thought, sometimes paralleling it, sometimes commenting acidly or humorously, always tiredly. It was a trapped thing, that talking mind, but it was articulate.

"... five-point-eight feet long over-all, an aerodynamic stream-line, with its largest diameter only two-point-three-seven feet. Slide One, please. As you have seen, it has one propelling and three supporting jets. These three are coupled directly to the same outlet valve, which is controlled by an absolute altimeter. The whole is, of course, gyro-stabilized. It is capable of trans-sonic speeds, but can very nearly hover, subject only to a small nutation which can probably be designed out."

It was going to be a mail rocket, commented his thought.

"Its equipment includes the usual self-guiding devices, a coding flight-recorder, and radio receivers tuned to various pre-selected FM, AM, and radar channels. In regard to radar, should it pick up any radar impulses close enough or strong enough to suggest detection, it changes course and speed radically. Should they persist, the Spy-Eye releases 'window'—aluminum-foil strips of various lengths—and returns to its starting point by preset and devious course.

"The spy device itself is relatively simple. It uses magnefilm, taking pictures of the source of any desired radio signal. When the signal is received, it locates the beam, aims the camera, and records the audio signal magnetically. Of course, the synchronization between the picture and the audio recording is perfect, because of the magnefilm."

"Will you explain magnefilm, please, Doctor?"

"Certainly, Captain. It was developed through research into the rather wide variation in dielectric characteristics of the early plastics—the styrenes, ureas, and so on. Molecular arrangement was altered in various plastics until a transparent conductor was developed. It was not very far from that to the production of a plastic with a remarkably high magnetic density. Once this was made in a transparent, strong, pliable form, it was simple to make photographic film of it. The audio impulses are impressed directly upon the film, as in any magnetic tape system." *And it was invented for 8-mm. movie addicts, so that they could have sound film,* added his thought. *Now it's a secret weapon.*

"The purpose of the Spy-Eye, of course, is to pick up short-range transmissions—vertically beamed walkie-talkies, line-of-sight FM messages, and the like. Since these are usually well beyond the range of the enemy's listening posts, they are seldom coded. Therefore, with this device, we have access to a wealth of intelligence that has so far been regarded as unreachable."

He signaled the projection room. The screen came to life. During the test, the various officers had spoken into the microphones of several AM and FM transmitters spotted within a quarter-mile. Unerringly, after a few spoken words, the screen showed the sources and their identification numerals, painted on large white signboards.

"In enemy territory," remarked the doctor dryly, "we shall probably have to do without the boards." There was polite laughter. "If you will remember, gentlemen, the selector was next set to pick up something on the broadcast band."

The screen, blank, gave an agonized groan. Then a child's voice said clearly, "What's the matter, Daddy? Has that old acid indigestion got you down again?" "Owoo," said the man's voice. The screen suddenly showed, far below, the tall towers of a transmitting antenna. "Honey child, you'd better go for the doctor. Your old Daddy's real poorly." "No need to be," rejoined the angelic little voice. "I took my ice-cream money and bought you a package of Bubble-Up, the fastest relief known to the mind of a man. It is only ten cents at the nearest drugstore. Here. Take one and drink this glass of water I brought you." *Glug-glug. Clink!* "Ah-h! I'm a new man!" "Now Daddy, here's my report card. I'm sorry. It's all D's." "Ha ha ha! Think nothing of it honey child. Here—take this dollar. Take five dollars! Take all the other kids down for a treat!"

"Cut!" said Dr. Simmons. "I would consider this conclusive evidence, gentlemen, that the Spy-Eye can spot a target for bombing."

Amid laughter and applause, the lights came on. The observers pressed forward to shake the physicist's hand. Colonel Simmons stood by until the rest went to a table, where a technician was explaining the flight-record tapes and the course and radio-band preselector mechanisms.

"Muscles, it's fine. Just fine! How about duplication? I know there can be no leaks out of here, but do you think *they* will be able to figure it out quickly enough to get something like it into production?"

Dr. Simmons rubbed his chin. "That's hard to say. Aside from the fuel and magnefilm, there's nothing new about the device except for the fact that old components are packed into a new box. The fuel can be duplicated, and magnefilm—well, that's a logical development."

"Well," said the colonel, "it can't matter too much. I mean, even if they have it already. We can blanket the earth with those things. There needn't be a single spot on the globe unobserved. The Spy-Eye doesn't have to detect radio alone, does it?"

"Lord, no! It could be built to seek infrared, or radioactivity, or even sound, though we'd have to tune the jets acoustically for that. The magnefilm's audio could pick our own directional beams and get a radio fix on anything we wanted it to take pictures of. The camera could be triggered to a time mechanism, or to anything that radiated or vibrated. So could the hunting mechanism."

"Oh, fine," said the colonel again. "There'll be no power on earth that can't be spotted and smashed within hours, once we get enough of these things out."

"No power on earth," nodded his brother. "You have every reason to be confident." *And no reason to be right,* his silent voice added.

The first signs of the war to come were in all the papers. But hardly anyone read them. They were inside, with small headings. The front pages were more exciting that day. They screamed of new international incidents. The tabloids were full of a photo-series of the mobbing of a bearded man called Koronsky. (He was English—Somerset—and spoke the buzzing brogue of his shire. His name had been Polish, three generations before. He was wearing a beard because of scars caused by a severe attack of barber's itch. These facts were not touched upon.) An Estonian student was wrapped in a U.N. banner and stoned for having sung "Ol' Man River" at a folk-song recital. An astonishing number of tea-leaf readers were hired overnight by restaurants in which beef Stroganoff suddenly became gypsy goulash.

The small notices in the papers dealt with the startling discovery by three experimenters, one in France and two in Canada, of a new noise in Jansky radiation, that faint hiss of jumbled radio frequencies which originates from somewhere in interstellar space. It was a triple blast of sound, each one two and two-fifth seconds in length, with two and two-fifths seconds of silence between the signals. They came in groups, three blasts each, a few fractions of a second under ten minutes apart. The phenomenon continued for seven months, during which time careful measurements showed an appreciable increase in amplitude. Either the signal source was getting stronger, or it was getting nearer, said the pundits.

During these seven months, and for longer, the Simmons brothers lapsed into their usual "got to write to him sometime" pattern in regard to each other. Both were busy. The colonel's life was a continuous round of conferences, research reports, and demonstrations, and the load on the physicist became heavier daily, as the demands of the Board of Strategy, stimulated by its research, its intelligence section, and the perilous political situation, reached his laboratories.

The world was arming feverishly. A few historians and philosophers, in their very few objective moments, found time to wonder what the political analysis of the future would have to say about the coming war. The First War was a war of economic attrition; the Second was too, but it was even more an ideological war. This incipient unpleasantness had its source in ideology, but, at the eve of hostilities, the battle of philosophies had been relegated to the plane of philosophy. In practice, each side—or rather, *all sides*—had streamlined themselves into fighting machines, with each part milled to its function, and all control centralized. The necessary process of kindling fire to fight fire had resulted in soviets where the proletariat did not dictate, and in democracies where the people did not rule. Indeed, since the increase of governmental efficiency everywhere had resulted in a new high in production of every kind, the economic and political aspects of the war had been all but negated, and it began to appear as though the war would be fought purely for the sake of fighting a war, and simply because the world was prepared for it.

30

* * *

On December 7, as if to perpetuate the memory of infamy, the first bomb was dropped.

It was *dropped*. It wasn't a self-guided missile. It wasn't a planted mine. It wasn't dust or bio, either; it was a blast-bomb, and it was a honey.

They got the ship that dropped it, too. A proximity-fused rocket with an atomic warhead struck it a glancing blow. That happened, spectacularly, over Lake Michigan. The ship, or what was left of it, crashed near Minsk.

It was Dr. Simmons' urgent suggestion which accounted for the ship. It had not been seen, but it had been spotted on radar on December 6, when it circled the earth twice. It was far inside Roche's Limit; the conclusion was obvious that it was self-powered. Simmons calculated its orbit, knowing that at that velocity it could not alter its course appreciably in the few hours it took to pass and repass any given point. The proximity rocket was launched on schedule, not on detection. Unfortunately, on its way to its rendezvous with fission, the ship dropped its bomb.

And when that happened, the world drew itself together like— like— Ever see a cat lying sleeping, spread out, relaxed and then some sound, some movement will put that cat on guard? It may not move a muscle, but it also isn't relaxed any more; it isn't asleep anymore. It has changed its pose from a slumber to a crouch, and you know that only because of the new shape of its eyes. The world did that.

But nobody started throwing bombs.

"Cool down, soldier-boy."

"Cool down, he says," fumed the colonel. "This is ... this ..." His words died into a splutter.

"I know, I know," said Dr. Simmons, trying not to grin. "You figured, and you figured, and you read all sorts of fantastic things and swallowed your incredulity and planned as if these things actually could happen. You worked all practicable statistical possibilities, and a lot more besides. And it has to start like this."

"Everybody *knows* Japan is neutral ground, and will stay that way. There's no *point* in it!" the colonel all but wailed. "The bomb didn't even land on a city, or even a depot! Just knocked off the top of a mountain in Makabe country on Honshu. There isn't a blasted thing there."

"I'd say there isn't an unblasted thing there at the moment," chuckled his brother. "Stop telling me how you feel and let's have what you know. Was the bomb traced?"

"Of course it was traced! We have recording radar all over. It came from that ship, all right. Muscles, it was a dinky little thing, that bomb. About like a two-hundred-fifty-pounder. But what a blossom.

"I heard the news report on it. Also seismographics. They had trouble picking up the Hiroshima bomb. They didn't have any with this one. It ran about seven hundred and forty-odd times as powerful."

"Officially," said the colonel, "it was well over nine hundred at the source."

"Well, well," said Dr. Simmons, in the tone of an orchid fancier noting red spots on a new hybrid. "Disruption, hm-m-m?"

"Disruption, and how," rejoined the colonel. "Look, Muscles. We've got disruption bombs, too—you know that. But just as a fission bomb blows away most of its fissionable material before it can be effective, so a disruption bomb blasts off that much more. We have bombs that make the old Baker-Day bomb look like a wet firecracker, sure; but the best we can do is about four hundred per cent. I thought that was plenty; but this thing— Anyhow, Muscles, I just don't get it. Who dropped it? Why? Great day in the morning, man! An egg like that would've thrown us into a ground-loop if it had landed on any one of our centers. No power on earth would be that careless. To miss, I mean. On the other hand, we can't even be sure it wasn't a wild throw by one of our allies. Nowadays, you know everything, and you know nothing; you know it ahead of time, or you know it too late."

"My, my," said Dr. Simmons mildly. "What about the ship?"

"The ship," repeated the colonel, and his face reddened again. "I just can't believe that ship. Who built it? Where? We have everything on earth spotted that's worth spotting. Muscles, that thing was fifteen hundred feet long according to the radar."

"Anybody photograph it?"

"Apparently not. I mean, lots of radar-directed cameras shot where it was, but it didn't show, except as a blur."

"How do you know it was that big, then? You know what 'window' does to radar, for example. I don't know just how, but that could be camouflage of some sort."

"That's what we thought at first. Until we saw the hole in the ground where it hit. That thing was *big!*"

"Saw it? I understand the Russians cordoned off the area and threatened mass bombing if anyone came smelling around."

"A thing called a Spy-Eye," said the colonel, "with a telescopic lens—"

"Oh," said the physicist. "Well—how much of the ship was left?"

"Not much. It exploded when it hit, of course. Apparently most of it was vaporized over Michigan. The Spy-Eye pix show something being dug up, though."

"Wish I had a piece of it," said Dr. Simmons longingly. "A thorough quantitative analysis would very soon show where it came from."

"We won't get it," said the colonel positively. "Not without the Russkis' cooperation anyway."

"Could that happen?"

"Certainly not! They're not stupid! They'll play this thing for all it's worth. If they can figure out where it came from, they'll know and we won't—one up for them in the war of nerves. If they can't, and the sample's worthless to them, we can't know it until we try, and we want to try. So they'll hold out for some concession or other. Whatever it is will cost us plenty."

"Leroy," said the physicist slowly, "have you heard about the so-called signals in the Jansky bands?"

"I know what you're driving at," snorted the colonel. "The answer is no. But really, *no*. That's no ship from outer space. We fixed on

33

these signals months ago, and had even the 200-incher and a whole battery of image orthicons on the indicated direction. The signal strength increased, but nothing could be seen."

"Uh-huh. And when it arrived, it couldn't be photographed."

"It— Oh. Oh-oh!"

"Well, you said yourself that if it had been built anywhere on Earth you'd have known it."

"Your phone," gasped the colonel. "I've got to find about those Jansky signals." He rushed to the corner of the room.

"They stopped," said the doctor. "Yes, Leroy. I've been following them all along. They cut out when we shelled the ship."

"Th-they did?"

"Yup."

"Well—that takes care of that, doesn't it? Even if it was something from outside—"

"Now," said Dr. Simmons relentlessly, "with that racket off the Jansky bands, it's possible to hear the new noises."

"New—"

"Three sets of 'em. By their amplitude, I'd judge that they're scheduled to be here in two, three, and five months respectively." The colonel gasped. "*I* think," added Dr. Simmons calmly, "that they're approaching faster than the first one."

"That can't be!" bellowed the colonel. "Haven't we enough to watch without fighting a Buck Rogers war as well? We just can't fight our own war and these invaders, too!"

"Come on," said Dr. Simmons gently. "Why not take it up with the Board, Leroy? They're ready for everything. You told me so yourself."

The colonel glared at him. "This is no time to needle me, Muscles," he growled. "What do you think's going to happen?"

The scientist considered. "Well, what do you think would happen if you sent out, say, a plane to investigate an island? The plane circles it a couple of times, and then without warning gets shot down. What would you do?"

"Send a squadron and bomb the—" He fell silent.

"Yes, Leroy."

"But—they dropped the bomb first!"

"How do you know what they were doing? Put it on other terms; you are walking in the woods and you come to a mound of dry earth. You wonder what it is. You stick a piece of wood into it." He shrugged. "Maybe it's an ant hill. It would seem to me that an atomic bomb would be an excellent method to get a quick idea of the elemental composition of a strange planet. There're all kinds of light from the disruption, you know. Screen off what radiation you can expect from your own bomb, and what's left will give you a pretty fair spectral analysis of the target."

"But they must have known the planet was inhabited. What right had they to bomb it?"

"Did the bomb do any damage?"

The colonel was silent.

"And yet we shot the ship down. Leroy, you can't expect them to like it."

The soldier looked up suddenly, narrowly at his brother. "It was your idea to shoot it down."

"It was not!" Dr. Simmons snapped. "I was asked how it could be done, and I said how it could be done. That was all. The order was given by some eager lad in your Board, if anyone." He made an impatient gesture. "That's beside the point, Leroy. We can come out of our caves in the brave new postwar world and fix the blame to our hearts' content. Our problem at the moment is what to do when the next contingent arrives. I rather think they'll be loaded for bear. That was, you say, a big ship, and what it dropped was a small bomb. You can guess what will happen if three ships drop a few whole sticks of bombs like that—say a thousand of them."

"Three hundred would be enough to make this planet look like the moon," said the colonel whitely.

"I remember a lecture, long ago," said Dr. Simmons reminiscently, "by a man named Dr. Szilard. Someone asked him if there was any conceivable defense against the atomic bomb. He laughed and said, 'Certainly. The Japanese discovered it in eight days.'"

"A defense? Oh. They surrendered."

"That's right. That stopped the bombs from coming over."

"How do you surrender to a force you can't communicate with?"

"Perhaps we can. We can try. But from their point of view we attacked first, and in all probability they'll hit first and talk later. You would."

"Yes," admitted the colonel. "I would. The thing to do, Muscles, is to try to organize some defense."

"With the world in the state it's in now? Don't be silly. There might be a chance if everyone believed, if every nation would cooperate. But if nobody trusts anybody—"

The colonel bolted to the door. "We'll have to do what we can. So long, Muscles. I'll keep you posted— What in blazes are you grinning for?"

"Don't mind me, please," said Dr. Simmons, half laughing. "It's nothing."

"Tell me what your nothing is so I can get to work with a clear mind," said the colonel irritably.

"Well, it's just that I've been expecting the well-known atomic doom for so *very* long, that I've covered every emotion but one over it. I've been afraid, even terrified. I've been angry. I've been disgusted. And now—it's funny. It's funny because of what you're going through. Of all the things you've guessed at, trained for, planned for—it has to come like this. Sitting ducks. An enemy you can't outthink, outweigh, outsmart, or terrorize. It was always inevitable; now even a soldier can see it."

"Very funny," growled the colonel, jamming his hat down. "Out of this world."

"Hey!" called the physicist. "That was good!"

Laughing, he went to his inner laboratory, the one where no one else ever went.

Their next contact was by telephone. Too much time had passed; at least, Dr. Simmons thought it was too much time. After he had determined to call his brother, it occurred to him that he did not know exactly how to go about it, so he called the War Department in Washington. It took two minutes and forty seconds to make the contact; but the doctor heard the Washington operator, the Chicago operator, the

Denver operator, the Gunnison operator, the Gunnison mobile operator, and an operations lieutenant passing along something called a crash pri. Dr. Simmons raised his eyebrows at this, and never forgot it.

"Hi, Muscles."

"Hello, Leroy. Listen. What's with the salvage situation? I want to do that analysis."

"The stinkers!" the colonel said heatedly. "They made a proposition. I turned 'em down. The Board backed me up."

"What was the proposition?"

"They wouldn't send a sample. They said if we had someone who could perform a definitive analysis, to send him to Russia."

"Aha! Mountain to Mahomet, eh? Why did you refuse?"

"Don't be silly! There are maybe a half-dozen men in this country who might be able to make a really exhaustive analysis, and come up with a reliable conclusion. And about five of 'em, we can't be sure."

"Send the other one, then."

"That's you, egghead. We're not going to run a risk like that."

"Why not?"

"They could use you, Muscles."

"I couldn't use anything they could give me."

"That isn't the point," the colonel assured him. "But they have ways—"

"Knock off the dramatics, Leroy. This isn't a grade-B movie. And there isn't time for fooling around. We have maybe six weeks."

There was a silence. Then, "Only six weeks?"

"That's right," said the doctor positively. "Tell you what. Make arrangements to get me to Minsk right away, and let me get on that analysis. At worst we can find out what the ship was made of, and get an idea of how advanced those people are. At the very best, we might find a defense. Tell the Russians that my work will be open and aboveboard. They can put on as many observers as they want to, and I will share my findings completely with them."

"You can't do that! That's just what we want to avoid!"

It was the physicist's turn to fall silent. *How do you like that!* he thought. *The Board is clinging to some faint hope that the invaders will*

37

do their dirty work for them. They think that we'll find a defense and no one else will. He said finally, speaking slowly and carefully as if to a child, "Leroy, listen. I'm just as anxious as you are to do something about this matter. I think I can do something. But either I do it my way, or I don't do it at all. Is that quite clear? Perhaps I'm more resigned than you are. Perhaps I think we deserve this ... are you there?"

"Yes." The doctor knew his brother had paused to lick his lips nervously. "You really think you can get something of value out of the analysis?"

"Almost certainly."

"I'll check with the Board. Muscles—"

"Yes, Leroy."

"Don't go mystic on us, hah?"

"Go see the Board," said Dr. Simmons, and hung up.

He went to Russia.

The colonel met him on his return, two weeks later, at a West Coast field. The unarmed long-range jet fighter and its bristling escort, which had accompanied it from Eniwetok, skimmed to the landing strip. The colonel had a two-place coupé sport plane waiting. Dr. Simmons, inordinately cheerful, refused a meal and said he wanted to take off right away for his laboratories. The colonel wanted him to appear before the Board for a report, but he smiled and shook his head, and the colonel knew that smile better than to argue.

When they reached traveling altitude, and the colonel had throttled down to stay under the sonic barrier, and they had the susurrus of driving jets to accompany them rather than the roar of climbing jets to compete, they talked.

"How was it, Muscles?"

"I had a ball. It was *fine.*"

The colonel shot a look at him. *He disapproves,* thought the doctor. *War is grim and businesslike, and for anyone to enjoy the business of war seems to him a sacrilege.*

"It looked pretty touchy at first. They all acted as if I had an A-bomb in my watch pocket. Then I ran into Iggy."

"Iggy?"

"Yup. I could recite his whole name if I tried hard, but it's a jaw-breaker. We used to drink forbidden sherry together in the dorm at the University of Virginia when I was a kid in school. We thrashed out all the truths of the cosmos together. He was a swell guy. I remember once when Iggy decided that the rule forbidding women in the dorm was unreasonable. He rigged up a—"

"What happened in Minsk?" asked the colonel coldly.

"Oh. Minsk. Well, Iggy's come a long way since college. He specialized in aerodynamics, and then got tired of it. For years he'd been fooling around with nuclear physics as a hobby, and during the Second War he got real high up in the field. Naturally he was called in when this ship nosed in at Minsk."

"Why naturally?"

"Well, the fragment retained much of its shape. That's aerodynamics. And it was hot—really hot. That's nuclear physics. He was a big help. According to his extrapolations, by the way, your radar was right. If that was part of the hull, as it probably was, and if was a more or less continuous curve, then the ship must've been all of fifteen hundred feet long, with a four-hundred-foot cross-section at max. Quite a piece of business."

"I can't say I'm happy to hear about it. Go on."

"Well, the high brass there apparently expected me to smell the fragment, taste it, and come up with a trade name. There was a lot of pressure to keep me away from testing equipment, if any. That's where Iggy came in. He apologized for my carelessness in not bringing my betatron and some distillation apparatus. They saw the point and got me to a laboratory. They have some nice stuff." He shook his head appreciatively.

Eagerly the colonel asked: "Anything we haven't got? Can we duplicate any of it? Where is this place? Did you see any defenses?"

"They have lots of stuff," said the doctor shortly. "Do you want me to finish? You do? All right. Well, we volatilized pieces of it, and we distilled it. We subjected it to reagents and reducers and stress analyses and crystallographic tests. We put it in magnetic fields and we tested its resistance and conductivity. We got plenty of figures on it." He laughed. Again the colonel looked impatiently at him.

39

"Well, what is the stuff?"

"There is no name for it, yet. Iggy wants to call it *nichevite*—in other words, 'never mind.' Leroy, it looks like dural, only it's harder and it's tougher. But it oxidizes very easily. It's metallic, but it has such a low conductivity that it makes like porcelain. It has heavy-isotope aluminum in it, and light copper, and it isn't an alloy. It's a compound. It's a blasted chemical compound, very stable, made of nothing but elements with a positive valence. It's stronger than any steel, and can withstand temperatures so high that you can forget about them. The atomic blast broke it; it didn't fuse it. We volatilized it only by powdering it and oxidizing it in an electric furnace, and then subtracting the oxygen from our calculations. That got us near enough to where we wanted to go. One thing is certain: no place on Earth you ever heard about was the source of that stuff. Iggy has sworn to his bunch that the material is of extra-solar origin. They're propagandizing it in Russia now. A good thing, too. The Russians were all ready to call the whole thing a Yankee trick."

"I've heard some of those broadcasts," said the colonel. "I was hoping we could keep that information to ourselves."

"Don't be childish," said the physicist, in as abrupt a tone as he ever used. "We're not out on maneuvers, sonny. Time and time again one person or another has told the world to wake up to reality. This once the world will wake up or else. You won't be able to keep it asleep any more. It's gone too far."

The threat from outside finally broke in the papers, but only after long and worried conferences in governmental and military head-quarters all over the world. The simple fact that the world would work together or face extinction made, at first, as much impression as it ever had—very little. It was not enough to overcome man's distrust of himself. Not at first.

But the die-hards yielded, gradually and with misgivings, and acquainted the people with the menace that faced them. There was little dangerous panic—controls were too tight to allow for it—but after the first thrill of excitement there came a unanimous demand for a plan of action which was too powerful to ignore.

Bulletins were posted hourly on the amplitude of the Jansky signals. As Dr. Simmons had pointed out, there were three sets of them, and it became increasingly evident that the three sources were in V formation, and coming fast—much faster than the first one had.

"They'll box us," said Colonel Simmons. "There won't be any circling this time. They'll take up equidistant positions around the planet, out of our range, and they'll fire at will."

"I think you're right," said his brother. "Well, that gives us two kinds of defense. They're both puny, but it'll be the best we can do. One's technological, of course. I don't know exactly which direction would be the best to take. We can build ships ourselves, and attack them in space. We can try to develop some kind of shield against their bombs, or whatever else they use against us. And we can try to build seeking torpedoes of some sort that'll go out and get 'em— bearing in mind that we might be out there ourselves sometime soon, and we don't want to fall prey to our own weapons."

"What's the other defense?"

"Sociological. In the first place, we must decentralize to a degree heretofore impossible. In the second place, we must pool our brains and our physical resources. No nation can afford to foot the bill of this kind of production; no nation can afford to take the chance of by-passing some foreign brain which might help the whole world. Leroy, stop puckering up like that! You look as if you're going to cry. I know what's bothering you. This looks like the end of professional militarism. Well, it is, in the national sense. But you have a bigger enemy than ever before, and one more worthy of the best efforts of humanity. You and your Board have been doing what seemed to be really large thinking. It wasn't, because its field was too small and too detailed. But now you have something worth fighting. Now your plans can be planetary—galactic—cosmic, if you like. Don't hanker after the past, soldier-boy. That attitude's about the only way there is to stay small."

"That's quite a speech," said the colonel. "I . . . wish I could argue with it. If I admit you're right, I can only admit that there is no solution at all. I don't believe the world will ever realize the necessity for cooperation until it's too late."

"Maybe it will. Maybe. I remember once talking to an old soldier who had been in the First War. In his toolshed he had a little trench shovel about eighteen inches long—a very flimsy piece of equipment it was. I remarked on it, and asked him what earthly good it was to a soldier. He laughed and said that when a green squad was deployed near no man's land and ordered to dig in, they gabbled and griped and scratched and stewed over the job. And when the first enemy bullets came whining over, they took their little shovels and they just *melted* into the ground." He chuckled. "Maybe it'll be like that. Who knows? Anyway, do what you can, Leroy."

"You have the strangest sense of humor," growled the colonel, and left.

They came.

The first was just a shape against the stars. It could be heard like a monster's breath in a dark place: *wsh-h-h-t wsh-h-h-t wsh-h-h-t* on the sixty-megacycle band, where before nothing had been heard but the meaningless hiss of the Jansky noise. But it could not be seen. Not really. It was just a shape. A blur. It did not reflect radar impulses very well; the response was indeterminate, but indicated that it was about the size and shape of the mysterious bomber which had dealt the first terrifying, harmless blow.

The world went crazy, but it was a directed madness. With the appearance of the Outsider, all talk of the advisability of defense ceased. There could be no discussion of priorities.

A Curie Institute scientist announced light-metal fission. A Hungarian broke his own security regulations with the announcement of an artificial element of heretofore unthinkable density which could be cast into fission chambers, making possible the long-awaited pint-sized atomic engine. A Russian scientist got what seemed to be a toe-hold on antigravity and set up a yell which resulted in a conclave of big brains in Denver—men from all over the world. He was wrong, but a valuable precedent was set. A World Trade Organization was established, with control of raw materials and manufactured goods and their routes and schedules. Its control was so complete that tariffs were suspended *in toto*—the regulation read "for the duration"—

and, since it is efficient to give a square deal, a square deal was given in such a clear-cut fashion that objectors were profiteers by definition. Russian ores began appearing in British smelters, and Saar coal was loaded into the Bessemers of Birmingham. Most important of all, a true International Police Force came into being with hardly a labor pain. Its members were free to go everywhere, and their duty was to stop anything which got in the way of planetary production. Individual injustice, faulty diet, poor housing, underpaying, and such items fell immediately into this category, and were dealt with quickly and with great authority.

Propaganda unified itself and came to a focus in the hourly bulletins about the Outsiders. Every radio station on Earth included that dread triple hiss in its station breaks.

And the Outsider stayed just where it was, just lay there, breathing, waiting for its two cohorts.

"It's makeshift," said Dr. Simmons, "but it might do. It just might do."

The colonel stepped past him and looked at the cradle, on which rested a tubby, forty-foot object like a miniature submarine.

"A satellite, you said?"

"Uh-huh. Loaded to the gills with direction-finders and small atomic rockets. It'll keep a continuous fix on the Outsider during its transit, and relay information to monitor stations on Earth. If one of the ships fires a torpedo, it will be detected and reported immediately and the satellite will launch an interceptor rocket. If the bomb or torpedo dodges, the interceptor will follow it. In the meantime, big interceptors can be on their way from Earth. If a torpedo comes close to the satellite, the satellite will dodge. If it comes too close, the satellite will explode violently enough to take the torp with it. We plan to set out three layers of these things, nine in each stratum, twenty-seven in all, so spaced as to keep a constant scanning in every direction."

"Satellites, hm-m-m? Muscles, if we can do this, why can't we go right out there and get the ships themselves?"

The physicist ticked the reasons off on his fingers. "First, because if they bracket us, as in every likelihood they will, they'd be foolish to come any closer than the one that's already here, and he's out of any range we can handle just now. We can assume that his ships, if not his bombs, will be prepared against our proximity devices. We'll try, of course, but I wouldn't be too hopeful. Second, we still haven't a fuel efficient enough to allow for escape velocity maneuvers without a deadly acceleration, so our chances of sending manned rockets up for combat are nil at the moment."

The colonel looked admiringly at the satellite and the crowd of technicians which swarmed around it. "I knew we'd come up with something."

His brother gave him a quizzical glance. "I don't know if you fully realize just how big a 'we' that is you just used. The casing of that satellite is Swedish steel. The drive is a German scientist's adaptation of the Hungarian baby fission engine. The radio circuits are American, except for the scanning relay, which is Russian. And those technicians—I've never seen such a bunch. Davis, Li San, Abdallah, Schechter, O'Shaughnessy—he comes from Bolivia, by the way, and speaks only Spanish—Yokamatsu, Willet, Van Cleve. All of these men, all these designs and materials, and all the money that make up these satellites, have been found and assembled from all over the earth in only the last few weeks. There were miracles of production during the Second War, Leroy, but nothing to match this."

The colonel shook his head dazedly. "I never thought I'd see it happen."

"You'll see more surprising things than this before we're done," said the scientist happily. "Now I've got to get back to work."

That was the week the second Outsider arrived. It took up a position in the celestial south, not quite opposing its fellow, and it lay quietly, breathing. If there was converse between them, it was not detectable by any known receiver. It was the same apparent size and had the same puzzling effect on radar and photographic plates as its predecessors.

In Pakistan, an unfueled airplane took off from a back-country airstrip, flew to twenty thousand feet, and came in for a landing. The projector which was trained on it had no effect on the approaching aircraft in the moment it took the plane to disappear behind a hillock and reappear on the other side. There was a consequent momentary power loss, and the plane lost too much altitude and had to make another pass. The wind direction dictated a climbing turn to the north, and the beam from the projector briefly touched the antenna of an amateur radio operator called Ben Ali Ra. Ben Ali Ra's rig exploded with great enthusiasm, filling the inside of his shack with spots and specks of fused metal, ceramic, and glass. Fortunately for him—and for the world—he was in the adjoining room at the time, and suffered only a deep burn in his thigh, which was struck by a flying fragment of a coil-form.

This was the first practical emergence of broadcast power.

Ben Ali was aware of the nature of the experiments at the nearby field, having eavesdropped by radio on some field conversations. He was also aware of certain aims and attitudes held by the local authority. Defying these, he left the area that night, on foot, knowing that he would be killed if captured, knowing that in any event his personal property would be confiscated, and in great pain because of his wound. His story is told elsewhere; however, he reached Benares and retained consciousness long enough to warn the International Police.

The issue was not that broadcast power was a menace; it had a long way to go before it could be used without shouting its presence through every loudspeaker within miles. The thing that brought the I.P. down in force on this isolated, all but autonomous speck on the map was the charge that the inventors intended to keep their development to themselves. The attachment of the device and all related papers by the Planetary Defense Organization was a milestone of legal precedent, and brought a new definition of "eminent domain." Thereafter no delays were caused by the necessity of application to local governments for the release of defense information; the I.P. investigated, confiscated, and turned the devices in question over to the Planetary Defense Organization, acting directly and paying fairly all parties involved. So another important step was taken toward the erasure of national lines.

Two weeks before the arrival of the third Outsider—excluding the one which had been shot down—the last of the twenty-seven satellites took up its orbit, and the world enjoyed its first easy breath since the beginning of the Attack, as it was called.

Because of high-efficiency circuits and components, the fuel consumption of the electronic set-up in the satellites was very small. They held their orbits without power, except for an occasional automatic correction-kick. They could operate without servicing for years. It was assumed that by the time they needed servicing, astrogation would have developed to the point where they could be refueled—and recharged—by man-carrying ships. If technology did not solve the problem, little harm could be done by the silent, circling machines; when, at long last, they slipped from their arbitrary orbits and spiraled in to crash, so many years would have passed that the question was, momently, academic.

And even before the twenty-seventh satellite was launched, factories were retooling for a long dreamed of project, a space station which would circle the Earth in an orbit close enough to be reached by man-carrying rockets, which would rest and refuel there and take off again for deep space without the crushing drag of Earth's gravity.

The third Outsider took up its position, as Dr. Simmons had prophesied, equidistant from the others with Earth in the center, rolling nakedly under them. As in the case of the arrivals of the other two, there was no sign of its presence but the increasing sound on the sixty-megacycle band. Radar failed utterly to locate it until, suddenly, it was in its position—a third blur against the distant stars, a third indeterminate, fifteen-hundred-foot shape on the radarscopes.

The Board of Strategy was happily, almost gleefully, busy again. Their earlier work within the field of the probability of human works faded to insignificance against the probabilities inherent in the Attack. There was another major difference, too: they came out in the open. They plastered the world with warnings, cautions, and notices, many of them with no more backing than vivid imaginings of some early science-fiction writer—plus probability. Although logic indicated that the first blows would be in the form of self-guided missiles, thousands of other possibilities were considered. Spy rays, for example; radio hams the world over were asked to keep winding coils, keep searching the spectrum for any unusual frequencies. Telepathic amplifiers, for another example; asylums were circularized for any radical changes in the quality and quantity of insanity and even abnormal conduct. The literary critics were called in to watch for any trends in creative writing which seemed to have an inhuman content. Music was watched the same way, as were the graphic arts. Farmers and fire wardens were urgently counseled to watch for any plant life, particularly predatory or prehensile or drug-bearing plant life, which might develop. Sociologists were dragged from their almost drunken surveys of this remarkable turn of social evolution, and were ordered right back into it again, to try to extrapolate something harmful to come from this functional, logical, unified planet. But only the nationalists found harm, and they were—well, unfashionable.

The bombs came about a month after the third Outsider took up his post.

The whole world watched. Everything stopped. Every television screen pictured radarscopes and the whip-voiced announcer at Planetary Defense Central in Geneva, which had at long last regained its place as a world center.

The images showed Outsiders A, B, and C in rapid succession. So well synchronized was the action that the three images could have been superimposed, and would have seemed like one picture. Each ship launched two bombs; of each two, one turned lazily toward Earth and the other hovered.

"Out of range of the satellites," said the announcer. "We shall have to wait. The satellites will detect the bombs when they are within two hundred miles, and will then launch their interceptors. Our Earth-based rockets are aiming now."

There was a forty-minute wait. Neighbor called neighbor; illuminated news banners on the sides of buildings gave the dreaded news. Buses and trains stopped while their passengers and crews flocked to televisors. There was a hushed tension, world-wide.

"*Flash!* Satellite 24 has released an interceptor. Stand by; perhaps we can get a recording of the scanner ... one moment please ... *Anything from Monitor 24b yet, Jim? On the air now? Check ...*

47

Ladies and gentlemen, if you can be patient a moment—we are recording pictures of the radarscope at Monitor 24b in Lhasa. It will be only a few ... here it is now."

Flickering at first, then clearing, came the Lhasa picture. The monitor station there kept a fix on Satellite 24 from horizon to horizon, as did the satellite's other two stations in San Francisco and Madrid. The picture showed the familiar lines of the satellite. Abruptly a short, thick tube began to protrude from the hull. When extended about eight feet, it swung over about forty degrees on its ball-and-socket base. From its tip shot a small cylinder; there was a brief flicker of jets. "The interceptor," said the loudspeakers unnecessarily.

The scene flashed to the Earth-based interceptor station at White Sands. A huge rocket mounted with deceptive slowness, balanced on a towering column of flame, and disappeared into the sky.

Then, bewilderingly, the scene was repeated for Monitor Stations 22c and 25a, as their satellites sensed the bombs coming from Outsiders B and C. White Sands sent two more giant rockets up as fast they could set the seeking gear.

Then, after an interminable four hours, came the picture which was to stand forever as the high point in newsreel coverage. It was the image picked up from the relaying television camera in the nose of Satellite 24's little interceptor.

It fixed the image of the Outsider's bomb, and it would not let go. The bomb, at first only a speck, increased in size alarmingly. It was a perfect cylinder, seen in perspective. There was nothing streamlined about it. It was quite featureless except for a strange indistinction around one end, as if it were not in focus. It was like a small patch of the substance of the Outsiders themselves.

The image grew. It filled the screen—

And then there was nothing.

But cameras all over Europe picked up and relayed the image of that awe-inspiring explosion. Silently a ball of light appeared in the sky, expanding, flickering through the entire spectrum, sending out a wheel of blue and silver rays. It lasted for a full fifteen seconds, growing in size and in brilliance, before it began to fade, and it left a pastel ghost of itself for a minute afterward. Speckles of random radiation cluttered the screens then, and there were no more actual pictures of the action.

The entire world gave a concerted shout of joy. In dozens of languages and dialects, the fierce, triumphant sound roared skyward. *Got one!* And the bells and whistles picked up the cry, frightening sleeping birds, sending crocodiles scuttling off river banks, waking children all over the world. It was like a thousand New Year's Eves, simultaneously.

What happened next happened quickly.

A White Sands rocket got the second bomb. For some reason there was no atomic explosion. Perhaps the proximity gear failed. Perhaps it was neutralized, though that would seem impossible, since the seeking gear obviously did not fail. It was not as spectacular as the first interception, but it was quite as effective. The purely physical impact as the huge interceptor struck the tiny bomb all but pulverized them both.

The third bomb breezed past its satellite interceptor, its White Sands interceptor, and a second-stratum satellite. It was observed that on getting within range of the seeking radar of each of these it became enveloped in the misty, coruscating field which characterized the Outsider ships. Apparently this field completely confused the radar; it was as if the radar detected it but didn't know what to do with it—"the same spot we were in a year ago," as Doctor Simmons remarked tersely.

The bomb entered the atmosphere—and burned up like a meteor.

Then it was that the most incredible thing of all happened. The three hovering bombs—one beside each Outsider—slowly retreated toward the parent vessels, as if being reeled in.

They recalled their bombs.

Thereafter they lay quietly, the three Outsiders. The did not move, they made no move. They gasped their triple pantings, and they filled thousands of photographic plates with their indeterminate muzziness, and that was all.

Four giant rockets out of the five sent after the invaders missed their mark completely. The fifth, which was equipped with an ingenious seeking device based on correlation of its target with an actual photographic transparency of the target, apparently struck Outsider

B. There was a splendid atomic display, and again the world went mad with joy.

But when the area could be observed again, Outsider B was still there. And there it stayed. There they all stayed.

A cyclic, stiffly controlled panic afflicted the world; as a sense of impending doom was covered by humanity's classic inability to fix its attention for very long to any one thing, the panic alternated to reactive terror, swung away from terror again because life must go on, because you must eat and he must love and they must make a bet on the World Series. . . .

Seven months passed.

Dr. Simmons plodded into his private office and shut the door. He was tired—much more tired than in the days earlier that year, when he was working an eighteen-hour day. *The more a man does, the more he can do,* he reflected wearily, *until the optimum is reached; and the optimum is way up yonder, if he cares about what he's doing.* He sat down at his desk and leaned back. *And if he takes just as much care as ever, but there just isn't as much to do, he gets tired. He gets very, very tired . . .*

He palmed his face, blinked his eyes, sighed, and leaning forward, flipped the annunciator switch. His night secretary said brightly: "Yes, Doctor?"

"Don't let anything or anybody in here for two hours. And take care of that cold."

"Yes, sir. Thank you, Doctor, I will."

A good kid. . . . He rose and went to the washroom which adjoined his office. Stepping into the shower stall, he lifted up the soap dish, which had a concealed hinge, and pressed a stud under it. He counted off four seconds, released the stud, and pulled on the hot water faucet. The back wall of the shower swung toward him. He stepped through into his own private laboratory—the one where no one else ever went.

He kicked the door closed behind him and looked around. *I almost wish I could do it all over again. The things that have happened here, the dreams . . .*

His thought cut out in a sudden, numbing shock.

"What are you doing here?"

The intruder accepted the question, turned it over, altered it, and gave it back. "What have *you* been doing here?" rasped the colonel.

The physicist sank into an easy-chair and gaped at his brother. His pulse was pounding, and for a moment his cheek twitched. "Just give me a second," he said wryly. "This is a little like finding someone in your bed." He took out a handkerchief and touched his dry lips with it. "How did you get in here?"

Leroy Simmons was sitting behind a worktable. He had his hat, with its polished visor, in the crook of his arm, and his buttons were brilliant. He looked as if he were sitting for a particular kind of portrait. The doctor jumped up. "You've *got* to have a drink!" he said emphatically.

The colonel put his hat on the table and leaned forward. The act wrinkled his tunic and showed up his bald spot. "What's the matter with you, Muscles?"

The doctor shook his head. *He doesn't look like a man of distinction any more,* he thought regretfully. "I feel a little better now," he said. "What brings you here, Leroy?"

"I've been watching you for months," said the colonel. "I've had to do it all myself. This is ... it's too big." He looked completely miserable. "I followed you and watched you and checked up on you. I took measurements all around these offices, and located this room. I was in here a dozen times, looking for the gimmick on the door."

"Oh, yes. Always dropping around to see me when I wasn't around, and saying you'd wait. My secretary told me."

"Her!" The syllable was eloquent. "She's no help. I never saw anyone harder to get information from."

"It's an unbeatable combination in a secretary," he grinned. "Infinite tact, and no facts. She's not in it, Leroy. No one is."

"No one but you. I notice you're not denying anything."

The doctor sighed. "You haven't charged me with anything yet. Suppose you tell me what you know, or what you think you know."

The colonel took a somber-backed little notebook out of his

pocket. "I have no associates," he said grimly, "either. It's all in here. Some of it is Greek to me, but some I understand—worse luck. I wish I didn't. You have something to do with the Outsiders, don't you?"

His brother looked at him for a long moment, and then nodded, as if he had asked and answered a question.

"Yes."

"You know where they come from, what they're going to do, how they operate—everything about them?"

"That's right."

"They have given you—information. They have given you a way to"—he referred to the book, his lips moving as he read; they always had—"expand and concentrate binding energy into a self-sustaining field."

"No."

"No? You have all the formulas. You wrote thousands of pages of notes on the subject. Your diary mentions it repeatedly—and as if it was an accomplished fact."

"It is. I didn't get it from the Outsiders. They got it from me."

There was a jolting silence. The colonel turned quite white. "That ... does ... it," he whispered. "I knew you were in contact with the enemy, Muscles. I tried my best to believe that you were simply working them for information, so that we could use it against them. A risky game, and you were playing it alone. After I went through your papers here, I just couldn't believe it any more. You seemed to be working along with them. And now you tell me that you are actually supplying them with devices we haven't got!"

The scientist nodded gravely.

The colonel's hand, under the table, moved to his wrist. He touched a button on the small transmitter there, and pulled a slide over.

Dr. Simmons said thickly, "Leroy. Would you mind telling me how you got on to this?"

"I'll tell you, all right. It started with a routine check-up of supplies and equipment into these laboratories, for auditing purposes. No production is run without cost accounting, even by the government. Even by a planetary one. It was brought to my attention that certain things came in here that apparently never went out. When I went over the reports and saw they were correct, I wrote a memo which cleared you completely on my authority, and I killed the investigation. I—picked it up myself."

"Good heavens, why?"

"If I found anything," the colonel said with difficulty, "I wanted to take care of it myself."

"Sort of keep the family name sweet and clean?"

"Not that. You're too clever. You always were. I . . . I'll tell you something. I was appointed to the Board because of you. I never could have made it otherwise. The Board figured I'd be an intimate link with you; that I could see you any time, when no one else could."

Of course I knew that, thought the doctor. "I didn't know that," he said. "I don't believe you."

"Oh, cut it out," said the colonel. "You played me for a sucker all along, and through me, the Board."

Correct again, the physicist thought. He said: "Nonsense, Leroy. I just withheld information from time to time."

"You gave us tips," said the colonel bitterly. "You sent us off on goose chase after goose chase. And we pushed the whole world around the way you wanted us to."

The boy's real sharp tonight, thought Dr. Simmons, and added to himself, *He's such a swell, sincere character. I hate to see him go through all this.* "And why does all this make you squelch the Board's investigation and pick it up yourself?"

"I know how slick you are," said the colonel doggedly. "You just might talk a jury or a court-martial out of shooting you. I don't see how you could, but I don't see how you could have done any of this either." He waved a hand around the secret lab. "You won't talk your way out of it with me."

"You're my judge, then, my jury. My executioner, too?"

"I'm . . . your brother," said the colonel in a low voice, "and, like always, I want you to get what you deserve."

"I could puddle up and bawl like a baby," said Dr. Simmons suddenly, warmly. "Let's stop playing around, Leroy, and I'll tell you the whole story."

"Is it true you've been working with the Outsiders?"

"Yes, you idiot!"

The colonel slumped back and said glumly: "Then that settles it. Go ahead and talk if you want to. It can't make any difference now." He looked at his watch.

The scientist rose and went to a wall panel, which he pulled out, revealing a compact tape-recording outfit. From a rack above it he selected a reel, set it on the peg, and drew the end of the tape into the self-threader. Without switching on, he returned to his chair.

"Just a couple of preliminaries, Leroy, and then you can have the whole story. I have done what I have done because of what you used to call 'dewy-eyed idealism.' It has worked. We live now in a unified world. It must remain unified until the threat of the Outsiders is done with; it has no alternative. I don't think that the Outsiders will be removed for a while yet, and the longer the world lives this way, the harder it will be for it to go back to the old cut-up, mixed-up way of life it has followed for the last fifteen thousand years or so.

"I'll tell you what will happen from now on. The space station will be completed and put into action. When the point of boredom is reached with that, new fuel will be developed. Shortly afterward, the three Outsiders will put out their hovering bombs again. It'll throw the world into a panic, but with the station and the new fuel and the whole world working at it, a fighting ship will leave the station—outbound.

"It will sling some torps at the Outsiders, and they won't go off, or they'll miss, or they'll explode prematurely. The Outsiders won't hit back. The warship will move in close, and when it gets close enough to do real damage, it will get a message.

"This message will be broadcast on the three most likely frequencies, and signals will go out all over the other bands advertising those three frequencies. The message will start like this: 'Stop and listen. This is the Outsider.' This will be repeated in English, French, Spanish, German, Arabic, and, for good measure, Esperanto. This is the message."

He rose again, put his hand on the switch, smiled, and turned to

54

face the colonel. "Funny ... this was designed only to speak to the future. And you're the first to hear it."

"Why is that funny?"

"You're the past." He flipped the switch. "You'll pardon the tone of it," he said gently. "I had a chance to make a deep purple oration, and I find I ramble on like an old lady over her knitting."

"*You?*"

"Me. The Outsider. Listen."

This is the message, as it came from the tape in Dr. Simmons' leisurely mellow voice.

I am the Outsider. Do not fear me. There will be no battle. I am your friend. Hear me out.

I am four ships and a noise in the Jansky radiations. The ships are not ships, and they came from Earth, not from outside. The Jansky signals do not come from the stars. Listen.

I am one man, one man only, without helpers, without any collaborators, except possibly thinkers—a little Thoreau, a little Henry George, maybe a smattering of H.G. Wells ... you can believe me. Archimedes once said, "Give me a lever long enough, and a place for a fulcrum, and I shall move the earth!" Given the tools, one man can do *anything*. There's plenty of precedent for this. Aside from the things which produce a man, aside from the multitude of factors which make his environment, if the man is capable, and if the environment provides tools and a time ripe for action, that man can use his tools to their utmost extent. Hitler did it. John D. Rockefeller and Jay Gould did it. Kathleen Winsor did it. Given the tools, mankind can do *anything*.

I was given the single greatest tool in history. I stumbled on it. I'll tell you the truth: I worked like a hound dog to find it, once I suspected it was there.

It's a theory and a device. The theory has to do with binding energy; the device releases and controls it. It is all completely and clearly explained elsewhere; I'll come to that in time. Roughly speaking, however, it is a controlled diffusion of matter. Any gas can be rarefied and diffused. So, I have discovered, can any matter. Further, it can be diffused analytically. Binding energy is actually a component of matter. If a close-orbit situation can be induced between the electrons and the nucleus of an atom, its binding energy can be withdrawn, if equally diffused, to form a field around the atom. The field is toroidal, and has peculiar qualities.

For one thing, it does crazy things to the apparent center of gravity of the mechanism producing the field. Any seeking device which tends to locate mass directs itself at the c.g. But on approaching a field of this sort, the closer it gets, the harder it becomes for it to find the c.g., since the apparent center of mass is out at the edges. When directed at the actual center of the device, your seeker veers violently to the edge—hard enough, generally, to make it pass the mechanism altogether.

The field distorts and reflects radio and light waves in an extremely complex fashion. These waves are led powerfully to follow the outlines of the toroid; but since the field is a closed one—closed as tightly as only binding energy can close anything—light and radio cannot penetrate, no matter how strong the temptation. And so they are thrown back, rather than reflected in reflection's ordinary sense, and return to their detectors—receivers, photographic plates, or what have you—in a rather distorted pattern.

The field also has a strange effect on valence, making it possible to build chemical compounds out of elements of similar valence. The atomic situation within the toroid—in the hole of the donut, as it were—is weird, and is the place where such compounding can be done. Exact data on this will also be given you.

Now, here is exactly what was done. Having found the way to generate this field, I debated the wisdom of giving it to a world on the verge of war. I contemplated destroying all my evidence, but could not; the thing was too big; humanity needed it too much. But it was too big for even a unified humanity on one planet. It's big enough for all of space, and needs a humanity big enough to control it. I felt that if humanity were big enough to unify, it would be big enough for this device. It is, now, or you spacemen would not be listening to me.

After having developed the binding-energy field, I invented another device—the Spy-Eye. I knew that the little eavesdroppers would be produced by the thousands, so that a few would not be missed. A half-dozen were launched with their selector circuits altered and some of their equipment replaced. Their fueling was different, too; there is a reaction-formula using the b.-e. field which will be found along with the rest of these things.

My half-dozen Spy-Eyes, powered vastly beyond any of their little brothers and sisters, went outside and took up their positions in space.

They are the Outsiders.

The noise in the Jansky radiation was pure propaganda, and its execution was simple—practically primitive. It was a trick once used by illegal radio stations during one of the wars, I forget which. Three of them, widely separated and synchronized, sent out the same signal, beamed to an Earth diameter. Direction-finders on Earth obediently pointed out their *resultant*—a direction in which they did not exist! The Spy-Eyes themselves were too small and too far away to be detectable, unless one knew exactly what to look for and where to look. The amplitude of the signals was raised gradually until it reached a pre-selected volume. Then one of the Spy-Eyes set up a b.-e. field and dropped toward Earth. It looked strange and huge. It came in close and circled Earth twice at a high velocity. I think I had more trouble there than at any other point, but I managed, finally, to wangle the Board of Strategy into firing on it. Their shell hit nothing; the b.-e. field disrupted its atomic warhead, for in the presence of a hard-radiation source, the field increases the effective critical mass. The Spy-Eye itself is what fell on Japan; it was armed, of course, and was mistaken for a little bomb. What made the explosion so intense was the fact that the field held the disrupting matter together for a fraction of a millisecond longer than it had ever done before. The object which fell near Minsk was a piece of stage-proppery I had made earlier. It, too, had a b.-e. field generator on its back. Again it exhibited its exclusiveness and its penetrating power; it acted like a thing of great mass when it hit the ground. It, too, had a b.-e. generator on its back. Again it exhibited its exclusiveness and its penetrating power; it acted like a thing of great mass when it hit the ground. The generator was, of course, blown to dust on impact, leaving only the supposed specimen.

The other three Outsider ships were Spy-Eyes, b.-e. field-equipped. The bombs were real bombs, however, they were supplied by Satellite 18, which, if examined, will be found inexplicably empty of its interceptors. I put guiding heads on them, and sent one to each of my "Outsider" Spy-Eyes.

I think that explains everything. If you question my motives, regard Earth as you deep-spacemen see it today—unified, powerful, secure within and without. Humanity is ready, now, to take the first steps toward greatness. Therefore:

Send my name—Simmons—in the old International Morse Code on 28.275 meters, from a distance of ten statute miles from any of the three Outsider ships, at one thousand watts power. Repeat the name four times. The field will break down; you may then locate the Spy-Eyes and pull them in. Dismantle them; inside you will find this recording and certain papers, which contain everything I know about the binding-energy field. Use it well.

Colonel Simmons leaned back in his chair. His face was gray. "Muscles—is this all true?"

"You know it is. You've seen it in action."

"Now what have I done?" muttered the colonel.

"Jumped to conclusions," said the doctor easily.

The colonel's mouth opened and closed spasmodically. Then in violent reaction, he swore. "You couldn't've done it!" he roared. "You set the timetable for this whole thing and built it into those Spy-Eyes. Well, what about all that was done here—the interceptors from White Sands, and the development of the satellites and all that?"

"Leroy, old horse, take it easy, will you? Who had charge of all that development? Who had the final say on design? Who outlined the exact use of each piece of equipment—by way, of course, of using it to its greatest efficiency?"

"You did. You did." The colonel covered his face. "All that power. All that control. You could have had the whole world for the taking, if you'd wanted it. Instead—"

"Instead, everyone on Earth has a job, enough food, good quarters, and an equal chance at education. I have it on good authority that the next session of Congress will unify divorce laws and traffic laws in this country. Russia has not only a second party but a third one. Social legislation is beginning to follow the lines of the Postal Union, and already a movement has started to have the governments pay the people their full wages during a six-week vacation. No communism, no fascism; function is the law, and social security—lower-case—is function."

"Shut up!" mouthed the colonel in a peculiar tone, half moan, half roar. He held his head and he rocked.

The doctor clasped his shoulder and laughed, "Listen to me, Leroy," he said, "and I'll tell you something funny. You know how little, stupid anecdotes will stick with you, like the limerick about the young lady from Wheeling, and the time you took the ball of tar to bed with you and we had to shave your head? Well, believe it or not, I honestly think that this job I have just done had its source in a couple—no, three—things that happened to me when I was young. When I think of them, and look at the world today—my!"

He took a turn around the floor. His brother sat still.

"Wells had something to do with it. Wells pointed out, mostly indirectly, that only a miracle could make humans work together. And sometimes his miracle was entertaining but untenable, because it constituted a common aim for mankind. That never did work. World peace is the finest aim a race could have, but it never tempted us much. Wells' other miracle was a common enemy—the Martian invasion, for example. Now, that makes sense. It did then and it does now.

"And here are the silly little things that have stuck with me. Remember that summer when I got a job as a dirt-moving foreman on a canal job? Two of the muckers got into a fight out by one of the machines. I got up into a dragline and dumped a load of sand on the two of them. They stopped fighting, ganged up on me, and punched the daylights out of me." He laughed.

"Then there was the other one. It was even sillier. It was in a restaurant, right after I started to teach at Drexel Tech. There were two bubble-headed little chicks sitting at a nearby table, verbally clawing each other's eyes out over a young man. Just as I was about to get up and move back out of the combat area, they spotted the young man in question submitting to the wiles of a very cute redhead. Whereupon the combatants were suddenly allies, and on the spot"—he laughed again—"concocted a devilish scheme to squirt ink on the contents of the redhead's clothesline!"

The colonel was looking at him dully.

"The common denominator," continued the doctor, "in the analysis of Wells, the fight on the canal job, and the feline fiddle-faddle in the café, was surprisingly valid, considering the wide difference in the nature of the fields of combat. It boils down to this: that human conflicts cease to be of importance in the face of a common enemy. 'Divide and rule' has its obverse; 'unite and conquer.' That's what the world has done during the Attack; except that instead of conquering the Outsider, it has conquered itself—still its common enemy."

"Wells," murmured the colonel. "I remember that. I was reading him and told you the miracle idea. I was in military prep, and you were a freshman in college."

"Gosh yes," said the doctor. "I remember, Leroy."

The colonel seemed to be thinking hard, and slowly. He spoke slowly. "Muscles," he said, "remember how I wore your freshman dinky when you came home for a weekend?"

"Do I!" chuckled the doctor. "You wouldn't give it back, and I spend the next six weeks sweeping out seniors' rooms because I showed up at school without it. Heh! Remember me strutting around in your gray cape when you were at the Point?"

"Yeh. We were always doing that. Your tie, my tie, our tie. Those were the days. You wouldn't fit my clothes now, Fatso."

"Is *that* so!" laughed the doctor, delighted to see his brother making some effort to come out of his doldrum. "Listen, son, you rate too much to be in shape. Too many flunkies to bend over for you when you want your shoes tied."

The colonel whipped off the coat with all those shiny buttons. "You couldn't button that around your fallen chest."

In answer the grinning doctor shucked out of his laboratory smock and put his arms into the uniform jacket. With some difficulty and a certain amount of sucking in and holding back, he got it buttoned. "The hat," he demanded. He put it on. It was too small.

Meanwhile the colonel slipped into the smock, with its solder-flux stains and its worn elbows. He flapped it in front of him. "What do you do with all this yardage? Smuggle stuff? Hey, Muscles; let's have a look in the cheval glass in the office. I want to see what I'd look like as a Great Brain."

They went into the office, through the door in the shower stall. The doctor, all aglitter in his brother's jacket, went first. There was a man standing just by the outside door. He had a black cloth over his nose and mouth and a silenced automatic in his hand.

The colonel, his smock flapping, pushed past his brother and walked out into the room. The man shot him twice and disappeared through the door.

"Leroy! Who did it, kid?"

"I did," said the colonel. "*No!* No doctor. Too late. Stay—"

"You . . . oh. *Oh!* That bullet was meant for me. The jacket switch! But why? Who was it?"

"Never mind . . . him," said the colonel. "Hired. Psychoed. Whole thing planned. Foolproof escape. All witnesses called away. He doesn't know you. Or me. My idea. Was very . . . careful."

"Why? Why?"

"Found out you . . . work with . . . enemy—" His voice trailed off. He closed his eyes sleepily and lay still for a moment. Then, his face twisted with effort, he sat suddenly upright. His voice returned—his normal, heavy, crackling tone. "I had proof—proof enough that you were a traitor, Muscles. I was afraid you'd get clear if you got a chance to work on a court. But I couldn't bring myself to kill you with my own hands. I figured it out this way."

"So he'd be there, and shoot me when we came out of the office. But why didn't you call him off?"

"Couldn't. He had orders to shoot the civilian. You were an officer for the moment. He didn't know us, I tell you. I radioed to a third party, who knows nothing. He gave this hood the starting gun." He raised his left hand. On the wrist was the miniature transmitter.

"I called him when you admitted you worked with the Outsiders ... then you explained ... and I couldn't call back; he was on his way here."

"Leroy, you fool! Why didn't you let him go ahead? Why did you make that silly switch? My work's done. Nothing can change it now."

"Muscles ... I'm ... old-line Army. Can't help it ... don't like this ... brave new ... never could. You're fit for it. You made it; you live in it. Besides, you'll ... appreciate the joke better than ... I would."

"What do you mean, kid?"

"You underestimated ... you thought you'd be dead when the ... spacemen heard your recording." He laughed weakly. "You won't be, you know. Things're moving too fast."

There was a sudden, horrible spell of coughing.

And then Dr. Simmons was alone, holding his dead brother's head in his arms, rocking back and forth, buffeted and drowning in an acid flood of grief.

And behind it—far, far behind it, his articulate mind said dazedly, *Great day in the morning, he's right! What'll they make of me—a saint, or a blood-red Satan?*

The Love of Heaven

WARNER STEPPED OUT over the moon-washed outcropping and cast about for the Danby Trail. Fellow trotted past him, stood and sniffed the hot, dark air, and looked up and back at Warner.

He leaned down and clapped the collie's shoulder. "You know where it is, dogface," he grinned. "Quit stalling. Let's go!"

The dog waited, and when he took a step forward, ran ahead to the black mouth of the forest trail. "Half hound, half homing pigeon," muttered Warner, and followed.

He stepped into the shadows and hesitated a moment, blinking, shifting the strap of his carbine to let his sticky shoulder breathe. "Fellow!"

Fellow's rumbling growl answered him.

Warner was quite familiar with Fellow's vocabulary; there were barks, yaps, whimpers and growls, and variations of all. He had heard this growl before—not often, but not to be ignored. Once it was a wildcat flattened on a limb above him. Once it was an impending ice slide. And once it was a man, crouched in the shadows of his porch, waiting for him after one of these night hunts. All three were killers. Warner was still very much alive.

Eyes wide, pupils round in the velvet dark, Warner stepped forward with the sliding, silent stride of the forester. His toe touched the dog. Slowly he half-knelt, and ran his hand over Fellow's quivering back. The collie was tense, low on the ground. Warner's hand felt the flattened ears, the curled lips.

"What is it, boy?"

Again there was the ominous rumble. Warner strained his eyes in the direction indicated by the dog's straining, sensitive nose. There was nothing to be seen but blackness, and a faint oval of moonlight somewhere off the trail.

Fellow inched forward, then was still again. Warner looked uselessly down at him, and, because it was the only thing to look at, back at the patch of light.

It moved.

Warner's back hair prickled. His tongue drove against his lower teeth, his nostrils flared, and a cold ball of terror nestled below his heart.

Moonlight has no face. Moonlight does not move toward you silently, taking shapes as it passes underbrush. Moonlight does not stand before you, looking like a naked man.

It stood looking at him, glowing softly. It was six and a half feet tall, too wide at the shoulder, too narrow at the hips, with arms and legs too thin and a head not too large, but too high.

But its face ...

It wore an expression of indescribable grief. Its face spoke of loss too great to bear, of the incontrovertible end of some great, sustaining hope. The despair was lined and underlined by the strength of that face. It was the face of a conqueror and of a sage, molded of the clay of power and understanding. And it was utterly defeated.

Warner was not an imaginative man, and he was schooled to danger. His frozen mind broke free almost instantly and told him *it's a ghost!*—for there was no time for any careful analysis, any testing of improbabilities.

"Control it," said the ghost, and pointed at Fellow, who snarled.

Warner's mind was more free than his tongue. His mind formed a demanding question, and his mouth managed only an interrogative grunt. And before he could lick his lips and reform them, Fellow was away from him and in midair, his long jaws hungry for the phantom's throat.

The apparition turned easily, bent backwards from the hips, and Fellow hurtled by, his teeth castanetting together. He squirmed around and landed facing the ghost, which watched calmly. Fellow snarled softly—it was like a purr—and bunched his feet together. The ghost braced its legs, ready for another spring. But Fellow did not spring. Close to the ground, he charged at the long, slender legs. The ghost dodged the dog's teeth, but could not move quite fast enough to avoid the furry flank, which thumped the calf of its leg.

Fellow spun to attack again—and kept spinning. He yelped and snapped viciously at his side. Close enough to the glowing figure to be visible by its strange light, Fellow bent like a caterpillar with a fire ant in its side, and crabbed away into the darkness, biting himself with teeth afroth in sudden foam; and he whimpered like a sick and pain-racked child.

"Fellow!"

The dog cried, somewhere in the darkness. Warner leapt toward the sound, caught his foot in a root and fell heavily. Oddly, his right hand turned under him and was driven into his solar plexus as he fell on it. The breath rushed out of him, and for seconds he lay helpless, frightened and furious, saying, "Uh! Uh!" through his knotted windpipe.

Then he could see again, because the specter had moved between him and the dog. Fellow was on his back, kicking feebly. The dog turned on his side once more, bit again at his quarter, and suddenly lay still. His eyes were open and rolled up, his tongue out, bloody, bitten half through.

Warner got to his knees.

"Do not touch it," said the ghost warningly.

Warner looked up at it. "You killed him," he whispered, and in one smooth motion shouldered out of the strap of his carbine and raised it.

The ghost disappeared.

I've gone blind, thought Warner. He stood up, knees flexed, head low, the carbine at the ready, prepared to snap a bullet at anything, or the sound of anything.

His chest began to hurt, and he remembered to breathe.

There was silence, and blackness, fear and fury, and the warm barrel on the heel of his left thumb, the formed grip of the stock embracing each of three right fingers. He turned his head slowly, turned from the waist, from the ankles, around and back, waiting, tense. The blackness was too much, too close. He raised his eyes up, and farther up, until he could see the ghostly second reflection of moonlight on the roof of leaves above. The dim, elusive light was good.

There was a faint sound to his right. The carbine breech came up to his cheek. Silence.

He blew from his nostrils. *"Move,* damn you!"

Something moved. Something whirred and thrashed in the underbrush. Warner fired three times, the gun snuggling more affectionately to shoulder and cheek each time.

Silence again. He lowered the gun to be free to turn his head. It was wrenched out of his unsuspecting fingers. He grabbed wildly at it, clutching nothing, and staggered. He whirled, whirled again, all but seeing the certain flash, feeling the inevitable thump of his own lead into his body. He dropped, then, and lay still, the way he had done at Tulagi.

There was light behind and above him. He cringed from it, gasping, dove for a dimly-seen trunk, and crouched behind it, not looking at the light until he had cover.

The ghost was standing twenty feet away, holding his carbine easily, watching him. He ducked back. Nothing happened. The light did not waver.

He peeped out again. The ghost stood there watching him with its tragic, wise eyes. It held the carbine at its hip, not aiming directly at him, certainly not aiming away. He knew it saw him, but it made no move. Looking at the strange, sad figure, Warner felt that it would wait there all night—all week. Time seemed to have nothing to do with that not-old, not-young, infinitely patient face.

Warner pressed his lips together, cleared his throat.

"Who are you?" he asked hoarsely.

The ghost answered, "I am—" It paused, searching Warner's face, hesitating as if choosing exactly the right word. "I am—regret."

"Regret?" Wild, extraneous references tumbled through Warner's brain. *"I am the ghost of Christmas Past"*—the masks of Comedy and Tragedy painted on the proscenium of his college auditorium. Mister Coffee-Nerves. What mummery was this?

The ghost was trying again. Warner could sense the effort for accuracy. "Not regret. I am—sorry. I am sorry your dog is death. Your dog is dead."

"Who are you?" barked Warner.

The ghost again searched his face. "I am you," it said, and waited. "No," it said, and muttered to itself, "I, you, he. It." It looked at Warner. "It is I," and it struck its chest with the carbine barrel.

Warner licked his lips. He could not know what this glowing thing was, but it was obviously demented. He asked: "Are you going to shoot me?"

"Shoot," said the ghost. "Shoot me." It looked suddenly at the carbine, as if it had just understood the reference. "Not shoot. Not you dead. Not . . . shoot . . . you . . . dead."

That's nice to know, thought Warner sardonically. *It'd be even nicer if he put the gun down.*

"Yes," said the ghost. It turned, leaned the carbine carefully against a tree, and walked a pace or two away. "Now you—" and it pointed to the ground in front of Warner's tree.

"You want me to come out?"

"Come out."

Warner considered carefully. He had no idea of the capabilities of this weird creature, but it seemed human, or near enough to being human that it might be possible to fool it. If he could keep it in conversation long enough, he might be able to edge over and get his hands on the carbine and, in two senses, put an end to this nightmare. He came out.

"You not. You not . . . can not . . . get gun, get the gun. A, an, the, some, them, those," said the ghost. "What those? What are those?"

"What?"

"A, an, the, and those."

"Oh. Articles, I guess you mean. You don't speak much English?"

The creature made that strange search of his face again. "Specific," it said suddenly. "Make general. What are 'a, an, the, dog, gun?'"

"Words," said Warner after a puzzled pause.

"Words," said the ghost. "Good. Words. Say me . . . say to me . . . tell . . . teach words to me."

Warner looked briefly at the carbine leaning against the tree. Fifteen, sixteen feet ... a sudden lunge might do it. He might have to grapple for a second, but—

"Do not touch gun," said the ghost.

In spite of himself, Warner almost grinned. "What are you—a mind reader?"

"I read. I hear-see-read. Mind, yes. I read mind. I read your mind. You make ... make—" He gazed at Warner's face. "You think, I read. Yes."

"Telepathy," said Warner informatively.

"Yes. Telepathy. You send, I ... I—"

"Receive?"

"Yes. You send, I receive. I send, you not receive."

"Why?"

"You not ... not ... you can not. I can. You ... man? Yes. You are a man. I are ... am ... I am not a man."

Warner's unquenchable humor curled to the surface. "You're kidding," he said, and to his astonishment the creature laughed uproariously.

"Give me general word, man."

"Gen ... oh. Human."

"Yes. You are human. I am not human."

"What are you?"

Again one of those searches. "Different," it said finally. "Human, but different ... kind." It turned suddenly and pulled up a shrub, deftly stripping it down to a stem and a fork. It searched him again—the process was quite without sensation to Warner—and, pointing to the stem, said: "This is primate." One long luminous finger ran up a side branch. "This is human, you." Indicating the other branch, "This human, me."

"Oh. You're a mutation."

"Yes. No."

"Maybe?"

"Maybe. Maybe you are a mutation."

"I don't understand."

The creature put its finger on the crotch of the stick. "Fifteens—fifteen hundreds generations past ... back ... ago."

"You mean the race branched fifteen hundred generations ago?"

"Yes. My generations. Long ones. One of me is three of you."

Warner translated this for himself: "Forty-five hundred generations ago the human race branched into your kind and my kind. That right?"

"Right."

"Then where on earth have you been all this time?"

"Not on Earth."

"Oh—ho! The Man from Mars!"

"Not Mars," said the specter seriously. "Not a planet of this sun. Human can not live on this sun's planets except this one."

"Where is it, then?"

It tried; he could see it trying. Suddenly he understood the searching process; the creature could get a word, or an idea, more easily if he brought it up to the surface of his mind. He visualized a star map; the ghost made an impatient sound. Warner's lips twitched; he had always had a very bad memory. He visualized the night sky.

"Yes," said the glowing man.

Warner thought of constellations; of the Cross, and Lyra, Scorpio, Sirius, and the Hyades. And when he visualized the Seven Sisters, the Pleiades, the ghost exclaimed. Warner could not remember how the Pleiades were placed, exactly, but he knew that five of the major stars were easily visible, the sixth fainter, and the seventh invisible except to the very best eyesight.

"Yes. Faint one," said the ghost. "But is not one star. Is many. Is not one group of stars; you see through stars near a line from here to there. My planet is not of faint Pleiades Sister; is through it, far away on other side. You are thinking about the gun again. Do not touch it."

Warner swore.

"Your dog is dead," said the glowing man. "I did not want to dead ... to kill your dog. You are the first man for me here. I not ... did not know you can ... could not hear-receive me. I heard you. I talked-thought to you. I told you to meet me. I told you not

69

to touch me. Your dog flew to me. I not ... did not want your dog to touch me. He would dead himself if he touch me. You will dead yourself if you touch me. Your dog is dead. I am sorry. I do not want you to be dead. I will be too sorry if you are dead. When I understand that you can not hear me except me ... I speak, I went ... dark and took away gun. Human with weapon never think."

Now I get sociological truths, thought Warner wryly. "Why will you kill me if I touch you?" he asked.

"Kill," said the other, and looked at his face. "Kill, die, murder, execute, slaughter. No. I will not kill you if you touch me. Kill is what you do with ... with desire, yes. I say a different thing. I say if you touch me you will die. I am sorry your dog is dead. I am more sorry if you are dead. I do not desire you dead. My ... me ... I am—"

"Poison?"

"Yes, poison. Poison. Almost all Earth things I poison. Very ... fast." And again came that surge of tragedy across the strange, tall face. "All things of Earth. All living things—"It still held the forked twig; it looked at it sadly and, without throwing it, with a gesture of will-lessness, let it slip from between its fingers to the ground. "That would be dead now, without ... even ... even if I did not break and pull away leaves. Just to touch it— My ... my feet ... footprints are dead places."

"But why? Why do you do it?"

"Why? I do not do it! I do not make and spread poison! I *am* poison!"

"I don't understand. What are you doing here? Why stay here if you kill everything you touch?"

"I will ... try. If you do not understand, tell me to ... to stop.

"We are different humans, and this is our place where we began ... this, this planet. We grew fast and got ... gained—"

"Evolved?"

"Evolved very fast, yes. We made a ... tools ... machines ... Think of men building. Think of what men must have to build. Yes!

Yes. Intelligence. Logic. Intuition? Yes, intuition? Yes, intuition too. We understood each other well. You do not understand each other. You work with you, he works with he. If you work together, you will build, but you are ... important. Or he is important. With us, the building was important. Thirty generations made us free from ... from things outside us."

"Environment?"

"Yes. Free. To have a ... problem was to find the way ... the way to solve it. It was ... different evolution. Evolution in plants, in animals, is try this, try that, this is good, that is no good, what is no good dies. We were different. We tried only what would be good, what would build. Understand?"

"I think so," said Warner. "We have built more in the last three hundred years than we did in the three thousand before that."

"Yes. It was the way, the way we began. We lived in a valley. We lived long, each of us, and very close. We were always few. We did not go to all the earth, like you-men. We stayed in our warm valley bottom and built. We did not build cities like you-men. We did not need them. We built inside"—it touched its head—"and a few machines, when we needed them. Then came a time when we knew our valley would be killed by the sea. It was below the sea. There was a thin mountain at the end, and it would break and the sea would come in.

"Some did not care. Some moved farther inland to be saved, and we never heard about them again. A few made a machine, and left this planet."

"A spaceship!"

"Not a ship. Not like the picture you are thinking. It would be good if you could hear ... see my thinks. No, it was a machine. It made ... solid things not-solid, and then made them solid again somewhere else. The me-men, and some women, went in the machine and the machine went away from this planet.

"The machine was built to ... to seek a planet like this one; this heavy, this warm, with this air. It went far."

"Did it take long?"

"There is no take-long in such a machine. It is not understood. No man has gone in the machine for a little way. Only a long way. I am the first to go away and to come back. To be in the machine is to set the part which seeks, and to start the machine. Then the machine is there. To be outside the machine is to watch it ... disappear. It is not known if it will come back soon, or fast, or not. Or not come back. I may come back when and where I left. Or later ... large later."

"Why have you come?"

"When me-men left this planet, the machine found another. It was like this and not like this. It was more warm. It was more dark. The sun had more ... more—"

"Radiation?"

"Not more. Different. We had mutation, some mutation. Not much. This—" and, shockingly, the light went out again. And came back. "Like small animal ... insect ... like firefly. Cold light. At will. But that was many generations.

"A thing happened. The machine came to that planet and broke. It is not understood what happened. Some dies then. The others made a place to live. Many more died. The plants were not right. The plants were the same building ... the same ... the same chemically as here. The animals were the same." A questing pause. "Colloidal. Carbohydrates. Yes. But a small different—

"Think of a thing, to give me the words ... a thing you eat, or you put inside you, and it makes you happy, or it makes you move fast, or it is a poison, or you sleep."

"Drugs?"

"Yes. Drugs. Not drugs. Like drugs. What can you make inside you that will do these things?"

"I don't think I ... hold on! Hormones?"

"Yes, yes, hormones. Plants make poisons to make animals sick, so the animals will not eat the plants. Some plants are always poison because no animal can make the same poison or the ... the ... antidote? Yes, antidote, but also the thing that makes the animal strong to the poison."

"You mean the animal gets a high enough tolerance for the poison so that the poison is harmless."

"Yes. Plants make hormone poisons; animals make hormones for tolerance. Yes. When me-men lived first on that planet they had no tolerance. Many died. Grass, trees, common, just like this"—the luminous hand waved—"were poison. Animals which ate those plants were poisoned. Most of the me-men died. Some did not."

"Survival of the fittest," said Warner unnecessarily.

"Not a law," said the creature, as if it had found a blue cigarette in a box of white ones. "A balance. A balance in fluxes.

"What was left was few, sick, weak. Necessary to fight hard to live. They became fewer every generation for too long. They lost the ... the ... thinks, the way to make machines, the big simple thinks behind the way to make machines, the big simple thinks behind the way to make machines. A long time before they were strong again, and when they were strong they were different.

"They knew they changed. But they knew where they came from, and that they were once strong, and they cared for the strength. For the many generations they were weak and sick and few, they held to one big thing—this planet, this Earth. This was the Beginning, this was the Source. For long, long, they had nothing great but this one think. They felt hard about it. They—"

"A religion?"

The other studied the word as it flowed from the convolutions of Warner's brain. "Like religion. You have in you some ... things— Think of the things you can not touch with your hands, things which are big. Yes. Yes— Religion, and more. Love. Pride. Courage. What is this one? Self-respect? Yes, we have that, but not self ... selves ... the thing me-men had was like all those in one central feeling, and all felt the same and could share. Earth was our greatness, and it would be our goal. A man, any kind of man, builds on a simple strong thing—an idea or a rock or a natural force. Earth was the thing of greatness to us, the source of our strength and the strength that we held when we were weak. We are strong again; we built strong, and we built around the idea of Earth. The thing we worked for was to be wise enough again to build another traveling machine.

73

We did. A small one. Big for one. Big enough for—me."

"We have had civilizations like that," said Warner thoughtfully. "Civilizations in which the government and the religion was the same, where customs and laws all sprang from worship."

"Worship. This was not worship."

"It wasn't? Sounds like Shinto to me," said Warner bluntly. "Ancestor-worship."

"Wrong," said the other, just as bluntly. "When we were weak, we were great, because we were great when we were strong. We were same thing, weak or strong, before and now. We were . . . are great. Ancestor worship is all in the past. We were . . . are . . . will be great. And Earth is at the beginning, and Earth is at the end." And again the tragedy swept that strange face.

"We have had trouble with races which thought they were better than any other," said Warner, his distaste evident.

"Better? You understand small things only. No me-man compares with other groups. A tree is a great tree because it does the most a tree can do, and it is no greater than a great grass. I hear . . . see a thing in you . . . yes. I see it. We do not fight against ourselves. Is the difference between us."

Warner's fear had long been replaced by curiosity, and then by wonder. For the first time he began to feel a respect. After a time he asked: "What are you going to do?"

"I shall go back," said the creature. "I shall go back and tell them that Earth is here, and that it is as the legends and records say, and that we can never come back. When I tell them that it will melt the . . . bones of our building."

Warner said: "For years many of us have worshiped in a way which includes a Paradise, a Heaven; and along with it the conviction that we can never achieve it in the flesh. That is, we go there when we die."

"That is not for us. Earth is our Paradise, I think; but it is one to be reached by us with our hands and legs and shoulders, to walk on, to live in, to be a part with. And if we come we must kill it."

74

Warner's mouth was dry. "The poison—it doesn't work both ways? The plants of your planet killed you. Now you have changed. Wouldn't Earth kill you?"

"No. We were harmless to our plants, but they killed us. We kill Earth things, but they can not harm us."

"Then why can't you come?"

"Because Earth is Earth, and we can not kill it."

"You mean you are not strong enough to kill it?"

"No. We are strong enough. We are a terrible enemy. We are like you, but we are like you thinking alike, and together. We could come and kill everything, and bring our plants and animals, and have the Earth."

"I don't understand. You seem to be difficult to stop once you want something. Why don't you come?"

The glowing stranger looked at him for a long time, quietly. "We rule our planet, and we despise it. When we lived on Earth, we were a part of Earth. We do not want Earth as a part of us; and we may have it no other way."

"Your tradition is that strong?"

"The bones of our building," said the creature again. "The base, the core, the beginning, the end, and the goal."

Warner shrugged. "You will have to find something new, then."

"We will die first."

And Warner knew that that was not a figure of speech.

Warner came back the next morning, to bury his dog. He concentrated on the things he was doing; the steps he took, the bite and lift and throw of his shovel, the gloved meticulousness with which he sponged off his carbine with a rag soaked in the bottle of bleach he brought with him. He was aware that he had given and received a farewell last night, and that he had been told about the bleach, and that, to the stranger, it simply did not matter whether he told his story or not. It could not matter.

These things were too much a part of that other experience, the thing which happened after the stranger's light went out, after five quiet minutes during which Warner sat in the blackness thinking nothing, nothing at all, just watching his etched memory of the shining, grieving face.

Then there had been that glare of red, and he had floundered and stumbled to it, to see the stranger sitting in a simple chair, clean-lined, hooded, with some barely-glimpsed controls on one desklike arm. The stranger was distorted, spread, flattened and—curved, curved like the surface of a sphere, going back and away, but in directions which could not be followed. Then the light was a whirlpool of incandescent blood, its inner surface dwindling away like a Dalinese perspective, its remote convergence a speck of glittering scarlet shaped like the stranger and his chair, tiny, or distant. Warner was numb, shocked, blasted by the enormity of that indescribable *direction*.

Therefore he concentrated on the simple, solid things he had to do—burying, cleaning, walking. His separation by a few hours from that vertiginous red distance was no separation at all, and perhaps it never would be. At the moment he watched it, he knew his consciousness could have gone down into it, or—*out* into it. And now, this morning, he felt that he could still lose himself in it if he let go.

Plodding through the dim wood toward the trail, he came to the spot at which he had had his strange encounter. Here on the moss, there on the side of a shrub, yonder on the rocks where the furry body of a dead mouse lay twisted, were patches of blight. Some of it looked like the work of a blowtorch, some of it looked like a rust; but wherever it was, something was dead.

He stopped. Fellow was dead, that mouse was dead, that moss and those leaves where dead. A man could be dead, a culture could be dead. He tried to understand a civilization built on a metaphysical concept, and could not. He tried to understand how a civilization could die when that concept was negated, and could not. He knew, however, that these things could be whether he understood or not. He knew, because, for a moment, he had looked in a direction which he did not understand.

He closed his eyes and frowned. "Keep it simple," he muttered. Those other-men, those creatures—they *had* to find something different. "We will die first." What would that death be? And what would come after the death?

Life after death.

He laughed. They'd die and go to Heaven.

Then he remembered what Heaven was to these people, and he stopped laughing. It wasn't funny. He looked at the blight. It wasn't funny at all.

He sat down on a rock where he could see the dead mouse, put his chin in his hands, and wondered how, how in the name of Heaven, he could tell anyone.

Till Death Do Us Join

SANDRA OPENED THE door. It was Golly. He walked in, kicked the door closed without looking at it, taking Sandra's arm as he passed her. He spun her around to him for a kiss.

She wiped her mouth. "I don't like that, Golly."

"I do." He kissed her again. His clothes were not very clean. Sandra stayed passive in his arms, waiting to be released. He pushed her away abruptly, and turned his back. "Paul's been here," he said.

She shook her head, making a tiny negative sound. Golly picked up a severely expensive handkerchief from the divan and tossed it to her. "Ain't yours."

"It is."

He sat down, lit a cigarette, and then looked at her. "With that P sewed on?" He compressed his lips. "I got no use for a two-timing woman, Sanny. Even less for a dumb one."

Sandra's forehead paled, heightening the red on her cheekbones. "If you don't like it, Golly—"

When Golly laughed, his teeth showed right up to the gums. He was wiry and slender, with shoulders a bit too wide for his hips. Sandra was always unnerved by his utter relaxation. With Paul, now, she was continually afraid of using bad grammar.

"What's funny?" she snapped.

"You," Golly said, not laughing any more at all. "You really think you can get rid of me just by telling me off?" He folded his arms. "If I ever catch Paul here, I'll kill him. You know that."

It was perfectly true, she thought, watching him, trying to build up some armor against his narrow gaze. "Tell *him* that," she said slowly. "He's your brother, not mine. Incidentally, I'm not married to either of you. Not likely to be, either, as long as this feud goes on."

She walked over to him, stood near, knowing that he would touch her if she came an inch closer, knowing that he wanted her to. Her hair was chestnut, and she wore it long, with a rakish part on the left. Her nose was aquiline and her mouth a little twisted when she relaxed her features. Her brows made her eyes look closer together than they were, so that in profile her face changed startlingly.

No one ever treated Sandra gently but Paul. Paul was funny, though. You never could tell about Paul.... Golly, now, was predictable. Golly was going to get sore, right away, when she got this off her chest. She spoke freely:

"Golly, I like Paul. Can you understand that? Yes, he was here. He'll be here any time he feels like it, any time I ask him to come. I won't have you telling me who can and who can't come here."

A smile sprang to his lips as if it were something caught from his shrugging shoulders. He rose and came toward her. She stepped back, and he continued across to the door.

"I'm not rushing you, Sanny," he said, "but you might as well get used to the idea of having me around. 'Night." The door closed behind him, then opened again. He leaned in and said very softly, "If you see Paul again, he won't live twenty-four hours. You can tell him that from me."

Sandra drew a breath to speak, put out her hand—but he was gone. She stood for a full minute looking at the door, and then went to the divan's end-table and viciously snubbed out his cigarette.

At a dance Sandra had met Paul. He was clean-cut, charming, and wore well cut, soft-toned clothes and perfect collars. From the very first Sandra sensed some lack in him, but could never determine quite what it was. She stopped wondering about it when she met Golly.

In the two brothers she found what she wanted. If Paul had ever reached for her suddenly, wordlessly, kissed her so that it hurt— Well, it would have been Paul. But he never did. Had Golly been soft-spoken and a little gentler, she could have loved him.

And they hated each other so much that it was dangerous for her to see either, once they both became interested.

They hated each other, and yet it was through Paul, in a way, that she first met Golly. She had a date one night with Paul and the bell rang twenty minutes early. She answered it.

"Paul, you're early. Why—you're not dressed. Or—that is Paul, isn't it?"

"It is not, and don't call me that. I'm Golly." He wore a thick black sweater and she did not think he was wearing a shirt.

"Golly? Oh—Paul's brother. He mentioned you once. Come in. Is Paul—"

"Will you stop talking about that dirty heel?" he snapped.

She was shocked. "Wh-what can I do for you?" she asked faintly.

"Nothin'. Hey, stand over here by the light. Hmmm. You're okay. Like to have me around once in a while?"

"Well, I— After all, Mr. Egan—"

"To you my name's Golly." His hands took out a cigarette and lit it, apparently without his knowledge. "Keep away from that big slob."

"Please!" She was certainly not prudish, but she had never met anyone like this before.

He did not apologize. Paul would have, for less. Paul often did. Sandra didn't like this Golly, this inscrutable, impulsive brother of Paul Egan. She didn't like him, and she didn't tell him to go.

He stayed for forty-five minutes and in that time kissed her twice. He left her suddenly without saying good-by, and she sat staring at his cigarette butts for nearly an hour, with her heart beating too fast, before she realized that Paul had broken their date.

Her annoyance turned to puzzlement, and then to the realization that Paul had stayed away because Golly came. She laughed, a conscious effort which made her feel more calm, and spent the evening ironing and wondering how such a poisonous hatred could develop between the two.

Afterward, Golly dropped in at highly irregular intervals. Always, when he entered, it would be with that flashing search of the room, that sniffing of atmosphere. Twice he had sensed Paul's recent presence, and the second time it happened was the occasion of his ultimatum. "If you see Paul again, he won't live twenty-four hours."

Sandra was frankly worried. Although admittedly dramatic, Golly could be extremely thorough. When he decided to kiss her, she got kissed. If he determined to kill Paul—but they're *brothers*, she thought in sudden panic. *Brothers don't kill each other.*

Do they?

Sandra began breaking dates with Paul. Golly, of course, came more often.

She liked him less each time—and she wanted to see him more. The powerful appeal of his arrogant manner almost offset her distaste for the things he did because of it. She deeply resented the advances he made, and in her heart resented him for avoiding those he could have made. She knew, too, that his casualness was neither restraint nor indifference, but a challenging half-interest. Sandra despised herself because she was affected by it but....

Paul came, finally. She ran to the door, thinking it was Golly, for Paul never came without phoning first. But it was Paul, standing abashed under the porch light.

"Paul! Oh, you idiot! I told you not to come!"

"I know," he said gently. "I know you did. But Sandra, I hád to know why, and you wouldn't say. Can't I come in for just a moment?"

She stood aside, reminded too vividly of the way Golly rang and then pushed past her. "For just a moment, then."

He came in and she took his coat wordlessly, nodding toward the divan. He sat down and began to pack his pipe neatly and nervously. Golly smoked cigarettes and left them burning on the edges of tables.

Sandra sat beside him, knowing a little disdainfully that he would come no closer. She waited for him to say something. The silence grew painful. Twice he licked his lips and opened his mouth, and twice he closed it against the pipestem.

Finally he said, "San, please. Why won't you tell me?"

"Tell you what?"

"Don't make it any harder than it is!" he barked, and she was startled by his tone. "Why won't you see me any more?" When she would not answer, he asked, "Have I done something?"

You haven't done anything, you fool, she thought acidly. She said, "No. It's something you won't talk about. You mentioned Golly once, when I asked you if you had any relatives around here. Since then you have always managed to change the subject."

His eyes widened. "Golly." After a long moment he breathed. "Oh. I see." The he was quiet for so long that she flared up.

"Well?"

"Sandra," he said with difficulty, "there are things that—that—"

"That can't be discussed." She stood up. "So why bother? Good night, Paul."

He stayed where he was, looking at her with wide suffering eyes. "Sit down, Sandra. I'll tell you as much as I can. I'd like you to understand."

She sat down, waited.

"Golly is—is—he hates me."

"I know." She had a sudden, shocking mental picture of Golly's slitted gaze, his quiet, deadly threat. "Why?"

"I don't know," Paul said, and ran his hand roughly through his carefully combed hair. His eyes closed. "You know how—how many stories there have been about—a man's not wanting to admit to a girl concerning—insanity in the family."

"Paul." Her voice was very gentle.

"Golly is a—a— He's dangerous, Sandra."

"I know that, too."

"If I could only—face him, talk to him, I could make him go away and never come back. But he—he—"

"He keeps away from you." She remembered, suddenly, the night Golly had come when Paul was due, and that Paul had not come at all. "Where does he work? Where does he live?"

"I don't know," said Paul worriedly. "The waterfront, a warehouse—somewhere around. I never know. I—Sandra!"

She turned with him. Their faces were close.

"There's a *good* thing in all this,": he said. "You wouldn't see me. You thought that if I came here he would kill me, and you wanted to make it—safe for me. You cared enough to—"

She looked at him, his sensitive brow, his tender mouth. "Don't flatter yourself!" she blazed. "I don't want to be the cause of any silly brawls, that's all. If you want to get killed, walk in front of a truck! But don't get me mixed up in it!"

The beginnings of a smile died on his face. He rose stiffly and went for his coat. At the door he paused, but when she did not speak, he went out, closing the door carefully behind him.

That was a lousy thing to do, she thought, and ran out on the porch. "Paul!"

He was at the gate, opening it. He turned and came back.

"I'm sorry, Paul. I flew off the handle."

"That's all right," he said softly. She knew he was still hurt because he did not offer to take the blame on himself. She drew him inside, but did not offer to take his coat.

"Listen, Paul. I'm sick and tired of having you two mess up my life. Tell me what's the matter and let's do something about it, once and for all. This thing can't go on any longer the way it is. What's the trouble between you and Golly, anyway?"

He licked his lips. "It's a—a sort of psychosis, Sandra. You've seen it before, surely, but in milder forms. Most brothers—and sisters, too—feel that they are a little incomplete as long as the other exists. This is only an extreme example of it." He put up a hand, for she was about to speak.

"No, San. Don't catechize me about it. It'll work out. You'll see. If I can once get to him, get to know why he—" He shook his head. "I'll make it all right. I'll get rid of him. Trust me, Sandra—please trust me."

She looked at him, and the lip which had begun to curl relaxed again. He was so very sincere, and, for the moment, so very helpless. But he would be able to do something. And he wanted to; he cared desperately about it. Golly, now, Golly didn't care much at all. Not enough to want to do anything but—but—

"I trust you, Paul. But do something quickly, quickly, darling." She leaned forward and kissed him on the mouth; then, crying, ran upstairs.

Paul called her, but she did not answer, and he went away. From her bedroom window she saw him go down the path with his head

83

bowed. At the gate he paused, turned, removed his hat and waved it high over his head. He always did that. Always.

Three nights later, when she came home, she found Golly on the porch steps, sprawled back as if he had been poured there and half-congealed.

"Well," she said, stopping before him.

"Hi," he said, his arm moving by itself to give her a vague salute. She walked up the steps, trying to pass him. He plucked her from her feet, landing her ungracefully in his lap.

"Damn you!" she said into his mouth. He moved his head away, looked at her somberly, and kissed her forehead. Then he set her on her feet.

Trembling, she marched up to the door and opened it. She knew it would be no use to slam it in his face, so she left it open. She took one arm out of her coat, paused, rubbed her cheek where his unshaven face had rasped it. Paul was always spotlessly clean, fresh-shaven when he came. Why did these two men remind her of each other so? What kind of half-men were they?

She slung her coat on the end of the divan—an act quite foreign to habit—and turned to look at Golly, who was teetering toe-to-heel in the center of the room, staring at her through those narrowed eyes. They were so like Paul's, and yet had such a different light.

"Golly," she said, "I'd like you a lot better if you tried just a little bit to act like a—a gentleman."

"Maybe I don't want you to like me any better."

"Wh-what?"

"Sure. I don't want dames tagging along after me."

"Don't flatter yourself!" She stopped, confused by her use of the same phrase she had hurled at Paul. "What do you want?"

He raised his eyebrows interrogatively and lit a cigarette.

"What did you come for? What do you want?"

"Hm. Peevish tonight," he grunted. He threw his match on the rug and came toward her. She ducked under his arm and picked up the match. He did not try to stop her.

She felt suddenly afraid—afraid with no sense of excitement, afraid even to run from him, because she knew she could never get away.

"You saw Paul the other night."

She had no denial, could find none, could find no voice for one. Her eyes were round.

He stepped close to her, stooped a little to look into her face with his veined-marble gaze, cupping her chin in his hard hand. When he spoke his voice was soft and very gentle, like Paul's. "Oh, Sandra, Sanny, I *told* you not to see him. I told you! Why did you do it?"

"Golly," she whispered. "Don't look at me like that. I—"

He slapped her across the face twice, with the front and back of his hand. When she raised her arms, he hit her hard in the pit of the stomach. As she began to sag, his fist crashed into the side of her jaw. She hurtled backward, struck the divan and slid to the floor.

Golly stood looking at her until he saw a rhythmic pulse in her neck. "Paul!" he said, and threw a bone-crushing right fist into his left palm. Then he walked out, leaving the door open.

Sandra lay there for over an hour, though she was not unconscious all that time. She reeled to her feet presently, with some vague notion of gong to the telephone. Instead she went up to the bedroom and fell asleep there.

She dreamed. A horrible thing, in which Paul and Golly circled around her. Paul was smiling and Golly was grinning and what made it horrible was that neither of them was all there. They were half-men, sometimes the top half and sometimes the right and sometimes the left, and where the real part ended there was blood.

She tossed and screamed, and she burst out laughing and woke herself up. She rose and showered and went to bed again, sleeping very late.

The next day she called Paul Egan. She spoke urgently, hurriedly, saying only that she wanted him, needed him. He agreed to come. When he arrived she was on the porch, waiting. She had been there a long time, looking down the road, a circle of words running through her mind, losing their meaning, losing everything but the power of hate they carried. Paul kills Golly kills Paul kills Golly kills Paul. . . .

It was dusk when he came. She caught his arm and drew him inside, reaching back for the switch of the hanging lamp in the foyer.

"You see, Paul? You see?"

He looked at the knobbed discoloration on her cheek and jaw and nodded. "The scum. The dirty scum. Why did he do it?"

"Because of you, Paul." She put her face in his shoulder, and his arms went around her, easily, quietly. "Paul, Paul, he's going to kill you."

Paul tightened his arms around her and then pressed her away. He shrugged out of his coat and hung it on the newel post. "When was he here?"

"Last night, early."

"I—had an idea." She wished she could see his face.

"You had? Paul, why didn't you come?"

He laughed a little. "Last time I was here you said you wanted no violence. Remember?"

"Yes. Well—I—got the violence. What are we going to do?"

"Have you any ideas?"

"I want him killed," she said dully, and cringed as if from herself. "Paul! I didn't mean that! I— Oh, I don't know what I'm saying!"

"Killing him wouldn't be a way out," Paul said in a harsh voice. "We've got to—I've got—" He clutched his face, rocking his head back and forth. "If I could only know what he was doing—find out how he—"

"There can't be a showdown, if that's what you mean," she said, coming to him, comforting him. "He'd be on you like a snake."

"Oh no. You don't understand. He wouldn't work that way, no matter how direct and violent he seems to you. He'd figure something out cleverly, set a trap for me. He wouldn't—do anything to me directly."

"He's afraid of you!"

"Perhaps he is," whispered Paul. His upper lip was wet. "I can't stand any more of this, Sandra, I can't. We'll have to force his hand. If he once tries to kill me and fails, I don't think he'll ever come back. It's as far as he can go."

"Why? I don't see why. Why don't you find him? Why don't you have him arrested? What kind of a man are you—" her hand strayed

86

to her bruised face—"that you can think of waiting for him to make the next move after *this?*"

He looked at her, and the twisted agony in his eyes wrung something within her. "Trust me, Sandra. I know what I'm up against. I tell you, if he tries and fails, you'll never see him again. I *know*. Trust me."

She took his hands. "He'll kill you."

"I think not. Not if I'm careful. Not if I watch every move I make. I know how he works. He will set some sort of trap somewhere where I do something regularly. I must do nothing quite the same until he tries to—to—Oh, Sandra! Why did this have to happen to you? I love you. You asked for none of this. Maybe it would be better if I went away and never—"

She closed his mouth with her hand. "I thought of that, Paul. Maybe I'm crazy—maybe something's wrong with me, I don't know; but nobody, nobody ever before was willing to risk being killed for me. You could run away and hide, but you're sticking to face it— for me. I'm not afraid."

There were no words in what they had to say to each other after that.

Later, he looked at his watch. "San, can you spend the night in town? I'll get a hotel reservation for you. You'll be quite safe. I'll have lunch with you, and dinner, and we'll go to a show. Then I'll bring you back here. He'll know, you see; and when we get back here tomorrow night, together, he'll try. I know him."

She rose. "You're sure, Paul?"

"I'm sure."

She ran to get her bag packed.

He phoned her, anxiously, at bedtime, and again the next morning. They had lunch together at the Criterion, and dinner at the Sable Antelope, and took in a show.

In the taxi on the way back to her house, they were tense and silent until she asked, "You think he will be there?"

He nodded. "He should be. He knows ... he must know."

She moved closer to him, and after a moment said, "Paul, don't— kill him."

"It isn't likely that I would," he said gently.

"Don't. Not for his sake, but—"

He held her close. "I know. I know," he murmured.

The cab deposited them at the curb and droned away with its life and its lights. They stood breathless, listening.

"I'm scared," she whispered. She felt his noiseless chuckle.

"Sure sign you're normal," he answered. "Come on."

She held back, questioning his sudden decisiveness. He bent and kissed her swiftly, a gesture so tender that again she was joltingly reminded of Golly's ruthlessness, and she gasped in terror, feeling Golly so close.

Paul held the gate open for her, and they tiptoed up the path. She would have mounted the steps, but he stopped her.

"This is the way we always come," he reminded her. "We must not do anything the same. I know him, darling. Some habit-pattern, some little, usual thing I do—that's where he'll ambush me. I *know*, Sandra. Uh—have you a key to the kitchen door?"

She nodded, and they crept around the house. Once a twig cracked somewhere, and once a dog howled down the road, and both times they froze and stood for minutes, their nerves strumming.

"Be funny if Golly wasn't around here at all," Paul breathed.

"Oh, he is, I know he is!" Sandra half sobbed. "Oh. I wish we were inside!"

"Don't be frightened!" he said, shaking her a little. "As long as you stay close to me he'll do nothing. If he wanted to kill you, he'd have done it the other night. It's me he's after. Hurry; open the door."

The key was annoyingly disobedient in her fingers, but she got the door open. She pulled him in and away from it and slid the bolt. Then she turned on the light and screamed at the looming bulk in the corner.

"Silly! It's just your raincoat!" Paul hissed.

It was, and the reaction was crushing. She clung to him, trembling.

When she had quieted, he spoke. "You're quite safe now, San. Turn out the light. I'll go. No one will see me slip out, it's so dark. I've outwitted him so far. If I can once get home, I can—lock myself in. But I wish he tries. I wish he tries to kill me, and fails. If he does, he will never come back."

"Oh Paul, I hope you're right! I hope you know what you're doing!" she cried.

"I do, darling. Truly I do. Trust me. And don't worry. I'll be careful. Good night, darling." He did not attempt to kiss her, and again she had that suffocating awareness of Golly's presence.

In the darkness he left her. A blacker piece of blackness, he glided out to the door and entered the garden.

She reshot the bolt, and ran to the front windows. She could just see him out there, stepping softly along the edge of the path, on the lawn, freezing suddenly as the willows rustled in the casual breeze.

After a long while he moved again, reached the gate, and instead of swinging it wide as he usually did, opened it only enough to let him slide through. He let it close, leaned back over it, and stared carefully all around him. Her eyelids strained in sympathy with his.

Then he stood erect, and with the old, endearing gesture, whipped off his hat and waved it high over his head. She smiled, and three jets of flame squirted toward him and he fell writhing to the sidewalk, his agonies drowning out the echoes of the gunshots.

It seemed to Sandra that he choked for a long, long time. Then she was conscious of the stillness and of the cramped muscles in her cheeks, holding her smile, and of the other, sharper pain of the long splinter she had driven under her fingernail when she clutched at the windowsill.

Then she walked to the telephone and called the police, and sat woodenly in the dark to wait.

There was a fatherly man who asked questions in a soft voice. He had pointed gray eyebrows, and came after all the others, the ones who took Paul away and the ones with floodlights and flash-bulbs.

The fatherly man asked her all about Paul and Golly, and how long she had known them, and how she felt about them, and many questions about herself. She answered them all, the answers seeming to come only from the front of her face. She kept her hands over her eyes, and spoke dully from between the heels of her hands.

When he had stopped his questions, he thought for minutes, silently. She took her hands down then, and began her own questions.

89

"Where was he?"

"Who?"

"Golly, of course!"

He looked at her sadly.

"There was no one there but Paul."

"But the guns—"

"The guns were tied to the trees on each side of the path, and to the eaves of the house. There were strings from their triggers, knotted together over the gate. When he waved his hat—"

"He always did that."

"Of course. He knew that the attempt would be made around some accustomed action—and he forgot to change that one."

She tossed her head miserably from side to side. "I don't understand!"

The kindly man spread his hands.

"You've heard about the psychosis that sometimes affects twins, haven't you? The thing that makes one feel incomplete as long as the other exists?"

"I—suppose so."

"Well, this is just an extension of the same thing."

"But that's crazy!"

The man shook his head slightly. "Paul Egan wasn't exactly all there."

"*Paul?*"

"Paul, yes. Paul Egan, the man who murdered himself."

She sprang up. "But it was Golly! It was Golly who killed Paul!"

"Sandra—you don't mind if I call you Sandra?—can't I make you understand? There was only one of them."

"Oh, no. No. Golly was—"

"—was Paul. Be quiet, now, and listen to me. Paul Egan was what is called a 'dissociative personality.' Some people have three or four very strong and quite separate personalities. Paul's divided quite sharply and completely."

"But didn't he know?"

"He knew, all right—but the chances are that he never remembered what he did when he was Golly."

90

"Why didn't he tell me?" she whispered.

"He loved you, I suppose."

"Why did he let Golly—why did he take that chance?"

The man shrugged. "I can only guess. From what you tell me, I gather that he was convinced that 'Golly's' failure in a murder attempt would be the end of Golly in his life. He probably reasoned that for the 'Golly' personality to be caught in an effort to do away with himself would be such a shock that 'Golly' would never return."

"Golly and Paul," she murmured. "You're playing with me!" she flared. "I don't believe it. I won't! I won't!"

He caught her wrists, pressed her gently back to her chair. "Listen to me, child. On the guns, on all of Golly's presents, on the tools that were used to make the booby-trap, and all over the house, are Paul Egan's fingerprints."

After a while, Sandra believed it.

The Perfect Host

I
As Told By
Ronnie Daniels

I WAS FOURTEEN then. I was sitting in the car waiting for dad to come out of the hospital. Dad was in there seeing mother. It was the day after dad told me I had a little sister.

It was July, warm, and I suppose about four in the afternoon. It was almost time for dad to come out. I half opened the car door and looked for him.

Someone called, "Mister! Mister!"

There was a red squirrel arcing across the thick green lawn, and a man with balloons far down the block. I looked at him. Nobody would call me mister. Nobody ever had, yet. I was too young.

"Mister!"

It was a woman's voice, but rough; rough and nasty. It was strong, and horrible for the pleading in it. No strong thing should beg. The sun was warm, too. The squirrel was not afraid.

The grass was as green and smooth as a jelly bean.

Mother was all right, dad said, and dad felt fine. We would go to the movies, dad and I, close together with a closeness that never happened when things were regular, meals at home, mother up making breakfast every morning, and all that. This week it would be raids on the icebox and staying up late sometimes, because dad forgot about bedtime and anyway wanted to talk.

"Mister!"

Her voice was like a dirty mark on a new collar. I looked up. She was hanging out of a window on the second floor of a near ell of the hospital. Her hair was dank and stringy, her eyes had mud in them, and her teeth were beautiful.

She was naked, at least to the waist. She was saying "Mister!" and she was saying it to me.

I was afraid, then. I got in the car and slammed the door.

"Mister! Mister! Mister!"

They were syllables that meant nothing. A "mis," a "ter"—sounds that rasped across the very wound they opened. I put my hands over my ears, but by then the sounds were inside my head, and my hands just seemed to keep them there. I think I sobbed. I jumped out of the car and screamed, "What? What?"

"I got to get out of here," she moaned.

I thought, why tell me? I thought, what can I do? I had heard of crazy people, but I had never seen one. Grown-up people were sensible, mostly. It was only kids who did crazy things, without caring how much sense they made. I was only fourteen.

"Mister," she said. "Go to—to.... Let me think, now. ... Where I live. Where I live."

"Where do you live?" I asked.

"In Homeland," she said.

She sank down with her forehead on the sill, slowly, as if some big slow weight were on her shoulderblades. I could see only the top of her head, the two dank feathers of her hair, and the point of an elbow. Homeland was a new residential suburb.

"Where in Homeland?" It seemed to be important. To me, I mean, as much as to her.

"Twenty," she mumbled. "I have to remember it ..." and her voice trailed off. Suddenly she stood bolt upright, looking back into the room as if something had happened there. Then she leaned far out.

"Twenty sixty-five," she snarled. "You hear? Twenty sixty-five. That's the one."

"Ron! Ronnie!"

It was dad, coming down the path, looking at me, looking at the woman.

"That's the one," said the woman again.

93

There was a flurry of white behind her. She put one foot on the sill and sprang out at me. I closed my eyes. I heard her hit the pavement.

When I opened my eyes they were still looking up at the window. There was a starched white nurse up there with her fingers in her mouth, all of them, and eyes as round and blank as a trout's. I looked down.

I felt dad's hand on my upper arm. "Ronnie!"

I looked down. There was blood, just a little, on the cuff of my trousers. There was nothing else.

"Dad...."

Dad looked all around, on the ground.

He looked up at the window and at the nurse. The nurse looked at dad and at me, and then put her hands on the sill and leaned out and looked all around on the ground. I could see, in the sunlight, where her fingers were wet from being in her mouth.

Dad looked at me and again at the nurse, and I heard him draw a deep quivering breath as if he'd forgotten to breathe for a while and had only just realized it. The nurse straightened up, put her hands over her eyes and twisted back into the room.

Dad and I looked at each other. He said, "Ronnie—what was— what ..." and then licked his lips.

I was not as tall as my father, though he was not a tall man. He had thin, fine obedient hair, straight and starting high. He had blue eyes and a big nose and his mouth was quiet. He was broad and gentle and close to the ground, close to the earth.

I said, "How's mother?"

Dad gestured at the ground where something should be, and looked at me. Then he said, "We'd better go, Ron."

I got into the car. He walked around it and got in and started it, and then sat holding the wheel, looking back at where we had been standing. There was still nothing there. The red squirrel, with one cheek puffed out, came bounding and freezing across the path.

I asked again how mother was.

"She's fine. Just fine. Be out soon. And the baby. Just fine." He looked back carefully for traffic, shifted and let in the clutch. "Good as new," he said.

I looked back again. The squirrel hopped and arched and stopped, sitting on something. It sat on something so that it was perhaps ten inches off the ground, but the thing it sat on couldn't be seen. The squirrel put up its paws and popped a chestnut into them from its cheek, and put its tail along its back with the big tip curled over like a fern front, and began to nibble. Then I couldn't see any more.

After a time dad said, "What happened there just as I came up?"

I said, "What happened? Nothing. There was a squirrel."

"I mean, uh, up at the window."

"Oh, I saw a nurse up there."

"Yes, the nurse." He thought for a minute. "Anything else?"

"No. What are you going to call the baby?"

He looked at me strangely. I had to ask him again about the baby's name.

"I don't know yet," he said distantly. "Any ideas?"

"No, Dad."

We rode along for quite a while without saying anything. A little frown came and went between dad's eyes, the way it did when he was figuring something out, whether it was a definition at charades, or an income tax report, or a problem of my school algebra.

"Dad. You know Homeland pretty well, don't you?"

"I should. Our outfit agented most of those sites. Why?"

"Is there a Homeland Street, or a Homeland Avenue out there?"

"Not a one. The north and south ones are streets, and are named after trees. The east and west ones are avenues, and are named after flowers. All alphabetical. Why?"

"I just wondered. Is there a number as high as twenty sixty-five?"

"Not yet, though I hope there will be some day ... unless it's a telephone number. Why, Ron? Where did you get that number?"

"I dunno. Just thought of it. Just wondered. Where are we going to eat?"

We went to the Bluebird.

I suppose I knew then what had gotten into me when the woman jumped; but I didn't think of it, any more than a redhead goes around thinking to himself "I have red hair" or a taxi-driver says to himself "I drive a cab."

I knew, that's all. I just knew. I knew the *purpose*, too, but didn't think of it, any more than a man thinks and thinks of the place where he works, when he's on his way to work in the morning.

II
As Told By
Benton Daniels

RONNIE'S NOT AN unusual boy. Oh, maybe a little quieter than most, but it takes all kinds. He's good in school, but not brilliant; averages in the low eighties, good in music and English and history, weak in math, worse in science than he could be if he cared a little bit more about it.

That day when we left the hospital grounds, though, there was something unusual going on. Yes, sir. I couldn't make head nor tail of it, and I must say I still can't.

Sometimes I think it's Ronnie, and sometimes I think it was something temporarily wrong with me. I'm trying to get it all straight in my mind, right from the start.

I had just seen Clee and the baby. Clee looked a little tired, but her color was wonderful. The baby looked like a baby—that is, like a little pink old man, but I told Clee she was beautiful and takes after her mother, which she will be and do, of course, when she gets some meat on her bones.

I came along the side path from the main entrance, toward where the car was parked. Ronnie was waiting for me there. I saw him as I turned toward the road, just by the north building.

Ronnie was standing by the car, with one foot on the running board, and he seemed to be talking with somebody in the second-floor window. I called out to him, but he didn't hear. Or he paid no attention. I looked up, and saw someone in the window. It was a woman, with a crazy face. I remember an impression of very regular white teeth, and scraggly hair. I don't think she had any clothes on.

I was shocked, and then I was very angry. I thought, here's some poor sick person gone out of her mind, and she'll maybe mark Ronnie for life, standing up there like that and maybe saying all sorts of things.

I ran to the boy, and just as I reached him, the woman jumped. I think someone came into the room behind her.

Now, look. I distinctly heard that woman's body hit. It was a terrible sound. And I remember feeling a wave of nausea just then, but for some reason I was sure then, and I'm sure now, that it had nothing to do with the thing I saw. That kind of shock-nausea only hits a person after the shock, not before or during. I don't even know why I think of this at all. It's just something I feel sure about, that's all.

I heard her body hit. I don't know whether I followed her body down with my eyes or not. There wasn't much time for that; she didn't fall more than twenty-five, maybe twenty-eight feet.

I heard the noise, and I when I looked down—*there wasn't anything there!*

I don't know what I thought then. I don't know if a man does actually *think* at a time like that. I know I looked all around, looking for a hole in the ground or maybe a sheet of camouflage or something which might be covering the body. It was too hard to accept that disappearance. They say that a dog doesn't bother with its reflection in a mirror because he can't smell it, and he believes his nose rather than his eyes. Humans aren't like that, I guess. When your brain tells you one thing and your eyes another, you just don't know what to believe.

I looked back up at the window, perhaps thinking I'd been mistaken, that the woman would still be up there.

She was gone, all right. There was a nurse up there instead, looking down, terrified.

I returned to Ronnie and started to ask him what had happened. I stopped when I saw his face. It wasn't shocked, or surprised, or anything. Just relaxed. He asked me how his mother was.

I said she was fine. I looked at his face and marveled that it showed nothing of the horrible thing that had happened. It wasn't blank, mind you. It was just as if nothing had occurred at all, or as if the thing had been wiped clean out of his memory.

I thought at the moment that that was a blessing, and, with one more glance at the window—the nurse had gone—I went to the car and got in. Ronnie sat next to me. I started the car, then looked back at the path. There was nothing there.

I suppose the reaction hit me then—that, or the thought that I had had a hallucination. If I had, I was naturally worried. If I had not, what had happened to Ronnie?

I drove off, finally. Ronnie made some casual small talk; I questioned him about the thing, carefully, but he seemed honestly to know nothing about it. I decided to let well enough alone, at least for the time being....

We had a quick dinner at the Bluebird, and then went home. I suppose I was poor company for the boy, because I kept finding myself mulling over the thing. We went to the Criterion, and I don't believe I heard or saw a bit of it. Then we picked up an evening paper and went home. He went to bed while I sat up with the headlines.

I found it at the bottom of the third page. This is the item:

WOMAN DIES IN HOSPITAL LEAP

Mrs. Helmuth Stoye, of Homeland, was found yesterday afternoon under her window at Memorial Hospital, Carstairs. Dr. R.B. Knapp, head physician at the hospital, made a statement to the press in which he absolved the hospital and staff from any charges of negligence. A nurse, whose name is withheld, had just entered Mrs. Stoye's room when the woman leaped to her death.

"There was no way to stop her," said Dr. Knapp. "It happened too fast."

Dr. Knapp said that Mrs. Stoye had shown known signs of depression or suicidal intent on admission to the hospital. Her specific illness was not divulged.

Mrs. Stoye, the former Grace Korshak of Ferntree, is survived by her husband, a well-known printer here.

I went straight to the telephone and dialed the hospital. I heard the ringing signal once, twice, and then, before the hospital could answer, I hung up again. What could I ask them or tell them? "I saw

Mrs. Stoye jump." They'd be interested in that, all right. Then what? "She disappeared when she hit the ground." I can imagine what they'd say to that. "But my son saw it too!" and the questions from hospital officials, a psychiatrist or two. . . . Ronnie being questioned, after he had mercifully forgotten about the whole thing . . . no. No; better let well enough alone.

The newspaper said Mrs. Stoye was found under her window. Whoever found her must have been able to see her.

I wonder what the nurse saw?

I went into the kitchen and heated some coffee, poured it, sweetened it, stirred it, and then left it untasted while I put on my hat and got my car keys.

I had to see that nurse. First I tore out the newspaper article—I didn't want Ronnie ever to see it.

III
As Told By
Lucille Holder

I HAVE SEEN a lot of ugly things as a trainee and as a nurse, but they don't bother me very much. It's not that the familiarity hardens one; it rather that one learns the knack of channeling one's emotions around the ugly thing.

When I was a child in England I learned how to use this knack. I lived in Coventry, and though Herr Hitler's treatment of the city seems to have faded from the news and from fiction, the story is still vividly written on the memories of us who were there, and is read and reread more often than we care to say.

You can't know what this means until you know the grim happiness that the chap you've dug out of the ruins is a dead 'un, for the ones who still live horrify you so.

So—one gets accustomed to the worst. Further, one is prepared when a worse "worst" presents itself.

And I suppose that it was this very preparation which found me jolly well unprepared for what happened when Mrs. Stoye jumped out of her window.

There were two things happening from the instant I opened her door. One thing was what I did, and the other thing was what I felt.

These are the things I did:

I stepped into the room, carrying a washing tray on my arm. Everything seemed in order, except, of course, that Mrs. Stoye was out of bed. That didn't surprise me; she was ambulant. She was over by the window; I suppose I glanced around the room before I looked directly at her.

When I saw her pajama top lying on the bedclothes I looked at her, though.

She straightened up suddenly as she heard me, barked something about "That's the one!" and jumped—dived, rather—right out. It wasn't too much of a drop, really—less than thirty feet, I'd say, but she went down head first, and I knew instantly that she hadn't a chance.

I can't remember setting down the washing tray; I saw it later on the bed. I must have spun around and set it there and rushed to the window.

I looked down, quite prepared for the worst, as I've said.

But what I saw was so terribly much worse than it should have been. I mean, an ill person is a bad thing to see, and an accident can be worse, and burn cases, I think, are worst of all. The thing is, these all get worse in one direction. One simply cannot be prepared for something which is bad in a totally unexpected, impossible way.

There was nothing down there at all. Nothing. I saw Mrs. Stoye jump out, ran to the window, it couldn't have been more than three seconds later; and there was nothing there.

But I'm saying now how I felt. I mean to say first what I did, because the two are so different, from this point on.

I looked down; there was no underbrush, no flowerbed, nothing which could have concealed her had she rolled. There were some people—a stocky man and a young boy, perhaps fourteen or fifteen—standing nearby. The man seemed to be searching the ground as I was; I don't remember what the boy was doing. Just standing there. The man looked up at me; he looked badly frightened. He spoke to the boy, who answered quietly, and then they moved off together to the road.

I looked down once more, still could not see Mrs. Stoye, and turned and ran to the signal-button.

I rang it and then rushed out into the hall. I must have looked very distraught.

I ran right into Dr. Knapp, all but knocking him over, and gasped out that Mrs. Stoye had jumped.

Dr. Knapp was terribly decent. He led me back into the room and told me to sit down. Then he went to the window, looked down and grunted. Miss Flaggon came in just then. I was crying.

Dr. Knapp told her to get a stretcher and a couple of orderlies and take them outside, under this window. She asked no questions, but fled; when Dr. Knapp gives orders in that voice, people jump to it. Dr. Knapp ran out, calling me to stay where I was until he came back. In spite of the excitement, he actually managed to make his voice gentle.

I went to the window after a moment and looked down. Two medical students were running across the lawn from the south building, and the orderlies with their stretcher, still rolled, were pelting down the path. Dr. Knapp, bag in hand, was close behind them.

Dr. Carstairs and Dr. Greenberg were under the window and already shunting away the few curious visitors who had appeared as if from out of the ground, the way people do after an accident anywhere. But most important of all, I saw Mrs. Stoye's body. It was lying crumpled up, directly below me, and there was no doubt of it that her neck was broken and her skull badly fractured. I went and sat down again.

Afterward Dr. Knapp questioned me closely and, I must say, very kindly. I told him nothing about the strange disappearance of the body. I expect he thought I was crying because I felt responsible for the death. He assured me that my record was in my favor, and it was perfectly understandable that I was helpless to stop Mrs. Stoye.

I apparently went quite to pieces then, and Dr. Knapp suggested that I take my two weeks' leave—it was due in another twenty days in any case—immediately, and rest up and forget this thing.

I said, "Perhaps I will."

I went out to the Quarters to bathe and change. And now I had better say how I *felt* during all this....

I was terrified when Mrs. Stoye jumped. When I reached the window right afterward, I was exactly as excited as one might expect.

But the instant I looked down, something happened. It wasn't anything I can describe, except to say that there was a change of attitude. That doesn't seem to mean much, does it? Well, I can only say this; that from that moment I was no longer frightened nor shocked nor horrified nor anything else. I remember putting my hands up to my mouth, and must have given a perfect picture of a terrified nurse.

I was actually quite calm. I was quite cool as I ran to the bell and then out into the hall. I collapsed, I cried, I sobbed, I produced a flood of tears and streaks for my face. But during every minute of it I was completely calm.

Now, I knew that was strange, but I felt no surprise at it. I knew that it could be called dishonest. I don't know how to analyze it. I am a nurse, and a profound sense of duty has been drilled into me for years. I felt that it was my duty to cry, to say nothing about the disappearance of the body, to get two weeks' leave immediately, and to do the other things which I have done and must do.

While I bathed I thought. I was still calm, and I suppose I behaved calmly; it didn't matter, for there was no one to see.

Two people had seen Mrs. Stoye jump beside myself. I realized that I must see them. I didn't think about the disappearing body. I didn't feel I had to, somehow, any more than one thinks consciously of the water in the pipes and heaters as one draws a bath. The thing was there, and needed no investigation.

But it was necessary to see that man and the boy. What I must do when I saw them required no thought either. That seemed all arranged, unquestionable, so evident that it needed no thought or definition.

I put away the white stockings and shoes with a feeling of relief, and slipped into underthings with a bit of lace on them, and sheer hose. I put on my wine rayon with the gored skirt, and the matching shoes. I combed my hair out and put it up in a roll around the back, cool and out of the way. Money, keys, cigarette case, knife, lighter, compact. All ready.

I went round by the administration offices, thinking hard. A man visits the hospital with his boy—it was probably his boy—and leaves the boy outside while he goes in. He would be seeing a wife, in all probability. He'd leave the boy outside only if the woman's condition was serious or if she were immediately post-operative or post-partum.

So many patients go in and out that I naturally don't remember too many of them; on the other hand, I can almost always tell a new patient or visitor ... marvelous the way the mind, unbidden, clocks and catalogs, to some degree, all that passes before it. . . .

The chances were that these people, the man and the boy, were visiting a new patient. Maternity would be as good a guess as any, to start with.

It was well after nine o'clock, the evening of Mrs. Stoye's death, and the administration offices were deserted except for Miss Kaye, the night registrar. It was not unusual for nurses to check up occasionally on patients. I nodded to Miss Kaye and went back to the files. The maternity admission file gave me five names for the previous two days. I got the five cards of of the patients' alphabetical and glanced over them. Two of these new mothers had other children; a Mrs. Korff, with three sons and a daughter at home, and a Mrs. Daniels who had one son. Here: "Previous children: One. Age this date: 14 yrs. 3 months." And further down: "Father age: 41."

It looked like a bull's eye. I remember feeling inordinately pleased with myself, as if I had assisted particularly well in an operation, or had done a bang-up job of critical first-aid.

I copied down the address of the Daniels family, and, carefully replacing all the cards, made my vacation checkout and left the building.

It seemed late to go calling, but I knew that I must. There had been a telephone number on the card, but I had ignored it. What I must do could not be done over the phone.

I found the place fairly easily, although it was a long way out in the suburbs on the other side of the town. It was a small, comfortable-looking place, set well back from the road, and with wide lawns and its own garage. I stepped up on the porch and quite shamelessly looked inside.

The outer door opened directly into the living room, without a foyer. There was a plate-glass panel in the door with a sheer curtain on the inside. I could see quite clearly. The room was not too large—fireplace, wainscoting, stairway in the left corner, big easy chairs, a studio couch—that sort of thing. There was a torn newspaper tossed on the arm of one fireside chair. Two end table lamps were lit. There was no one in the room.

I rang the bell, waited, rang again, peering in. Soon I saw a movement on the stairs. It was the boy, thin-looking and tousled, thumping down the carpeted steps, tying the cord of a dark-red dressing gown as he came. On the landing he stopped.

I could just hear him call "Dad!" He leaned over the bannister, looking up and back. He called again, shrugged a shrug which turned into a stretch, and, yawning, came to the door. I hid the knife in my sleeve.

"Oh!" he said, startled, as he opened the door. Unaccountably, I felt a wave of nausea. Getting a grip on myself, I stepped inside before I spoke. He stood looking at me, flushing, a bit conscious, I think, of his bare feet, for he stood on one of them, trying to curl the toes of the other one out of sight.

"Daniels. . . ." I murmured.

"Yes," he said, "I'm Ronald Daniels." He glanced quickly into the room. "Dad doesn't seem to be . . . I don't . . . I was asleep."

"I'm so sorry."

"Gosh, that's all right," he said. He was a sweet little chap, not a man yet, not a child—less and less of a child as he woke up, which he was doing slowly. He smiled. "Come in. Let me have your coat. Dad ought to be here now. Maybe he went for cigarettes or something."

It was as if a switch had been thrown and a little sign had lit up within him—"Remember your manners."

Abruptly I felt the strangest compulsion—a yearning, a warming toward this lad. It was completely a sexual thing, mind you—completely. But it was as if a part of me belonged to a part of him . . . no; more the other way round. I don't know. It can't be described.

And with the feeling, I suddenly knew that it was all right, it was all quite all right.

I did not have to see Mr. Daniels after all. That business would be well taken care of when the time came, and not by me. Better—much better—for him to do it.

He extended his hand for my coat. "Thank you *so* much," I said, smiling, liking him—more than liking him, in this indefinable way—"but I really must go. I—if your father—" How could I say it? How could I let him know that it was different now; that everything might be spoiled if his father knew I had come here? "I mean, when your father comes back. . . ."

Startlingly, he laughed. "Please don't worry," he said. "I won't tell him you were here."

I looked at his face, his round, bland face, so odd with his short slender frame. That thing like a sense of duty told me not to ask, but I violated it. "You don't know who I am, do you?"

He shook his head. "Not really. But it doesn't matter. I won't tell dad."

"Good." I smiled, and left.

IV
As Told By
Jennie Beaufort

YOU NEVER KNOW what you're going to run up against when you're an information operator, I mean really, people seem to have the craziest idea of what we're there for. Like the man called up the other day and wanted to know how you spell conscientious—"Just conscientious," he says, "I know how to spell objector," and I gave him the singsong, you know, the voice with a smile, "I'm soreee! We haven't that infor*may*—shun!" and keyed him out, thinking to myself, what a schmoe. (I told Mr. Parker, he's my super, and he grinned and said it was a sign of the times; Mr. Parker's always making jokes.) And like the other man wants to know if he gets a busy signal and hangs on to the line, will the signal stop and the bell ring when the party he is calling hangs up.

I want to say to him, what do you think I am, Alexander Graham Bell or something, maybe Don Ameche, instead of which I tell him, "One moment, sir, and I will get that information for you?" (not that I'm asking a question, you raise your voice that way because it leaves the customers breathless) and I nudge Sue and she tells me, Sue knows everything.

Not that everything like that comes over the wire, anything is liable to happen right there in the office or in the halls to say nothing of the stage-door Johnnies with hair oil and cellophane boxes who ask all the girls if they are Operator 23, she has such a nice voice.

Like the kid that was in here yesterday, not that he was on the prowl, he was too young, though five years from now he'll be just dreamy, with his cute round face and his long legs. Mr. Parker brought him in to me and told me the kid was getting up a talk for his civics class in high school, and tells the kid to just ask Miss Beaufort anything he wants to know and walks off rubbing his hands, which I can understand because he has made me feel good and made the kid feel good and has me doing all the work while he gets all the credit.

Not that I felt good just at that particular moment, my stomach did a small flip-flop, but that has nothing to do with it; it must have been the marshmallow cake I had for my lunch, I should remember to keep away from the marshmallow when I have gravy-and-mashed, at least on weekdays.

Anyway this kid was cute, with his pleases and his thank you's and his little almost bows-from-the-waist like a regular Lord Calvert. He asked me all sorts of questions and all smart too, but he never asked them right out, I mean, he would say, "Please tell me how you can find a number so *fast?*" and then listen to every word I said and squiggle something down in his notebook. I showed him the alphabeticals and the central indexes and the assonance file (and you can bet I called it by its full name to that nice youngster) where we find out that a number for Meyer, say, is listed as Maior. And he wanted to know why it was that we never give a street address to someone who has the phone number, but only the other way around, and how we found out the phone number from just the street address.

So I showed him the street index and the checking index, which has the numbers all in order by exchanges with the street addresses, which is what we use to trace calls when we have to. And lots more. And finally he said he wanted to pretend he was me for a minute, to see if he understood everything. He even blushed when he said it. I told him to go ahead and got up and let him sit down. He sat there all serious and bright-eyed, and said, "Now, suppose I am you, and someone wants to know the number of—uh—Fred Zimmerman, who lives out at Bell Hill, but they have no street number."

And I showed him how to flip out the alphabetical, and how to ask the customer which one he wants if there should be more than one Fred Zimmerman. He listened so carefully and politely, and make a note in his book. Then he asked me what happens of the police or somebody has a phone number and wants the address, we'll say, out in Homeland, like Homeland 2050. I showed him the numerical index, and whipped it out and opened it like an old hand. My, he caught on quickly. He made another note in his book ... well, it went on like that, and all in twenty minutes.

I bet he could take over from me any time and not give Mr. Parker a minute's worry, which is more than I can say for some of the girls who have been working here for years, like that Patty Mawson with her blonde hair and her awful New Look.

Well, that boy picked my brains dry in short order, and he got up and for a moment I thought he was going to kiss my hand like a Frenchman or a European, but he didn't. He just thanked me as if had given him the crown jewels or my hand in marriage, and went out to do the same for Mr. Parker, and all I can say is, I wish one-tenth of the customers showed as much good house-breaking.

V
As Told By
Helmuth Stoye

Grace ... Grace ... *Grace!*

Oh, my little darling, my gentle, my soft little bird with the husky voice. Miss Funny-Brows. Little Miss Teeth. You used to laugh such a special laugh when I made up new names for you, Coral-cache, Cadenza, Viola-voice ... and you'll never laugh again, because I killed you.

I killed you, I killed you.

Yesterday I stopped all the clocks.

I couldn't stand it. It was wrong; it was a violation. You were dead. I drew the blinds and sat in the dark, not really believing that it had happened—how *could* it happen? You're *Grace,* you're the humming in the kitchen, the quick footfalls in the foyer as I come up the porch steps.

I think for a while I believed that your coming back was the most real, the most obvious thing; in a moment, any moment, you would come in and kiss the nape of my neck; you would be smelling of vanilla and cut flowers, and you'd laugh at me and together we'd fling up the blinds and let in the light.

And then Tinkle struck—Tinkle, the eight-foot grandfather's clock with the *basso profundo* chime. That was when I knew what was real. It was real that you were dead, it was real....

I got angry at that violation, that sacrilege, that clock. What right had the clock to strike, the hands to move? How could it go on? It was wrong. I got up and stopped it. I think I spoke to it, not harshly, angry as I was; I said, "You don't know, do you, Tinkle? No one's told you yet," and I caught it by its swinging neck and held it until its ticking brain was quiet.

I told all the clocks, one by one, that you were dead—the glowing Seth Thomas ship's clock, with its heavy threads and its paired syllables, and Drowsy the alarm, and the cuckoo with the cleft palate who couldn't say anything but "hook-who!"

A truck roared by outside, and I remember the new surge of fury because of it, and then the thought that the driver hadn't been told yet ... and then the mad thought that the news would spread from these silent clocks, from these drawn blinds, spread like a cloud-shadow over the world, and when it touched birds, they would glide to the ground and crouch motionless, with no movement in their jeweled eyes; when it touched machines they would slow and stop; when it touched flowers they would close themselves into little soft fists and bend to knuckle the earth; when it touched people they would finish that stride, end that sentence, slowing, softening, and would sink down and be still.

There would be no noise or confusion as the world slipped into its stasis, and nothing would grow but silence. And the sun would hang on the horizon with its face thickly veiled, and there would be eternal dusk.

That was yesterday, and I was angry. I am not angry today. It was better, yesterday, the sitting in turmoil and uselessness, the useless raging up and down rooms so hollow, yet still so full of you they would not echo. It got dark, you see, and in good time the blinds were brighter than the walls around them again. I looked out, squinting through grainy eyelids, and saw a man walking by, walking easily, his hands in his pockets, and he was whistling.

After that I could not be angry any more, not at the man, not at the morning. I knew only the great cruel pressure of a fact, a fact worse than the fact of emptiness or of death—the fact that nothing ever stops, that things must go on.

It was better to be angry, and to lose myself in uselessness. Now I am not angry and I have no choice but to think usefully. I have lived a useful life and have built it all on useful thinking, and if I had not thought so much and so carefully Grace would be here with me now, with her voice like a large soft breeze in some springtime place, and perhaps tickling the side of my neck with feather-touches of her moving lips ... it was my useful, questing, thirsty thought which killed her, killed her.

The accident was all of two years ago—almost two years anyway. We had driven all the way back from Springfield without stopping, and we were very tired. Grace and Mr. Share and I were squeezed into the front seat.

Mr. Share was a man Grace had invented long before, even before we were married. He was a big invisible fat man who always sat by the right-hand window, and always looked out to the side so that he never watched us.

But since he was so fat, Grace had to press up close to me as we drove.

There was a stake-bodied truck bowling along ahead of us, and in the back of it was a spry old man, or perhaps a weatherbeaten young man—you couldn't tell—in blue dungarees and a red shirt. He had a yellow woolen muffler tied around his waist, and the simple strip of material made all the difference between "clothes" and "costume."

Behind him, lashed to the bed of the truck just back of the cab, was a large bundle of burlap. It would have made an adequate seat for him, cushioned and out of the wind. But the man seemed to take the wind as a heady beverage and the leaping floor as a challenge.

He stood with his arms away from his sides and his knees slightly flexed, and rode the truck as if it were a live thing. He yielded himself to each lurch and bump, brought himself back with each recession, guarding his equilibrium with an easy virtuosity.

Grace was, I think, dozing; my shout of delighted laughter at the performance on the bounding stage before us brought her upright. She laughed with me for the laugh alone, for she had not looked through the windshield yet, and she kissed my cheek.

He saw her do it, the man on the truck, and he laughed with us.

"He's *our* kind of people," Grace said.

"A pixie," I agreed, and we laughed again.

The man took off an imaginary plumed hat, swung it low toward us, but very obviously toward Grace. She nodded back to him, with a slight sidewise turn of her face as it went down that symbolized a curtsey.

Then he held out his elbow, and the pose, the slightly raised shoulder over which he looked fondly at the air over his bent arm, showed that he had given his arm to a lady. The lady was Grace, who, of course, would be charmed to join him in the dance ... she clapped her hands and crowed with delight, as she watched her imaginary self with the courtly, colorful figure ahead.

The man stepped with dainty dignity to the middle of the truck and bowed again, and you could all but hear the muted minuet as it began. It was a truly wonderful thing to watch, this pantomime; the man knew the ancient stately steps to perfection, and they were unflawed by the careening surface on which they were performed.

There was no mockery in the miming, but simply the fullness of good, the sheer, unspoiled sharing of a happy magic.

He bowed, took her hand, smiled back into her eyes as she pirouetted behind him. He stood back to the line waiting his turn, nodding slightly to the music; he dipped ever so little, twice, as his turn came, and stepped gracefully out to meet her, smiling again.

I don't know what made me look up. We were nearing the Speedway Viaduct, and the truck ahead was just about to pass under it. High up over our heads was the great span, and as my eyes followed its curve, to see the late afternoon sun on the square guard posts which bounded the elevated road, three of the posts exploded outward, and the blunt nose of a heavy truck plowed through and over the edge, to slip and catch and slip again, finally to teeter to a precarious stop.

Apparently its trailer was loaded with light steel girders; one of them slipped over the tractor's crumpled shoulder and speared down toward us.

Our companion of the minuet, on the truck ahead, had finished his dance, turned to us, was bowing low, smiling, looking up through his eyebrows at us. The girder's end took him on the back of the head. It did not take the head off; it obliterated it. The body struck flat and lay still, as still as wet paper stuck to glass. The girder bit a large piece out of the tailgate and somersaulted to the right, while I braked and swerved dangerously away from it. Fortunately, there were no cars coming toward us.

There was, of course, a long, mixed-up, horrified sequence of the two truck drivers, the one ahead and the one who came down later from the viaduct and was sick. Ambulances and bystanders and a lot of talk ... none of it matters, really.

No one ever found out who the dead man was. He had no luggage and no identification; he had over ninety dollars in his pocket. He might have been anybody—someone from show business, or a writer perhaps, on a haywire vacation of his own devising. I suppose that doesn't matter either. What does matter is that he died while Grace was in a very close communication with what he was doing, and her mind was wide open for his fantasy. Mine is, generally,

I suppose; but at that particular moment, when I had seen the smash above and the descending girder, I was wide awake, on guard. I think that had a lot to do with what has happened since. I think it has everything to do with Grace's—with Grace's—

There is no word for it. I can say this, though. Grace and I were never alone together again until the day she died. Died, died, Grace is dead.

Grace!

I can go on with my accursed useful thinking now, I suppose.

Grace was, of course, badly shaken, and I did what I could for her over the next few weeks. I tried my best to understand how it was affecting her. (That's what I mean by useful thinking—trying to understand. Trying and trying—prying and prying. Arranging, probing, finding out. Getting a glimpse, a scent of danger, rooting it out—bringing it out into the open where it can get at you.) Rest and new clothes and alcohol rubdowns; the theater, music and music, always music, for she could lose herself in it, riding its flux, feeling and folding herself in it, following it, sometimes, with her hushed, true voice, sometimes lying open to it, letting it play its colors and touches over her.

There is always an end to patience, however. After two months, knowing her as I did, I knew there was more here than simple shock. If I had known her less well—if I had cared less, even, it couldn't have mattered.

It began with small things. There were abstractions which were unusual in so vibrant a person. In a quiet room, her face would listen to music; sometimes I had to speak twice and then repeat what I had said.

Once I came home and found supper not started, the bed not made. Those things were not important—I am not a fusspot nor an autocrat; but I was shaken when, after calling her repeatedly I found her in the guest room, sitting on the bed without lights. I had no idea she was in there; I just walked in and snapped on the light in the beginnings of panic because she seemed not to be in the house; she had not answered me.

And at first it was as if she had not noticed the sudden yellow blaze from the paired lamps; she was gazing at the wall, and on her face was an expression of perfect peace. She was wide awake—at least her eyes were. I called her: "Grace!"

"Hello, darling," she said quietly. Her head turned casually toward me and she smiled—oh, those perfect teeth of hers!—and her smile was only partly for me; the rest of it was inside, with the nameless things with which she had been communing.

I sat beside her, amazed, and took her hands. I suppose I spluttered a bit, "Grace, are you all right? Why didn't you answer? The bed's not—have you been out? What's happened? Here—let me see if you have a fever?"

Her eyes were awake, yes; but not awake to me, to here and now. They were awake and open to some *elsewhere* matters. . . . She acquiesced as I felt her forehead and cheeks for fever, and while I was doing it I could see the attention of those warm, pleased living eyes shifting from the things they had been seeing, to me. It was as if they were watching a scene fade out while another was brought in on a screen, so that for a second all focusing points on the first picture were lost, and there was a search for a focusing point on the second.

And then, apparently, the picture of Helmuth Stoye sitting next to her, holding one of her hands, running his right palm across her forehead and down her cheek, came into sharp, true value, and she said, "Darling! You're home! What happened? Holiday or strike? You're not sick?"

I said, "Sweetheart, it's after seven."

"No!" She rose, smoothed her hair in front of the mirror. Hers was a large face and her appeal had none of the doll qualities, the candy-and-peaches qualities of the four-color ads. Her brow and cheekbones were wide and strong, and the hinges of her jaw were well-marked, hollowed underneath. Her nostrils were flared and sensuously tilted and her shoulders too wide to be suitable for fashion plates or pinups. But clothes hung from those shoulders with the graceful majesty of royal capes, and her breasts were large, high, separated and firm.

Yet for all her width and flatness and strength, for all her powerfully-set features, she was woman all through; and with clothes or without, she looked it.

She said, "I had no idea ... after seven! Oh, darling, I'm sorry. You poor thing, and no dinner yet. Come help me," and she dashed out of the room, leaving me flapping my lips, calling, "But Grace! Wait! Tell me first what's the mat—"

And when I got to the kitchen she was whipping up a dinner, efficiently, deftly, and all my questions could wait, could be interrupted with "Helmuth, honey, open these, will you?" "I don't know, b'loved; we'll dig it out after supper. Will you see if there're any French fries in the freezer?"

And afterward she remembered that *The Pearl* was playing at the Ascot Theater, and we'd missed it when it first came to town, and this was the best night ... we went, and the picture was fine, and we talked of nothing else that night.

I could have forgotten about that episode, I suppose. I could have forgotten about any one of them—the time she turned her gaze so strangely inward when she was whipping cream, and turned it to butter because she simply forgot to stop whipping it when it was ready; the times she had the strong, uncharacteristic urges to do and feel things which had never interested her before—to lose herself in the distances from high buildings and tall hills, to swim underwater for long, frightening minutes; to hear new and ever newer kinds of music—saccharine fox-trots and atonal string quartets, arrangements for percussion alone and Oriental modes.

And foods—rattlesnake ribs, moo goo gai pan, curried salmon with green rice, *Paella*, with its chicken and clams, headcheese, *cannoli*, sweet-and-pungent pork; all these Grace made herself, and well.

But in food as in music, in new sensualities as in new activities, there was no basic change in Grace. These were additions only; for all the exoticism of the dishes, for example, we still had and enjoyed the things she had always made—the gingered leg of lamb, the acorn squash filled with creamed onions, the crêpes suzettes.

She could still be lost in the architecture of Bach's "Passacaglia and Fugue" and in the raw heartbeat of the Hagard-Bauduc "Big

Noise from Winnetka." Because she had this new passion for underwater swimming, she did not let it take from her enjoyment of highboard diving. Her occasional lapses from efficiency, as in the whipped cream episode, were rare and temporary. Her sometime dreaminess, when she would forget appointments and arrangements and time itself, happened so seldom, that in all justice, they could have been forgotten, or put down, with all my vaunted understanding, to some obscure desire for privacy, for aloneness.

So—she had everything she had always had, and now more. She was everything she always had been, and now more. She did everything had always done, and now more. Then what, what on earth and in heaven, was I bothered, worried, and—and afraid of?

I know now. It was jealousy. It was—one of the jealousies.

There wasn't Another Man. That kind of poison springs from insecurity—from the knowledge that there's enough wrong with you that the chances are high that another man—any other man—could do a better job than you in some department of your woman's needs. Besides, that kind of thing can never be done by the Other Man alone; your woman must cooperate, willfully and consciously, or it can't happen. And Grace was incapable of that.

No; it was because of the sharing we had had. My marriage was a magic one because of what we shared; because of our ability to see a red gold leaf, exchange a glance and say never a word, for we knew so well each other's pleasure, its causes and expressions and associations. The pleasures were not the magic; the sharing was.

A poor analogy: you have a roommate who is a very dear friend, and together you have completely redecorated your room. The colors, the lighting, the concealed shelves and drapes, all are a glad communion of your separate tastes. You are both proud and fond of your beautiful room ... and one day you come home and find a new television set. Your roommate has acquired it and brought it in to surprise you. You are surprised, and you are happy, too.

But slowly an ugly thing creeps into your mind. The set is a big thing, an important, dominating thing in the room and in the things for which you use the room. And it is *his*—not mine or ours, but *his*. There is his unspoken, undemanded authority in the choice of programs in the evenings; and where are the chess games, the folk singing with your guitar, the long hours of phonograph music?

They are there, of course, ready for you every moment; no one has taken them away. But now the room is different. It can continue to be a happy room; only a petty mind would resent the new shared riches; but the fact is that the source of the riches is not shared, was not planned by you both. This changes the room and everything in it, the colors, the people, the shape and warmth.

So with my marriage. A thing had come to Grace which made us both richer but I did not share that source; and damn, damn my selfishness, I could not bear it; if I could not share it I wanted her deprived of it. I was gentle; beginning with, "How do you feel, sweetheart? But you aren't all right; what were you thinking of? It couldn't be 'nothing' . . . you were giving more attention to it than you are to me right now!"

I was firm, beginning with, "Now, look, darling; there's something here that we have to face. Please help. Now, exactly why are you so interested in hearing that Hindemith sketch? You never used to be interested in music like that. It has no melody, no key, no rhythm; it's unpredictable and ugly. I'm quoting you, darling; that's what you used to say about it. And now you want to soak yourself in it. Why? Why? What has changed you? Yes—people must grow and change; I know that. But—growing so fast, so quickly, in so many different directions! Tell me, now. Tell me exactly why you feel moved to hear this thing at this time."

And—I was angry, beginning with, "Grace! Why didn't you answer me? Oh, you heard me, did you? What did I say? Yes; that's right; you did . . . then why didn't you answer? Well? Not important? You'll have to realize that it's important to me to be answered when I speak to you!"

She tried. I could see her trying. I wouldn't stop. I began to watch her every minute. I stopped waiting for openings, and made them myself. I trapped her. I put on music in which I knew she would be lost, and spoke softly, and when she did not answer, I would kick over my chair with a shout and demand that she speak up. She tried. . . . Sometimes she was indignant, and demanded the peace that should be her right. Once I struck her.

That did it. Oh, the poor, brutalized beloved!

Now I can see it, *now!*

She never could answer me, until the one time. What could she have said? Her "I don't know!" was the truth. Her patience went too far, her anger was not far enough, and I know that her hurt was without limits.

I struck her, and she answered my questions. I was even angrier after she had than I had been before, for I felt that she had known all along, that until now she had withheld what she knew; and I cursed myself for not using force earlier and more often. I did. For not hitting *Grace* before!

I came home that night tired, for there was trouble at the shop; I suppose I was irascible with the compositors, but that was only because I had not slept well the night before, which was because— anyway, when I got home, I slammed the door, which was not usual, and, standing there with my raincoat draped over one shoulder, look- ing at the beautiful spread on the coffee table in front of the fire- place, I demanded, "What's that for?"

There were canapés and dainty round and rolled and triangular sandwiches; a frosty bluish beverage twinkling with effervescence in its slender pitcher; there were stars and flowers of tiny pickles, pastes and dressings, a lovely coral potato chip dip, and covered dishes full of delicate mysteries. There were also two small and vivid bowls of cut blooms, beautifully arranged.

"Why, for us. Just for us two," she said.

I said, "Good God. Is there anything the matter with sitting up to a table and eating like a human being?" Then I went to hang up the coat.

She had not moved when I came back; she was still standing fac- ing the door, and perhaps a quarter of her welcoming smile was frozen on her face.

No, I said to myself, no you don't. Don't go soft, now. You have her on the run; let's break this thing up now, all at once, all over the place. The healing can come later. I said, "Well?"

She turned to me, her eyes full of tears. "Helmuth . . ." she said weakly. I waited. "Why did you . . . it was only a surprise. A pretty surprise for you. We haven't been together for so long . . . you've been . . ."

"You haven't been yourself since that accident," I said coldly. "I think you like being different. Turn off the tears, honey. They'll do you no good."

"I'm *not* different!" she wailed; and then she began to cry in earnest. "I can't stand it!" she moaned, "I can't, I can't . . . Helmuth, you're losing your mind. I'm going to leave you. Leave you . . . maybe for just a while, maybe for . . ."

"You're going to *what?*" I whispered, going very close to her.

She made a supreme effort and answered, flatly, looking me in the eye, "I'm going, Helmuth. I've got to."

I think if she'd seen it coming she would have stood back; perhaps I'd have missed her. I think that if she'd expected it, she would have fled after I hit her once. Instead she stood still, unutterably shocked, unmoving, so it was easy to hit her again.

She stood watching me, her face dead, her eyes, and, increasingly, the flames of the fingermarks on her bleached cheeks burning. In that instant I knew how she felt, what her mind was trying frantically to do.

She was trying to think of a way to make this a dream, to explain it as an accident to find some excuse for me; and the growing sting in her beaten cheeks slowly proved and reproved that it was true. I know this, because the tingling sting of my hand was proving it to me.

Finally, she put one hand up to her face. She said, *"Why?"*

I said, "Because you have kept a secret from me."

She closed her eyes, swayed. I did not touch her. Still with her eyes closed, she said:

"It wants to be left alone. It feeds on vital substance, but there is always an excess . . . there is in a healthy person, anyway. It only takes a small part of that excess, not enough to matter, not enough for anyone but a jealous maniac like you to notice. It lives happily

118

in a happy person, it lives richly in a mind rich with the experiences of the senses, feeding only on what is spare and extra. And you have made me unfit, forever and ever, with your prodding and scarring, and because you have found it out it can never be left alone again, it can never be safe again, it can never be safe while you live, it can never be content, it can never leave me while I live, it can never, it can never, it can never."

Her voice did not trail off—it simply stopped, without a rise or fall in pitch or volume, without any normal human aural punctuation. What she said made no sense to me.

I snarled at her—I don't think it was a word—and turned my back. I heard her fall, and when I looked she was crumpled up like a castoff, empty, trodden-on white paper box.

I fought my battle between fury and tenderness that night, and met the morning with the dull conclusion that Grace was possessed, and that what had possessed her had gone mad ... that I didn't know where I was, what to do; that I must save her if I could, but in any case relentlessly track down and destroy the—the— No, it hadn't a name ...

Grace was conscious, docile, and had nothing to say. She was not angry or resentful; she was nothing but—obedient. She did what she was told, and when she finished she stopped until she was told to do something else.

I called in Doc Knapp. He said that what was mostly wrong with her was outside the field of a medical doctor, but he didn't think a little regimented rest and high-powered food therapy would hurt.

I let him take her to the hospital. I think I was almost glad to see her go. No I wasn't. I couldn't be glad. How could I be glad about anything? Anyway, Knapp would have her rested and fed and quieted down and fattened up and supplied with two alcohol rubs a day, until she was fit to start some sort of psychotherapy. She always liked alcohol rubs. She killed her—she died just before the second alcohol rub, on the fourth day ... Knapp said, when he took her away, "I can't understand it, Helmuth. It's like shock, but in Grace that doesn't seem right at all. She's too strong, too alive."

Not any more, she isn't.

My mind's wandering. Hold on tight, you ... Hold. ...

Where am I? I am at home. I am sitting in the chair. I am getting up. Uh! I have fallen down. Why did I fall down? Because my leg was asleep. What was it asleep? Because I have been sitting here all day and most of the night without moving. The doorbell is ringing. Why is the doorbell ringing? Because someone wants to come in. Who is it? Someone who comes visiting at two o' eight in the morning, I know that because I started the clock again and Tinkle says what time it is. Who visits at two o' eight in the morning? Drunks and police and death. There is a small person's shadow on the frosted door, which I open. "Hello, small person, Grace is dead."

It is not a drunk it is not the police it is Death who has a child's long lashes and small hands, one to hold up a blank piece of paper for me to stare at, one to slide the knife between my ribs, feel it scrape on my breastbone ... a drama, Enter Knife Left Center, and I fall back away from the door, my blood leaping lingering after the withdrawn blade, Grace, Grace, treasure me in your cupped hands—

VI
As Told By
Lawrence Delehanty

I GOT THE call on the car radio just before half-past two. Headquarters had a phone tip of some funny business out on Poplar Street in Homeland. The fellow who phones was a milk truck dispatcher on his way to work. He says he thought he someone at the door of this house stab the guy who came to the door, close the door and beat it.

I didn't see anyone around. There were lights on in the house—in what seemed to be the living room, and in the hallway just inside the door. I could see how anyone passing by could get a look at such a thing if it had happened.

I told Sam to stay in the prowl car and ran up the path to the house.

I knocked on the door, figuring maybe there'd be prints on the bell push. There was no answer. I tried again, and finally opened the door, turning the knob by the shaft, which was long enough for me to get hold of without touching the knob.

It had happened all right. The stiff was just inside the door. The guy was on his back, arms and legs spread out, with the happiest look on his face I ever saw. No kidding—that guy looked as if he'd just been given a million dollars. He had blood all over his front.

I took one look and went back and called Sam. He came up asking questions and stopped asking when he saw the stiff. "Go phone," I told him, "and be careful. Don't touch nothin'."

While he was phoning I took a quick squint around. There was a few dirty dishes in the kitchen sink and on the table, and half a bottle of some liqueur on an end table in the living room, sitting right on the polished wood, where it'd sure leave a ring. I'd say this guy had been in there some time without trying to clean up any.

I inched open the drawer in the big sideboard in the dining room and all the silver was there. None of the drawers in the two bedrooms were open; it looked like a grudge killing of some kind; there wasn't no robbery I could see.

Just as I came back down the stairs the doorbell rang. Sam came out of the front room and I waved him back. "There goes our prints on the bell," I said. "I'll get it." I pussyfooted to the door and pulled it wide open, real sudden.

"Mr. Stoye?" says a kid standing there. He's about fourteen, maybe, small for his age. He's standing out there, three o'clock in the morning, mind you, smiling real polite, just like it was afternoon and he'd come around to sell raffle tickets. I felt a retch starting in my stomach just then—don't know why. The sight of the stiff hadn't bothered me none. Maybe something I ate. I swallowed it down and said, "Who are you?"

He said, "I would like to see Mr. Stoye."

"Bub," I said, "Mr. Stoye isn't seeing anybody just now. What do you want?"

He squinted around me and saw the stiff. I guess I should've stopped him but he had me off guard. And you know, he didn't gasp or jump back or any of the things you expect anyone to do. He just straightened up, and he smiled.

"Well," he says, sort of petting his jacket pocket, "I don't s'pose there's anything I can do now," and he smiles at me, real bright. "Well, good night," he says, and turns to go.

I nabbed him and spun him inside and shut the door. "What do you know about all this?" I asked him.

He looked at the stiff, where I nodded, and he looked at me. The stiff didn't bother him.

"Why, nothing," he said. "I don't know anything at all. Is that really Mr. Stoye?"

"You know it is."

"I think I did know, all right," he said. "Well, can I go home now? Dad doesn't know I'm out."

"I bet he doesn't. Let's see what you got in your pockets."

He didn't seem to mind. I frisked him. Inside the jacket pocket was a jump knife—one of those Army issue paratrooper's clasp knives with a spring; touch the button and *click!* You've got four and a half inches of razor steel sticking out of your fist, ready for business. A lot of 'em got out in war surplus. Too many. We're always finding 'em in carcasses.

I told him he'd have to stick around. He frowned a little bit and said he was worried about his father, but I didn't let that make no difference. He gave his name without any trouble. His name was Ronnie Daniels. He was a clean-cut little fellow, just as nice and polite as I ever saw.

Well, I asked him all kinds of questions. His answers just didn't make no sense. He said he couldn't recall just what it was he wanted to see Stoye about. He said he had never met Stoye and had never been out here before. He said he got the address from knowing the phone number; went right up to the telephone company and wormed it out of one of the girls there. He said he didn't remember at all where he got the number from. I looked at the number just out of curiosity; it was Homeland 2065, which didn't mean nothing to me.

After that, there wasn't anything to do until the homicide squad got there. I knew the kid's old man, this Daniels, would have to get dragged into it, but that wasn't for me to do; that would be up to the detective looey. I turned the kid over to Sam.

I remember Sam's face just then; it turned pale. I asked him what was the matter but he just swallowed hard and said he didn't know; maybe it was the pickles he had with his midnight munch. He took the kid into the front room and they got into a fine conversation about cops and murders. He sure seemed to be a nice, healthy, normal kid. Quiet and obedient—you know. I can't really blame Sam for what happened.

The squad arrived—two carloads, sirens and all, making so much noise I thought sure Stoye would get up and tell 'em to let him rest in peace—and in they came—photogs, print men, and the usual bunch of cocky plainclothesmen. They swarmed all over.

Flick was the man in charge, stocky, tough, mad at everybody all the time, especially on the night detail. Man, how he hated killers that worked at night and dragged him away from his pinochle!

I told the whole story to him and his little book.

"His name's Tommy," I said, "and he says he lives at—"

"His name's Ronnie," says Sam, from behind me.

"Hey," I says. "I thought I told you to stay with him."

"I had to go powder my nose," says Sam. "My stomach done a flip-flop a while back that had me worried. It's okay. Brown was dusting in the room when I went out. And besides, that's a nice little kid. He wouldn't—"

"Brown!" Flick roared.

Brown came out of the living room. "Yeah, chief."

"You done in the front room?"

"Yeah; everything I could think of. No prints except Stoye's, except on the phone. I guess they'd be Sam's."

"The kid's all right?"

"Was when I left," said Brown, and went back into the living room. Flick and me and Sam went into the front room.

The kid was gone.

Sam turned pale.

"Ronnie!" he bellows. "Hey you, Ronnie!"

No answer.

"You hadda go powder your big fat nose," says Flick to Sammy. Sam looked bad. The soft seats in a radio car feel good to a harness bull, and I think Sam decided right then that he'd be doing his job on foot for quite a while.

It was easy to see what had happened. Sammy left the room, and then Brown got finished and went out, and in those few seconds he was alone the kid had stepped through the short hall into the kitchen and out the side door.

Sam looked even worse when I suddenly noticed that the ten-inch ham slicer was gone from the knife rack; that was one of the first things I looked at after I saw Stoye had been stabbed. You always look for the kitchen knives in a home stabbing.

Flick returned to Sam and opened his mouth, and in that moment, believe me, I was glad I was me and not him. I thought fast.

"Flick," I said, "I know where that kid's going. He was all worried about what his old man would think. Here—I got his address in my book."

Flick snapped, "Okay. Get down there right away. I'll call what's-his-name—Daniels—from here and tell him to wait for the kid and hold him if he shows up before you do. Get down there, now, and hurry. Keep your eyes peeled on the way; you might see him on the street. Look out for that knife. Kelly, get a general alarm out for that kid soon's I'm off the phone. Or send it from your car."

He turned back to me, thumbed at Sam. "Take him with you," he says, "I want him out of my sight. And if hot damned nose gets shiny again see he don't use your summons book."

We ran out and piled into the car and took off. We didn't go straight to Daniels' address. Sam hoped we would see the kid on the way; I think he had some idea of a heroic hand-to-hand grapple with the kid in which maybe he'd get a little bit stabbed in the line of duty, which might quiet Flick down some.

So we cut back and forth between Myrtle Avenue and Varick; the kid could've taken a trolley on one or a bus on the other. We found out soon enough that he'd done neither; he'd found a cab; and I'd like to know who it was drove that hack.

He must've been a jet pilot.

It was real dark on Daniels' street. The nearest streetlight was a couple hundred feet away, and there was a big maple tree in Daniels' front yard that cast thick black shadows all over the front of the house. I missed the number in the dark and pulled over to the curb; I knew it must be somewhere around here.

Me and Sam got out and Sam went up on the nearest porch to see the house number; Daniels was two doors away. That's how we happened to be far to the left of the house when the killer rang Daniels' bell.

We both saw it, Sam and me, that small dark shadow up against Daniels' front door. The door had a glass panel and there was some sort of night light on inside, so all we saw was the dark blob waiting there, ringing on the bell. I guess Daniels was awake, after Flick's phone call.

I grabbed Sam's arm, and he shook me free. He had his gun out. I said, "What are you gonna do?" He was all hopped up, I guess.

He wanted to make an arrest or something. He wanted to be The Man here. He didn't want to go back on a beat. He said, "You know how Stoye was killed. Just like that."

That made sense, but I said, "Sam! You're not going to shoot a kid!"

"Just wing him, if it looks—"

Just then the door opened. There wasn't much light. I saw Daniels, a stocky, balding man with a very mild face, peering out. I saw an arm come up from that small shadowy blob. Then Sam fired twice. There was a shrill scream, and the clatter of a knife on the porch. I heard Ronnie yell, "Dad! Dad!"

Then Sam and I were pounding over to the house. Daniels was frozen there, staring down onto the porch and the porch steps.

At the foot of the steps the kid was huddled. He was unconscious. The ham slicer gleamed wickedly on the steps near his hand.

I called out, "Mr. Daniels! We're the police. Better get back inside."

And together Sam and I lifted up the kid. He didn't weigh much. Going inside, Sam tripped over his big flat feet and I swore at him.

We put the kid down on the couch. I didn't see any blood. Daniels was dithering around like an old lady. I pushed him into a chair and told him to stay there and try to take it easy.

Sam went to phone Flick. I started going over the kid.

There was no blood.

There were no holes in him, either; not a nick, not a graze. I stood back and scratched my head.

Daniels said, "What's wrong with him. What happened?"

Inside, I heard Sam at the phone. "Yeah, we got 'im. It was the kid all right. Tried to stab his old man. I winged him. Huh? I don't know. We're looking him over now. Yeah."

"Take it easy," I said again to Daniels. He looked rough. "Stay right there."

I went to the door, which was standing open. Over by the porch rail I saw something shining green and steel blue. I started over to it, tripped on something yielding, and went flat on my face. Sam came running out. "What's the—*uh!!*" and he came sailing out and landed on top of me. He's a big boy.

I said, "My goodness, Sam, that was careless of you," or words to that effect, and some other things amounting to maybe Flick had the right idea about him.

"Damn it, Delehanty," he says, "I tripped on something. What are you doing sprawled out here, anyway?"

"I was looking for—" and I picked it up, the green and steel blue thing. It was a Finnish sheath knife, long and pointed, double razor edges, scrollwork up near the hilt. Blood, still a bit tacky, in the scroll-work.

"Where'd that come from?" grunted Sam, and took it. "Hey! Flick just told me the medic says Stoye was stabbed with a two-edged knife. You don't suppose—"

"I don't suppose nothin'," I said, getting up. "On your feet, Sam. Flick finds us like this, he'll think we were playing mumblety-peg . . . tell you what, Sam; I took a jump knife off the kid out there, and it only had a single edge."

I went down the steps and picked it up. Sam pointed out that the kid never had a chance to use the ham slicer.

I shrugged that off. Flick was paid the most for thinking—let him do most of the thinking. I went to the side of the door and looked at the bell push to get an idea as to how it might take prints, and then went inside. Sam came straight in and tripped again.

"Pick up ya feet!"

Sam had fallen to his knees this time. He growled something and, swinging around, went to feeling around the porch floor with his hands. "Now it's patty-cake," I said. "For Pete's sake, Sam—"

Inside Daniels was on the floor by the couch, rubbing the kid's hands, saying, real scared like, "Ronnie! Ronnie!"

"Delehanty!"

Half across the room, I turned. Sam was still on his knees just outside the door, and his face was something to see. "Delehanty, just come here, will you?"

There was something in his voice that left no room for a wise-crack. I went right to him. He motioned me down beside him, took my wrist and pushed my hand downward.

It touched something, but—*there was nothing there.*

We looked at each other, and I wish I could write down what that look said.

I touched again, felt it. It was like cloth, then like flesh, yielding, then bony.

"It's the Invisible Man!" breathed Sam, bug-eyed.

"Stop talking nonsense," I said thickly. "And beside, it's a woman. Look here."

"I'll take your word for it," said Sam, backing away. "Anyhow, I'm a married man."

Cars came, screaming as usual. "Here's Flick."

Flick and his mob came streaming up the steps.

"What's going on here? Where's the killer?"

Sam stood in front of the doorway, holding his hands out like he was unsnarling traffic. He was shaking. "Walk over this side," he said, "or you'll step on her."

"What are you gibbering about? Step on who?"

Sam flapped his hands and pointed at the floor. Flick and Brown and all the others looked down, then up again. I don't know what got into me. I just couldn't help it. I said, "He found a lady-bug and he don't want you to step on it."

Flick got so mad, so quick, he didn't even swear.

We went inside. The medic was working over the boy, who was

127

still unconscious. Flick was demanding, "Well! Well? What's the matter with him?"

"Not a thing I can find out, not without a fluoroscope and some blood tests. Shock, maybe?"

"Shot?" gasped Daniels.

"Definitely not," said the M.O.

Flick said, very, very quietly, "Sam told me over the phone that he had shot the boy. What about this, Delehanty? Can you talk sense, or is Sam contagious?"

I told him what we had seen from the side of the house. I told him that we couldn't be sure who it was that rang the bell, but that we saw whoever it was raise a knife to strike, and then Sam fired, and then we ran up and found the kid lying at the bottom of the steps. We heard a knife fall.

"Did you hear him fall down the steps?"

"No," said Sam.

"Shut up, you," said Flick, not looking at him. "Well, Delehanty?"

"I don't think so," I said, thinking hard. "It all happened so fast."

"It was a girl."

"What was a girl? Who said that?"

Daniels shuffled forward. "I answered the door. A girl was there. She had a knife. A long one, pointed. I think it was double-edged."

"Here it is," said Sam brightly.

Flick raised his eyes to heaven, moved his lips silently, and took the knife.

"That's it," said Daniels. "Then there was a gunshot, and she screamed and fell."

"She did, huh? Where is she?"

"I— I don't know," said Daniels in puzzlement.

"She's still there," said Sam smugly. I thought, oh-oh. This is it.

"Thank you, Sam," said Flick icily. "Would you be good enough to point her out to me?"

Sam nodded. "There. Right there," and he pointed.

"See her, lying there in the doorway," I piped up.

Flick looked at Sam, and he looked at me. "Are you guys trying to—*uk!*" His eyes bulged, and his jaw went slack.

Everyone in the room froze. There, in plain sight on the porch, lay the body of a girl. She was quite a pretty girl, small and dark. She had a bullet hole on each side of her neck, a little one here and a great big one over here.

VII
Told by the Author
Theodore Sturgeon

I DON'T MUCH care for the way this story's going.

You want to write a story, see, and you sit down in front of the mill, wait until that certain feeling comes to you, hold off a second longer just to be quite sure that you know exactly what you want to do, take a deep breath, and get up and make a pot of coffee.

This sort of thing is likely to go on for days, until you are out of coffee and can't get more until you can pay for same, which you can do by writing a story and selling it; or until you get tired of messing around and sit down and write a yarn purely by means of knowing how to do it and applying the knowledge.

But this story's different. It's coming out as if it were being dictated to me, and I'm not used to that. It's a haywire sort of yarn; I have no excuses for it, and can think of no reasons for such a plot having unfolded itself to me. It isn't that I can't finish it up; far from it—all the plot factors tie themselves neatly together at the end, and this with no effort on my part at all.

This can be demonstrated; it's the last chapter that bothers me. You see, I didn't write it. Either someone's playing a practical joke on me, or— No. I prefer to believe someone's playing a practical joke on me.

Otherwise, this thing is just too horrible.

But about that demonstration, here's what happened:

Flick never quite recovered from the shock of seeing that sudden corpse. The careful services of the doctor were not required to show that the young lady was dead, and Flick recovered himself enough to start asking questions.

It was Daniels who belatedly identified her as the nurse he had seen at the hospital the day Mrs. Stoye killed herself. The nurse's name was Lucille Holder. She had come from England as a girl; she had a flawless record abroad and in this country. The head doctor told the police on later investigation that he had always been amazed at the tremendous amount of work Miss Holder could turn out, and had felt that inevitably some sort of a breakdown must come. She went all to pieces on Mrs. Stoye's death, and he sent her on an immediate vacation.

Her movements were not difficult to trace, after she left the administrative office, where she ascertained Mr. Daniels' address. She went first to his house, and the only conclusion the police could come to was that she had done so on purpose to kill him. But he was not there; he, it seems, had been trying to find her at the hospital at the time! So she left. The following night she went out to Stoye's, rang the bell, and killed him.

Ronnie followed her, apparently filled with the same unaccountable impulse, and was late. Miss Holder went then to Daniels' house and tried to kill him, but was shot by the policeman, just as Ronnie, again late, arrived.

Ronnie lay in a coma for eight weeks. The diagnosis was brain fever, which served as well as anything else. He remembered little, and that confused. He did, however, vouch for the nurse's visit to his home the night of Mrs. Stoye's death. He could not explain why he had kept it a secret from his father, nor why he had had the impulse to kill Mr. Stoye (he admitted this impulse freely and without any horror), nor how he had happened to think of finding Stoye's address through the information operator at the telephone company.

He simply said that he wanted to get it without asking any traceable questions. He also admitted that when he found that Mr. Stoye had already been killed, he felt that he must secure another weapon and go and kill his father. He says he remembers thinking of it without any emotion whatsoever at the time, though he was appalled at the thought after he came out of the coma.

"It's all like a story I read a long time ago," he said. "I don't remember doing these things at all; I remember seeing them done."

When the policeman shot Miss Holder, Ronnie felt nothing; the lights went out, and he knew nothing until eight weeks later.

These things remained unexplained to the participants:

Mrs. Stoye's disappearing body. The witnesses were the two Daniels and Miss Holder. Miss Holder could not report it; Ronnie did not remember it; Mr. Daniels kept his own counsel.

Lucille Holder's disappearing body. Daniels said nothing about this either, and for the rest of his life tried to forget it. The members of the homicide detail and the two prowl car men tried to forget it, too. It was not entered into the records of the case. It seemed to have no bearing, and all concerned were happy to erase it as much as possible. If they spoke of it at all, it was in terms of mass hypnosis—which was reasonably accurate at that. . . .

Lucille Holder's motive in killing Mr. Stoye and in trying to kill Mr. Daniels. This could only be guessed at; it was simple to put it down to the result of a nervous breakdown after overwork.

Mrs. Stoye's suicide. This, too, was attributed to a mounting mental depression and was forgotten as quickly as possible.

And two other items must be mentioned. The radio patrolman Sam was called on the carpet by Detective Lieutenant Flick for inefficiency in letting the boy Ronnie go. He was not punished, oddly enough. He barely mentioned the corpse of Lucille Holder, and that there were witnesses to the fact that *apparently* the lieutenant had not seen it, though he had stepped right over it on the way into Daniels' house. Flick swore that he was being framed, but let Sam alone thereafter.

The other item has to do with Miss Jennie Beaufort, an operator in the Information Office of the telephone company. Miss Beaufort won a prize on a radio quiz—a car, a plane, two stoves, a fur coat, a diamond ring, a set of SwingFree shoulder pads, and a 38-day South American cruise. She quit her job the following day, took the cruise, enjoyed it mightily, learned on her return that income tax was due on the valuation of all her prizes, sold enough to pay the tax, and was so frightened at the money it took that she went back to work at her old job.

* * *

So, you see, these tangled deaths, these mad actions, were all explained, forgotten, rationalized—made to fit familiar patterns, as were Charles Fort's strange lights and shapes in the night, as were the Flying Discs, the disappearance of Lord Bathurst, the teleportation of Kaspar Hauser, and the disappearance of the crew of the *Marie Celeste*.

I leave it to the reader to explain the following chapter. I found it by and in my typewriter yesterday afternoon (I'd been writing this story all the previous night). Physically, it was the most extraordinary looking manuscript I have ever seen.

In the first place the paper bails had apparently been released most of the time, and letters ran into each other with wild abandon. In the second place there were very few capital letters; I was reminding of Don Marquis's heroic Archy the cockroach, who used to write long effusions while Mr. Marquis was asleep, by jumping from one key to the other.

But Archy was not heavy enough to operate the shift key, and so he eschewed the upper case characters. In the third place, the spelling was indescribable. It was a mixture of phonetics and something like Speed-writing, or ABC shorthand. It begins this way:

> i mm a thngg wch livz n fantsy whr tru fantsy z fond in th mynz v mn.

I couldn't possibly inflict it all on you in its original form. It took me the better part of two hours just to get the pages in order—they weren't numbered, of course.

After I plowed through it myself, I undertook a free translation. I have rewritten it twice since, finding more rhythm, more fluidity, each time, as I become familiar with the extraordinary idiom in which it was written. I think that as it now stands it closely follows the intent and mood of the original. The punctuation is entirely mine; I regard punctuation as inflection in print, and have treated this accordingly, as if it were read aloud.

I must say this: there are three other people who could conceivably have had access to this machine while I was asleep. They are Jeff and Les and Mary.

I know for a fact that Jeff, who is an artist, was busy the entire time with a nonobjective painting of unusual vividness and detail; I know how he works, and I know what the picture looked like when I quit writing for the night, and what it looked like when I woke up, and believe me, he must have been painting like mad the entire time—he and no one else.

As for Les, he works in the advertising department of a book publisher, and obviously has not the literary command indicated by this manuscript.

And Mary—I am lucky enough to say that Mary is very fond of me, and would be the last person in the world to present me with such a nasty jolt as is innate in this final chapter. Here it is; and please forgive me for this lengthy but necessary introduction to it, and for my intrusion; this sort of thing is strictly against the rules.

VIII
"?"

I AM A Thing which lives in fantasy, where true fantasy lives in the minds of men.

What fumbling is this, what clumsiness, what pain.... I who never was a weight, who never turned, coerced, nor pressed a person, never ordered, never forced—I who live with laughter, die with weeping, rise and hope and cheer with man's achievements, yet with failure and despair go numb and cold and silent and unnoticeable—what have I to do with agony?

Know me, mankind, know me now and let me be.

Know the worst. I feed on you. I eat and breathe no substance but a precious ether. No, not souls (but where a soul is strong and clean I live my best). I take this guarded essence where I can, and thrive on it; and when I choose a host I am imprisoned, for I may not leave him while he lives, and when he dies I must locate another to inhabit. And I have ... powers.

But know this too: The thing that I take is the essence of joy—and in joy is created an excess of that which I need. I drink in your reservoir, yes; but when there is drought and the level is low, and your needs are increased, and the water turns bitter with flavors of worry, and anger, and fear, then I shrink and I soften, and lose all my hunger; and then if you grieve, if your spirit is broken, if you should forget all the pleasure and glory and wonder of being a man—then I die. . . .

Such a death is not death as you know it. It is more a waiting unmoving within a soul's winter, to wake with the spring of the heart. But where people grieve over years, or let fear share their souls with me, then I must wait for the walls of my prison to crumble.

Then, after the death of my host I go drifting, seeking another. That is my Search, and in it, for me, is the ultimate cold. No human can know such a thing, for death, for a human, is kinder.

I am and I am not a parasite. I feed on your substance; yet what living thing in the world does not feed on the substance of others? And I take only excess—take only that which you radiate gaily when you feel joy.

When you feel otherwise, then I must wait, or must sleep, or must die. Where is the evil in being a parasite, when I take only a product which you never need? I demand only sustenance; that is the right of all living things. I ask in addition a thing which is simple enough—I ask to be left to myself, to encyst or to flower or be joyful, without any devilish probing.

I do not know how old I am; I do not know if there are others like me. I do not know how many hosts I have inhabited, or whether I was born or hatched, or whether, like a human, I must one day truly die. I shall, no doubt; I am alive, and nothing lives forever. I know my years are thousands, and my hosts have been in the scores of hundreds. I have no interest in statistics.

Yet you must know me. . . . I think my origins were like a plant's— an accidental seed of sensuality perhaps. My infancy was passed in dreams, in sightless stirrings when the stimulation merited, and blacknesses between. I think that when my hosts passed on, my knotted insubstantial cyst just drifted like a petal on a roiling stream, it bumped and nuzzled and at last slipped in when chance presented hosts which qualified.

To qualify, in those uncaring phases, men had but to show an openness and nothing more. And when I gained experience and consciousness increased, and realization came to me, and I was grown and had ability to choose, I gained as well the power of rejection.

And after that I was no longer bound to sickly children, open to me through their thirst for colors, senses, odors, vivid to them through unsaid convictions that the end was near. I became increasingly meticulous in choosing; I became an expert in detecting signs of whimsy-richness in its earliest potential. I have powers. . . .

You have powers too, you human ones. You can change the color of a life by vicious striking at a stranger-child. You can give away a thing you treasure, making memories which later might compose a symphony. You can do a thousand thousand things you never do; you never try; there is no reason to depart from paths you have established. When, however, circumstances force you into it, you do the "superhuman."

Once my host was Annabelle, a woman on a farm. (She loved the birds!) In a blizzard she was lost; she was old and had a crippled knee, and could not find the road, and could not last the night. She stumbled on a post which stood erect and lonesome on the prairie, and, without a conscious thought of bravery, or what mankind might say to her, she put her hand upon the weathered wood, and in the blowing snow and bitter cold, she walked around the post—around and around, in spite of age and pain and growing numbness, walked around the post until the sun came up in blowing gray, then growing cold.

They found her and they saved her, when in truth she saved herself. There was about her such a cloud of pure achievement, such a joy at having cheated wind and cold! (I fed that day; I still possess the energies she radiated!) . . . I have powers; all have powers, when we're forced to use them. I have powers, you have too, which you have never catalogued.

I have powers—now I use them!

I have no host. Such bitterness and agony as I have just experienced I never want again. My Search, this time, will be a thorough one and for it, now, I make my sacrifice. I am unknown; but with this script, these purposely hypnotic words, *I shall be known!* I sacrifice my privacy, my yearning for the pleasant weightless dark where I have dwelt. I challenge mankind's probing, for, through these bright words and burnished continuities, I shall locate a host who will defend me!

I had a man—he had me, possibly—who would have fought for me. And after him I dwelt within a woman's mind—the richest and most magical of all. The man was one of those who, on maturing, never lost the colorful ability to wonder like a child. And one day, miming, imitating a precise and dainty minuet in joyful incongruity (he danced alone upon the bouncing platform of a truck) a falling girder struck him and he died. I had no warning and no way to make a Search; I flung myself into the mind of one who was nearby in close communion with my dead host's whimsy.

Grace had a mind that was magic throughout. Never in thousands of years have I seen such a shimmering jewel; never in thousands of pages of words found in thousands of languages could such a trove be described. All that she saw was transmuted in sibilant subtleties; all that she heard was in breath-taking colors and shapes. What she touched, what she said, what she saw, what she felt, what she thought—these were all blended in joy.

She was the pinnacle; she was the source of the heady exuberant food which in flavor eclipsed my most radiant memories. She, like the blizzard of Annabelle—she was the suitable circumstance, bringing about the release of the powers I held all untried.

I stirred in her mind. I found I could reach out and touch certain sources of hunger—sights that she never had seen and sensations she never had turned to, things which should surely delight a sensitive soul.

I found to my joy that with care I controlled them, the hungers for things I remembered in hosts less responsive. I practiced this skill as she broadened her life, and I led her to music and poems and thoughts which she never, perhaps, could have found by herself. She had every reason for happiness with all these riches, and I—oh, I gloried in bringing things to her, as many a gifted composer has brought new music to some virtuoso.

But her husband was Stoye.

Stoye was a devil. He hated me for what I was, before he could define it. His mind was quite as rich as hers, but something curbed it. Growing with her was impossible; he sensed with rare perception that a Thing had come to her, and since that Thing was not of him, he hated it. It mattered not to him that she was better for it. Brutally he turned away from sharing what I brought into his home.

And she—I could not take her from him. How I tried! Poor treasure trove, she was at last a battleground between that questing creature and myself. He hounded me through her, and I struck back by taking her to rare enchantments in which he could not share.

He was the very first—the very first—of all the humans I have known, to recognize me and to seek me out. This recognition was intolerable; all my life I have avoided it, and lived in war and secret joyfulness. He goaded me until I evidenced myself; I never realized I could make a human speak, but Grace spoke for me when she said that "It only wants to be let alone."

She might as well have died, right then and there, for all the sustenance I got from her thereafter. I knew that she would kill herself; between us, her and me, there was a madness caught from Stoye.

Stoye put her, numb and docile, into the hospital. I started to encyst, for Grace's well was dry to me. I found a likely subject in the nurse, who seemed as sensitive as Grace (but lacked that fine capacity for whimsy) and I poised myself to make the change. While waiting, then, I thought of Stoye—and realized that, with Grace's death, he would not rest until he found me and destroyed me, either by attacking all my hosts, or if he learned the way of it, by closing minds against me by his printed propaganda. He had to be destroyed.

Grace killed herself; her one blind foolishness, her love for Stoye and all her stupid thoughts that she had lost it, made her do it. I might have stopped her; but why should I, when I needed a release from all her bitterness? Believe me, it was just as strong as all her joys had been ... before she leaped she tried to warn him, tried to send some crazy message to him through a youngster standing down below.

My connection with her was not close just then; I am not sure; she still was set on death as an escape but wished her husband to be watchful and protect himself. And then she leaped.

And then it came—that awful amputation.

I could not know that Ronnie was so strong a host, potentially—that so well suited to me was he that, as I flashed upward to the nurse, to take possession, I was torn apart!

I have no substance; yet I am an entity, with limits and with boundaries. These were ruptured; while my greater part found room within the nurse's mind, a fragment nestled into Ronnie's.

At first I felt a transcendental pain and dizziness; and then I did the things I could to be protected. I hid the crumpled body with a forced hypnotic wave (this is no subtle mystery; a thousand men can do it) to keep the wave of terror all confused with curiosity, for terror undiluted quite inhibits my possession of a host.

I settled into Lucille Holder's mind and tested the controls which Stoye had forced me to develop. Lucille was far less strong than Grace had been, and forcing her was easy. I was wounded, I was maddened, and at last I drank, with purpose and a new dark joy, the thing called hate.

Stoye had to die. The man called Daniels, Ronnie's father, saw Grace leap and was a witness. Possibly he might become too curious, with his son possessed, and be another probing devil. He must die. Ronnie had a part of me, and I did not think he could release it while he lived. So he must die.

To test my new controls, I sent the nurse at first to do the minor task. The elder Daniels was not there; and when I found myself confronted with that other part of me, I nearly died of yearning. And I realized, in that closeness, that the boy could be controlled as well, and that he could destroy his father quite at my convenience, while Lucille could kill him later. Satisfied, I went away.

I spent that night and all next day securing my controls, and practicing. And late the night that followed, I killed Stoye, and two strange things happened.

One was when Stoye died; I felt a wave of powerful protectiveness about him as he fled his body, and I sensed again the fullest, richest magic that was Grace. I was terrified of it; I had never known before that humans could outlive their carcasses. . . .

The other thing was the arrival of Ronnie, apparently moved by the part of me carried within him. Yet since he possessed but a fragment, his effort was late and his motive was weak, and I feared that he might make a botch of the killing of Daniels. I therefore sent Lucille to do it; Ronnie, again weak and tardy, followed my orders.

The gunshot, the bullet which shattered the neck of the nurse, was quite unexpected. I was flung unprepared into cold, in my nakedness, cold indescribable, cold beyond bearing. Yet I was glad; for the fraction of me that was Ronnie's came streaming toward me as I was exploded away from the nurse. The wrench it gave Ronnie must have been dreadful; when I settle into a host my roots go down deep.

I hid Lucille's body and searched all the minds in the house for a suitable host. Ronnie was perfect, unconscious and closed. Daniels was fretful; I can't abide fear. I fought back the cold, drew inward, contracted, and formed, at long last, a new cyst. I let Lucille's body be seen, and ignoring the others—their whimsy was as flat as their oversized feet—I withdrew.

And I have been thinking.

Some things were important that now cannot matter. I am different because of the searchings of Stoye—I blame him for all that has happened, and that is a thing which can no longer matter.

I know how to hate now, and how to make murder; the taste of these things is still bitter, but so is the taste of good stout when first taken, and stout has a taste worth acquiring. Like Grace I still have all my earlier qualities—the sun on a mountain or watching the curve of the wing of a gull (through a host) certainly has all the zest for me that it has ever had. Now I have more, though; and that is a thing which can matter very much indeed.

I have been selfish. It never occurred to me, back in the days of the man who did minuets joyfully, that I might do something *for* him whom I chose as a host. Grace taught me that, purely by feeding me richly through her experiences, purely by being a subject for my schooled suggestions. There may have been many who carried me who were susceptible to my control.

I could not know without trying, and I never tried this command until Grace took me in. And since then I hunger, I thirst for the richness and beauty and shifting and changing of colors and sounds which she brought me, and never again will rest and be fed and be happy to have just enough to sustain me.

I drift, now, encysted, but testing my powers when never before had I thought of them. I find I am mobile; also, to certain degrees, I can move things—this writing machine, for example, though it is slow and laborious. I find I can whisper to humans and fit some strange thoughts and ideas to each other.

I'll find, soon, a person, a man or a woman, or even a sensitive child. This one will be mine and I'll lead him to wonders of sense and of music and heady adventure. I think I am learning to savor the tartness of terror, the bloody salt flavor of killing with purpose. My host will exist in a series of colorful pageants and move in a world of emotional riches, all of my carefulest choosing.

And for this I sacrifice that which I guarded—my passion for quiet and secret enjoyments. I say to you, Know me! Suspect me! For by your suspicion you open yourself to my coming. And when some great mural is painted by someone who never did passable work in his life before that, suspect me. And when in a prison some cringing psychotic says, over and over, "A voice said to do it!" suspect me.

Whenever you walk in the street and feel a strange spasm of nausea, suspect me indeed; for then I am injured, and what you have seen is a part-host like Ronnie; and know that that person must die—and can kill if I will it.

I am so cold. . . .

I write this because in my search for a host who is perfect, I find that one segment of humans is almost entirely open. These are the readers and tellers of tales of the dark and of terror and madness. The one who has written these chapters would serve as a host—but I fear he would turn on me, feed on my memories, use me for piddling profit in plying his trade.

Besides, he's a bit superficial for one of my tastes. I know his intentions, however, and what he will do with this script. I know he is frightened because of the way this long tale has unfolded. I know, too, that nothing will keep him from seeing it printed.

When it is read, though, by thousands of like-minded people over the world, and he hears of the music and murder created by someone who fell to me only through reading it, then he will curse and will wish he were dead, and wish he had torn this to pieces.

The Martian and the Moron

IN 1924, WHEN I was just a pup, my father was a thing currently known as a "radio bug." These creatures were wonderful. They were one part fanatic, one part genius, a dash of childlike wonderment, and two buckets full of trial-and-error. Those were the days when you could get your picture in the paper for building a crystal set in something smaller and more foolish than the character who had his picture in the paper the day before. My father had his picture in there for building a "set" on a pencil eraser with a hunk of galena in the top and about four thousand turns of No. 35 enameled wire wrapped around it. When they came around to take his picture, he dragged out another one built into a peanut. Yes, a real peanut which brought in WGBS, New York. (You see, I really do remember.) They wanted to photograph that too, but Dad thought it would be a little immodest for him to be in the paper twice. So they took Mother's picture with it. The following week they ran both pictures, and Dad got two letters from other radio bugs saying his eraser radio wouldn't work and Mother got two hundred and twenty letters, forwarded from the paper, twenty-six of which contained proposals of marriage. (Of course Mother was a YL and not an OW then.)

Oddly enough, Dad never did become a radio ham. He seemed satisfied to be the first in the neighborhood to own a set, then to build a set—(after the spiderweb coil phase he built and operated a one-tube regenerative set which featured a UX-11 detector and a thing called a vario-coupler which looked like a greasy fist within a lacquered hand, and reached his triumph when he hooked it into a forty-'leven-pound "B-eliminator" and ran it right out of the socket like a four-hundred-dollar "electric" radio) and first in the state to be on the receiving end of a court order restraining him from using his equipment (every time he touched the tuning dials—three—the

141

neighboring radios with which Joneses were keeping up with each other, began howling unmercifully). So for a time he left his clutter of forms and wire and solder-splattered "bathtub" condensers shoved to the back of his cellar workbench, and went back to stuffing field mice and bats, which had been his original hobby. I think Mother was glad, though she hated the smells he made down there. That was after the night she went to bed early with the cramps, and he DX'd WLS in Chicago at 4:30 one morning with a crystal set and wanted to dance. (He learned later that he had crossed aerials with Mr. Bohackus next door, and had swiped Mr. Bohackus' fourteen-tube Atwater-Kent signal right out of Mr. Bohackus' gooseneck-megaphone speaker. Mr. Bohackus was just as unhappy as Mother to hear about this on the following morning. They had both been up all night.)

Dad never was one to have his leg pulled. He got very sensitive about the whole thing, and learned his lesson so well that when the last great radio fever took him, he went to another extreme. Instead of talking his progress all over the house and lot, he walled himself up. During the late war I ran up against security regulations—and who didn't—but they never bothered me. I had my training early.

He got that glint in his eyes after grunting loudly over the evening paper one night. I remember Mother's asking him about it twice, and I remember her sigh—her famous "here we go again" sigh—when he didn't answer. He leapt up, folded the paper, got out his keys, opened the safe, put the paper in it, locked the safe, put his keys away, looked knowingly at us, strode out of the room, went down into the cellar, came up from the cellar, took out his keys, opened the safe, took out the paper, closed the safe, looked knowingly at us again, said, "Henry, your father's going to be famous," and went down into the cellar.

Mother said, "I knew it. I *knew* it! I should have thrown the paper away. Or torn out that page."

"What's he going to make, Mother?" I asked.

"Heavens knows," she sighed. "Some men are going to try to get Mars on the radio."

"Mars? You mean the star?"

"It isn't a star, dear, it's a planet. They've arranged to turn off all the big radio stations all over the world for five minutes every hour so the men can listen to Mars. I suppose your father thinks he can listen too."

"Gee," I said, "I'm going down and—"

"You're going to do no such thing," said Mother firmly. "Get yourself all covered with that nasty grease he uses in his soldering, and stay up until all hours! It's almost bedtime. And—Henry—"

"Yes, Mother?"

She put her hands on my shoulders. "Listen to me, darling. People have been—ah—teasing your father." She meant Mr. Bohackus. "Don't ask him any questions about this if he doesn't want to talk, will you, darling? Promise?"

"All right, Mother." She was a wise woman.

Dad bought a big shiny brass padlock for his workshop in the cellar, and every time Mother mentioned the cellar, or the stars, or radio to him in any connection, he would just smile knowingly at her. It drove her wild. She didn't like the key, either. It was a big brass key, and he wore it on a length of rawhide shoelace tied around his neck. He wore it day and night. Mother said it was lumpy. She also said it was dangerous, which he denied, even after the time down at Roton Point when we were running Mr. Bohackus' new gasoline-driven ice cream freezer out on the beach. Dad leaned over to watch it working. He said, "This is the way to get things done, all right. I can't wait to get into that ice cream," and next thing we knew he was face down in the brine and flopping like a banked trout. We got him out before he drowned or froze. He was bleeding freely about the nose and lips, and Mr. Bohackus was displeased because Dad's key had, in passing through the spur-gears in which it had caught, broken off nine teeth. That was six more than Dad lost, but it cost much more to fix Dad's and showed, Mother said, just how narrow-minded Mr. Bohackus was.

Anyway, Dad never would tell us what he was doing down in the cellar. He would arrive home from work with mysterious packages and go below and lock them up before dinner. He would eat abstractedly and disappear for the whole evening. Mother, bless her, bore it with fortitude. As a matter of fact, I think she encouraged it. It was better than the previous fevers, when she had to sit for hours listening to crackling noises and organ music through big, heavy, magnetic earphones—or else. At least she was left to her own devices while all this was going on. As for me, I knew when I wasn't needed, and, as I remember, managed to fill my life quite successfully with clock movements, school, and baseball, and ceased to wonder very much.

About the middle of August Dad began to look frantic. Twice he worked right through the night, and though he went to the office on the days that followed, I doubt that he did much. On August 21—I remember the date because it was the day before my birthday, and I remember that it was a Thursday because Dad took the next day off for a "long weekend," so it must have been Friday—the crisis came. My bedtime was nine o'clock. At nine-twenty Dad came storming up from the cellar and demanded that I get my clothes on instantly and go out and get him two hundred feet of No. 27 silk-covered wire. Mother laid down the law and was instantly overridden. "The coil! The one coil I haven't finished!" he shouted hysterically. "Six thousand meters, and I have to run out of it. *Get* your clothes on this instant, Henry, number twenty-seven wire. Just control yourself this once Mother and you can have Henry stop standing there with your silly eyes bulging and get dressed you can have any hat on Fifth Avenue *hurry!*"

I hurried. Dad gave me some money and a list of places to go, told me not to come back until I'd tried every one of them, and left the house with me. I went east, he went west. Mother stood on the porch and wrung her hands.

I got home about twenty after ten, weary and excited, bearing a large metal spool of wire. I put it down triumphantly while Mother caught me up and felt me all over as if she had picked me up at the foot of a cliff. She looked drawn. Dad wasn't home yet.

After she quieted down a little she took me into the kitchen and fed me some chocolate-covered doughnuts. I forget what we talked about, if we talked, and at the bottom of the steps I could see a ray of yellow light. "Mother," I said, "you know what? Dad ran out and left his workshop open."

She went to the door and looked down the stairs.

"Darling!" she said after a bit, "Uh—wouldn't you like to—I mean, if he—"

I caught on quick. "I'll look. Will you stay up here and bump on the floor if he comes?"

She looked relieved, and nodded. I ran down the steps and cautiously entered the little shop.

Lined up across the bench were no less than six of the one-tube receivers which were the pinnacle of Dad's electronic achievement. The one at the end was turned back-to-front and had its rear shielding off; a naked coil-form dangled unashamedly out.

And I saw what had happened to the two alarm clocks which had disappeared from the bedrooms in the past six weeks. It happened that then, as now, clocks were my passion, and I can remember clearly the way he had set up pieces of the movements.

He had built a frame about four feet long on a shelf at right angles to the bench on which the radios rested. At one end of the frame was a clock mechanism designed to turn a reel on which was an endless band of paper tape about eight inches wide. The tape passed under a hooded camera—Mother's old Brownie—which was on a wall-bracket and aimed downward, on the tape. Next in line, under the tape, were six earphones, so placed that their diaphragms (the retainers had been removed) just touched the under side of the tape. And at the other end of the frame was the movement from the second alarm clock. The bell-clapper hung downwards, and attached to it was a small container of black powder.

I went to the first clock mechanism and started it by pulling out the toothpick Dad had jammed in the gears. The tape began to move. I pulled the plug on the other movement. The little container of black powder began to shake like mad and, through small holes, laid an even film of the powder over the moving tape. It stopped when it had put down about ten inches of it. The black line moved slowly across until it was over the phones. The magnets smeared the powder, which I recognized thereby as iron filings. Bending to peer under the tape, I saw that the whole bank of phones was levered to move downward a half an inch away from the tape. The leads from each of the six phones ran to a separate receiver.

I stood back and looked at this goldberg and scratched my head, then shook same and carefully blew away the black powder on the tape, rewound the movements, refilled the containers from a jar which stood on the bench, and put the toothpick back the way I had found it.

I was halfway up the stairs when the scream of burning rubber on the street outside coincided with Mother's sharp thumping on the floor. I got to her side as she reached the front window. Dad was outside paying off a taxi-driver. He never touched the porch steps at all, and came into the house at a dead run. He had a package under his arm.

"Fred!" said Mother.

"Can't stop now," he said, skidding into the hallway. "Couldn't get 27 anywhere. Have to use 25. Probably won't work. Everything happens to me, absolutely everything." He headed for the kitchen.

"I got you a whole reel of 27, Dad."

"Don't bother me now. Tomorrow," he said, and thumped downstairs. Mother and I looked at each other. Mother sighed. Dad came bounding back up the stairs. "You *what?*"

"Here." I got the wire off the hall table and gave it to him. He snatched it up, hugged me, swore I'd get a bicycle for my birthday (he made good on that, and on Mother's Fifth Avenue hat, too, by the way) and dove back downstairs.

We waited around for half an hour and then Mother sent me to bed. "You poor baby," she said, but I had the idea it wasn't me she was sorry for.

Now I'd like to be able to come up with a climax to all this, but there wasn't one. Not for years and years. Dad looked, the next morning, as if he had been up all night again—which he had—and as if he were about to close his fingers on the Holy Grail. All that day he would reappear irregularly, pace up and down, compare his watch with the living-room clock and the hall clock, and sprint downstairs again. That even went on during my birthday dinner. He had Mother call up the office and say he had Twonk's disease, a falling of the armpits (to whom do I owe this gem? Not my gag) and kept up his peregrinations all that night and all the following day until midnight. He fell into bed, so Mother told me, at one ayem Sunday morning and slept right through until suppertime. He still maintained a dazzling silence about his activities. For the following four months he walked around looking puzzled. For a year after that he looked resigned. Then he took up stuffing newts and moles. The only thing he ever said about the whole crazy business was that he was born to be disappointed, but at least, this time, no one could rib him about it. Now I'm going to tell you about Cordelia.

This happened the above-mentioned years and years later. The blow-off was only last week, as a matter of fact. I finished school and went into business with Dad and got mixed up in the war and all that. I didn't get married, though. Not yet. That's what I want to tell you about.

I met her at a party at Ferris's. I was stagging it, but I don't think it would have made any difference if I had brought someone; when I saw Cordelia I was, to understate the matter, impressed.

She came in with some guy I didn't notice at the time and, for all I know, haven't seen since. She slipped out of her light wrap with a single graceful movement; the sleeve caught in her bracelet, and she stood there, full profile, in the doorway, both arms straight and her hands together behind her as she worried the coat free, and I remember the small explosion in my throat as my indrawn breath and my gasp collided. Her hair was dark and lustrous, parted widely in a winging curve away from her brow. There were no pins in it; it shadowed the near side of her face as she bent her head and turned it down and toward the room. The cord of her neck showed columnar and clean. Her lips were parted ever so little, and showed an amused chagrin. Her lashes all but lay on her cheek. They stayed there when she was free and turned to face the room, for she threw her head back and up, flinging her hair behind her. She came across to my side of the party and sat down while the Thing who was with her went anonymously away to get her drink and came unnoticeably back.

I said to myself, "Henry, my boy, stop staring at the lady. You'll embarrass her."

She turned to me just then and gave me a small smile. Her eyes were widely spaced, and the green of deep water. "I don't mind, really," she said, and I realized I had spoken aloud. I took refuge in a grin, which she answered, and then her left eyelid dropped briefly, and she looked away. It was a wink, but such a slight, tasteful one! If she had used both eyelids, it wouldn't have been a wink at all; she would have looked quickly down and up again. It was an understanding, we're-together little wink, a tactful, gracious, wonderful, marvelous, do you begin to see how I felt?

The party progressed. I once heard somebody decline an invitation to one of Ferris's parties on the grounds that he had *been* to one of Ferris's parties. I had to be a little more liberal than that, but tonight I could see the point. It was because of Cordelia. She sat still, her chin on the back of her hand, her fingers curled against her white throat, her eyes shifting lazily from one point in the room to another. She did not belong in this conglomeration of bubbleheads. Look her—part Sphinx, part Pallas Athene ...

Ferris was doing his Kasbah act, with the bath towel over his head. He will next imitate Clyde McCoy's trumpet, I thought. He will then inevitably put that lampshade on his head, curl back up his upper lip, and be a rickshaw coolie. Following which he will do the adagio dance in which he will be too rough with some girl who will be too polite to protest his big shiny wet climaxing kiss.

I looked at Cordelia and I looked at Ferris and I thought, no, Henry; that won't do. I drew a deep breath, leaned over to the girl, and said, "If there were a fire in here, do you know the quickest way out?"

She shook her head expectantly.

"I'll show you," I said, and got up. She hesitated a charming moment, rose from her chair as with helium, murmured something polite to her companion, and came to me.

There were French doors opening on to the wide terrace porch which also served the front door. We went through them. The air was fragrant and cool, and there was a moon. She said nothing about escaping from fires. The French doors shut out most of the party noises—enough so that we could hear night sounds. We looked at the sky. I did not touch her.

After a bit she said in a voice of husky silver,

"Is the moon tired? she looks so pale
Within her misty veil:
She scales the sky from east to west,
And takes no rest.

"Before the coming of the night
The moon shows papery white;
Before the drawing of the day
She fades away."

It was simple and it was perfect. I looked at her in wonderment. "Who wrote that?"

"Christina Rosset-ti," she said meticulously, looking at the moon. The light lay on her face like dust, and motes of it were caught in the fine down at the side of her jaw.

"I'm Henry Folwell and I know a place where we could talk for about three hours if we hurry," I said, utterly amazed at myself; I don't generally operate like this.

She looked at the moon and me, the slight deep smile playing subtly with her lips. "I'm Cordelia Thorne, and I couldn't think of it," she said. "Do you think you could get my wrap without anyone seeing? It's a—"

"I know what it's," I said, sprinting. I went in through the front door, located her coat, bunched it up small, skinned back outside, shook it out and brought it to her. "You're still here," I said incredulously.

"Did you think I'd go back inside?"

"I thought the wind, or the gods, or my alarm clock would take you away."

"You said that beautifully," she breathed, as I put the coat around her shoulders. I thought I had too. I notched her high up in my estimation as a very discerning girl.

We went to a place called the Stroll Inn where a booth encased us away from all of the world and most of its lights. It was wonderful. I think I did most of the talking. I don't remember all that passed between us but I remember these things, and remember them well.

I was talking about Ferris and the gang he had over there every Saturday night; I checked myself, shrugged, and said, "Oh well. *Chacun à son goût,* as they say, which means—"

And she stopped me. "Please. Don't translate. It couldn't be phrased as well in English."

I had been about to say "—which means Jack's son has the gout." I felt sobered and admiring, and just sat and glowed at her.

And then there was that business with the cigarette. She stared at it as it lay in the ashtray, followed it with her gaze to my lips and back as I talked, until I asked her about it.

She said in a soft, shivery voice, "I feel just like that cigarette." I, of course, asked her why.

"You pick it up," she whispered, watching it. "You enjoy some of it. You put it down and let it—smolder. You like it, but you hardly notice it . . ."

I thereupon made some incredibly advanced protestations.

And there was the business about her silence—a long, faintly amused, inward-turning silence. I asked her what she was thinking about.

"I was ruminating," she said in a self-deprecating, tragic voice, "on the futility of human endeavor," and she smiled. And when I asked her what she meant, she laughed aloud and said, "Don't you know?" And I said, "Oh. That," and worshipped her. She was deep. I'd have dropped dead before I'd have admitted I didn't know what specifically she was driving at.

And books. Music, too. When were at the stage where I had both her hands and for minutes on end our foreheads were so close together you couldn't have slipped a swizzle stick between them, I murmured, "We seem to think so much alike. . . . Tell me Cordelia, have you read Cabell?"

She said, "Well, really," in such a tone that, so help me, I apologized. "Lovely stuff," I said, recovering.

She looked reminiscently over my shoulder, smiling her small smile. "So lovely."

"I knew you'd read him," I said, struck with sweet thunder. "And Faulkner—have you read any of Faulkner?"

She gave me a pitying smile. I gulped and said, "Ugly, isn't it?"

She looked reminiscently over my other shoulder, a tiny frown flickering in her flawless brow. "So ugly," she said.

In between times she listened importantly to my opinions on Faulkner and Cabell. And Moussorgsky and Al Jolson. She was wonderful, and we agreed in everything.

And, hours later, when I stood with her at her door, I couldn't do a thing but shuffle my feet and haul on the hem of my jacket. She gave me her hand gravely, and I think I stopped breathing. I said, "Uh, well," and couldn't improve on it. She swept her gaze from my eyes to my mouth, from side to side across my forehead; it was a tortured "No!" her slightly turning head articulated, and her whole body moved minutely with it. She let go my hand, turned slowly toward the door, and then, with a cry which might have been a breath of laughter and which might have been a sob, she pirouetted back to me and kissed me—not on the mouth, but in the hollow at the side of my neck. My fuse blew with a snap and a bright light and, as it were, incapacitated my self-starter. She moved deftly then, and to my blurred vision, apparently changed herself into a closed door. I must have stood looking at that door for twenty minutes before I turned and walked dazedly home.

I saw her five more times. Once it was a theater party, and we all went to her house afterward, and she showed great impartiality. One it was a movie, and who should we run into afterward but her folks. Very nice people, I liked them and I think they liked me. Once it was the circus; we stayed very late, dancing at a pavilion, and yet the street was still crowded outside her home when we arrived there, and a handshake had to do. The fourth time was at a party to which I went alone because she had a date that night. It devolved that the date was the same party. The way she came in did things to me. It wasn't the fact that she was with somebody else; I had no claim on her, and the way she acted with me made me feel pretty confident. It was the way she came in, slipping out of her wrap, which—caught on her—bracelet, freezing her in a profile while framed in the doorway. . . . I don't want to think about it. Not now.

I did think about it; I left almost immediately so that I could. I went home down and slumped down in an easy chair and convinced myself about coincidences, and was almost back to normal when Dad came into the room.

"*Argh!*" he said.

I leapt out of the chair and helped him to pick himself up off the middle of the rug. "Blast it, boy," he growled, "Why don't you turn on a light? What are you doing home? I thought you were out with your goddess. Why can't you pick up your big bony feet, or at least leave them somewhere else besides in the doorway of a dark room?" He dusted off his knees. He wasn't hurt. It's a deep-piled rug with two cushions under it. "You're a howling menace. Kicking your father." Dad had mellowed considerably with the years. "What's the matter with you anyhow? She do you something? Or are you beginning to have doubts?" He wore glasses now, but he saw plenty. He'd ribbed me about Cordelia as can only a man who can't stand ribbing himself.

"It was a lousy party," I said.

He turned on a light, "What's up, Henry?"

"Nothing," I said. "Absolutely nothing. I haven't had a fight with her, if that's what you're digging for."

"All right, then," he said, picking up the paper.

"There's nothing wrong with her. She's one of the most wonderful people I know, that's all."

"Sure she is." He began to read the paper.

"She's deep, too. A real wise head, she is. You wouldn't expect to find that in somebody as young as that. Or as good-looking." I wished he would put his eyebrows down.

"She's read everything worth reading," I added as he turned a page a minute later.

"Marvelous," he said flatly.

I glared at him. "What do you mean by that?" I barked. "What's marvelous?"

He put the paper down on his knee and smoothed it. His voice was gentle. "Why Cordelia, of course. I'm not arguing with you, Henry."

"Yes you—well, anyway, you're not saying what you think."

"You don't want to hear what I think."

"I know what I want!" I flared.

He crackled the paper nervously. "My," he said as if to himself, "this is worse than I thought." Before I could interrupt, he said, "Half of humanity doesn't know what it wants or how to find out. The other half knows what it wants, hasn't got it, and is going crazy trying to convince itself that it already has it."

"Very sound," I said acidly. "Where do you peg me?"

He ignored this. "The radio commercial which annoys me most," he said with apparent irrelevancy, "is the one which begins, 'There are some things so good they don't have to be improved.' That annoys me because there isn't a thing on God's green earth which couldn't stand improvement. By the same token, if you find something which looks to you as if it's unimprovable, then either it's a mirage or you're out of your mind."

"What has that to do with Cordelia?"

"Don't snap at me, son," Dad said quietly. "Let's operate by the rule of reason here. Or must I tear your silly head off and stuff it down your throat?"

I grinned in spite of myself. "Reason prevails, Dad. Go on."

"Now, I've seen the girl, and you're right; she's striking to look at. Extraordinary. In the process of raving about that you've also told me practically every scrap of conversation you've ever had with her."

"I have?"

"You're like your mother; you talk too much," he smiled. "Don't get flustered. It was good to listen to. Shows you're healthy. But I kept noticing one thing in these mouthings—all she's read, all the languages she understands, all the music she likes—and that is that you have never quoted her yet as saying a single declarative sentence. You have never quoted her as opening a conversation, changing the subject, mentioning something you both liked *before* you mentioned it, or having a single idea that you didn't like." He shrugged. "Maybe she is a good listener. They're—"

"Now wait a minute—"

"—They're rare anywhere in the world, especially in this house," he went on smoothly. "Put your hands back in your pockets, Henry, or sit on 'em until I've finished. Now, I'm not making any charges about Cordelia. There aren't any. She's wonderful. That's the trouble. For Pete's sake, get her to make a flat statement."

"She has, plenty of times," I said hotly. "You just don't know her! Why, she's the most—"

He put up his hands and turned his head as if I were aiming a bucket of water at him. "Shut up!" he roared. I shut. "Now," he said, "Listen to me. If you're right, you're right and there's no use defending anything. If you're wrong you'd better find it out soon before you get hurt. But I don't want to sit here and watch the process. I know how you tick, Henry. By gosh, I ought to. You're like I was. You and I, we get a hot idea and go all out for it, all speed and no control. We spill off at the mouth until we have the whole world watching, and when the idea turns sour the whole world gets in its licks, standing around laughing. Keep your beautiful dreams to yourself. If they don't pan out, you can always kick yourself effectively enough, without having every wall-eyed neighbor helping you."

A picture of Mr. Bohackus with the protruding china-blue eyes, our neighbor of long ago, crossed my mind, and I chuckled.

"That's better, Henry," said Dad. "Listen. When a fellow gets to be a big, grown-up man, which is likely to happen at my age, or never, he learns to make a pile of his beloved failures and consign them to the flames, and never think of them again. But it ought to be a private bonfire."

It sounded like sense, particularly the part about not having to defend if it was right enough to be its own defense. I said, "Thanks, Dad. I'll have to think. I don't know if I agree with you ... I'll tell you something, though. If Cordelia turned out to be nothing but a phonograph, I'd consider it a pleasure to spend the rest of my life buying new records for her."

"That'd be fine," said Dad, "if it was what you wanted. I seriously doubt that it is just now."

"Of course it isn't. Cordelia's all woman and has a wonderful mind, and that's what I want."

"Bless you, my children," Dad said, and grinned.

I knew I was right, and that Dad was simply expressing a misguided caution. The Foxy Grandpa routine, I thought, was a sign of advancing age. Dad sure was changed since the old days. On the other hand, he hadn't been the same since the mysterious frittering-out of his mysterious down-cellar project. I stopped thinking about Dad, and turned my mind to my own troubles.

I had plenty of time to think; I couldn't get a Saturday date with her for two weeks, and I wanted this session to run until it was finished with no early curfews. Not, as I have said, that I had any doubts. Far from it. All the same, I made a little list . . .

I don't think I said ten words to her until we were three blocks from her house. She quite took my breath away. She was wearing a green suit with surprising lapels that featured her fabulous profile and made me ache inside. I had not known that I was so hungry for a sight of her, and now she was more than a sight, now her warm hand had slipped into mine as we walked. "Cordelia . . ." I whispered.

She turned her face to me, and showed me the tender tuggings in the corners of her mouth. She made an interrogative sound, like a sleepy bird.

"Cordelia," I said thickly. It all came out in a monotone. "I didn't know I could miss anybody so much. There's been a hollow place in my eyes, wherever I looked; it had no color and it was shaped like you. Now you fill it and I can see again."

She dropped her eyes and her smile was a thing to see. "You said that beautifully," she breathed.

I hadn't thought of that. What I had said was squeezed out of me like toothpaste out of a tube, with the same uniformity between what came out and what was still inside.

"We'll go to the Stroll Inn," I said. It was where we met. We didn't meet at the party. We just saw each other there. We met in that booth.

She nodded gravely and walked with me, her face asleep, its attention turned inward, deeply engaged. It was not until we turned the corner on Winter Street and faced the Inn that I thought of my list; and when I did, I felt a double, sickening impact—first, one of shame that I should dare to examine and experiment with someone like this, second, because item 5 on that list was "You said that beautifully ..."

The Stroll Inn, as I indicated before, has all its lights, practically, on the outside. Cordelia looked at me thoughtfully as we walked into their worming neon field. "Are you all right?" she asked. "You look pale."

"How can you tell?" I asked, indicating the lights, which flickered and switched, orange and green and blue and red. She smiled appreciatively, and two voices spoke within me. One said joyfully, " 'You look pale' is a declarative statement." The other said angrily, "You're hedging. And by the way, what do you suppose that subtle smile is covering up, if anything?" Both voices spoke forcefully, combining in a jumble which left me badly confused. We went in and found a booth and ordered dinner. Cordelia said with pleasure that she would have what I ordered.

Over the appetizer I said, disliking myself intensely, "Isn't this wonderful? All we need is a moon. Can't you see it, hanging up there over us?"

She laughed and looked up, and sad sensitivity came into her face. I closed my eyes, waiting.

" 'Is the moon tired? She looks so pale—' " she began.

I started to chew again. I think it was marinated herring, and very good too, but at the moment it tasted like cold oatmeal with a dash of warm lard. I called the waiter and ordered a double rum and soda. As he turned away I called him back and asked him to bring a bottle instead. I needed help from somewhere, and pouring it out of a bottle seemed a fine idea at the time.

Over the soup I asked her what she was thinking about. "I was ruminating," she said in a self-deprecating, tragic voice, "on the futility of human endeavor." Oh, brother, me too, I thought. Me too.

Over the dessert we had converse again, the meat course having passed silently. We probably presented a lovely picture, the two of us wordlessly drinking in each other's presence, the girl radiating an understanding tenderness, the young man speechless with admiration. Look how he watches her, how his eyes travel over her face, how he sighs and shakes his head and looks back at his plate.

I looked across the Inn. In a plate-glass window a flashing neon sign said bluely, "nnI llortS. NnI llortS."

"Nnillorts," I murmured.

Cordelia looked up at me expectantly, with her questioning sound. I tensed. I filled the jigger with rum and poured two fingers into my empty highball glass. I took the jigger in one hand and the glass in the other.

I said, "You've read Kremlin von Schtunk, the Hungarian poet?" and drank the jigger.

"Well, really," she said pityingly.

"I was just thinking of his superb line, 'Nni llorts, nov shmoz ka smörgasbord,'" I intoned, "which means—" and I drank the glass.

She reached across the table and touched my elbow. "Please. Don't translate. It couldn't be phrased as well in English."

Something within me curled up and died. Small, tight, cold and dense, its corpse settled under my breastbone. I could have raged at her, I supposed. I could have coldly questioned her, pinned her down, stripped from her those layers of schooled conversational reactions, leaving her ignorance in nakedness. But what for? I didn't want it ... And I could have talked to her about honesty and ethics and human aims—why did she do it? What did she ever hope to get? Did she think she would ever corral a man and expect him to be blind, for the rest of his life, to the fact that there was nothing behind this false front—nothing at all? Did she think that—did she think? No.

I looked at her, the way she was smiling at me, the deep shifting currents which seemed to be in her eyes. She was a monster. She was some graceful diction backed by a bare half-dozen relays. She was a card-file. She was a bubble, thin-skinned, covered with swirling, puzzling, compelling colors, filled with nothing. I was hurt and angry and, I think, a little frightened. I drank some more rum. I ordered her a drink and then another, and stayed ahead of her four to one. I'd have walked out and gone home if I had been able to summon the strength. I couldn't. I could only sit and stare and bathe myself in agonized astonishment. She didn't mind. She sat listening as raptly to my silence as to my conversation. Once she said, "We're just *being* together, aren't we?" and I recognized it as another trick from the bag. I wondered how many she might come up with if I just waited.

She came up with plenty.

She sat up and leaned forward abruptly. I had the distinct feeling that she was staring at me—her face was positioned right for it—but here eyes were closed. I put my glass down and stared blearily back, thinking, now what?

Her lips parted, twitched, opened wide, pursed. They uttered a glottal gurgling which was most unpleasant. I pushed my chair back, startled. "Are you sick?"

"Are you terrestrial?" she asked me.

"Am I *what?*"

"Making—contact thirty years," she said. Her voice was halting, filled with effort.

"What are you talking about?"

"Terrestrial power quickly going," she said clearly. "Many—uh—much power making contact this way very high frequencies thought. Easy radio. Not again thought. Take radio code quickly."

"Listen, toots," I said nastily, "This old nose no longer has a ring in it. Go play tricks on somebody else." I drank some more rum. An I.Q. of sixty, and crazy besides. "You're a real find, you are," I said.

"Graphic," she said. "Uh—write. Write. Write." She began to claw the table cloth. I looked at her hand. It was making scribbling motions. "Write write."

I flipped a menu over and put it in front of her and gave her my pen.

Now, I read an article once on automatic writing—you know, that spiritualist stuff. Before witnesses, a woman once wrote a long letter in trance in an unfamiliar (to her) hand, at the astonishing rate of four hundred and eight words a minute. Cordelia seemed to be out to break that record. That pen-nib was a blur. She was still leaning forward rigidly, and her eyes were still closed. But instead of a blurred scrawl, what took shape under her flying hand was a neat list or chart. There was an alphabet of sorts, although not arranged in the usual way; it was more a list of sounds. And there were the numbers one to fourteen. Beside each sound and each number was

158

a cluster of regular dots which looked rather like Braille. The whole sheet took her not over forty-five seconds to do. And after she finished she didn't move anything except her eyelids which went up. "I think," she said conversationally, "that I'd better get home, Henry. I feel a little dizzy."

I felt a little more than that. The rum, in rum's inevitable way, had sneaked up on me, and suddenly the room began to spin, diagonally, from the lower right to the upper left. I closed my eyes tight, opened them, fixed my gaze on a beer-tap on the bar at the end of the room, and held it still until the room slowed and stopped. "You're so right," I said, and did a press-up on the table top to assist my legs. I managed to help Cordelia on with her light coat. I put my pen back in my pocket (I found it the next morning with the cap still off and a fine color scheme in the lining of my jacket) and picked up the menu.

"What's that?" asked Cordelia.

"A souvenir," I said glumly. I had no picture, no school ring, no nothing. Only a doodle. I was too tired, twisted, and tanked to wonder much about it, or about the fact that she seemed never to have seen it before. I folded it in two and put it in my hip pocket.

I got her home without leaning on her. I don't know if she was ready to give a repeat performance of that goodnight routine. I didn't wait to find out. I took her to the door and patted her on the cheek and went away from there. It wasn't her fault....

When I got to our house, I dropped my hat on the floor in the hall and went into the dark living-room and fell into the easy-chair by the door. It was a comfortable chair. I felt about as bad as I ever had. I remember wondering smokily whether anyone ever loves a person. People seem to love dreams instead, and for the lucky ones, the person is close to the dream. But it's a dream all the same, a sticky dream. You unload the person and the dream stays with you.

What was it Dad had said? "When a fellow gets to be a big grown-up man ... he learns to make a pile of his beloved failures and consign them to the flames." "Hah!" I ejaculated, and gagged. The rum tasted terrible. I had nothing to burn but memories and the lining of my stomach. The latter was flaming merrily. The former stayed where they were. The way she smiled, so deep and secret ...

Then I remembered the doodle. Her hands had touched it, her mind had— No, her mind hadn't. It could have been anyone's mind, but not hers. The girl operated under a great handicap. No brains. I felt terrible. I got up out of the chair and wove across the room, leaning on the mantel. I put my forehead on the arm which I had put on the mantel, and with my other hand worried the menu out of my pocket. With the one hand and my teeth I tore it into small pieces and dropped the pieces in the grate, all but one. Then I heaved myself upright, braced my shoulder against the mantel, which had suddenly begun to bob and weave, got hold of my lighter, coaxed a flame out of it and lit the piece I'd saved. It burned fine. I let it slip into the grate. It flickered, dimmed, caught on another piece of paper, flared up again. I went down on one knee and carefully fed all the little pieces to the flame. When it finally went out I stirred the ashes around with my finger, got up, wiped my hands on my pants, said, "That was good advice Dad gave me," and went back to the chair. I went back into it, pushed my shoes off my feet, curled my legs under me and, feeling much better, dozed off.

I woke slowly, some time later, and with granulated eyelids and a mouth full of emory and quinine. My head was awake but my legs were asleep and my stomach had its little hands on my backbone and was trying to pull it out by the roots. I sat there groggily looking at the fire.

Fire? What fire? I blinded and winced; I could almost hear my eyelids rasping.

There was a fire in the grate. Dad was kneeling beside it, feeding it small pieces of paper. I didn't say anything; I don't think it occurred to me. I just watched.

He let the fire go out after a while; then he stirred the ashes with his finger and stood up with a sigh, wiping his hands on his pants. "Good advice I gave the boy. Time I took it myself." He loomed across the shadowy room to me, turned around and sat down in my lap. He was relaxed and heavy, but he didn't stay there long enough for me to feel it. "Gah!" he said, crossed the room again in one huge bound, put his back against the mantel and said, "Don't move, you, I've got a gun."

"It's me, Dad."

"Henry! Bythelordharry, you'll be the death of me yet. That was the most inconsiderate thing you have ever done in your entire self-ish life. I've a notion to bend this poker over your Adam's apple, you snipe." He stamped over to the book case and turned on the light. "This is the last time I'll ever—Henry! What's the matter? You look awful! Are you all right?"

"I'll live," I said regretfully. "What were you burning?"

He grinned sheepishly. "A beloved failure. Remember my preachment a couple weeks ago? It got to working on me. I decided to take my own advice." He breathed deeply. "I feel much better, I think."

"I burned some stuff too," I croaked. "I feel better too. I think," I added.

"Cordelia?" he asked, sitting near me.

"She hasn't got brain one," I said.

"Well," he said. There was more sharing and comfort in the single monosyllable than in anything I have ever heard. He hadn't changed much over the years. A bit heavier. A bit grayer. Still intensely alive, though. And he'd learned to control those wild projects of his. I thought, quite objectively, "I like this man."

We were quiet for a warm while. Then, "Dad—what was it you burned? The Martian project?"

"Why, you young devil! How did you know?"

"I dunno. You look like I feel. Sort of—well, you've finally unloaded something, and it hurts to lose it, but you're glad you did."

"On the nose," he said, and grinned sheepishly. "Yup, Henry— I really hugged that project to me. Want to hear about it?"

Anything but Cordelia, I thought. "I saw your rig," I said, to break the ice. "The night you sent me out for the wire. You left the workshop open."

"I'll be darned. I thought I'd gotten away with it."

"Mother knew what you were up to, though she didn't know how."

"And you saw how."

"I saw that weird gimmick of your, but it didn't mean anything to me. Mother told me never to mention it to you. She thought you'd be happier if you were left alone."

He laughed with real delight. "Bless her heart," he said. "She was a most understanding woman."

"I read about the Martian signals in the papers," I said. "Fellow named—what was it?"

"Jenkins," said Dad. "C. Francis Jenkins. He built a film-tape recorder to catch the signals. Primitive, but it worked. Dr. David Todd of Amherst was the man who organized the whole project, and got the big radio people all over the world to cooperate. They had a five-minute silence every hour during Mars' closest proximity—August 1 to 3."

"I remember," I said. "It was my birthday, 1924. What got you so teed off?"

"I got mad," said my father, folding his hands over his stomach. "Just because it had become fashionable to use radio in a certain way on earth, those simple souls had to assume that the Martian signals—if any—would come through the same way. I felt they'd be different."

"Why should they be?"

"Why should we expect Martians to be the same? Or even think the same? I just took a wild stab at it, that's all. I tuned in on six wavelengths at the same time. I set up my rig so that anything coming through on any one wavelength would actuate a particular phone."

"I remember," I said, trying hard. "The iron filings on the paper tape, over the ear-phones."

"That's right. The phone was positioned far enough below the tape so that the magnetic field would barely contain the filings. When the diaphragm vibrated, the filings tended to cluster. I had six phones on six different wavelengths, arranged like this," and he counted them out on the palm of his hand:

$$
\begin{array}{cc}
1 & 2 \\
3 & 4 \\
5 & 6
\end{array}
$$

"What could you get? I don't figure it, Dad. There'd be no way of separating your dots and dashes."

"Blast!" he exploded. "That the kind of thinking that made me mad, and makes me mad to this day! No; what I was after was something completely different in transmission. Look; how much would you get out of piano music if all the strings but one were broken? Only when the pianist hit that note in the course of his transmission would you hear anything. See what I mean? Supposing the Martians were sending in notes and chords of an established octave of frequencies? Sure—Jenkins got signals. No one's ever been able to interpret them. Well, supposing I was right—then Jenkins was recording only one of several or many 'notes' of the scale, and of course it was meaningless."

"Well, what did you get?"

"Forty-six photographs, five of which were so badly under-exposed that they were useless to me. I finally got the knack of moving the tape carefully enough and lighting it properly, and they came out pretty well. I got signals on four of the six frequencies. I got the same grouping only three or four times; I mean, sometimes there would be something on phones 1, 2, and 4, and sometimes it would only be on 4, and sometimes it would be on 2 and 6. Three and 5 never did come through; it was fantastic luck that I picked the right frequencies, I suppose, for the other four."

"What frequencies did you use?"

He grinned. "I don't know. I really don't. It was all by guess and by Golly. I never was an engineer, Henry. I'm in the insurance business. I had no instruments—particularly not in 1924. I wound a 6000-meter coil according to specs they printed in the paper. As for the others, I worked on the knowledge that less turns of heavier wire means shorter wave-lengths. I haven't got the coils now and couldn't duplicate 'em in a million years. All I can say for sure is that they were all different, and stepped down from 6000.

"Anyway, I studied those things till I was blue in the face. It must've been the better part of a year before I called in anyone else. I wrote to Mr. Jenkins and Dr. Todd, too, but who am I? A taxidermical broker with a wacky idea. They sent the pictures back with polite letters, and I can't say I blame them ... anyway, good riddance to the things. But it was a wonderful idea, and I wanted so much to be the man who did the job.... Ever want something so badly you couldn't see straight, Henry?"

"Me?" I asked, with bitterness.

"It's all over now, though. I'm through with crazy projects, for life. Never again. But gosh, I did love that project. Know what I mean?"

"No," I said with even more bitterness.

He sat straight. "Hey, I'm sorry, fellow. Those were rhetorical questions. Maybe you'd better spill it."

So I told it to him—all of it. Once I started, I couldn't stop. I told him about the moon poem and the "well, really" gimmick and the "please don't translate" routine, and the more I talked, the worse I felt. He sat and listened, and didn't say "I told you so," and the idea was worming its way into the back of my mind as I talked that here sat one of the most understanding people ever created, when he screamed. He screamed as one screams at the intrusion of an ice-cube into the back of one's bathing-suit.

"What's the matter?" I said, breaking off.

"Go on, go on," he gabbled. "Henry you idiot don't tell me you don't know what you're saying for Pete's sake tell it to—"

"Whoa! I don't even remember where I was."

"What she said to you—'Are you a terrestrial?'"

"Oh, don't get so excited, Dad. It doesn't mean anything. Why bother? She was trying to interest me, I suppose. I didn't let it get to me then and I won't now. She—"

"*Blast* her! I'm not talking about her. It was what she said. Go on, Henry! You say she wrote something?"

He wormed it all out of me. He forced me to go over it and over it. The windows paled and the single light by the book case looked yellow and ill in the dawn, but still he pounded at me. And I finally quit. I just quit, out of compounded exhaustion and stubbornness. I lay back in the big chair and glared at him.

He strode up and down the room, trying to beat his left hand to a pulp with a right fist. "Of course, of course," he said excitedly. "That's how they'd do it. The blankest mind in the world. Blank and sensitive, like undeveloped film. *Of course!* 'Making contact thirty years' they said. 'Much power making contact this way—very high frequencies thought.' A radionic means of transmitting thought, and it uses too much power to be practical. 'Easy radio. Not again thought.'"

He stopped in front of me, glaring. "'Not again thought,'" he growled. "You—you *dope!* How could my flesh and blood be so abjectly stupid? There in your hands you held the interplanetary Rosetta Stone, and what did you do with it?"

I glared back at him. "I was quote consigning one of my beloved failures to the flames end quote," I said nastily.

Suddenly he was slumped and tired. "So you were, son. So you were. And it was all there—little Braille, you said. A series of phonetic symbols, and almost a certainly a list of the frequency-octave they use. And—and all my pictures. . . . I burned them too." He sat down.

"Henry—"

"Don't take it so hard, Dad," I said. "Your advice was good. You forget your Martians and I'll forget my moron. When a fellow get to be a grown-up man—"

He didn't hear me. "Henry. You say her folks like you?"

I sprang to my feet. "NO!" I bellowed. "Dad, I will not, repeat, *not* under any circumstances woo that beautiful package of brainless reflexes. I have had mine. I—"

"You really mean it, don't you?"

"That I do," I said positively.

"Well," he said dejectedly, "I guess that's that."

And that old, old fever came back into his face.

"Dad—"

He slowly straightened up, that hot "Land ho!" expression in his eyes. My father is hale, handsome, and, when he wants to be, extremely persistent.

"Now, Dad," I said. "Let's be reasonable. She's very young, Dad. Now, let's talk this thing over a little more, Dad. You can't go following a girl all over the house with a notebook and pencil. They said

they wouldn't use the thought contact again. Dad. Now Dad—"
"Your mother would understand if she were alive," he murmured.
"No! You can't!" I bawled. "Dad, for heaven's sake use your head! Why you—Cordelia—Dad, she'd make me call her *Mummy!*"
Now what am I going to do?

Die, Maestro, Die!

I finally killed Lutch Crawford with a pair of bolt-cutters. And there was Lutch—all of him, all his music, his jump, his public and his pride, in the palm of my hand. Literally in the palm of my hand—three pinkish slugs with horn at one end and blood at the other. I tossed 'em, caught 'em, put 'em in my pocket and walked off whistling *Daboo Dabay,* which had been Lutch's theme. It was the first time in eight years I had heard that music and enjoyed it. Sometimes it takes a long while to kill a man.

I'd tried it twice before. I tried it smart, and failed. I tried it sneak, and failed. Now it's done.

Whistling it, I can hear the whole band—the brass background: "Hoo Ha Hoo Ha" (how he used to stage that on the stand, the skunk—Lutch, I mean, with the sliphorns and trumpets turning in their chairs, blowing the "hoo" to the right with cap-mutes, swinging around, blowing the "ha" at the left, open) and then Lutch's clarinet a third above Skid Portly's gimmicked-up guitar: "Daboo, dabay, dabay daboo . . ." You know, spotlights on Lutch, a bright overflow of light on Skid and his guitar, light bronzing and scything from the swinging bells of the trombones here and the trumpets over there . . . the customers ate it up, they loved it, they loved him, the bubbleheaded bunch of bastiches . . . and Fawn at the piano, white glow from the spot running to her, gold flashes lighting up her face when the brasses swung, lighting up the way she cocked her head to one side, half smiling at Lutch, stroking the keyboard as if it was his face, loving him more than anybody there.

And up in the back, in the dark, out of sight but altogether needed, like a heart, there was always Crispin, crouching over the skins, his bass a thing you felt with your belly rather than heard, but the real beat coming through his hands, pushing out one crushed ruff for

167

each beat, shifting from center to edge—not much—matching the "hoo ha" of the brass. You couldn't see Crispin, but you could feel what he made. They loved it. He made love with the skins. He was loving Fawn with the pedal, with the sticks, there in the dark.

And I'd be out front, off to one side, seeing it all, and I can see it now, just whistling the theme. It was all there—Lutch, everything about Lutch, everything that Lutch was. There was the swinging brass, and Crispin loving Fawn, and Fawn loving Lutch, and Lutch giving theme solo to Skid's guitar, taking the foolish obbligato for himself. And there was Fluke, and that's me. Sure, in the dark. Always keep Fluke in the dark; don't show them Fluke's face. Fluke has a face that kept him out of the United States Army, didn't you know? Fluke has a mouth only as big as your two thumbnails, and all his teeth are pointed.

I was as much a part of it as any of them, but I didn't make anything. I just worked there. I was the guy who waited for ten bars of theme, and then coming in with the beat, holding the microphone just off my cheek like a whisper-singer, saying "Lutch is here, Lutch is gone, man, gone." Lutch used to say old Fluke had a voice like an alto-horn with a split reed. He called it a dirty voice. It was a compliment. "Gone, man, gone," I'd say, and then talk up: "Top o' the morn from the top o' the heap, Kizd. This the Fluke, the fin of the fish, the tail of the whale, bringin' you much of Lutch and such ... Lutch Crawford and his Gone Geese, ladies and gentlemen, from the Ruby Room of the Hotel Halpern in ..." (or the Rainbow, or the Angel, or wherever). That was me, Fluke. I hadn't wanted the buildup, all that jive about "fin and the fish." That was Lutch's idea. That was Lutch, like giving his theme solo to Skid's guitar, instead of taking it himself. He even hauled me into his recording dates— you know that. That was the thing about that band; it was a machine; and some will drive a machine, and some will ride it, and Lutch, he rode.

I *had* to kill him.

I'll tell you about the time I tried it smart.

Five years ago, it was. We had an ivory man who was pretty good. Name was Hinkle. He arranged a lot—he was the one who styled the band the way you know it. You can forget him; he was killed. Went down to a dance pitch in the South Side to hear a bass-player who was getting famous, and some drunk started an argument and pulled a gun and missed the cat he aimed at and hit Hinkle. It was none of Hinkle's argument—he didn't even know anybody there. Anyway, he got iced and we had to play a date without a piano. We got along, strictly ho-hum.

Then about eleven o'clock this baby shuffles up to the stand, all big eyes and timidity. She pulled Lutch's swallow-tail between numbers, dropped it like it was hot, and stood there blushing like a radish. She was only about seventeen, cute-fat, with long black hair and pink lips like your kid sister. It took her three tries to lay out what she wanted, but the idea was she played a little piano and thought she might fill out a number for us.

Lutch was always an easy fall for anyone who looked like he wanted something real hard. He didn't think five seconds. He waved her over to the ivory, and called for "Blue Prelude," which had enough reed, soon enough, that we could cover the piano if it soured.

We didn't cover up a thing. The kid played Hinkle, perfect, pure and easy; close your eyes and Hinkle was there, walking bass and third-runs, large as life.

The rest of the date turned over to the kid, far as the band was concerned. She pulled out a bag of tricks that I'll never forget. She had style and good wrists. She read like lightning and memorized better, and she had a touch. Hell, I don't have to tell you about Fawn Amory . . . anyhow, we had a powwow, and Lutch had dinner with her folks. Fawn had every disk Lutch Crawford had ever waxed— that was how she knew Hinkle's style—and she'd been playing piano since she was a pup. Lutch hired her with her daddy's blessing, and we had us a piano again.

We began to get big about then. It wasn't so much Fawn's playing—she wasn't brilliant, she was just terrific—but it was what she was to the band. The music business is full of roundheels and thrushes who feed on seed; this kid was from fresh air. She made the band worth staying with. Turnover just stopped, except for a couple of times when a side-man would carry too much altitude and make a pass. That never happened more than once per man. Then one or the other of us would happily pull the wolf's teeth. Once Skid busted a four hundred dollar guitar over a guy's head for that. (A good thing in the long run; he went into electrics seriously after that; but the electric guitar comes later.) And once I gave a spare lip to a trumpet man, pushing three teeth out under his nose, when his right hand forgot what his left was hired for.

She had this wide-eyed yen for Lutch when she joined us, and it was there for anyone to see. But clean, dig me? Lutch, he treated her like the rest of the sides. He kept it just like it was, and we went places. I don't think I was the only one who lost sleep. As long as no one made a move, everything stayed the same and the band as a whole jatoed. We rose, Jack.

It was Fawn who made the break. Looking back, I guess it could've been expected. We were all pretty wise; we did what we did because we thought it out. But she was just a kid. She'd been eating her heart out for too long, I guess, and she had no muscles for a pitch like that. We were in Boulder City that night, taking fifteen about two in the morning at a roadhouse. There was all kinds of moon. I was in a wild hassle with myself. Fawn was under my skin clear down to the marrow by then. I went into the bar and slurped up a boiler-maker—they always make me sick, and I wanted a small trouble to concentrate on. I left the rest of the sides jaw-jamming around a table and walked outside. There was a gravel path, the kind that gives a dry belch under your feet. I stayed off it. I walked on the grass and looked at the moon, which was bad for me, and felt the boilermaker seething under my low ribs, and felt but rugged. You know.

It wasn't only Fawn. I realized that. It was something to do with Lutch. He was so—sure of himself. Hell. I never could be that. Never until now, when I've got what was coming to me. Now I'm damn sure where I'm going, and I did it with my own hands. Not every-body can say that. But Lutch, he could. He had talent, see—big tal-ent. He was the real musician. But he didn't use it, only to guide with his fingertips. He styled Hinkle still, and another man soloed his theme. He was like that. He was so sure of himself that he didn't

170

have to hog anything. He didn't even have to reach out and pick up anything that he knew he could have. Now me, I never could know till I tried. There shouldn't be guys like Lutch Crawford, guys that never have to wonder or worry. Them as has, gits, they say. There can't be any honest competition with a guy like that. He'll win out, or you will. If he does, he'll do it easy as breathing. If you do, it's only because he let you. Guys like that shouldn't be born. If they are, they ought to be killed. Things are tough enough with an even break. Lutch, he had a pet name for the band. He called it the unit. That doesn't sound like a pet name, but it was. Fluke was his barker, and part of the unit . . . it didn't matter that the band would be just as good without me. Any one of us could be dropped or replaced, and it would still be Lutch Crawford's Gone Geese. But Fluke was in, and Skid, and Crispin and the rest, and that's the way he wanted it to stay. I was in the bucks, with a future—thanks to him. Thank you very much to him for every damn thing.

So I was standing on the grass looking at the moon and feeling all this, when I heard Fawn sob. Just once. I went that way, walking on the grass, sliding my feet so that left shoe wouldn't squeak.

She was standing at the corner of the building with Lutch. She was crying without making any more noise and without covering her face. It was wet and sort of pulled down and sidewards as if I saw it through a wavy glass.

She said, "I can't help it, Lutch, I love you."

And he said, "I love you too. I love everybody. It's nothing to get sick over."

"It isn't . . ." The way she said that, it was a question and a whole flood of detail about how sick you can get. "Let me kiss you, Lutch," she whispered. "I won't ever ask you again. Let me this once. Once, I got to, Lutch, I got to, I can't go on much longer like this . . ."

Now, I hated him, and I think I hated her a little, for a second, but you know, I'd of kicked him clear to Pensacola if he hadn't done what she said. I never had a feeling like that before. Never. I don't want it again.

Well, he did. Then he went back inside and got his clarinet and hit a blue lick or two to call us back in, the same as always. He left her out there, and me too, though he didn't know I was there. Difference was, he left me alone ...

We finished the date somehow, Crispin and his heartbeat drums, and Skid throwing that famous gliss all over the finger-board—he could really glissando with that new guitar, that Crispin helped him design, but I'm coming to that—and the horns and Fluke. Yeah, Fluke, real smooth: "Sweet Sue now, kizd, the sweetest Sue we ever knew, featuring Fawn Amory, the breeze on keys ..." And Fawn ripples into the intro, and I give her a board-fade on the p.a. system, and sigh in with, "Oh kizd, ain't we got Fawn ..." and cut back to full volume on the piano mike. And I kept spooning that corn back and back to myself, "Ain't we got Fawn, ain't we got—"

Crispin was a big blond guy who was a graduate electrical engineer. He earned his way through school playing drums, and after he graduated went right on playing. If he'd gone into electronics the way he'd planned, he'd of kept on playing drums. By the same token nothing could keep him from messing with electronics while he was a trap man. He was forever rehashing our p.a. system, and Skid's git-box was like peanuts to him; he kept coming back for more. Skid was amplified when he started with us—a guitar's pretty nowhere with a pickup in a band nowadays—but all he had was a simple magnetic pickup clamped onto a regular concert guitar. He had a few gimmicks too— a pedal volume control and a tone-switch on the box that gave him a snarl when he wanted it. Trouble was, at high volumes that pickup picked up everything—the note and the scratch of the plectrum and the peculiar squeak of Skid's calloused left fingers when he slid them on the wound strings, so that a guitar solo always had a background of pops and crackles and a bunch of guys whistling for taxicabs.

Crispin, he fixed that. He was a big, good-natured cat that everybody liked on sight, and sometimes when we went into a new town Crispin would go down to Radio Row and talk some repairman into the use of his shop for a couple days. Crispin would drag in Skid's guitar amplifier and haul its guts out and attach tone generators and oscilloscopes and all like that, and after that would spend good sleeping time telling Skid how to run the thing. After a couple of years Skid had an instrument that would sit up and typewrite. He had a warble-vibrato on it, and a trick tailpiece that he operated with his elbows that would raise a six-string chord a halftone while he held it, and some jazz called an attenuator that let him hit a note that wouldn't fade, just like it was blown out of an organ. Skid had a panel beside him with more buttons, switches, and controls on it than a custom-built accordion has stops. He used to say that the instrument was earning his keep—any three-chord man from a hill-billy band could take his spot if he got that instrument. I thought he was right. For years I thought he was right when he said that.

It was before rehearsal the next day, that time in Boulder City, that Crispin came to me and talked like with my mouth. I was in the sun-porch thinking about that moon last night and all that went with it, about Lutch and the way everything came so easy to him, he never had to make up his mind. Crispin lounged up next to me and said,

"Fluke, did you ever see the time when Lutch couldn't make up his mind?"

I said, "Brother," and he knew I meant no.

He looked at his thumb, threw it out of joint. "Cat gets every-thing he wants without asking for it. Never has to think of asking for it."

"You're so right," I said. I didn't feel like talking.

He said, "He rates it. I'm glad." He was, too.

I said, "I'm glad too." I wasn't. "What brings up all this jive, Crispin?"

He waited a long time. "Well, he just asked me something. He was all—all—ah, he was like a square at the Savoy, shuffling his feet and blushing."

"*Lutch?*" I demanded. Lutch usually came on like coke, all steam, no smoke. "What was it?"

"It was about Fawn," he said.

I felt something the size and weight of a cueball drop into my stomach. "What's with Fawn?"

"He wanted to know what the sides would think if he and Fawn got married."

"What'd you tell him?"

"What could I tell him? I said it would be fine. I said it didn't have to make any difference. It might even be better."

"Better," I said. "Sure." Much better. Even if it was out of your reach, at least you could dream. You could hope for some break, some way. Lutch and Fawn ... they wouldn't fool around with this marriage kick, now. They'd do it up right.

"I knew you'd think the same way," he said. He sounded as if there was a load off his mind. He slapped my back—I hate that— and walked off whistling *Daboo Dabay*.

That was when I made up my mind to kill Lutch. Not for Fawn. She was just part of it—the biggest part, yes; but I couldn't stand this one more trip his way of the silver platter. I remember once when I was a kid hitch-hiking. It was cold and I'd been at a crossroads near Mineola for a long time. I began to wish real hard, hard like praying. A long time later I remember what it was I wished for so hard. Not for a ride. Not for some guy with a heater in his car to stop. What I wished for was a whole bunch of cars to come along so I could thumb them. Dig me? The biggest break I ever wanted was to have the odds raised for me, so I could make my own way easier. That's all anyone should have. Lutch, born talented, good-looking, walking through life picking up gold pieces ... people like that shouldn't live. Every minute they live, a guy like us gets his nose rubbed in it.

For a second there I thought I'd quit, walk off, get clear. And then I remembered the radio, the jukes, people humming in front of elevator doors—and I knew I'd never get away from him. If he was dead it would be different; I could be glad when I heard that jive. No, I had to kill him.

But I'd play it smart.

For a couple of days I thought about it. I didn't think about much else. I thought about all the ways I'd ever heard about, and all the tricks they use in whodunits to catch up on all the ways. I had about decided on an auto accident—he was all the time driving, either with the band or on quick trips for mail or spare reeds or music and all like that, and the law of averages was in my favor; he never had accidents. I was actually out casing the roads around there in Lutch's car when I had one of those fantastically unexpected pieces of luck that you dream about if you've got a good imagination.

I'd just turned into the highway from the Shinnebago side road when I heard sirens. I pulled over right away. A maroon Town-and-Country came roaring around the bend of the highway at about eighty. There were bullet holes in the windshield and the driver was hunched low. There were two cats in the back blasting away with automatics. Behind them came a State Police car, gaining. I didn't wait and watch; I was out and under before I knew what I was doing. Peering around the rear of my machine, I looked up just as one of the men in the Town-and-Country straightened up, holding his right forearm. Just then the driver hauled the car into the road I'd just left. It couldn't be done at that speed but he did it, the tires scream-ing from Dizzy Gillespie; and the man who was hit went sling-shotting out of the car. First he bounced and then he slid. I thought he'd never stop sliding. About the time he hit the road, the police car flashed by me with the right front tire flat. It was crabbing left and crabbing right, and this time the tires were from Stan Kenton.

The important thing is that that cat's gun flew straight up in the air when he was hit and landed in the weeds not twenty feet from me. I had it before those cops got their car stopped. They never saw me. They were busy, then with the car, afterward with the stiff. I walked down there and talked to them. Seems these characters had been robbing gas stations and motorists. They'd already killed two. One of the cops growled about these war souvenir guns, and he'd be glad when all that foreign ammo was used up. They said they'd get the guys who'd gotten away soon enough; just a matter of time. I said sure. Then I got back in Lutch's machine and drove away, real thoughtful. I knew I'd never have another chance like this.

The next afternoon I told Lutch I'd go in town with him. He was picking up the mail and I said I had to go to the drug store. He didn't think anything about it. I went and got the gun and stuck it in the sleeve of my jacket, under my armpit. It stayed there fine. It was a big Belgian automatic. It had four shots left in it.

I felt all right. I thought I was doing okay until Lutch looked over at me—he was driving—and asked me if I felt all right. Then I realized I had sweat on my upper lip. I looked in the rear view mirror. I could maybe two miles—we were out in the flats—and there wasn't car in sight. I looked ahead. There was a truck. It passed. Then the road was cleared.

I said, "Pull over to the side, Lutch. I want to talk to you."

He looked at me, surprised. "I can listen and drive, Fluke. Shoot."

Shoot, he said. I almost laughed. "Pull over, Lutch." I meant to sound normal but it came out as a hoarse whisper.

"Don't be silly," he said. He had that big easy open-handed way about him, Lutch had. "Go on, Fluke, get it off your chest."

I took out the gun and kicked off the safeties and poked it into his ribs. "Pull over to the side, Lutch."

He pulled up his arm and looked down under it at the gun. "Why, sure," he said, and pulled over and stopped. He switched off, leaned back into the angle of the seat and the door so he half faced me, and said, "Lay it on me, Fluke. You fixing to kill me with that?" He didn't sound scared, and that was because he wasn't. He really wasn't. Nothing like this had ever happened to him, so nothing ever could. He wasn't prodding me, either. He was talking to me like at rehearsal. Lutch was a very relaxed cat.

"Yes, I am," I told him.

He looked at it curiously. "Where'd you get it?"

I told him that too. If he'd only started to sweat and cry, I'd have shot him then. I hated him too much to just shoot him easy. I told him all about it. "They haven't caught those jokers yet," I said. "The cops'll dig one of these slugs out of you and it'll be the same as the ones in those other killings. They'll think those hoods did it."

"They will? What about you?"

"I'll have one of the slugs, too. In the arm. It'll be worth it. Anything else you want to know?"

"Yes. Why? Fluke, *why*? Is it—Fawn?"

"That's right."

He sort of shook his head. "I hate to say this, Fluke, but I don't think killing me will help your chances any. I mean, even if she never finds out."

I said, "I know that, Lutch. But I'll have an even break; that's all I ever want. I can't get it with you around."

His face was sorry for me, and that's absolutely all. "Go on, then," he told me.

I pulled the trigger. The gun bucked in my hand. I saw him spin, and then everything went black, like I was under a baby spot and the fuse blew.

When I came to my eyes wouldn't straighten out. The whole world was full of dazzly black speckles and something globular was growing out of the back of my head.

I was still in the front seat of the car. Something was scratching and chafing at my wrist. I pulled it away and put my head in my head in my hands and groaned.

"How you doing?" Lutch said. He bent forward, peering anxiously in my face.

I got my handkerchief out and put it behind my heat and looked at it. There was blood—just a speck. "What happened, Lutch?"

He grinned. It was a little puckered, but still a grin. "You'll never make a gunman, Fluke. I seen you twice with the gang in shooting galleries. You're afraid of guns."

"How did you know that?"

"You always close your eyes real tight, screw 'em down before you pull a trigger. I was half-turned toward you as it was, and it was easy to twist aside. Turning made the gun ride around and slip back under my arm. Then I hit you with my shoulder and ran your head back against the door post. Does it hurt much?"

"I didn't shoot you."

"You tore hell out of my shirt."

"God damn you, Lutch," I said quietly.

He sat back with the arms folded, watching me, for a long time, until I asked, "What are we waiting for?"

"For you to feel well enough to drive."

"Then what?"

"Back to the club."

"Come on Lutch; lay it on me. What are you going to do?"

"Think," said Lutch. He opened the door and got out and walked around the car. "Shove over," he said. He was carrying the gun. He wasn't pointing it, but he was holding it ready to use. I shoved over.

I drove slowly. Lutch wouldn't talk. I didn't dig him at all. He was doing just what he said—thinking. Once I took a hand off the wheel. His eyes were on me immediately. I just felt the lump on my head and put the hand back. For the time being I was hogtied.

When we stopped in front of the club he said, "Go on up to my room." We had quarters over the hall. "I'll be right behind you with the gun in my side pocket. If anyone stops you, don't stall. Shake 'em naturally and go on up. I'm not afraid of guns and I'll shoot you if you don't do what I say. Do I mean it?"

I looked at his face. He meant it. "Well, all reet," I said, and got out.

No one stopped us. When we were in his room he said, "Get in that closet."

I opened my mouth to say something but decided not to. I got in the closet and closed and locked the door. It was dark.

"Can you hear me?" he said.

"Yup."

In a much softer voice he said, "Can you hear me now?"

"I can hear you."

"Then get this. I want you to listen to every word that is said out here until I open the door again. If you make a noise I'll kill you. Understand?"

"You're in, Jack," I said. My head hurt.

A long time—maybe two or three minutes—passed. From far away I heard him calling, but couldn't make out what he was saying. I think he was in the stair landing. I heard him come in and shut the door. He was whistling between his teeth. *Daboo, Dabay.* Then there was a light knock on the door.

"Come in!"

It was Fawn. "What's cookin', good-lookin'?" she sang.

"Sit down, chicken."

The chair was wicker. I could hear it plain.

Lutch Crawford always talked straight to the point. That's how he got so much work done. "Fawn, about the other night, with all that moon. How do you feel now?"

"I feel the same way," she said tightly.

Lutch had a little habit of catching his lower lip with his teeth and letting go when he was thinking was hard. There was a pause about long enough to do this. Then he said, "You been hearing rumors about you and me?"

"Well I—" She caught her breath. "Oh, Lutch—" I heard the wicker, sharp and crisp, as she came up out of it.

"Hold on!" Lutch snapped. "There's nothing to it, Fawn. Forget it."

I heard the wicker again, slow, the front part, the back part. She didn't say anything.

"There's some things too big for one or two people to fool with, honey," he said gently. "This band's one of 'em. For whatever it's worth, it's bigger than you and me. It's going good and it'll go better. It's about as perfect as a group can get. It's a unit. Tight. So tight that one wrong move'll blow out all its seams. You and me, now— that'd be a wrong move."

"How do you know? What do you mean?"

"Call it a hunch. Mostly, I know that things have been swell up to now, and I know that you—we—anyway, we can't risk a change in the good old status quo."

"But—what about me?" she wailed.

"Tough on you?" I'd known Lutch a long time, and this was the first time his voice didn't come full and easy. "Fawn, there's fourteen cats in this aggregation and they all feel the same way about you as you do about me. You have no monopoly. Things are tough all over. Think of that next time you feel spring fever coming on." I think he bit at his lower lip again. In a soft voice like Skid's guitar with the bass stop, he said, "I'm sorry, kid."

"Don't call me *kid!*" she blazed.

"You better go practice your scales," he said thickly.

The door slammed.

After a bit he let me out. He went and sat by the window, looking out.

179

"Now what did you do that for?" I wanted to know.

"For the unit," he said, still looking out the window.

"You're crazy. Don't you want her?"

What I could see of his face answered that question. I don't think I'd realized before how much he wanted her. I don't think I'd thought about it. He said, "I don't want her so badly I'd commit murder for an even chance at her. You do. If anyone wants her worse than I do, I don't want her enough. That's the way I see it."

I could of told him then that it wasn't only him and Fawn that bothered me; that that was just part of it. Somehow it didn't seem to make no never mind just then. If he wanted to play the square he was welcome to it. "I'll go pack," I said.

He jumped up. "You'll do no such a damn thing!" he roared. "Listen, hipster; you've seen how far I'll go to keep this unit the way it is. You taught me something today, the hard way, and by the Lord you're not going to kick over this group just when you've taught it to me!" He walked over and stood close; I had to crease the back of my neck to see his face. He jabbed his fingers at my nose. "If you walk out on the unit now, so help me, I'll track you down and hound you to death. Now get out of here."

"All right," I told him, "But listen. I'll take a raincheck on that last. You're riding a high riff right now. Think it over quiet, and tell me tonight if you want me to stay. I'll do what you say."

He grinned the old grin again. "Good, Fluke. See ya."

It's hard to hate a joe like that. But if you can make it, you can do a job.

I made it.

So. That was the time I tried it smart. Next time I tried it sneaky.

We played the Coast, up and back. We did two rushes in feature pictures and thirteen shorts. We guested on some of the biggest radio shows going. We came back East after a lick at Chicago, where there was a regular Old Home Week with Fawn's folks, and we got three consecutive weeks at the Paramount. We played 'em sleek, and had the old folks smiling into each other's eyes. We played 'em frantic, and blew the roof. You know.

And every dollar that fell into our laps, and every roar of applause, and every line of print in the colyums that drooled over us, I hated, and there was plenty to hate. The Geese played so many different kinds of music there was no getting away from it anywhere. I once saw a juke-box with seven Crawford plates in it at once! There was Lutch with the world throwing itself at his head because he was a nice guy. And here I was in the gravy because he was good to me. And the whole world was full of the skunk and his music, and there'd never be any rest from it anywhere. (Did you hear the Hot Club of France's recording of *Daboo Dabay?*) A great big silk-lined prison for old Fluke; a padded cell. Lutch Crawford built a padded cell and was keeping old Fluke in it.

Fawn got a little haggard, after that time in Boulder City, but she gradually pulled up out of it. She was learning, the rest of us had learned, to feel one way and act another. Well, isn't that the rock-bottom starting point for anyone in show business? She was the better for it ...

We started West again, and South, and the time I tried it sneaky was in Baton Rouge.

It was a road club again, real razzle, with curved glass and acoustic ceilings and all that jazz. I can't say that anything particular keyed me off—it was just that I'd made up my mind a long time ago how I was going to do it and I needed a spot near running water. Baton Rouge has a fair-sized creek running past its front door, and Old Man River, he don't say nothin'.

It was very simple—it's surprising how simple some things can be, even things you've been eating your heart out over for years, when they get fixed up at last ... Lutch got a letter. The hat-check girl at the club turned away to hang up a coat and when she turned back the letter was there by the tip-plate. There were plenty of people in and out through the lobby. I was, myself. The powder-room was downstairs; I was sick that night. Everyone knew about it; they were laughing at old Fluke. I am allergic to shrimps, and here I had to go and gulp up a pound or more of New Orleans fried shrimp and rice: I had the hives that grease-paint would barely cover, and could just about navigate, and I had to take a trip down below every twenty minutes or so. Sometimes I stayed a long while ...

Lutch got the letter. It was sealed, addressed with a typewriter. No return address. The hat-check girl gave it to the head-waiter who gave it to Lutch. Lutch read it, told Crispin and Fawn he'd be back, he didn't know when, put on his hat and left. I don't know what he thought about on the way. The letter, I guess. It said

Dear Lutch,
First, don't show this to anyone or tell anyone about it yet. Make sure no one is looking over your shoulder or anything like that.
    Lutch, I'm half out of my mind over something I've heard. I think a serious danger threatens my daughter Fawn, and I must talk to you. I am in Baton Rouge. I don't want Fawn to know it yet.
    Maybe there is nothing in this business but it is best to play it safe. I am waiting for you near a warehouse above Morrero—that is just down-river from Baton Rouge. The warehouse has LE CLERC ET FILS painted on the street side. I am in the office out near the end of the wharf. I think you might be followed. Take a cab to the depot at Morrero and walk to the river. You can't miss it. But watch for a shadow, you can't be too careful. I hope all this turns out to be for nothing.
    Bring this with you. If what I fear is true it would not be safe even to burn it at the club. Please hurry.
Anxiously
JOHN AMORY.

I'm proud of that letter. Fawn's pop and Lutch were real buddy-buddy, and the old man would never ask a favor unless it were real important. The letter was the only evidence there was and Lutch brought it with him. A nice job, if I do say so myself.

No one saw Lutch. The cab-driver didn't know who he was or if he did he never mentioned it later. Lutch came as soon as he could, knocked at the door of the office. There was a dim light inside. No one answered. He came in and closed the door behind him. He called out, softly, "Mr. Amory!"

I whispered, from inside the warehouse, "In here."

Lutch went to the inner door, stepped into the warehouse and stopped, with the light from the office showing up the strip of skin between his collar and his hair just fine. I hit him there with a piece of pipe. He never made a sound. This time I wasn't going to talk it over with him.

I caught him before he hit the floor and carried him over to the long table beside the sink. The sink was already full of water, and I had seen to it that it was river water, just in case. I put the pipe where I could reach it in case I had to hit him again, and spread him out on the table with his head over the sink. Then I dunked it, and held it under.

Like I thought, it revived him and he began to kick and squirm. The burlap sacks I had laid on the table muffled that all right, and I had him pretty firmly around the shoulders, with my elbow at the back of his neck forcing his head under. I had one leg hooked under the sink support. He didn't have a chance, though it was hard work for a few minutes.

When he was quiet again, and with five minutes or so over for good measure, I got the small-boat anchor chain—an old rusty one it was— and wound it around him secure but careless-like; it could be by acci-dent. I got the letter out of his pocket and burned it, grinding all the ashes down on a small piece of roofing tin which I dropped into the river. I rolled Lutch in after it. There was quite a current running—he started downstream almost before he was under the surface. I said, "So long, superman," straightened myself, locked up the warehouse and, picking up the car I'd parked two blocks away, drove back to the club. It was easy to climb in the basement window into the stall of the men's room I'd left locked, and to come back upstairs without being noticed. The whole thing had taken just forty-three minutes.

I was happy about the whole thing. The chain would hold him under, that and the mud, and the catfish would make quick work of him. But if, by some fluke, the body should be found, well, the chain could be an accident, and he certainly died of drowning. In river water. The bump on the back of his neck—that was nothing.

But Lutch Crawford was hard to kill.

I don't have to tell you about the next month or so, with the head-lines and all that jive that went on. The band went right ahead; Lutch's hand was always so light on it that his absence made almost no difference. The sides worried some about him, but it took them three days to get really panicked. By that time my mind was easy. No amount of police work and private detective shenanigans could do a thing about it. The whole band alibied me, and the hat-check girl too, with my hives. Matter of fact, no one even thought to ask me any questions, specially. No one remembered exactly what time Lutch left the club; there had been nothing to call it to anyone's atten-tion. A clean job.

The next thing I wanted to do was to get clear of the whole aggre-gation and go live by myself. I was careful, though, and made no move until someone else did it first.

It came to a head six weeks after Lutch disappeared. We'd moved on to Fort Worth, Texas. Fawn and Crispin hadn't wanted to leave Baton Rouge, but finally decided that Lutch, wherever he was, knew our schedule as well as we did and would come back when he was ready to.

We had a big powwow in Fort Worth. Crispin took the floor. Everyone was there.

Fawn still looked bad. She'd lost a lot of weight. Skid Portly looked five years older.

Crispin came to the point as quick as Lutch used to.

"Gang," he said, "don't get your hopes up; I didn't call you because I have any new ideas about Lutch or where he might be. There's no word.

"What brings this up is that after two weeks at Brownsville and a week at Santa Monica, this tour is over. We have our pick of sev-eral offers—I'll go over them with you later—and we've got to decide right now what we're going to do. Lutch isn't here and there's no way of knowing when he will show. We can either take a vacation after the Santa Monica date, and hang up the fiddle until Lutch shows up, or we can go on. What do you say?"

"I could use a rest," I said.

"We could all use a rest," said Crispin. "But what has us tuck-ered out is this business of Lutch. If it wasn't for that we wouldn't think of a break until next summer."

Fawn said, "What would Lutch want us to do?"

Moff—Lew Moffatt, that was, the reed man—said, "I don't reckon there's any doubt about that."

There was a general mumble of agreement. Lutch would have gone on.

"Then we go on?"

Everybody said yes but me. I didn't say. No one noticed.

Crispin nodded. "That leaves a big question. As far as perfor-mances are concerned, we can get along. But someone has to take over booking, contracts, a lot of the arranging, hotel accommoda-tions, and so on."

"What do you mean some*one?*" asked Skid. "Lutch did four men's work."

"I know," said Crispin. "Well, do you think we can make it? How about the arrangements? Skid, you and Fawn used to help him the most."

Skid nodded. Fawn said, "We can do it."

Crispin said, "I'll handle the business, if it's okay with you." It was. "Now, how about billing? We can't phony it up; Lutch's dis— uh—absence has had a flock of publicity, and if Lutch doesn't come back before we start, we can't bill him. The customers wouldn't like it."

They chewed that over. Finally Skid said, "Why'n't you take it, Crisp?"

"Me? I don't want it."

The rest of them all started talking at once. Lutch and Crispin had worked very close together. The general idea was that they wanted him to do it.

Crispin had been lounging back against a long table. Now he stood up straight. He said,

"All right, all right. But listen. This band is Lutch Crawford's Gone Geese, and if it's all the same to you it'll stay that way. We can bill as Don Crispin and Lutch Crawford's Gone Geese if you like; but I want it so that wherever Lutch is, he'll know that it's still his band. That means, too, that any new arrangement or novelty or what have you, is going to be done the way Lutch would do it, to the very best of our ability. If any one of you hears something in the band that doesn't sound like Lutch, speak up. I want it so that when Lutch comes back—damn it, I won't say *if*—when Lutch comes back he can pick up the baton in the middle of a number and take over from there. Are you with it?"

They were. After the fuss had died down Koko deCamp, the hot trumpet man, spoke up sort of timid. "Crispin," he said, "I don't want to cause any hard feelings, but I have a standing offer with the King combo. My contract with Lutch is up at the end of this tour, and I think I could do myself more good with the King. That's only—" he added quickly, "if Lutch don't come back."

Crispin frowned and scratched his head. He looked over at Fawn. She said again, "What would Lutch want him to do?"

Crispin said, "There it is. Lutch would let you do whatever you thought you wanted. He never stopped anyone who wanted to leave."

I could of told him. I didn't.

Crispin went on, "There's the code word, kizd, 'What would Lutch want?' Start from there. Anyone else want out? There'll be no hard feelings."

The bass man—we'd only had him a couple of months—said he thought he'd go. Then I spoke up.

Fawn said, "Oh, no!"

"Why, Fluke?" asked Crispin. They all stared at me.

I spread my hands. "I want out, that's all. Do I have to fill out a questionnaire?"

"There won't be any 'Gone Geese' without Fluke," said Skid.

He was so right. The way they billed it was "Don Crispin and the Lutch Crawford Orchestra." Crispin and Fawn did their best to make me stay with it, but no. Oh no. I was over, out and clear. I think Fawn figured that it hurt me to stay close to the band, after Lutch had been so good to me. Hell. I wanted to laugh, that was all, and I couldn't do that where the band could see me.

We broke up at Santa Monica after the date there. I thought I'd take it easy for a year or so and look around, but what should drop into my lap but a gold-plated offer from a radio station in Seattle, for a night record-jockey stand. That was made to order. My voice and delivery and savvy of the sharps and the flats were perfect for it, and best of all, I could work where people didn't have to look at my face. Sometimes I think if I had been in radio from the start, I wouldn't of—I might not have become the kind of cat who—ah, that's useless chatter now.

I got twenty-six weeks with options and could have upped the ante if I'd wanted to argue, which I didn't. Crispin and the rest of Lutch's sidemen went all out for me, sending me telegrams during my show, giving me personal appearances, and plugging me in their clubs. Seemed like, dead or alive, Lutch kept on being kind. I didn't let it get me. I'd lived long enough to know you can't break clean from any close contact with a human being. Quit a job, get a divorce, leave a home town, it drags on in shreds and tatters that haunt you. I held tight to laughing. Lutch was dead.

Then one night I got that advance shipment of Mecca records. Six sides of Crispin-Crawford.

I gave it a big hello in the old Fluke style: "Aha, lil kizd—a clump of jump for bacon to crisp-in; Crispin and Crawford, and six new plates for gates. Just like old times for Fluke the Juke.... This spinner's a winner: old *Deep Purple* in the Crispin crunchy style."

I played it off. I hadn't heard any of these plates yet, though they were cleared for broadcast; they'd been delivered just before air time. *Deep Purple* was the old bandstand arrangement that Lutch had done himself. Moff was playing Lutch's clarinet, and there wasn't enough difference to matter. In the double-time ride in the third chorus, Skid slipped in a lick on guitar that I hadn't heard before, but it was well inside the Crawford tradition. The other platters showed up the same way; Crispin took a long drum solo in *Lady Be Good* that was new, but strictly Crawford. I held out the two new ones until last.

I mean new. There was a blow-top novelty called *One Foot in the Groove* that I had never heard; the by-line was Moff and Skid Portly. The other one was an arrangement of *Tuxedo Junction*. We'd always used a stock arrangement for that one; this was something totally new. In the first place it let in some bop sequences, and in the second place it really exploited an echo chamber—the first that had been done on a Crawford record. I listened to it bug-eyed.

It was good. It was *very* good. But the thing that tore me all apart was that it was Lutch Crawford, through and through. Lutch had never used an echo before. But he would—he *would,* because it was a new trend. Just like the be-bop continuities. I could imagine the powwow before the recording session, and Fawn saying "What would Lutch want?"

Listening to it, I saw Lutch, wide shoulders, long hands, pushing the brass this way, that way, reaching up and over to haul the sound of the drums up and then crush them down, down to a whispering cymbal. I could see him hold it down there with his right hand flat in the air in front of him as if he had it on a table, long enough for him to catch his lower lip between his teeth and pull it loose, and suddenly, then, like a flash-bulb going off, dazzle the people with an explosion of scream-trumpet and high volume guitar.

The turntable beside me went quietly about its work, with the sound-head pulsing a little like a blood-pressure gauge. It hypnotized me, I guess. Next thing I knew my engineer was waving frantically at me through the plate glass, giving me a 'dead-air' sign, and I realized that the record had been finished for seconds. I drew a thick rattling breath and said the only thing in the world that there was—a thing bigger than me, clearer than my scriptsheets or the mike in front of me or anything else. I said stupidly, "That was Lutch. That was Lutch Crawford. He isn't dead. *He isn't dead....*"

Something in front of my eyes began bobbing up and down. It was the engineer again, signalling. I had been staring straight at him without seeing him. I was seeing Lutch. The engineer pointed downward, waggled his finger round and round. That meant a record. I nodded and put on a Crosby plate, and sat back as if I'd been lanced in the gut with a vaulting pole.

My phone light flashed. I took calls on the show; the phones were equipped with lights instead of bells so they wouldn't crowd the mike. I picked up the receiver, saying automatically, "Fluke the Juke."

"One moment please." An operator. Then, "Fluke? Oh, Fluke
…" Fawn. It was Fawn Amory.

"Fluke," she said, her words tumbling over each other the way
notes did on her keyboard, "Oh Fluke, darling, we heard you, we
all heard you. We're in Denver. We cut a date to catch your show.
Fluke honey, you said it, Fluke, you said it!"

"Fawn—"

"You said he isn't dead. We know that, Fluke—we all do. But
the way you said it; you don't know how much that means to us!
We did it, you see? *Tuxedo Junction*—we worked and worked—
something that would be new and would be Lutch too. Lutch can't
die as long as we can do that, don't you see?"

"But I—"

"We're going to do more, Fluke. More Lutch, more real Lutch
Crawford. Will you come back, Fluke? We want to do more 'Gone
Geese' records and we can't without you. Won't you please, Fluke?
We *need* you!" There was a murmuring in her background. Then,

"Fluke? This is Crispin. I want to double that, boy. Come on
back."

"Not me, Crispin. I'm done," I managed to say.

"I know how you feel," said Crispin quickly. He knew I was about
to hang up on him. "I won't push you, hipster. But think it over, will
you? We're going to keep on, whatever happens, and wherever Lutch
is, alive or—wherever he is, he'll have a band, and as long as he has
a band, he's here."

"You're doing fine," I croaked.

"Just think it over. We can do twice as well if you'll come back.
Keep in touch. Here's Fawn again."

I hung up.

I'll never know how I got through that show. I know why I did.
I did because I was going to make my own way. That was why I had
wanted to kill Lutch. Come sick, come ça, as the man said, this was
my kick—making my own way without Lutch Crawford.

Six o'clock was closing time for me, and I imagine I got through
the routines all right; no one said anything to me about it. And if
didn't answer the phone, and ignored requests, and played all the

long stuff I could get my hands on so I wouldn't have to talk, well, they took it the way any outfit will take guff from a guy they pay too highly.

I walked, I don't know where. I suppose I frightened a lot of kids on their way to school with that face of mine, and got a lot of queer looks from women scrubbing their porch steps. I wouldn't know. *Lutch isn't dead* was the only thing that made. I can't tell you all the things I went through; there was a time of fear, when I thought Lutch was after me for what I'd done, and a time of calm, when I thought it couldn't matter less—I could just go on minding my own business and let Lutch die altogether, the way everybody has to. And there was a time of cold fury, when I heard that new *Tuxedo Junction* with the echoing guitar, and knew that Crispin would keep turning new Lutch out—real Lutch, that no one else in the music business could imitate. Lutch, he was talented like three or four people, and there happened to be three or four people with just those talents in his band. Anyway, it's all a haze.

About ten o'clock it all clicked into the clear. I found myself on Elliott Avenue away out near Kinnear Park—I must've walked miles—and everything was squared away. *I hate Lutch Crawford*—I was left with that, the old familiar feeling. And I still had to do something about it because Lutch wasn't dead.

I walked into a telegraph office and wired Crispin.

They started by giving me something I didn't want—but wasn't that the whole trouble? This time it was a sort of surprise party and testimonial dinner. I guess I was a little sour. They didn't understand. Crispin, he tried to make me feel better by guaranteeing that he'd see to it I was paid twice over for breaking my radio contract. Fawn— well, Fawn shouldn't have been so sweet to me. That was a huge mistake. Anyway, there was a dinner and some drinks and Crispin and Skid and Moff and them got up one by one and said what a fine cat I was. Then they all sat around playing "remember when" and passing remarks to the empty chair at the head of the table where Lutch's clarinet was. It was a fine party.

After that I went to work. What they saw me doing was "Is

190

coming a sizzle-swizzle for *Rum and Coca Cola,* featuring the Id-kid, Skid, and his supercharged git-fiddle, so look out!" And "We got a dream-scheme, kizd, all soft and lofty, smooth, forsooth, but full of nerve-verve. Hey Moff, stroke these quiet cats with *Velvet Paws ...*" So—I helped them.

What I was doing was trying to find Lutch so's I could kill him. You should have been a fly on the wall to hear those slave-sessions. Take a tune, find old Lutch, mix 'em up, make 'em be something new that's styled like something they wouldn't let be dead. So—they helped me.

I could have killed Lutch by killing the lot of them. I never did discard that idea. But maybe I'm lazy. Somewhere in that aggregation was the essence of what was Lutch. If I could smoke that out and kill it, he'd be dead. I knew that. It was just a matter of finding out what it was. It shouldn't have been much trouble. Hell, I knew that outfit inside out—performers, arrangements, even what they liked to eat. I told you—there was damn little turnover there. And in the music business people show up real soon for what they are.

But it wasn't easy.

That outfit was like a machine made for a very special purpose—but made all out of standard parts you could buy on the open market. That isn't to say that some of the parts weren't strictly upper-bracket; all of them were machined to a millionth. But I couldn't believe that what Lutch called "unit" was the thing that made the group an individual, great one. If Lutch had been around, you could've said that Lutch made the difference between a good machine and something alive. But Lutch wasn't around, and the thing still lived. Lutch had put the life in it, by choosing the right pieces and giving them the right push. After that the thing ran under its own power—the power of life—and Lutch Crawford wouldn't be dead until that life was gone. It was going to be him or me.

So I helped them. We had club and hotel dates, and we made records, and in keeping Lutch alive, I helped them.

And they helped me. Every time a new tune started climbing the top ten, every time someone came up with a number that looked like a winner, we'd arrange it for the band; and in those sessions the band

and workings of every least part were torn down and inspected and argued over. I never missed a word of this, so—they helped me.

It was hell for me. If you've got guts enough to kill a man, you've got to finish the job. Lutch was alive. It was bad away from the band, with every radio and juke-box in the whole world blasting out Crawford creations. It was bad with the band—sometimes you could *see* him!

Theme time at a club, and the lights the way they always were, and the band the same, except that now Crispin's luggage was front and center. The swinging bells of the brass and their "hoo ha" and then Skid's solo *Daboo Dabay* with Moff taking the obbligato on the clarinet. Moff never stood out front to play, though. He was out of sight like Crispin used to be. Crispin, crushing the beat, whisper-drumming, stared up and out the way he used to when he was in the blackness, and Skid was no different, watching his fingers . . . all the books say a good guitarist never watches his fingers but I guess Skid never read them . . . but you could see he was following *some-one,* and it wasn't Crispin, from under his pulled-down eyebrows. But Lutch was there most of all for Fawn, Fawn with the flickering golden light touching and leaving her face, and her head tilted to one side so the heavy hair swung forward past her round bare shoulder; and on her face that look, that half-smile, half-hungry look— hungry like Lutch was there looking at her, not like he was away.

Daboo dabay . . . it hypnotized those cats. We always opened with it, and sometimes we had as many as three half-hour network spots, and that meant theme opening and closing. It was always the same. I often wondered if the customers who faithfully spattered out their applause at the drop of a *hoo ha* had any idea that this was different, this was a—a resurrection, maybe eight times a night.

First I was sure it was the brass—the low brass, where that peculiar vitality came from. You see, that was my protection—Lutch was strong in everything we did, but you couldn't *see* him in anything but the theme. When we did the theme I concentrated on what I heard, not on what it meant. Anyway, night after night I waited for the theme, and cut out everything but that low brass as I listened. It wasn't notes I was listening for, but tone—style—*Lutch.* After a week or so I pinned it down to the second trumpet and a trombone. I was sure I was right; the Crawford quality was somewhere down there where the tone was low and full.

I got a break on it. So did Karpis and Heintz, the sliphorn and trumpet men I'd singled out. See, they roomed together in a hotel we used during Convention Week in Spokane. So one night they didn't get to the club in time to open. The hotel was an old firetrap—no escapes. The only way out of their room was through the door. No phone. Small transom, and that jammed and painted over. Locking the door from outside, putting a twist of coat hanger in the key so it couldn't turn, that was easy. It was forty minutes before a bellhop let them out.

I heard the theme twice without those two sides. Crispin put it in a nutshell when I asked him about it later. "Thin," he said, "but it's still Lutch." That was what I thought.

No one found out who had locked those boys in, of course. I don't operate so I can be found out. No one knew who was responsible when two trumpets and a reed man got left miles behind us when we went to St. Louis. We'd hired a bus and a couple of cars—we had a quartet and two vocalists by then. And one of the cars just quit back there in the fog. Who watered the gasoline? Some shmoe at a gas station, and let's forget it.

The theme wasn't the theme on that date. I hadn't knocked out the thing that was Lutch—I'd knocked out the orchestra by pulling those men; we were just nothing. That was no answer. I had to find the heart of Lutch, and stop it, stop it so it could never beat again.

Somebody slugged Stormy, the bass, while he was asleep the second afternoon in St. Louis. He went to the hospital and they got another man quick. He wasn't Stormy, but he was good. You could hear that the bass was different—but the orchestra was still Lutch.

How long can you keep it up? Sometimes I thought I'd go crazy. Actually. Sometimes I wanted to run out into the tables and smash the customers around, because I thought that maybe they knew what I was looking for. I was so close to it. That thing that was Lutch could cut in and cut out during a number, and I'd never notice it, being so busy listening to one instrument or combo. Someone out there could know, right in the same room with me, and I wouldn't. Sometimes I thought I was going out of my mind.

I even got us a new piano player for a night. I had to come out in the open for that, but it was safe. I hung around the conservatory until I latched on to a kid who was all starry-eyed about Lutch Crawford. I made like a talent scout. The kid was good-looking, with pimples. A jack-rabbit right hand, like Art Tatum, or it would be in a few years. I told Fawn about the boy, and said he was pining away. I laid it on. You know. You know how old Fluke. And Fawn, her and her soft heart! she not only agreed to let the kid in, but persuaded Crispin to let him take a one-night stand!

He did. He was good. He read like crazy, and he played every note that was on the paper and played 'em right; and he played a lot more he dreamed up, and they were right too. But he wasn't for the Geese. Now, here's a funny thing. It's aside from the business of killing Lutch. This kid was wrong for us, but so good Crispin spoke to Forway, the tour manager, and today that kid's making records that sell three quarters of a million each. All because of the break I got him by way of getting Fawn off the ivory for a night. Now what do you think of that?

I found out that night, though, that Fawn wasn't the "Lutch" thing that I was hunting. The band sounded like Lutch Crawford with the wrong piano, that's all. It wasn't wrong enough to keep Lutch from being there, somewhere in the sharps and flats. I wanted to run up to the stand and rip the music apart with my hands and yell, "Come out of there, you yellow skunk! Come out and let me get to you!"

I was glad it wasn't Fawn. I'd have stopped her, if it was, but I wouldn't have liked doing it much . . .

And I *found* him. I found him!

He had been right there all the time, looking at me, me looking at him, and I hadn't wits enough to see him.

Virus X and I found him. Virus X is something like flu, and something like dysentery, and it's no fun. It swept through us like a strong wind. I got it first, and it only lasted a couple of days. Moff, now, he was out two weeks. We only had to close for two nights, though. We made it the rest of the time, sometimes with something like a full band, sometimes with a skeleton. One of the short-timers was the guy who played guitar—Skid Portly.

Skid always said that any hill-billy could do what he did, given his guitar. I believed him. Why not? I'd diddled around with the instrument myself. Put your finger behind a fret, pluck the string. With a pedal you could make it louder or softer. With push-buttons you could make it warble or snarl or *whuff!* out with a velvet sound. With a switch you could make it sound exactly like a harpsichord or an organ. With a lever under your arm you could make all six strings rise in pitch like six fire sirens rising together, to almost full tone. You didn't play it. You operated it.

Skid came down with Virus X, and called in a character called Sylviro Giondonato, a glossy-haired, olive-skinned cat from East St. Louis. He was bugeyed at the chance, like the pianist I'd found. He played a whole mess of guitar, and when he got his hands on Skid's instrument I thought he was going to cry. He spent ten hours in Skid's hotel room learning the gimmicks on that box, with Skid, who was feeling rotten, coaching him every step of the way. I know he did things on that guitar that Skid wouldn't dare to do. Giondonato had one of those crazy ears like Rheinhardt or Eddie South—not that Eddie plays guitar.

The band played that night without Lutch.

Gionni—Johnny, we called him—was a star. The customers all but clawed down the ceiling-beams. A big hit. But it wasn't Lutch.

Crispin ripped off a momma-daddy on the tom after a while, our signal to take fifteen. I don't think I heard it. I was crouching at the corner of the stand thinking over and over, *No Lutch! No Lutch!* and trying not to laugh. It had been a long time.

When Crispin touched my shoulder I almost jumped out from behind my teeth. "No Lutch!" I said. I couldn't help it.

"Hey," said Crispin. "Level off, Fluke. So you noticed too?"

"Brother."

"You wouldn't think one man's work would make that much difference, would you?"

"I don't get it," I said. I meant that. "Johnny's a hell of a guitar player. Man, I think he's *better* than Skid."

"He is," Crispin said. "But—I think I know why Lutch doesn't show when he plays. Johnny plays terrific guitar. Skid plays terrific electric guitar. Dig me? The two are played pretty much the same— and so are a cello and a viola. But the attack is 'way different. Johnny exploits the guitar as good as I've heard it anywhere so far. But Skid plays that instrument out there."

"What's that to do with Lutch?"

"Think back, Fluke. When Skid came with us, he was amplified, period. Look what he's got now—and look where we are now. You know how much we've depended on him."

"I thought we were depending on his guitar."

Crispin shook his big, straight-nosed head. "It's Skid. I don't think I realized it myself until now."

"Thanks," I told him.

He looked at me curiously. "For what?"

I threw up my hands. "For—well, I feel better now, that's all."

"You're a large charge of strange change, Fluke," he said.

I said, "Everybody knows that."

Three nights later I slugged Skid Portly from behind. I killed Lutch Crawford with a pair of bolt-cutters. And there was Lutch—all of him, all his music, all his jump, his public and his pride, in the palm of my hand—three pinkish slugs with horn at one end and blood at the other. I tossed 'em, caught 'em, put 'em in my pocket and walked off whistling *Daboo Dabay*. It was the first time in eight years I had heard that music and enjoyed it. Sometimes it takes a long time to kill a man.

Rehearsal next day was pretty dismal.

Crispin had everything set up. When we were all there, sort of milling around, he got up on the lower tier of the stand. Everyone shut up, except me, but then, I wasn't laughing out loud.

Crispin's mouth was tight. "I asked Fawn what to do," he said abruptly, "just like Lutch used to. She said, 'What would Lutch do?'"

I think Lutch would first see if we could make it the way we are—find out how bad we're hurt. Right?"

Everybody uh-huhed. That's what Lutch would do. Someone said, "How's Skid?"

Crispin barked, "You play trumpet. How'd you feel if someone sliced off your lip?" Then he said, "I'm sorry, Riff."

Riff said, "Gosh, that's okay."

They took their places. Fawn looked like the first week after Baton Rouge. Giondonato started for the guitar. Crispin waved him back. "Stand by, Johnny." He glanced at the guitar. It was ready to go, resting neck upward on the seat of Skid's chair. Crispin touched it, straightened it up a bit, lovingly. He bent and shifted the speaker outward a little. Then he went to his luggage. "Theme," he said. He looked over at me. I picked up my mike, puffed into it, adjusted the gain.

Crispin gave a silent one-two. Fawn stroked a chord. The brasses swung right: *Hoo*

And left: *Ha*

Fawn crowded the beat with her chord. I looked at her.

For the very first time she wasn't looking at that spot on the floor in front of the band. She was looking at Crispin.

Hoo Ha

Moff raised his clarinet, tongued it, laid his lips around the mouthpiece, filliped the stops nervously, and then blew.

And with the first note of the clarinet, shockingly, came the full, vibrato voice of Skid's guitar: *Daboo, Dabay, Dabay, Daboo . . .*

And right on top of it there was a thunderous, animal, coughing gasp, and a great voice screaming, screaming, sobbing like peals of laughter. The sound was huge, and crazy, and it dwindled to an echoing, "He isn't dead, he isn't dead . . ."

And then I had to breathe, and I realized that the sounds had come from me, that I was standing frozen, staring at Skid's glittering guitar, with the mike pressed close to my cheek. I began to cry. I couldn't help it. I threw down the microphone—it made a noise like thunder—and I took the rolled-up handkerchief out of my pocket and hurled it at the guitar, which was playing on and on and on,

Lutch's theme, the way Lutch wanted it played, by somebody else. The handkerchief opened in the air. Two of them hit the instrument and made it thrum. One stuck to the cloth and went cometing under the chair.

Moff ran over there. I was screaming, "Use these, damn you!" Moff bent as if to pick up something, drew back. "Crispin—it's the—the fingers . . ." and then he folded up and slumped down between the chairs.

Crispin made a noise almost like the first one I had blown into the mike. Then he rushed me. He caught me by the front of the coat and the belt and lifted me high in the air. I heard Fawn scream, *"Don!"* and then he threw me on the floor. I screamed louder than Fawn did.

I must have blacked out for a moment. When I opened my eyes I was lying on the floor. My left arm had two elbows. I couldn't feel it yet. Crispin was standing over me, one foot on each side. He was shoving the rest of them back. They were growling like dogs. Crispin looked a mile high.

"Why did you do that to Skid?" Crispin asked. His voice was quiet; his eyes were not. I said, "My arm . . ." and Crispin kicked me.

"Don! Don, let me—" and people began to jostle and push, and Fawn broke through. She went to her knees beside me. "Hello, Fluke," she said, surprisingly.

I began to cry again. "The poor thing's out of his mind," she said.

"The poor thing?" roared Stormy. "Why, he—"

"Fluke, why did you do it?"

"He wouldn't die," I said.

"Who wouldn't, Fluke? Skid?"

They made me sore. They were so dumb. "Lutch," I said. "He wouldn't be dead."

"What do you know about Lutch?" gritted Crispin.

"Leave him alone," she blazed. "Go on, Fluke."

"Lutch was living in Skid's guitar," I said patiently, "and I had to let him out."

Crispin swore. I really didn't know he ever did that. My arm began to hurt then. Fawn got up slowly. "Don . . ."

Crispin grunted. Fawn said, "Don, Lutch used to worry all the time about Fluke. He always wanted Fluke to know he was wanted for himself. Fluke had something that no one else had, but he wouldn't believe it. He always thought Lutch and the rest of us were sorry for him."

The guitar was still playing. It rose in crescendo. I twitched. "Skid—" I yelled.

"Moff, turn that thing off," said Crispin. A second later the guitar stopped. "I knew it would trap somebody," he said to me, "but I never thought it would be you. That's a recording played through the guitar amplifier. I made hundreds of 'em when I was running tests on Skid's guitar. I've been worried for a long time about the luck we've been having—a choir missing this night, a side missing that night, a combo out the next night. The more I thought of it the more it took a pattern. Someone was doing it, and when that happened to Skid, I had an idea that someone'd give himself away, if only for a second, when that guitar began to play. I never expected *this!*"

"Leave him alone," said Fawn tiredly. "He can't understand you." She was crying.

Crispin turned to her. "What do you want to do with him? Kiss and make up?"

"I want to kill him!" she shrieked back at him. She held out her polished nails, crooked, like claws. "With these. Don't you know that?"

Crispin stepped back, stunned.

"But that doesn't matter," she went on in a low voice. "We can't stop saying it now, of all times— What would Lutch want?"

It got very quiet in there.

"Do you know why he was rejected from the army during the war?" she asked.

Nobody said anything.

Fawn said, "Extreme ugliness of face. That was a ground for deferment. Look it up if you don't believe me." She shook her head slowly and looked at me. "Lutch was always so careful of his feelings, and so were we all. Lutch wanted him to have his face made over, but he didn't know how to suggest it to Fluke—Fluke was psychopathically sensitive about it. Well, he waited too long, and I waited too long, and now look. I say let's have it done now, and save what little is left of the—creature."

Stormy said, "This good-for-evil kick can go just so far." The rest of them growled.

Fawn raised her hands and let them fall. "What would Lutch do?"

"I killed Lutch," I said.

"Shut up, you," said Crispin. "All right, Fawn. But listen. After he gets out of the hospital, I don't care if he looks like Hedy Lamarr— he stays out of my way or by God I'll strap him down and take him apart with a blunt nailfile."

At long, long last I blacked out.

There was a time of lying still and watching the white, curve-edged ceiling stream past, and a time of peeping through holes in the bandages. I never said another word, and very little was said to me. The world was full of strangers who knew what they were doing, and that was okay with me.

They took the bandage off this morning and gave me a mirror. I didn't say anything. They went away. I looked myself over.

I'm no bargain. But by the Lord I can cite you hundreds of people now who are uglier than I am. That's a change from not knowing a single one.

So I killed Lutch Crawford?

Who was the downy-clown, the wise-eyes, the smarty-party, the gook with a book and his jaws full of saws, who said, "The evil that men do lives after them . . ."? He didn't know Lutch Crawford. Lutch did good.

Look at the guy in the mirror. Lutch did that.

Lutch isn't dead. I never killed anybody.

I told you and told you and told you that I want to make my own damn way! I don't want this face! And now that I have all this written down I'm going out. You couldn't make me a big guy too, could you, Lutch? I'm going out through the top sash. I can get through. And then six floors, face first.

Fawn—

The Dark Goddess

... More to a Marriage ...

AGNES VAN CREEFT moved noiselessly to the doorway and peered
inside. Jessie was lying quite still—no, not quite; her long nervous
hands palmed and stroked the blanket as if they could not get enough
of the touch of it. Jessie had lived every hour of her forty-odd years
in this same hungry, tactile way, and she would, to the end. There were
few enough hours left. The electric vitality of the woman was dimmed,
but definitely present in the room; a glowing rebellion, a refusal to
accept—not death; she seemed not to mind that—but dying.

The corners of Jessie's deep-set eyes told her, apparently, that
there was more in the doorway than the bulk of drapes. Her head
jerked to it, swift as always.

Agnes was tall, large, with a soft face and a hard mouth. She
came into the room with small motions of silent feet. "Jessie?" she
murmured. "You're awake?"

Jessie turned on her side and propped herself on one elbow.
"Agnes! Well, what do you know. Where's Tommie? Come in, girl.
Sit down. No, here on the bed. Smoke? Oh, that's right; you don't
smoke. Or drink. Or—what was that other thing?" She grinned up
puckishly.

"I suppose you mean dance," said Agnes. She sat carefully on the
edge of the bed. "I sent Tommie on an errand. I wanted to talk to
you. . . . Really, Jessie, you should take better care of yourself—
bouncing and shouting like this."

"What for?"

"You're a very sick woman," said Agnes. "*I* think you should
have stayed at the hospital."

"What for?" Jessie said again. "I want to be here with my own things while I—wait. You're sitting between me and my ashtray."

Agnes turned troubled eyes to the wide night-table. On it was a black-enamelled, pedestalled figurine of softly gleaming bronze—a seated nude, with the legs crossed above the knees, the shoulders tilted, the arms raised, bent, holding the palms out to right and left, delicately. The face, bland and secretive, pouting, would have been staring straight into Agnes's had the carven eyes been open. Agnes made a small grimace and reached around the thing, being careful not to touch it, to get the heavy smoking-set which lay beside it.

With the tray in her hand, Agnes checked herself. "Jessie, do you think you really ought—"

"Give it here," said Jessie, scooping it up and thumping it on the sheet beside her. She thumbed out a cigarette and lit it, drawing quickly and hard with her cheeks. The pulsing hollows and the sur-mounting double arches of her deep eye-sockets stressed her emaci-ation, and Agnes felt the familiar helplessness which had keyed her regard for this swift, slender, wiry creature ever since they had met. "Jessie, smoking can't possibly—"

"Can't possibly make me any worse than I am unless I set fire to my bed, and I can't do that while I'm chaperoned. Now, Aggie, what's on your mind?"

Agnes made her mouth even smaller. "Well, I—it's a delicate sort of—I mean, I don't want to intrude, Jessie, Tommie's a grown man and all that, but he is my brother, and I have only his best—his best—and there's not very much, that is, very long ..." She floun-dered to a stop.

Jessie regarded her quizzically. "'Sometimes I feel so *sorry* for you, Aggie. Great day, woman! Life gets so complicated even when a person *tries* to keep it simple! You know what you want to say, and yet you're all fouled up with your sensibilities. Keep it clean, kid. Let's have it."

Agnes took an immaculate, preparatory handkerchief from her buttoned sleeve. "I—hardly know how to begin."

"I can see that," said Jessie dryly. "Maybe I can help. The day after tomorrow, or the day after that, I'll be dead."

Agnes winced. "Please, Jessie—"

"And you want me to do something before then. What is it?"

"You—you quite take my breath away, Jessie. But then, you always did. I never could understand you."

"I know. What do you want me to do?"

"You—you're very hard to deal with, Jessie. You make it quite difficult for me."

"I'm very reasonable to deal with and I'm making it very easy. Now, then . . . Come on, girl! You're wasting time. You don't want to waste time, do you, Agnes?"

Agnes felt trapped—trapped into the very thing she had come here to do. She was ten years older than Jessie, and yet Jessie had always been able to rap her knuckles, to make her stand in the corner like a bewildered child. "I want you to marry Tommie," she blurted.

Jessie turned her head until she was looking straight upward from the wide pillow. "Well, for Pete's sake," she breathed. Slowly she began to smile. "What on earth for?"

"Oh, it would be so much better—can't you see, dear? In every way; the way Tommie would remember you, the way all his publishers and—and—"

"And his sister?"

"That has nothing—" Agnes faced those deep eyes; and for all their smiling, for all their incorruptible clear-sightedness, there was no mockery there. She finished, "Well, yes. For me too, of course."

"Was this Tommie's idea?"

"No."

"His publishers ask you to come around?"

"No! How could they? Why should you ask a thing like that?"

"Those happened to be the people you mentioned. That leaves you. Why should I do a thing like this for you?"

Agnes moved her lips but they made no words.

"Agnes, why fret about it at this late date? I am Mrs. Thomas Davis van Creeft. That's the way I've been getting my mail for twenty-two years. I'm Tommie's wife; even under the law it's all nice and legal—now."

And they both turned to look at the figurine—Jessie lovingly,

Agnes inadvertently. Then Agnes moved, on the edge of the bed, so that she presented a large curved back to the object. "I know *that* story," she said.

"No you don't," said Jessie, and shook her head. "You couldn't ... anyway," she added abruptly, "it doesn't make any difference now. We're married—ask anyone."

"Anyone won't do," said Agnes stonily. "Tommie told me about it years ago."

"I know he did." She laughed, "Poor Tommie! Always defiant, and the defiance was not good unless he could jolt somebody with it. Generally, you."

"Generally—me."

The warmth crept back into Jessie's voice. "It was one of the things—the many, many things—he could depend on you for, Agnes. He shocked you, and frightened you, and worried you, but you never stopped being devoted to him, and he knew it. And you never tried to interfere once he had made up his mind."

For the first time since she had entered the room, Agnes smiled. It was a surprisingly full smile, and was proper to the lines of her gentle face. "It wouldn't have made much difference," she said.

Jessie laughed her sudden, barking laugh. "You're so right. I don't know what makes you think he'd say a formal 'I do' after all these years."

"He'd do it for you."

"He would," Jessie admitted, "and down inside he'd be thinking I'd reneged on something, and was taking advantage of my strategic position." She waved a hand to include the room, the bed, and her current situation.

Agnes was visibly shocked. "Jessie, I do wish you wouldn't!"

"I don't have the proper respect for the dying, I guess. Oh, Agnes, I'm sorry, I'm very thoughtless." A gleam came into her eyes. "But you see how it feels to have me take advantage of my circumstances ... Why bother with this wedding thing now, of all times, Agnes? How could it possibly matter?"

"Oh, I don't know, I don't know, I just wish it could be," Agnes all but sobbed. "I—do know, Jessie. M—maybe it's because I've never married. It's just that—marriage is too big a thing to make a funny sophisticated game out of. I know I'm old-fashioned, Jess, but I've always seen this thing of yours as a sort of horrible mockery. You've been so—so—"

"Unrepentant?"

"Yes, and then there's *that* horrible thing," and she gestured over her shoulder with her now-moist handkerchief toward the statuette which pouted at her broad back. " 'There's our marriage-license,' Tommie used to say—that naked, pagan thing . . ."

"Shh. She'll hear you."

"I don't—Oh, Jessie, *don't* play! I never could understand your kind of joke—or your friends, or your ideas, or your way of life. And I've tried *so* hard not to interfere."

Jessie caught her hand and squeezed it. "Agnes, don't cry. You're a dear. You always were. I wish I knew a million like you; they don't make 'em straighter. Sometimes I think things are simpler and cleaner for you than they are for me, for all my bragging. You go by what's laid down, and I go by what seems best for all concerned. Sometimes I wish I was like you."

"If you were, you couldn't make a charade out of a thing like marriage. It's too *big* to be smeared by any one person, or by a couple, Jessie! Marriage is the founda—"

"You don't have to sell me that package," said Jessie, her husky voice crackling. Agnes stopped as if the other had thrown a switch.

"I bought it a long time back," said Jessie, quietly. "I wrapped it up and kept it shiny and clean for twenty-two years. Shut up," she said, without changing her inflection, as Agnes tried to speak. "Now I'm going to talk. You just sit quiet and listen to me."

She turned over on her back and put her hands behind her head. As she spoke her eyes shifted from this point to that on the shadowed ceiling, finding memories, some dim, some bright and clear, each reflecting its corresponding amount of light into her face.

"Did you know I'd only known Tommie two weeks before we were—married? That's all it was. It doesn't seem so long ago, yet people have been born and grown up and married since then—people who are already older than we were when we met . . .

THE PERFECT HOST

"You remember the late 'twenties. Those were wild days. It was the last gasp of Prohibition, and a lot of things went on that people tried not to notice at the time and have since tried to forget. Roadhouse parties were one of those things. The one we were on was big, and, like a lot of 'em, got smaller as we went along. We wanted to drink, that was all—not because we liked the stuff, but because we were told we couldn't. There were plenty of places just north of New York, up through Connecticut and Rhode Island, where anyone in a car could reach all the liquor and jazz music he wanted, or thought he wanted. I suppose we knew it was stupid, childish, and vicious, but we did it anyway, partly to rebel, partly to be fashionable. Silly kids!

"I remember every detail of that evening. Tommie doesn't. He's like that. That's why he doesn't drink now, hasn't for years. When Tommie drinks he doesn't know what he's doing at the time, doesn't remember afterward what he's done, and feels rotten the next morning.

"Tommie had just sold a magazine story and was full of money and high spirits. He wanted to buy me a present, but I didn't feel that way about Tommie—I thought if he gave me anything, something important might be spoiled. He compromised on Miss O'Casey there—" she jabbed a finger toward the statuette— "and bought it at one of those funny little antique stores in Connecticut. We hauled her to one roadhouse after another, setting her up on the tables and buying her drinks—you know."

"We woke up next morning at my place. You could hardly call it a rosy nuptial morning. Tommie felt terrible. The evening before was nothing to him but a large black cloud with streaks of lightning through it; I don't think he wasted a minute trying to remember how he happened to be in my bed when he woke up, or what, if anything, had happened between us. He lay blinking dully at the dark goddess, which was sitting on my vanity table looking very bland and peaceful, and he groaned because his head hurt him. I fed him some breakfast and kissed him and sent him home. I wasn't too happy about the whole thing. I was crazy about Tommie, and I didn't want it spoiled, and I was afraid that now it was.

206

"He was back again in a couple of hours. Poor, mixed-up, mismanaged Tommie! He didn't know what to do, or where to turn. He'd arrived home—he lived in a rooming-house uptown—to discover what little he had piled up on the sidewalk. He just hadn't gotten around to paying his rent, and you know how it was with him in those days—forty dollars this week, fifty dollars next, nothing for three weeks, a hundred the week after. It was just after the stock-market crash, and landladies were getting very particular about that week's rent in advance, and Tommie simply didn't have any money just then. That money he'd spent the night before was all he had. He didn't even have a bank account!"

"He could have come to me," said Agnes stiffly.

"He'd've starved first," said Jessie. "Not because he disliked you, or even because of his pride, but just because he didn't want to hear the truth about himself that you were so ready to tell him. Let's face it, Agnes: Tommie didn't become a big grown-up adult as fast as most of us. He got there—but it took time.

"Well, I won't go into too many details. First I let Tommie bring his stuff over, because he had nowhere else to store it. I invited him to dinner. When he came, he had a tragic story of hunting for some place to hang his hat, and it just wasn't possible without money. So—he stayed over that night. And the next one. Finally I told him to stop wasting so much time in house-hunting and make himself some money. The quickest way for him to do that was to write, so he set up his old typewriter in a corner of my living-room—I had a four-room place, and my roommate had just left to get married—and he got to work.

"The first story bounced, and the second, and the third. The days ran into weeks. I went to work every day, and Tommie would begin pounding on the typewriter as I left. I'll admit it—I loved every minute of it. I guess I have a soft spot in me somewhere, and just don't operate completely unless there's something I can take care of. Tommie kept a little black book—I think he still has it somewhere—and carefully put down every little thing that he ate and smoked and drank, and added half the rent and gas and power, with a little over because he used the radio while he was working. It was cute.

"It was wonderful, but it couldn't go on forever. I got so I almost dreaded the day he'd sell a story. I didn't want him under my thumb, but—just to have him there was— Well, finally, when he'd been with me about six weeks, a check came in. When I got home he'd made dinner—oh, Aggie, you should have seen it! Candles on the table, and he'd roasted some squab. There was champagne! The idiot ... the potatoes weren't quite done, and we had to gulp the shrimp-cup so the squab wouldn't burn; but it was the most wonderful dinner I ever had." She flicked at her eyes and laughed.

"And then he solemnly presented me with an envelope containing slips of paper with columns of figures, and some money—down to the penny, his share of the expenses while he'd been there. He was so proud of it! It was the first time in his whole life he'd ever kept any kind of an account. He sat me down on the settee and showed me every item, and on some of them he quizzed me, with his face all puckered up with anxiety, as to the price of apples or how much gas I thought it took to roast a leg of lamb.

"I had to take the money. He'd've felt like a whipped pup if I hadn't. Then I said I guessed he'd be leaving me now. He shuffled his feet and said, well, he guessed he should. I can't tell you how I felt. Suddenly it occurred to me to ask him, 'Tommie! How much money have you got left?'

"He admitted it, finally. He had three dollars and ninety cents. My darling budget-master—three dollars and ninety cents!

"I think I laughed for half an hour. He thought—and probably still thinks—that I was laughing because I thought he was funny. But I was laughing because I knew I could make him stay. Finally he began to laugh too, and he stayed.

"After that the question of his getting a place came up less and less often. He still took care of the budget, bless him ... you know, I think that had a lot to do with his growing up in all the other ways? He began keeping his income-tax straight, and thinking ahead about getting his clothes pressed before he had to wear them, and keeping himself stocked up with typewriter ribbons and stamps. There are some old friends who say I made him over. Well, I didn't. He did it all by himself."

"But why didn't you get married?"

Jessie smiled up into the place where the ceiling met the wall. "Tommie was terrified of the idea. At the end of seven months, when he was back on his feet and free to do what he wanted, we talked it out. He cared so terribly much about the thing we had together, Agnes. Tommie's a strange man. Maybe that's why his books are so popular.... I'd cut my tongue out before I'd advise anyone else to do what we did. I don't think it would work for anyone else ... anyway, Tommie was—and is—a sentimentalist of the first water. If we went to a restaurant and had a really perfect meal—I mean perfect in every last detail—Tommie wouldn't go back. He'd made a memory, and anything placed on it would mar it for him. He wanted to keep that memory untarnished and unchanged in the little jewel-box he kept in the back of his dear fuzzy head.

"'We're together because we want to be together,' he would say. 'The very fact that we're in this room together proves that there's no place in all the world where either of us want to be but here, together. We don't need a piece of paper to keep us together like two hot-dogs from the butcher-store. If we had that piece of paper, we could never know if we were together because we wanted to be, or if it was because society made it the easiest thing to do.' Sometimes he'd mention the jail. He'd been walking along the street when a man right in front of him was killed by gangsters, and he was held for four days as a witness—mostly for his own protection; those were wild days. 'That jail cell wasn't bad, Jess,' he told me. 'It wasn't very big, but it was clean. The fellow in there with me wasn't bad company. They fed us regularly—not a lot, but quite enough—and they let us smoke all we wanted to, and there were magazines and candy-bars to be had at the commissary. The beds weren't inner-spring, but they were clean, and it was warm enough at night. I've been lots worse off than I was there. There was just one thing about it—a thing that drove me half out of my mind while I was there—a think that made that place a hell on earth. The door was locked. *The door was locked!* If they'd left it open—or even unlocked—I'd have been willing to stay in there indefinitely. Marriage is like that, Jess. We have ours, but the door is open. As long as we know it is, we never have to go through it to see what's on the other side. A marriage license would lock it.'"

Jessie shifted restlessly. "Children would have locked it, too ... and if we could have had them, it would have been locked, and the whole story would be different. But we couldn't, worse luck—worse, worse luck ...

"Anyway, as far as the world was concerned, we were married. That began early, when I had to tell the landlady why I had a man in my place—I blurted it out, and that was the end of it. Tommie was very upset about that, but realized he could kick the whole story over with a word. So—hardly anyone ever got to know. You wouldn't have known if he hadn't been compelled to tell you."

"I wish he hadn't," said Agnes. "I do. I've always liked you, Jessie. Really I have, though I've never been able to understand you. But when Tommie told me about your—your—about it, it blighted my whole attitude toward both of you."

"I know it did. I was always sorry about that. It was one of the more infantile things that Tommie pulled, the darling. Anyway, we appointed Miss O'Casey there—" she thumbed at the statue— "Official Keeper of the Compact." O.K.C., get it? Miss O'Casey. She was in on it from the beginning. I told you Tommie's a sentimentalist. Well, maybe I am too, a little. He built a shelf in the little hallway between the living room and the bedroom and put her up there, where she could see and be seen, always. Tommie sometimes called her One-up, because of that raised finger—one up for the common people. Sometimes I called her Gigglepuss, just because her face is so placid and somber. But you say we made a joke of it—it wasn't a joke, Agnes. Never that. Miss O'Casey and what she stood for was—is—a very serious thing indeed. Look at her, Aggie. Please do. Look at her carefully."

With an expression of martyred patience, Agnes turned to look at the statue. She ran her eyes primly over the naked torso and bent to peer into the face. "She does look—strong," she confessed at length, "strong and very peaceful."

"She's made that kind of marriage for us," said Jessie quietly. "I can't describe to you the look that passes between Tommie and me when we hear of some old friends getting a divorce—and there have been so many of them, so terribly many! You know, they come to us, sometimes to one, sometimes to both of us, and ask us how we've made it all these years. They ask *us!* And what can we tell them?" She shrugged. "Only to have someone like Miss O'Casey here—and then keep faith with her. She does her part."

Agnes turned again to look at the statue. Behind her, Jessie, said, almost sleepily, "There's more to a marriage than a wedding, Agnes."

"I—don't think I ever realized that before, in just that way," said Agnes. She looked profoundly troubled. "I don't see how you *did* it! Where was your security—how could you know he would always stay with you? What guarantees—"

"The guarantees were between us; we had our faith and ourselves to answer to, first and above all," snapped Jessie. "And—there it is again—as long as I had Miss O'Casey, I could be sure. I'm no super-woman, Agnes. I did nothing that any other married woman hasn't done; I just played it a little differently, that's all, because my man was happier when I did. He's been happy, Agnes."

"Yes," said Agnes, "he has." She rose slowly. "I've been here too long, Jess. I didn't mean to tire you. I wish you could do as I asked, but I can see now why you wouldn't—why, at least according to your way of thinking, you don't have to. I can't condone it; I'm sorry as I can be. I wish I could feel easy in my mind about it, but I can't. I'm sorry, Jessie, more sorry than I can say." She sighed, and rose slowly, feeling her weight, her years.

"Aggie—"

"Yes, Jess."

"Aggie—I can't have you feeling this way, when it's all so simple ... Aggie, for all Tommie told you—did we have a marriage?"

Agnes stood between the bed and the door, fighting something within herself, a battle between two definitions of a word.

"Aside from the wedding, Agnes—*was it a marriage?*"

"I—I think it was," Agnes whispered.

And then Jessie began to cry.

Agnes stared at her, completely bewildered. For years she had been convinced that Jessie couldn't cry. For many of those years she had been certain that Jessie was so hard, so tough, she couldn't be hurt, couldn't be reached.

"Jessie! What is it?"

"I'm—I'm *happy,* damn it. B-because of what you said. Here, get me Miss O'Casey. Put her right down on the bed."

Thunderstruck, quite beyond thought, Agnes lifted the statuette and put it on the sheet. Jessie toppled it on its side.

"She's Balinese," she said. "The top part, the figure itself. Quite old. The little man in the antique shop told us. But the pedestal is American, Victorian. And—"

She put one hand on the elaborate head-dress of the dark goddess, and the other under the base. There was a faint click, and then Jessie gave the base a quarter turn to the right. It fell away.

"He showed us that, too, but Tommie didn't remember. He didn't remember anything that happened that night. Here."

From the depths of the statue, Jessie drew a folded square of paper and extended it to the other.

Agnes absently found her spectacles and perched them on her nose. "What is it?"

"Read it!"

"*This is to certify . . .*" she read haltingly, "*before me this day of . . . Jessica Mavis Tortelle and Thomas Davis van Creeft . . . holy matrimony . . .* Jessie! A license! A marriage license!" She fell down on her knees by the bed. "Why didn't you tell me? Why?"

Jessie tangled her fingers in the other's obedient hair. "Honey," she said huskily, "You'd've blabbed to Tommie. It meant too much to you. You couldn't have helped yourself."

"But—you mean Tommie doesn't know, at all?"

"He does not. Look: I wanted to be married to Tommie. But he was so scared of marriage he couldn't see straight. If I'd told him this—" she struck the license with her knuckle— "that first morning, he'd have been ashamed of it. I won't have anyone ashamed of any marriage of mine. And—afterwards, you know, Agnes, Tommie's a writer, but he's no bohemian. At heart, he's a timid, clean-cut, conventional citizen. Thinking he was living in sin has made him a gay dog, a little cut above the rest of 'em. It's done wonders for his work; his books are full of tolerance for the way the other fellow lives, because he wants that tolerance for himself." She plunged the paper back into its hiding place and deftly fitted the statuette together again. "Miss O'Casey is the Official Keeper of the Compact, Agnes; and now she has a partner. You. Guard it well."

Agnes put the figure back on the night table, and her hands lingered on the glossy back surface. "Jessie," she said, "I'll never understand you."

"Don't try," said Jessie, sinking back into the pillow. Her eyes closed. Agnes stared down at her through her misted spectacles. Where had she seen that expression of strength, and of peace? Oh, yes . . .

Suddenly Jessie's eyes sprang open, and they blazed. "And if you ever tell him," she rapped, "so help me, Aggie, I'll come back and haunt you!"

"I won't, dear; oh, I won't!" and, impulsively, she did something she never would have allowed herself to do ordinarily, for fear of a bruising rebuff: she bent and kissed her sister-in-law. The thin arms came up from the bed and went round her; Jessie hugged her, hard.

The funeral was short, and full of music and flowers—what Jessie would have called "happy flowers, not sad flowers." Drapes were drawn back to let in the light, and the room was fragrant and warm and waiting for laughter; none of your shadows and silences, wax and lilies for Jessie van Creeft.

The coffin lay on a long, low trestle, covered with white silk, and, at its foot, on a glass-topped table, stood the dark goddess. If the attending priest regarded it as a pagan thing, then he had faith in the power of his own doctrines, and said nothing against its presence.

After the words were spoken, Agnes stood for a long time looking at the coffin and at the statue. Suddenly she stepped to the lowboy, and from a vase took two or three rosebuds. She dropped them on the table before the dark goddess, and left the room.

A man followed her. He was tall, timid, balding, gentle. "Agnes."

"Yes, Tommie."

"I saw you put the flowers there. I was—I ... Why did you do it, Agnes? Will you tell me?"

She looked at her gloves. "I just—thought Miss O'Casey deserved it," she said softly. "It was a real marriage."

He put his arm around her. "Sis," he whispered, "I didn't know you knew that."

"I haven't known it long," she said into his lapel, "And oh, Tommie, I wish I'd known before!"

Scars

THERE IS A time when a thing in the mind is a heavy thing to carry, and then it must be put down. But such is its nature that it cannot be set on a rock or shouldered off on to the fork of a tree, like a heavy pack. There is only one thing shaped to receive it, and that is another human mind. There is only one time when it can be done, and that is in a shared solitude. It cannot be done when a man is alone, and no man aloof in a crowd ever does it.

Riding fence gives a man this special solitude until his throat is full of it. It will come maybe two or three weeks out, with the days full of heat and gnats and the thrum of wire under the stretcher, and the nights full of stars and silence. Sometimes in those nights a chunk will fall in the fire, or a wolf will howl, and just then a man might realize that his partner is awake too, and that a thing in his mind is growing and swelling and becoming heavy. If it gets to be heavy enough, it is put down softly, like fine china, cushioned apart with thick strips of quiet.

That is why a wise foreman pairs his fence riders carefully. A man will tell things, sometimes, things grown into him like the calluses from his wire cutters, things as much a part of him, say, as a notched ear or bullet scars in his belly; and his hearer should be a man who will not mention them after sun-up—perhaps not until his partner is dead—perhaps never.

Kellet was a man who had calluses from wire cutters, and a notched ear, and old bullet scars low down on his belly. He's dead now. Powers never asked to hear about the scars. Powers was a good fence man and a good partner. They worked in silence, mostly, except for a grunt when a post-hole was deep enough, or "Here," when one of them handed over a tool. When they pitched for the night, there was no saying "You get the wood," or "Make the coffee." One or

the other would just do it. Afterward they sat and smoked, and sometimes they talked, and sometimes they did not, and sometimes what
they said was important to them, and sometimes it was not.

Kellet told about the ear while he was cooking one evening. Squatting to windward of the fire, he rolled the long-handled skillet deftly,
found himself looking at it like a man suddenly scanning the design
of a ring he has worn for years.

"Was in a fight one time," he said.

Powers said, "woman."

"Yup," said Kellet. "Got real sweet on a dressmaker in Kelso
when I was a bucko like you. Used to eat there. Made good mulligan."

They were eating, some ten minutes later, when he continued.
"'Long comes this other feller, had grease on his hair. He shore smelt
purty."

"Mexican?"

"Easterner"

Powers' silence was contributory rather than receptive at this
point.

"She said to come right in. Spoons him out what should be my
seconds o' stew. Gets to gigglin' an' fussin' over him." He paused
and chewed, and when the nutritious obstacle was out of the way,
spat vehemently. "Reckon I cussed a little. Couldn't he'p m'self. Next
thing you know, he's a-tellin' me what language not to use in front
of a lady. We went round and round together and that ended quick.
See this ear?"

"Pulled a knife on you."

Kellet shook his big, seamed head. "Nup. She hit me a lick with the
skillet. Tuk out part o' my ear. After, it tuk me the better part of an hour
with tar soap to wash the last o' that hair grease offen my knuckles."

One bullet made the holes in his stomach, Kellet told Powers
laconically while they were having a dip in a cold stream one
afternoon.

"Carried a leetle pot-belly in them days," said Kellet. "Bullet went
in one side and out t'other. I figgered fer a while they might's well
rack me, stick me, bleed me, and smoke me fer fall. But I made it.
Shore lost that pot-belly in the gov'ment hospital though. They

wouldn't feed me but custards and like that. My plumbin' was all mixed up and cross-connected."

"Feller in th' next bed died one night. They used t'wake us up 'fore daylight with breakfast. He had prunes. I shore wanted them prunes. When I see he don't need 'em I ate 'em. Figgered nobody had to know." He chuckled.

Later, when they were dressed and mounted and following the fence, he added, "They found the prune stones in m'bandages."

But it was at night that Kellet told the other thing, the thing that grew on like a callus and went deeper than bullet scars.

Powers had been talking, for a change. Women. "They always got a out," he complained. He put an elbow out of his sleeping bag and leaned on it. Affecting a gravelly soprano, he said, "I'd like you better, George, if you'd ack like a gentleman."

He pulled in the elbow and lay down with an eloquent thump. "I know what a gentleman is. It's whatever in the world you cain't be, not if you sprouted wings and wore a hello. *I* never seen one. I mean, I never seen a man yet where *some* woman, *some* time, couldn't tell him to ack like he was one."

The fire burned bright, and after a time it burned low. "I'm one," said Kellet.

Powers sensed that thing, that heavy growth of memory. He said nothing. He was awake, and he knew that somehow Kellet knew it.

Kellet said, "Know the Pushmataha country? Nuh—you wouldn't. Crick up there called Kiamichi. Quit a outfit up Winding Stair way and was driftin'. Come up over this little rise and was well down t'ord th' crick when I see somethin' flash in the water. It's a woman in there. I pulled up pronto. I was that startled. She was mother-nekkid.

"Up she goes on t'other side 'til she's about knee-deep, an' shakes back her hair, and then she sees me. Makes a dive fer th' bank, slips, I reckon. Anyway, down she goes an' lays still.

"I tell you, man, I felt real bad. I don't like to cause a lady no upset. I'd as soon wheeled back and fergot the whole thing. But what was I goin' to do—let her drown? Mebbe she was hurt.

"I hightailed right down there. Figured she'd ruther be alive an' embarrassed than at peace an' dead.

"She was hurt all right. Hit her head. Was a homestead downstream a hundred yards. Picked her up—she didn't weigh no more'n a buffalo calf—an' toted her down there. Yipped, but there wasn't no one around. Went in, found a bed, an' put her on it. Left her, whistled up my cayuse, an' got to me saddlebags. When I got back she was bleedin' pretty bad. Found a towel for under her head. Washed the cut with whiskey. Four-five inches long under the edge of her hair. She had that hair that's black, but blue when the sun's on it."

He was quiet for a long time. Powers found his pipe, filled it, rose, got a coal from the dying fire, lit up, and went back to his bedroll. He said nothing.

When he was ready, Kellet said, "She was alive, but out cold. I didn't know what the hell to do. The bleedin' stopped after a while, but I didn't know whether to rub her wrists or stand on m' head. I ain't no doctor. Finally I just set there near her to wait. Mebbe she'd wake up, mebbe somebuddy'd come. Mebbe I'd have my poke full o' trouble if somebuddy did come—I knowed that. But what was I goin' to do—ride off?

"When it got dark two-three hours later I got up an' lit a tallow-fat lamp an' a fire, an' made some coffee. Used my own Arbuckle. 'Bout got it brewed, heard a funny kind of squeak from t'other room. She's settin' bolt upright lookin' at me through the door, clutchin' the blanket to her so hard she like to push it through to t'other side, an' makin' her eyes round's a hitchin' ring. Went to her an' she squeaked ag'in an' scrambled away off into the corner an' tole' me not to touch her.

"Said, 'I won't, ma'am. Yo're hurt. You better take it easy.'

" 'Who are you?' she says. 'What you doin' here?' she says.

"I tol' her my name, says, 'Look, now, you're bleedin' ag'in. Just you lie down, now, an' let me fix it.'

"I don't know as she trusted me or she got faint. Anyway down she went, an' I put a cold cloth on the cut. She says, 'What happened?'

"Tole her, best I could. Up she comes ag'in. 'I was bathin'!' she says. 'I didn't have no—' and she don't get no further'n that, just squeaks some more.

"I says, straight out, 'Ma'am, you fell an' hurt yo're head. I don't recall a thing but that. I couldn't do nought but what I did. Reckon it was sort of my fault anyway. I don't mean you no harm. Soon's you git some help I'll leave. Where's your menfolks?'

"That quieted her down. She tole me about herself. She was homesteadin'. Had pre-emption rights an' eighteen months left t' finish th' term. Husband killed in a rock-slide. Swore to him she'd hold th' land. Didn't know what she'd do after, but spang shore she was a-goin' to do that first. Lot o' spunk."

Kellet was quiet again. The loom of the moon took black from the sky and gave it to the eastward ridge. Powers' pipe gurgled suddenly.

"Neighbor fourteen mile downstream was burned out the winter before. Feller eight mile 'tother way gone up to Winding Stair for a roundup, taken his wife. Be gone another two months. This little gal sweat out corn and peas for dryin', had taters put by. Nobuddy ever come near, almost. Hot day, she just naturally bathed in the crick.

"Asked her what about drifters like me, but mebbe gunmen. She reached under the bed, drug out a derringer. Says, 'This's for sech trash.' An' a lettle pointy knife. 'This's for me,' she says, just like that. I tol' her to keep both of 'em by her. Was that sorry for her, liked her grit so, I felt half sick with it.

"Was goin' to turn in outside, by the shed. After we talked some an' I made her up some johnny-cake, she said I c'd bunk in th' kitchen if I wanted. Tol' her to lock her door. She locked it. Big wooden bar. I put down m'roll an' turned in."

The moon was a bead on the hill's haloed brow; a coronet, then a crown.

Powers put his pipe away.

"In the mornin'," said Kellet, "she couldn't get up. I just naturally kicked the door down when she wouldn't answer. Had a bad fever. Fast asleep an' couldn't wake up but for a half minute, an' then she'd slide off ag'in. Set by her 'most all day, 'cept where I saw to my hoss an' fixed some vittles. Did for her like you would for a kid. Kept washin' her face with cold water. Never done nothin' like that before; didn't know much what to do, done the best I could.

"Afternoon, she talked for a hour or so, real wild. Mostly to her man, like he was settin' there 'stead o' me. He was a lucky feller. She said . . .

"Be damned to you what she said. But I . . . tuk to answerin' her oncet in a while, just 'Yes, honey,' when she got to callin' hard for him. Man a full year dead, I don't think she really believed it, not all the way down. She said things to him like—like no woman ever thought to say to me. Anyway . . . when I answered thataway she'd talk quiet. If I didn't she'd just call and call, and git all roiled up, an' her head would bleed, so what else you expect me to do?

"Next day she was better, but weak's a starveling colt in a blowin' drought. Slept a lot. I found out where she'd been jerkin' venison, an' finished it up. Got some weeds outen her black-eye peas. Went back ever' now an' then to see she's all right. Remember some red haw back over the ridge, rode over there and gathered some, fixed 'em to sun so's she'd have 'em for dried-apple pie come winter.

"Four-five days went by like that. Got a deer one day, skinned it an' jerked it. Done some carpenterin' in th' shed an' in th' house. Done what I could. Time I was fixin' the door to the kitchen I'd kicked down that first mornin', she lay a-watchin' me an' when I was done, she said I was good. 'Yo're good, Kellet,' she said. Don't sound like much to tell it. Was a whole lot."

Powers watched the moon rise and balance itself on the ridge, ready to float free. A single dead tree on the summit stood against it like a black-gloved hand held to a golden face.

Kellet said, "Just looka that ol' tree, so . . . strong-lookin' an' . . . so dead."

When the moon was adrift, Kellet said, "Fixed that door with a new beam an' good gudgeons. Man go to kick it down now'd have a job to do. She—"

Powers waited.

"—she never did use it. After she got well enough to get up an' around a bit, even. Just left it open. Mebbe she never thought about it. Mebbe she did, too. Nights, I'd stretch out in my bedroll, lay there, and wait. Pretty soon she'd call out, 'Good night, Kellet. Sleep good, now.' Thing like that, that's worth a passel o' farmin' an' carpenterin' . . .

"One night, ten-'leven days after I got there, woke up. She was cryin' there in the dark in t'other room. I called out what's the matter. She didn't say. Just kept a-bawlin'. Figgered mebbe her head hurt her. Got up, went to th' door. Asked her if she's all right. She just keeps a-cryin'—not loud, mind, but cryin' hard. Thing like that makes a man feel all tore up.

"Went on in. Called her name. She patted the side o' the' bed. I set down. Put my hand on her face to see if she was gettin' the fever ag'in. Face was cool. Wet, too. She tuk my hand in her two an' held it hard up ag'in her mouth. I didn't know she was so strong.

"Set there quiet for two-three minutes. Got m'hand loose. Says, 'What you bawlin' for, ma'am?'

"She says, 'It's good to have you here.'

"I stood up, says, 'You git back to yo're rest now, ma'am.' She—"

There were minutes between the words, but no change in his voice when he continued.

"—cried mebbe a hour. Stopped sudden, and altogether. Mebbe I slept after that, mebbe I didn't. Don't rightly recall.

"Next mornin' she's up bright an' early, fixin' chow. First time she done it since she's hurt. Tole her, 'Whoa. Take it easy, ma'am. You don't want to tucker yo'reself out.'

"She says, 'I coulda done this three days ago.' Sounded mad. Don't rightly know who she's mad at. Fixed a powerful good breakfast.

"That day seemed the same, but it was 'way differ'nt. Other days we mostly didn't talk nothin' but business—caterpillars in th' tomato vines, fix a hole in the smoke shed, an' like that. This day we talked the same things. Difference was, we had to try hard to keep the talk where it was. An' one more thing—didn't neither of us say one more word 'bout any work that might have to be done—tomorrow.

"Midday, I gathered up what was mine, an' packed my saddle-bags. Brought my hoss up to th' shed an' watered him an' saddled him. Didn't see her much, but knowed she's watchin' me from inside th' house.

"All done, went to pat m'hoss once on the neck. Hit him so hard he shied. Right surprised m'self.

221

"She come out then. She stood a-lookin' at me. Says, 'Good-bye, Kellet. God bless you.'

"Says good-bye to her. Then didn't neither of us move for a minute. She says, 'You think I'm a bad woman.'

"Says, 'No sech a damn thing, ma'am! You was a sick one, an' powerful lonesome. You'll be all right now.'

"She says, 'I'm all right. I'll be all right long as I live,' she says, 'thanks to you, Kellet. Kellet,' she says, 'you had to think for both of us an' you did. Yo're a gentleman, Kellet,' she says.

"Mounted, then, an' rode off. On the rise, looked back, saw her still by the shed, lookin' at me. Waved m'hat. Rode on."

The night was a white night now, since the moon had shucked its buoyant gold for its traveling silver. Powers heard Kellet turn over, and knew he could speak now if he cared to. Somewhere a mouse screamed briefly under an owl's silent talons. Distantly, a coyote's hungry call built itself into the echoing loneliness.

Powers said, "So that's what a gentleman is. A man that c'n think for two people when the time comes for it?"

"Naw-w," drawled Kellet scornfully. "That's just what she come to believe because I never touched her."

Powers asked it, straight, "Why didn't you?"

A man will tell things, sometimes, things grown into him like the calluses from his wire-cutters, things as much a part of him as, say, a notched ear or bullet scars in his belly; and his hearer should be a man who will not mention them after sun-up—perhaps not until his partner is dead—perhaps never.

Kellet said, "I cain't."

Messenger

THE TWO GUNS spoiled the lines of Bentow's carefully fitted coat. No one but he and his tailor would have noticed it, but he would be happy when he had used them and had done with the whole business.

He stepped out of the administrative corridor into the south end of Generator Room No. 5, and glanced down its enormous length. The great dynamos crouched off into distance like an avenue of hulking houses. A slight movement in the gleaming street between them made Bentow step back into the corridor.

After an interminable wait old Zeitz, the section night watchman, trudged by, his eyes cast down, his ancient legs transmuting these indoor distances into his rounds just as mechanically as the purring monsters about him turned motion into power.

When he had gone, Bentow put his sleek head out of the corridor again, and then stepped into the room. Staying close to the aluminum-clad wall, he walked quickly to the end of the room and along it to the open doorway of Condenser Station No. 48, where his inspection route charts had shown him that Auckland Ford should be.

Ford, straight and gray, was there standing with his level eyes on the instrument panel inside. He turned in surprise as Bentow stepped inside.

"Well," he said, smiling. "You're about the last person I ever expected to see where the work gets done."

Bentow forced himself to return the smile. "Public relations isn't all cocktails and stuffed shirts, Mr. Ford," he said. "I worked right through midnight tonight, and since I was at the plant, I thought I'd bone up a little on how things work. You'd be surprised how many technical questions are asked at those cocktail parties."

"So this is research? Well, I'm glad to help. This is the first thing you've done that I can like, Bentow."

"You really do dislike me, don't you?" Bentow said, frowning.

"I didn't say that," said Ford. "I just don't give a hang one way or the other. Hope I'm not being too frank."

"Not at all," said Bentow stiffly. He wet his lips. "Your daughter appears to have a certain amount of respect for me."

"That isn't respect," said Ford bluntly. "She's too young to know what respect is. She can understand authority and she knows who brings the feed pan. But if she wants to marry you, it's all right with me. You're not a bad catch. You've got a good income, a really impressive array of false front, and plenty of good looks. Dorcas is a sweet kid, but I faced the fact long ago that she's not too bright."

"She is everything in the world I want," said Bentow solemnly.

"Good," said Ford. "And, by Heaven, I expect you to behave accordingly, or you'll answer to me!"

Overhead a horn honked—a series of five unpleasant *beeps*.

"That's my call," said Ford. "Early. My report's not due for another ten minutes. Just a second, Bentow."

He stalked out the low doorway and took down the phone which hung outside. Bentow shuffled his feet nervously and then moved to the far bulkhead, where he would be out of sight of the generator room. Ford was back in a moment.

"Just a reminder that the manifold in eighty-seven needs a special inspection," he said.

"Did you tell them I was here?" Bentow asked.

"I did not. It wasn't a social call."

"But you'll make your routine report ten minutes from now?"

"Of course."

"Just wondered," said Bentow, and thought to himself, "I'd better wait until after he reports. Killing ten minutes will give me a little practice. Do my killing by stages—"

"Well, what did you want to know?" asked Ford.

"Oh—I know pretty much the general principles," said Bentow. "A mercury-vapor power plant using the atomic-pile heat from the transmutation factory. But tell me about these condenser stations, just as if I were some curious bubblehead at a cocktail party."

Ford gave him a somewhat pitying look, and finally said, "All right, Mr. Curious Bubblehead from a cocktail party." He grinned while Bentow winced. "These stations are not the condensers themselves; those are all underneath. But the mercury lines pass through here—high-pressure ones to the turbines, low-pressure ones to the exhaust chambers of the condensers. These stations check the pressures on each, all the time."

"What exactly for?" Bentow queried.

"Well, the pressure data are matched with generator output to determine the working efficiency; with mercury-flow checks to determine the volatilization rate—that has everything to do with the chemical purity of the mercury—and, most of all, to check for leaks."

"Yes. I know that's important. The stuff is quick poison at those pressures."

"Mercury vapor is poison at any pressure," said Ford. "But at these pressures—" he pointed to the great trunks of the ducts which led through the back wall and down into the floor— "750 pounds per square inch to the turbines, and a mere 60 pounds for exhaust, the vapor can reach a lethal concentration like *that!*" and he snapped his long fingers. "The tiniest pin hole in one of those trunks over there would mean a deadly concentration of vapor here in seconds!"

"And how long would it take to kill a man?" Bentow asked curiously.

"Only a few minutes."

"But any of you operators can smell the stuff before it gets dangerous, can't you?"

"No. A concentration of only one part in one hundred thousand in air is dangerous. A man would be seriously poisoned by the time he felt anything at all," said Ford.

Bentow thought this over for a moment before asking, "Well, what protects you?"

Ford pointed to a small box, screened, on a shelf. Blue-white light hovered around it. "Ikey does," he said.

"Oh, yes—the spectral detector. Just how does it work?"

"Well, you know how dark lines show up on a spectroscope?"

"I think so," said Bentow. "If you put a sheet of cadmium-tinted glass over your spectroscope and shoot the sun, you'll get dark lines on the cadmium sector of the solar spectrum."

"That's roughly the idea. Well, Ikey there has a photo-electric cell with a mercury filter over it. Trained on it is a mercury-vapor lamp. If any trace of mercury vapor occurs in the air in here, the value of the light that reaches the cell changes because of the spectral lines which occur behind the filter. Then Ikey goes into action."

Bentow looked at his elaborate wrist watch. He knew all this, but it didn't hurt to check again while he waited.

"Well, first of all he sets up a yell," Ford continued. "There are screechers all around the plant; if you've ever heard one once you'll never forget it. Then he automatically shuts the door to this station and starts blowers to change the air."

"Shuts the door? But suppose someone is in here?"

"There's a push-button outside the door, but the phone."

"Oh yes," said Bentow. "I noticed it. It has a light over it."

"That's right. Well, when I come in here I push it. The light lights, and if anything should happen in here the door will stay open until I can get out and push the button. If I should be hurt, someone else will be along but quick, fish me out, and close the door. But if no one is here, the door will close as soon as the alarm starts."

"Ah," said Bentow. "And suppose you forget to push the button when you first come in?"

"You *don't* forget," said Ford grimly.

The overhead horn sounded a series of five beeps again.

"My report," said Ford.

"Don't mention that I'm here," said Bentow swiftly. "This is a little irregular, you know."

"More irregular for me than for you," said Ford. "I'm working. Don't worry, I won't." He went out.

Bentow shifted the guns in his side pockets tensely, and leaned back against the bulkhead. "I'm working," he muttered under his breath. Why should Auckland Ford work? he wondered. The man was brilliant; had been ever since his youth, when, as the winner of a talent search, he had done that phenomenal job on heat-transfer devices. A lot of that work was built into this very plant—the slow viscous flow of Fordium, as it was called, from the pile jackets to the mercury boilers was Ford's development. The heavy stuff was incredibly stable, and absorbed little radiation from the hellish fury of the piles. It transferred plenty of heat and a negligible amount of radiation to the boilers.

Ford was a wealthy man—one of the wealthiest in this part of the world. But what did he do with his money? Gave it away, a lot of it. The rest moldered in banks, awaiting yet another of his fantastically generous impulses. The charity called Providence had benefited, no one knew how much, from Ford's gifts.

Providence, with its subsidies of pure science, or applied science in any field which furthered the humanities—such as a lie-detector which was now accepted by the courts; nine specialized cancer cures, a bombardment technique which preserved food in cellophane jackets without refrigeration, and so on and on.

And now, according to the word that Ford's pretty but slightly stupid daughter had dropped, Ford was going to will everything he owned to Providence, as soon as Julius, his attorney, returned from the coast, which would be this week. And what did he, Bentow, want with that empty-headed doll without her enormous inheritance?

Bentow glanced around the bare room. There were the two huge mercury trunks. There was Ikey, the detector, who would start to yell when one part of mercury vapor in two billion of air showed itself. He would like very much to impair Ikey's efficiency, but did not dare. Ikey would be one of the first things inspected after the "accident."

Aside from the pressure indicators, there was very little else in the room, except a spanner or two and a small first-aid kit. Bentow nodded in satisfaction.

Ford came in, his long gray eyes going immediately to the gauges. Apparently satisfied, he turned to Bentow.

"Anything else you wanted to know?" he asked.

"Only one thing I wanted to be sure of. If there's a leak and the doors close, how long do they stay closed?"

"Twelve hours, as a matter of safety. The boiler lines are diverted as soon as three others can be slowed down and this boiler's output diverted to them."

"During that time, you say the blowers will be replacing the air in here," Bentow said. "Does the alarm keep on sounding until the concentration is down below one part in two billion?"

"Gosh, no!" grinned Ford. "We'd be out of our minds if it did. No—as soon as the door closes, the alarm is shut off, except for light signals which indicate which station has the trouble. Unless, of course, the concentration continues to rise. Then Ikey sounds off again."

"I see," said Bentow, who had known it before, but was glad of the final check. "One more thing—and this is just personal curiosity; don't answer me unless you want to. But why do you work here?"

Ford smiled, and his cool gaze pinioned Bentow. "I wouldn't really expect you to understand," he said quietly. "It's just that I found out very early that there is nothing that can destroy a human being but excess. Alcohol won't hurt you, drunkenness will. Work won't hurt you, exhaustion will. And so on through everything a man eats, thinks, drinks, and breathes.

"And there is such a thing as too much success and too much money," he went on. "You don't believe that, I know. I've worked all my life. I don't live a Spartan existence—that's an extreme—but I haven't let myself get soft. My company pension comes due soon, and it'll be enough. I'm getting rid of everything else. I don't need it. I have my home and my lab and a lot of things to interest me. That's all I want. But there are thousands of other people who want and need my surplus money; they can have it. It'll do them good and it could only harm me—like any excess."

"It really is true, then, that you're turning over everything you have to Providence?" Bentow questioned.

"That's right. Did Dorcas tell you?"

"Yes. But why Providence?"

Ford laughed. "I don't know why I tell you this. No one else knows. Providence is mine. I founded it."

Bentow's eyes popped, and Ford laughed again.

"But that must have taken millions!" Bentow gasped.

"I just had some good ideas." Ford's eyes speared into Bentow. "I know what you're thinking. That money meant so much rich living, so much yachting, so much social climbing—not for me, Bentow. I'm a working man."

Bentow's eyes glowed strangely. "I think you're crazy."

Ford shrugged. "You would. You have never learned the meaning of 'enough.'"

"Does Dorcas feel the same way you do?"

"She doesn't feel," said Auckland Ford positively. "Easy come, easy go—she's always been a happy, or slap-happy, child. Maybe some day she'll get a jolt big enough to give her some sense. I don't believe in jolting people who are close to me, personally. It's useless to talk sense to your intimates. They'll only listen to strangers." He shrugged. "Dorcas is *good,*" he said. "Sooner or later, that will show up."

Bentow took the gun from his left jacket pocket. A corner of his mind appreciated the fact that his jacket now fell to its correct cut.

Ford said, in surprise, "That's mine!"

"Dorcas took me on an extensive tour of your laboratory," said Bentow. "These long evenings at home, when you're on the night shift—"

"That gun will never be good for anything," said Ford. "Not as a weapon, anyway. Industrially it might have some use—if anyone wants a tool that will penetrate fifty inches of molyb steel with a hole a thousandth of an inch in diameter."

"What about this one?" Bentow drew the other, and the sartorial corner of his mind heaved a satisfied sigh.

"I don't deal in weapons," said Ford. "Can't say I'm crazy about the idea of your just picking these up."

"No one knows I've got them—not even Dorcas," said Bentow. "This one," he added persistently. "A paralysis device, isn't it?"

"That's what it turned out to be," said Ford glumly. I was fooling with subsonics for anaesthetic purposes. I suppose you know the police now carry that one as standard equipment. Causes a temporary derangement of the motor centers. What the deuce are you doing with it?"

Bentow smiled. "Only this," he said, and pressed the thumb-stud.

Ford stood stiffly, almost as he always stood. But now his mouth opened slowly, his tongue protruded and began to oscillate violently. His long, narrow eyes widened until they were almost perfectly round. His hands curled, tensed, straightened, stiffened. He overbalanced slowly, like a tall tree just sawed through, fell to lean stiffly a moment against the bulkhead, and then jackknifed to the floor.

"I know you can hear me," said Bentow smugly, putting away the paralysis gun. "You just can't move. Don't worry, that will only last two or three minutes. I wish I could be here to see what the great Brain will do then. The place will be full of mercury vapor, and that so carefully designed hermetically sealed door will be closed. Pound against it all you wish—no one will hear you. The phone's outside, the door controls are outside, and no one will know you're here."

He paused, cocking his shining head to one side as if listening.

"Oh," he said, pretending the other had spoken. "You want to know why? Well, Mr. Brilliant Scientist, it seems that you are about to leave all of your considerable fortune to a thing called Providence, with the bland idea that I shall be able to support your dear daughter on my wages in the manner to which she has become accustomed. My dear Mr. Ford, I intend to do much better than that—with the money which she will now inherit!"

He still held the other gun. He walked over the trunk duct marked "HP" for "High Pressure" and fired twice. There was no sound—simply a line of blue light so fine it was almost invisible.

"Those," he said, putting the gun in his pocket, "will be attributed to pressure leakage. Because you were afraid that this thing would be used as a weapon, you have kept its performance characteristics secret, and I assure you that all of your records will be destroyed before I go on my honeymoon.

"I must go now." An ugly smirk was on his face. "I am sincerely sorry that I cannot stay to see what you do when you come out of the paralysis. I would, but I can't think of jeopardizing the health of your future, if post-mortem, son-in-law."

He waved his hand jauntily and stepped into the generator room. He called back, "What amuses me most in this dramatic situation is that you are being killed by two of your own inventions, in a plant which is possible because of a third. A happy suicide to you!"

He stood tensely by the doorway. Turning, he pushed the button there. The light went out. Then he sprinted to the corner and down the generator room to the administrative corridor.

There he waited until there came a harrowing mechanical scream which went on and on and on. A red light flared over the door of the station he had just left, and its ponderous door slid shut with a clang. Through the clamor of the screecher he could hear the pound of running feet. He turned and sprinted up the corridor to his office. The light still burned there.

He opened the closet and took out his overcoat. With one arm into it, he went to the door which gave on to the general offices and opened it a crack. There were voices outside.

"A leak," someone said out there. It was old Zeitz, the night watchman. "Stay right here, Sam. There was a blowoff out Hancord oncet where they phonied up an alarm to get the guards outen the offices, so's they could steal secret files. You stay right here till I git back, and' grab anyone thet come in, no matter who."

"I got you," said a bass voice.

Peering around the door, Bentow could see the shadowy hulk of the younger guard, and knew immediately that his, Bentow's, kind of brains would be useless against that particular one hundred and ninety pounds.

Bentow shucked out of his coat and put it away. He was not going to go out into the generator room, with guards and techs converging on Condenser Station No. 48, and he couldn't leave while that big guard was out there. His office was soundproof; he would simply pretend to be working late until all of the excitement died away, or express profound regret about the whole thing if someone came in accidentally.

Not that anyone would. In a technological emergency, no one would dream of calling the public relations office, even during office hours.

He settled back into his swivel chair, and smiled.

A half an hour later he screamed when Auckland Ford tottered into his office.

Ford, with his long face flushed and his once-clear eyes shot with blood, smiled a ghastly smile. Bentow screamed again, tried to huddle away, upset his swivel chair and cowered in a sobbing heap in the corner.

Men poured in, to catch Ford as he fell, to snatch the sodden Bentow to his feet and hold him.

From a deep easy-chair, with solicitous technicians around him, Ford glared redly at Bentow. "Well, Bentow, did you hear it?" he said.

"Hear what?" quavered Bentow.

Jackson, the swarthy plant super, said, "He means the screecher, when it gave his code call."

"This office is soundproof," said Bentow. "I don't know what you're talking about."

Ford's breath took on a wheeze. Jackson said, "I'll tell you, Bentow. Ford doesn't want to go to the hospital until he knows you've been told what happened. Can't say I blame him." His lips curled. He went on, "He found himself locked in that cell with the vapor concentration mounting. He'd been knocked down by a paralyzer but—" awe entered his voice— "that didn't keep his brain from working. When he could move again he found himself in a real spot."

"I'd have written your name on the floor," rasped Ford at Bentow, "but I didn't have anything to write with. Not even a spanner would make an impression on the stuff."

"You rest easy," said a guard, with his hand on Ford's shoulder.

"Yeah, I'll tell it," said Jackson. He turned back to the sweating Bentow. "He tried to write on the floor, first of all, and lost minutes at it. When I *think* of it!" he exploded. "All of us milling around outside, and the door closed, and none of us dreaming that there might be anyone inside! The screecher giving the alarm, and then dying out and all of us nodding at each other and saying, 'Well, we'll get to her at noon tomorrow.' And all the while he—"

He thumbed over his shoulder at Ford, who grinned weakly.

"The medicine chest," Ford whispered. "Only thing there was in the place." He laughed horribly. "I took a—" He began to cough.

Jackson said again, "I'll tell it. We were about to go back to our stations when the screecher started up again. That meant only that the leak was getting ahead of the blowers, at first. But none of us had ever heard the screecher like that. Hinks here spotted it."

Hinks, the guard, nodded and, oddly, blushed. "It went *Awk. Awk-awk-awk. Awk.*"

His imitation of the alarm screecher was so startlingly accurate that every man in the room jumped. Hinks blushed again and tittered, pulled himself together and said:

"It done it again, and a third time, and all of a sudden I remembered that was Mr. Ford's code-call on the beeper."

"Very—" said Bentow, and then his voice failed him. He swallowed hard and tried again. "Very ingenious. What has that to do with me?"

"It was Ikey," said Ford from his chair. "Ikey's like a light meter. Hold one candle one foot away, the meter'll say one foot-candle. Hold twenty candles twenty feet away, it'll still say one foot-candle." He ran out of breath.

"Yeah," said Jackson, "all Ikey knows is the concentration of mercury vapor in that little air space between the light and the cell. Mr. Ford took a thermometer—why they put a fever thermometer in all these local first aid kits I'll never know, but they're standard—and he broke it and held a little pool of mercury smaller'n a dime under the beam of Ikey's light."

"Shielded it off with a piece of my shirt," whispered Ford. "As primitive as Indian smoke signals. The little bit of mercury that vaporizes at room temperature drove Ikey into hysterics when it was that close to the beam."

"I still don't see what this has to do with me," said Bentow.

"You will," snapped Jackson. "Mr. Ford told us what you said about killing him with his own inventions. Watch what happens to you when you run into the lie-detector in court. He invented *that,* too!"

The door from the general offices opened. The guard-captain stood flat-footed and looked at every face in the room in one swift sweep. Then he pointed his finger at Bentow.

"His," he said tersely.

"I asked the captain to get the thumb-print from that push-button outside Station Number 48," Jackson explained, "and match it if he could in the company files. It's yours all right."

Bentow opened his mouth, put his hands to his face, and slumped down in a near faint.

"I think," said Ford harshly, "that my haywire kid Dorcas is going to get that jolt I was talking about." Then, oddly, he began to laugh. He laughed until Hinks nudged him anxiously.

"I'm all right," whispered Ford. "Maybe I'm delirious. I was just thinking about getting that message through to you fellows. Did you know I'm leaving everything to Providence?"

There was a bumble of approving excitement in the room.

"Providence," said Ford, "has had a lot of names at one time or another—a lot of 'em. D'you remember what the name of Jupiter's messenger was, Jackson?"

Jackson frowned.

"Uh—Hermes?"

"No, son. It was Mercury!"

Ford shook his head and laughed again.

Minority Report

This is the strange story of Dr. Falu Englehart's change of heart and the truth of how he turned from a dedicated lifetime to tear down his dream. It can be told now because, in the matter of the Titan invasion, humanity has shown itself, en masse, to have come of age— to have reached a stage of understanding.

For we in this twenty-eighth century are a strange race, only now entered upon our Third Phase, the first being an age of faith—and ignorant superstition—and the third of understanding and tolerance. The years between are a hell and a horror—the accursed five centuries which began in the eighteenth century, and which ended in near suicide in the twenty-second—years in which faith was destroyed and understanding not yet achieved.

It can be told now because it cannot hurt us. Had the story been circulated in the mad years of the Second Phase, it would have dealt a blow to humanity's belief in itself from which it might never have recovered. Humans knew what they were, even then; but during that violent adolescence they went to insane lengths to prove that they were otherwise—that they were supreme.

When the Titans descended upon us fifty years ago and dealt their insignificant portion of death and ruin, we answered as an understanding people would. We recognized in them our counterparts, a race in the throes of the disease called conquest. We are a peaceful species, close to the land; and they did not understand that our farms and our city-less planet represented, not a primitive society, but a society fulfilled. They took our achievement for a stasis or a recidivism, our decentralization as a sign of the primitive. When we immobilized them without machines—and like all very young humanoids, they worshipped machines—and defended ourselves by the simple expedient of teaching them their own terrible acquisitive history, why, we did not dam their stream and drive it back, like sweating savages; we dried it up. So much for that well-known tale; it does, however, demonstrate one of the ways in which we have proven our maturity, and our fitness to hear the strange story of Dr. Englehart.

Falu Englehart was born, to quote Umber's epic poem on his life, "with stars in eyes that were myopic to all earthly things." At nine he built his first telescope, and at twelve he developed a new technique for cataloguing novae.

He lived in the uneasy peace of the twenty-first century, when the world was an armed mechanical thing which seized upon a race to the stars as a means to absorb its overproduction while maintaining its technology.

The Gryce Expedition lit a fire in the boy Englehart which nothing could extinguish—nothing but his own incalculable energy, which he turned so strangely on it when he put it out. The epic is in error when it states that Gryce taught the boy; they never met. But Englehart followed Gryce's every move in the newspapers, on the air—by a prepathic device known as radio—and through more esoteric talks with astronomers who had fallen under the spell of his exuberant genius. Englehart's feeling for Gryce was an exaggerated hero-worship. When Gryce's interstellar drive was announced, it is said that the boy, then thirteen, burst into tears of joy; and when a professional writer dared to challenge Gryce's theories on the grounds that interplanetary travel had not yet been developed, and said that Gryce was a visionary and a mountebank, the youth traveled fifteen hundred miles by begging rides from travelers, and physically attacked the writer.

Gryce took off in his ship the *Falu*—so named from the initials of the society which built it, the First Antares League Union, and not, as Umber so flamboyantly put it, "In honor of the burning infant genius of Englehart." Englehart, whose given name was Samuel, took the name of Falu after the ship, for he identified himself completely with it, and wanted no one to identify him otherwise.

At eighteen Falu Englehart, purely by the violence of his own desires, secured a menial position with the Gryce Laboratories and soon was at work on the counterpart of the interstellar drive which had taken Gryce away—forever. Of his years with Gryce Laboratories there is little record, and it is a temptation to succumb, as Umber did, to the manufacture of such a record out of Englehart's prodigious enthusiasm and the act of his departure in his own ship, *Gryce,* thirty years later.

It is certain, however, that he clung to the hope that Gryce would return longer than anyone else alive, and that he transmuted his hope into a determination to follow, and find out what had happened to the great man. One may learn something of the utter dedication of Englehart's life by realizing that he regarded his own genius, which far outshone that of Gryce, as a secondary thing—perhaps a negligible one. But Englehart's talent was more than a scientific one; in the trouble days of the ship *Gryce's* departure, the lush days of government grants and popular subscriptions were over, and the union of local Antares Leagues had withered and died with the fading hope of Gryce's return. Somehow or other Englehart took the wreckage and leavings of Gryce's work and built with them; somehow he took upon himself the appalling task of financing the work; somehow he procured materials, met payrolls, and kept men working for him in the heat and light of his incandescent purpose.

When the *Gryce* was ready for launching, Englehart was nearly fifty years old, and in those days, fifty years marked the autumn of middle age. Umber's poetry sketches him vaguely, but gives me an impression of a tall, compelling man, a voice like deep music, eyes filled with the immensities. Actually, Englehart was a pudgy little man of fifty, nearly bald, unmarried—and this was not a difficult state to maintain for him or for the few women he met—and, for all his monomania, a gentle-spoken citizen save when he was crossed; and then his compulsion was not that of magnetism, but of sheer nuisance.

He was nearly as forgotten by the world as Gryce, at launching time, except for sensationalist writers who drew on his manifest folly for humorous material from time to time. There was a stir of interest when it was known that he was gone, and his epitaph was written in pity and laughter, and in one or two cases, with an expression of genuine respect for his astonishing dynamism. No one respected his purpose, his goal.

And then he did the most astonishing thing of his surprising life. He came back.

His ship materialized inside the orbit of Mars, causing a warping-eddy perilously close to a primitive exploring ship, one of those pioneer interplanetary reaction-drive contraptions that had been developed since Gryce's disappearance. Englehart himself made no calls, but the pioneers did, and Earth was ready for him when he warped in. He was welcomed as a hero, as a conquistador, a demigod. He was none of these. He was a man who, for half a century, should have been exhausted, but had never thought of it until now. It would seem that even the irony of his return, not only from the grave, but from obscurity, escaped him completely. He showed no emotion whatsoever except a dogged determination to destroy his ship, its drive, and everything pertaining to them; to spend the rest of his life in preventing mankind from ever again trying to reach the stars.

That he did this effectively, we know. For years he had had sole possession of the Gryce premises and records, and the men who had helped him and Gryce never had been able to understand, fully, the principles of the drive. Neither Gryce nor Englehart were teachers; they were doers, and apparently certain esoteric syntheses were done by no one else.

Englehart landed in the Chesapeake Bay in Old North America and was taken off, along with one of the two men who had gone with him—one of them had died on the trip—by the hysterically cheering crew of a towing-craft of some description. The *Gryce* was anchored, and Englehart was seen to lock the port with a magnekey. That same night the *Gryce* pulled her moorings, mysteriously took off out of control, and crashed into the ocean three hundred kilometers off shore. She apparently sank to the bottom and then exploded horrendously; nothing recognizable was ever found of her.

And, shortly after Englehart returned to the old Gryce plant, which had been under lock and key during his absence, there was an explosion and fire there which destroyed everything.

He made as few statements as he possibly could; the gist of them was that he had not found Gryce, though he still would not admit that Gryce was dead; that he had emerged from his drive "capsule" in a portion of space which he did not recognize, and had spent the entire four years of his trip in an attempt to find his way back; that certain one-in-a-billion combinations of space stresses had made his flight possible at all, that the odds were incalculable against its ever being done again. He published these statements along with a short thesis on the mathematical theory of his drive, and a series of patently sequential formulae which proved the drive impracticable, the directional control impossible, and his return miraculous. The mathematical philosopher who discovered his reasoning fallacious, and further proved that the fallacy was purposely brought into the calculations, was not born for another two hundred years, and by that time there was hardly industry left on Earth to produce a clock, much less an interstellar drive. We could build such a thing today, certainly; and certainly we shall not. And the debt we owe Falu Englehart is beyond measure.

This pudgy colossus had a crew of two, a man of forty named Horton or Hawton who was an engineer, and a creature called Gudge, who was apparently some sort of menial, a twisted being of great strength. What his background was is not known. He was feted on his return to Earth with Englehart; and little as Englehart said, Gudge said so much less that it was believed that he was deaf and dumb. This is not true. He was certainly warped in body and mind, a man of intense secretiveness, and the possessor of a mad philosophy of ego-isolation which is beyond understanding. He had one amusement, and until very recently no one ever suspected it. He wrote.

He had, apparently, the dexterity of those who write long passages of verse on grains of rice, and he must have been able to do it in the dark. Certainly Englehart never dreamed that he was doing it. If he had, Englehart would have come back alone. We must picture for ourselves the great, ugly hulk of Gudge, curled on his bunk around his knotted careful hands, while his stylus made studied, microscopic marks on enduring vellumplex. There must have been no detectable sound, and no motion but his controlled breathing and the tiny jumping of a muscle at the base of his thumb. Certainly it is a picture that Gudge never drew for us; no man ever had less to say about himself. And the events that led up to the entombment of the script, cast into a block of plastic that was carved, possibly by Gudge himself, into the only replica of the ship *Gryce* ever preserved—the concealment of the many sheets somewhere about his misshapen person, the risk he ran on leaving the ship with Englehart while carrying them, and his motivation in concealing them in an artifact that he knew would be preserved intact—these are things, also, at which we must guess. One wonders what the poet Umber would have done with the information. Gudge probably would have found his way into the epic as a doughty Boswell, and the murder of Hawton would have provided a fine counterplot of mutiny.

Much of Gudge's writing is maundering in his own idiom: without background or references, it is impossible to decipher. "They talked about loyalty," he wrote, near what, in order of pages at least, seems to be the beginning. "You do what you do because it is the last part of what you have done, and the first part of what you will do. Loyalty is the problem of minds which can think of stopping before the end, to take up something else after it has begun."

And "Gryce is a lover, pursuing the stars, and Falu, who never knew a mother, wants to be the mother of Gryce."

Between and among these extraordinary reflections, Gudge wrote enough about the trip so that a narrative emerges.

"Falu said to sleep in the ship. I thought there would be more boxes to pack but when I saw his face, his mouth so tight, his upper lip ballooning with the pressure inside, his eyes with bright tears in them behind the thick glasses, the glasses so thick the glass was frosted at the edges—why, I knew where we were going, and I did not ask about the boxes. I went into the ship and Hawton was there and Falu came after. And he did not take Pag and Freehold and the three Poynters, but locked the port. I saw them out there, understanding and frightened, and they ran away."

Who were these five, and where did they go? And had they thought they were to leave with the ship?

"The noise of the jets was always a terror; a scream first, and then a blowtorch, and as we moved, a great blowtorch in a barrel. I fell and was hurt. Horton came to me, holding to the corridor rails.

I could hear his hands crackling. He put me to a bunk, and straps. He strapped himself, too. We were very heavy."

So they blasted off—how far, and for how long, it is hard to tell. Probably it was a long time. There is a brief reference to Saturn "like two hats covering their mouths, one with another," and a period after that. Then there is one of the few references to Gudge himself, and his strange attitude. "Horton struck me, which did not hurt me and which made him foolish. He said I should have shown him the leg so it could be cured. I think a man should die if he cannot mend himself. Hawton put me on the bunk and with rays and a paste, mended me."

How long had it been—two months—three, since Gudge hurt himself on the takeoff? And yet he had no complaint to make then, nor when it got worse, nor when Horton struck him for it, nor when he treated the leg. One cannot help wondering whether Gudge was animal-like, abject, broken, or whether he had a strange, ascetic dignity.

"Falu put on the big ones. They started slowly, down in the belly of the ship, and Falu stood in the control room watching the meters. The big ones rumbled and rumbled, and though it never grew louder, it crept into the blood; the heart was pumping the rumble, the water we drank was full of the rumble, rumble.

"Hawton was white and sweaty. He put his hands on his temples and squeezed, and cried to Falu, 'Englehart, in Heaven's name, how much more of this do we have to take?' and Falu talked to the instruments and said, 'Not much more. We take off from the peak of one of these vibrations, but we've got to be vibrating in unison, or we'll never get together in one piece.'

"A gong sounded, and light flashed on the board. Falu reached and chopped off the ignition, and the jets were silent, which was a terrible thing, for it left the big ones shrieking. I could hear them, and I could not, and they seemed to be tearing my blood apart. Horton cried.

"Falu was wet but quiet. He braced his knees between the chart table supports and passed his hand over the spot of light."

(This was undoubtedly some sort of photoelectric control, installed in anticipation of the devastating effects of the capsule-entry on the motor center. It is remarkable that Falu could direct his hand to it at such a time.)

"Then we were blind," Gudge wrote, "and I heard them fall as I fell. We could not see and we could not move, but we were glad, because the silence was blessed."

There is a gap here in the narrative. Apparently some time—ship's time—passed, and their sight and motive power returned to them. Gudge wrote a great deal about the insubstantial appearance of everything aboard, and the changing shapes of utensils and stanchions. It would seem that Gudge's ordinary observations, even in normal space, were somewhat similar; that is, everything, to him, was wavering and distorted, and he was more fit to adjust to the strange conditions of an encapsulated ship. Englehart doggedly and stolidly went about the ship's business with a furious pretense of normalcy. There is no mention of Horton, and it is probable that he simply withdrew into himself.

And then they emerged. "Never was there such hurt," wrote the man who had not complained of a takeoff injury for months, "never such bathing in pain, such twisting and writhing. Hawton's arm tensed against itself and I heard the bone break. Falu sat at the chart table, his hands frozen to the edges, pulling himself on to it until thought he would cut himself in two. He screamed more than Hawton."

They lay in space for some time, recovering from the brutal transition. Near them was a reddish sun. In all likelihood it was Antares; it was for Antares that Gryce had set his course, and the one-time popular Antares Leagues had that star as their goal, once the etheric drift theory showed that for all its distance it would be easiest to reach. It is difficult to be sure, however, since there is no record of the capsule-time Englehart spent, nor any real indication of his temporal directions.

They fired up the reaction drive and began to move toward the sun. With the restoration of gravity, Horton found it impossible to keep his food down, and Englehart complained of a splitting headache. These conditions apparently continued until the return.

Englehart ate and slept and lived at his instruments. And one day—

"I brought him his broth, and just as I set it down, Falu's breath whistled suddenly, once, through a tight throat. He stared at the screen and cried for Horton.

"The screen was the large one for seeing ahead. It had colors. Space, outside the corona of the sun, was the color of a purple bruise, and beyond that black; and in the black floated a planet like Earth.

"But what made Falu cry out was the sight of the glimmering bowls, like parachutes without shrouds, which rushed toward us. I think there were seven.

" 'Ships!' shouted Hawton. 'Englehart—are they ships?'

"Falu said nothing then, but made us heavy as usual."

(This odd phrase probably means that he cut the drive to one Earth gravity.)

"The bowl-ships were in a single line, but as we watched, they deployed, the leader rising, the last dropping, the others flanking, until they approached us as a ring.

" 'They're going to box us,' Hawton said. He was frightened. Falu said, 'They can't, at our combined speeds. Watch.'

"He set the starboard jet to roaring, and the ring of bowl-ships began to march sidewise across the screen as we turned.

"But Falu was wrong. The ring of bowl-ships, quite unchanged, began to shift with us, and it seemed that the planet and the stars were moving instead, and that the ring was painted on our screen.

"Falu shook his head and peered at them through his thick glasses. 'How can they do it without killing everyone aboard them?'

"Horton said something about overcoming inertia. He said that perhaps there was nothing alive aboard the ships. He glistened with fear.

"When the ring of ships was centered on our screen again, Falu put his hand to the board and drove us harder so that we were heavy again. The ships began to grow, the ring widened, but with nearness. Falu said, through closed teeth, 'Then we'll go through them. Turning like that is one thing; to stop and follow is something else again.'

" 'They'll fire on us,' Hawton whimpered. 'Falu—use the capsule drive!'

Falu snarled like an animal, and his voice was like a whip for animals. 'Don't be stupid. It takes three days to build up resonance for the capsule. They'll be on us in an hour. Sit down and be quiet.'

"The ships grew and the ring widened until we could see the markings on their silver sides, red and blue, and the triangular openings around their bottom edges. Falu clicked on the small screens—sides, above, below—as we entered the ring.

"And at the instant we entered the ring, there were two ships above us, and two high on each side, and two low on each side, and one beneath—and they stayed with us. They approached us, they stopped and reversed to go with us, all in that instant of surrounding.

"Falu tried his forward jets, and then one side and the other, but the ring of ships stayed around us. They had no jets.

"And then, in the next hour, the ring began to shift, with those high on the right coming closer to us, and those low on the left moving away. Falu watched them, leaving his controls alone, while Hawton danced about him, mouthing advice. Falu did not answer him, but at last called me. 'Gudge—get him out of sight.' I went to Horton and pointed to his bunk room. He pushed me away. I hit him on the neck and put him on the bunk. I was careful of his broken arm. I think the pain he had been through had soured him through and through, like old warm milk.

"Falu waited and watched, while the ships above came closer and closer, and those below on the other side drifted away. Falu muttered, 'They'll crash us if they keep that up.' And closer they came, and Falu watched them and I stood behind him, watching, too.

"At last Falu grunted and turned to his controls. The near ships seemed close enough to touch with the hand. Falu jetted away from them, down and away to the center of the ring. And it happened that that put the nose of our ship again on the planet; and now the ring of ships stayed equally distant from us as we drove toward this new world. Twice more in the next twenty hours Falu tried to change course, but each time the strange ships led us back toward the planet.

"Hawton cried to be freed. Falu told me to unstrap him. Hawton was angry. He told me he would kill me if I ever touched him again. I said nothing and thought my own thoughts. He went to the control room and stared silently at the screens. Falu said, 'Try to keep your head, Horton. Those ships want us to go to the planet. We were going there anyway; Gryce probably went there, too. So far these ships have made no hostile move except to keep us on course. They outnumber us and there is nothing we can do but go along with them.'

"Horton looked at the screens and trembled, and said nothing about the ships at all. Instead he said 'What did you bring that stupid slug along for?' He meant me.

"Falu said, 'Because he does his work and he keeps his mouth shut. Try it.' I knew then that Horton would hate me as long as he lived. He went to the settee by the port bulkhead and sat there with this arms folded around his hate."

There follows, in Gudge's account, another of those indeterminate periods of idiomatic reflection, in which Falu Englehart, Horton, and the lost Gryce expedition have no part. Probably some days passed, in which there was little to do except wait until they reached wherever it was that the bowl-ships intended to take them. Perhaps nine days passed—it may have been more. In any case, Gudge interrupted in mid-sentence an extraordinary series of thoughts on the similarity of his reactions to sound and to color: "They say all anger is red. Anger is not red while Red is peace in a bright light with your eyes closed—" to write:

"It looked like Earth at first, but not as blue. There were ice-caps and seas, and many clouds. Falu turned the magnescope on it, and when it could find rifts in the roiling clouds, valleys could be seen, and mountains, and once a rapid river. There were cities, too. I saw no life in them.

"The bowl-ships forced us around the planet. Falu said we were in a closed orbit. We stopped using the jets, and drifted weightless around the planet.

"Two of the ships fell away from the ring and dropped toward the blue world. Before them a great green light fanned out, and where it touched the clouds they were gone. Down and down they went, circling around each other and destroying the clouds beneath us until we could see perhaps a quarter of a planet.

"The planet had a burned face. Burned and pitted and twisted, gouged out, melted, blasted. For miles around a boiling hell-pit which threw molten gobs of rock high in the air, the land was sere and smoking. The planet had a face like my face. The two ships came back up to airlessness, and clouds swirled in and mercifully covered the planet's face.

"The two ships flashed past us, spacewards, and the other five began nudging us to follow. Falu ignited the jets, and Horton, who was taking courage now, helped him trim the ship to keep it inside the ring formation. They talked of the blasted planet, wonderingly. Earth had never seen such a cataclysm.

" 'They showed it to us,' breathed Falu. 'They just showed it to us, and then took us away. Why? Who are they? Why don't they attack or free us? Why have we never seen ships like this in our System? Their science—' and he fell silent, awed. Falu was awed."

Falu's awe is the only thing on which Gudge expresses astonishment. Apparently it shook Gudge to his roots, sending him off into a wild metaphysical orgy on the subject of constancy in the universe, and the half-dozen things he had felt he could rely upon to remain unchanged—the color of interstellar space; each man's threshold of pain; what he called "the touch of greenness"; and two other items which are abbreviated and undecodable. If Gudge were not completely mad, he had a set of sensitivities completely alien to any human norm.

At this point in his narrative it is necessary to fill in certain movements which must have occurred, unmentioned by the chronicler. For his next mention of their trip describes four of the five escort ships deployed in a square before them, with the fifth above, and the other two holding a body, "a rock as big as our factory on Earth" between them by orange beams of light. These must have been the two ships which went down to disperse the clouds, and which led the flotilla out from the planet. Apparently they went to capture this asteroid and bring it to a rendezvous in space. At the rendezvous, the seven ships were motionless in relation to the *Gryce*.

"The four ships made a square, perhaps two miles on a side. There was a dim purple glow from a single plate on each side of each ship, and from this purple spot a blackness gathered and spread. Whether it was gas or dust or a substance, we could not tell. It reached out from the four ships, filling the square of space between them, blotting out the stars, until it lay like a great black blanket in space.

"And then lights appeared on the expanse of blackness—a yellow triangle, a red circle, a series of coruscating amber lines, moving and merging, writhing about, forming mosaic and kaleidoscopic patterns. We were all three spellbound, watching them, and this, apparently, was what the aliens wanted of us.

"For they began to show us pictures, and never have there been such pictures, such blendings of color and proportion. The black velvet of the screen on which they were projected—or which projected them to us—lent a depth that made the screen more a vast window through which we looked at happenings, rather than a mere picture. I could understand why Falu cried out wordlessly and leapt to his feet when the designs faded away and were replaced suddenly, brilliantly, by the picture that had burned in his brain since he was a downy youth; for here, with colors and depth, was the shape of his dream.

"A ship. An Earth ship.

"The *Falu* herself.

"She was shown from behind and above, gleaming and beautiful, and before her were the edge of the red sun and the cloudy planet we had seen.

"We saw the planet come nearer, but with the action speeded up so that it swelled visibly, and we understood that this would be a re-enactment of what had happened to the *Falu*.

"Until the planet was a great curving mass filling the lower half of the picture, the *Falu's* broad shining back was in the foreground, but now it receded from us, curving down and away toward the clouds. And suddenly the picture was gone.

"It was replaced by another view of the cloudy sphere, and in a moment there was a rift in the clouds through which we saw a valley, not brown like the ones we had actually seen, but green and lush. There was a river set about with groves of feathery trees, and there were rolling fields under cultivation. Some of these were blood-red, some fallow, some pale blue with blossoms. It was a rich and peaceful valley.

"The view followed it upstream. There were boats on the water, moving rapidly without sails or turbulence in their wakes, and soon there was a city.

"It was a low, wide city of low, wide houses, not crowded together like Earth cities, but parklike. The water's edge was not bunioned with cramped and rusty sheds and quays, but forest and lawn. We could see the prim openings here and there into which towboats and barges slipped into the bank and disappeared, probably to underground terminals.

"The view, the camera-eye, swept down into the city and slowed, as if one were driving through the wide streets. As it swung from side to side, we saw the planet's people.

"They were not human. They were bipeds with strange flexible legs having two knee-joints each. Their arms were set low on their bodies, and were jointed differently from those of humanity, bending up and downward like the claws of a mantis, rather than down and forward like the arms of a man. Their heads and faces were tiny and grotesquely human, except for the placement of ear-flaps where cheekbones should be. Their bodies extended downward past the hips, terminating in a flattened point on which they sat, bracing themselves with legs folded to make a three-point support; they used no chairs.

"They were busy people. We saw pictures of them making metal beams in great automatic forges, growing food in tanks, and making paint and tools. There were beds of truly gorgeous flowers, and parks in which were shapes of stone that must have been sculpture, though none resembled the people; but people walked among them.

"Through the city the pictures took us, and it was a wondrous thing. It made one realize that this was a people completely in command of itself; that it used its resources and did not abuse them; that the stretches of wild country we saw around the city were so because the people wanted it so, and not because there was any frontier which they could not conquer.

"Outside the city again the pictures showed us a wide expanse that at first view seemed to be an airfield; indeed it was so, but it was something more. There were launching cradles on which rested great ships—ships ten times the size of the *Falu* and the *Gryce,* though of roughly the same pattern; and in addition were the bowl-ships, a row of perhaps thirty of them. There were some small ones, but most of them were two hundred feet or more across.

"Then, in a beautifully synthesized picture diagram, we saw one of the ovoid ships leave its cradle in a cloud of flame, and mount the sky; and behind it appeared a silver dotted line, while the whole picture contracted as if the camera were leaping away from the planet, back and back, until it was a ball again, and the dotted line showing us the course of the ship; and still back and back, until the red sun itself was a small disk and the cloudy planet a dot, and the dotted silver line reached outward until it touched another planet.

"And suddenly, making us gasp with the brilliance of it, the same dotted silver lines appeared throughout a system of the red sun and seven planets—a great silver network of them.

"Hawton said, 'I don't understand.'

"Falu Englehart growled at him, without turning his face from the screen, 'Their commerce, stupid. They're showing us that they have a highly developed space commerce.'

"The pictures changed again; again we saw the spaceport, and the aircraft, and the rocketship ramps, and the camera swung to show us the bowl-ships. One of them lifted; but here was no screaming flame, no gout of dust. Here was simply the balloonlike lifting of the whole sweetly curved structure of the ship, up and up into the iridescent sky. And now there was a golden dotted line; and again we had the breathtaking recession from the planet. But this time it was a greater one; this time it left the red sun, and the stars about it rushed together, until we saw a whole segment of the galaxy, thousands of suns. And yet the golden line went out and out, until at last it touched a blue-white star. And then there was a network again, this time golden, and so vast that one wanted to cry. For the whole galaxy seemed woven together with a fabric of golden threads.

"Hawton snorted. 'I don't believe it. That simply can't be. They're lying to us. If they had a commerce like that, we'd have had them on Earth thousands of years ago.'

"Falu said, 'Wait.'

"The cosmic picture winked out, and after a moment of that total blackness, we saw again the picture of Gryce's ship, the *Falu*, spinning down into the clouds of the planet we had visited.

"As she entered the gaseous envelope, a flame appeared, purple, but blue-white at the center, around the *Falu*. And in a moment, the whole side of the planet seemed to open outward in one furious, hellish blast. Falu grunted and covered his eyes against that terrible radiance, and Horton closed his and wrinkled up his face, turning away.

"Down and down the picture-eye took us, to the infuriated clouds. It swept us along the valley we had seen before, and as we reached the same city street, we saw the people stop in the shops, in the factories and parks, and turn as one to the sky. A great glare, purple and white, filled the scene, and the ground came up once, twice, again, hurling the people off their feet, bringing the buildings down on them. Here an inhabitant holding two young ones was crushed; there another fell into the gaping mouth of a crack in the Earth, which closed on him.

"Out we were taken, to the spaceport. We saw a rocket blast off just as its cradle crumpled, and the ship wavered, turned, and crashed into the row of bowl-ships. Great ravines appeared on the smooth landing area; and then we saw, in the distance, a gleaming cliff that was not a cliff, but a towering continent of water, rushing toward us. So real was this that as it approached the picture's foreground, we all found ourselves in our own control cabin, shaken and looking at each other foolishly.

"Now the picture was of the planet again, back and back from the planet with its ravening scar, back to show the whole system of the red sun. Again we saw the silver network, and part of the greater, golden one; and where they based on the cloudy planet, those lines dimmed and died out, until at last the planet lay deserted, alone, unwanted, and dead.

"Once more the picture brought us to the planet, only briefly, to show up again the wrack and ruin, the burned, broken, murdered thing that we had seen before with our own eyes, when the two bowl-ships had opened the clouds for us. And then the great screen went dark.

" 'I don't understand,' whispered Hawton. 'Gryce went to that planet and something happened, something that—'

" 'Wait,' Falu said again.

"And now the two bowl-ships which bore between them, on beams of orange light, the great rock which was as big as our factory on Earth, came forward. They swung the rock between us and the strange black screen steadied it, and their orange rays disappeared. The ships withdrew to a point above us.

"There was a picture again on the huge screen, a picture of our ship, seen from a point just at the other side of the floating rock. We saw, at the side of the image of our ship, a movement, as something came from it toward the rock. It drifted out until it touched the rock, and just before it touched, we saw it was a piece of metal, a block. Then the picture disappeared, to be replaced immediately by the same scene, the only difference being that the object, when it came near enough to see, was a metal disk. Again the picture disappeared and repeated itself, but this time the object which came from our ship was a cube.

"Again and again this was repeated, this scene of some object being projected from our ship to the rock, and each time the object was different. Sometimes it was metal with a silver or golden luster, and sometimes it was a smaller piece of rock, and sometimes a red or green or yellow lump of plastic. I understood what they wanted of us, but said nothing."

(Why did Gudge never, or almost never, speak?)

"Falu, watching this reiteration for the twentieth time, said, 'They want us to do something. They want us to throw something out to that rock. I wonder what exactly they want us to throw?'

"And Hawton said, 'From the looks of those pictures, it might be almost anything.'

"Falu said, 'Well, let's throw something. Gudge—'

"But I had already gone, as soon as Falu said he wanted it done. In the after storeroom was a dense roll of insulex for space repair. There was more. It weighed four hundred pounds on Earth, but nothing here, of course. I cast off its buckle-clamps and brought it out to the disposal chute. Beside it I put a pressure-bottle of carbon dioxide. Then I waited. Falu came aft to watch me, and said, 'You know, Gudge, sometimes I wonder just where the limits of your mind are. Yes, I'll turn the ship.' He was always surprised when I understood anything before he did. Hawton was never surprised. He forgot it, time and time again, because he wanted to.

"With the steering jets Falu gently nudged the ship over so that the disposal lock pointed directly at the rock. As soon as his jets appeared, the pictures on the black screen ceased, and all of the ships around us withdrew perhaps a hundred miles, in a single instant.

"I put the roll of insulex and the bottle in the disposal lock, tripped the trigger on the bottle, and slammed the inside port as the carbon dioxide began whistling out. In a moment the bottle was empty and the lock full of gas under pressure. When Falu had steadied the ship and called out to me, I turned the valve that opened the outer port, and with a *whoosh* the gas swept out, taking the insulex with it. Then I went to the control room and stood again behind Falu, where I could see the forward visiscreen.

"The bulky roll turned slowly end over end as it flew, in the spot of light that Hawton kept on it with the pistol-grip control over the chart table. It needed no light when it struck, though—

"And I thought it was going to miss! It barely touched, and yet—

"Before us, we saw a miniature of what had happened to the cloudy planet—a miniature, because it was only a roll of insulex and a fragment of rock compared with the mass of the *Falu* and an entire planet. But it was a miniature close to our eyes, too close. Had we known, we could have put the filters up over the viewing cells; at least we could have looked away.

"In the split second before the cells went out, we got a flash of that white and purple radiance that was knives in our eyes, and then blindness, for our ship and for us. And I know that as I lie dying I shall carry still a tattered shard of that frightful brilliance in my old eyes. In that moment there was nothing to do, no thought to pass, no move to make but to claw at the eyes which had captured and held white flame behind their lids.

"It was an hour before we could see dimly again, and six before we could ship new cells on the forward and low starboard viewers.

"And there on the restored screen we saw the seven bowl-ships, patiently and passively waiting some sign from us. Falu shoved the trembling, red-eyed Hawton aside and grasped the searchlight grip. 'I want the rest of it,' he said. His face was deeply scored, pouchy. The loss of his dream of finding Gryce was as much as he could bear—all the burden he could ever carry. Anything else he might learn would be a small thing indeed. He blinked the light.

"The four bowl-ships had restored, or rebuilt, the great screen. Again we saw the shifting patterns and mosaics, which were apparently their 'ready' signal. And then there were more pictures.

"First a picture of our roll of insulex and the rock, and then, in that bewildering fashion, the picture became a diagram. The roll of insulex turned into a glowing ruby color, ran together, separated into two blobs which in turn became two cubes. They approached each other, touched, separated, touched again, separated and were still.

"Then the rock was shown, and it turned a shimmering yellow; and it, too, ran together into a formless mass, separated into two cubes. And these too, came together and moved apart.

"Next, all four cubes were shown, the two red and the two yellow, the red above, the yellow below; and a red and yellow cube changed places. A red cube moved and touched a yellow—and both dissolved in ghastly, glaring flame. And again, the remaining yellow cube moved and touched the red one, and they married in purple-white violence and were gone. And Falu breathed, 'I think I see—'

"The pictures then repeated the scene of Gryce's ship, the *Falu*, approaching the cloudy world. And then the scene was frozen into a still photograph, and the *Falu* turned the same glowing red as had the insulex, while the planet was shown in the shimmering yellow.

"The red ship moved down to the yellow planet and devastated it.

"We were then shown a picture of our own ship as it released the insulex. Ship and insulex turned red as the rock fragment and the bowl-ships turned yellow; and when our red property touched the yellow rock, the hell was loosed again.

"And now we saw the great expanding chart of the galaxy, and on it again were superimposed the shining networks of dotted gold and silver lines, showing the wide commerce of these people. And suddenly every sun and planet was the shimmering yellow—every one, except for a scattering of red here and there near the edges of the galaxy.

"The eye of the camera moved to one of these red spots, expanded it, and we saw Sol and her planets, all untouched by the shining network, and all of them but the retrograde moon of Uranus, in glowing ruby.

"We saw a new kind of dotted line, the deadly red this time, leave the third planet, and followed it across the corner of the universe to the cloudy planet, and saw for the third time the picture of the *Falu* plunging into the deadly clouds.

"After that, the black screen dissolved and the seven ships took up their ring position around us again.

"Slowly, with sick hands, Falu Englehart fired the jets and swung the ship about. Hawton cried, 'What are you doing?'

"Tiredly, Falu said, 'Going back, Horton. Back.'

"Hawton ran to the screen. 'They'll kill us! They'll kill us!'

"Falu glanced briefly at the seven ships. They were not moving. Still in a ring, they were motionless, letting us leave them behind. 'They'd kill us if we went toward their planets, or any other sun in the universe but Sol—or one or two others. They won't kill us if we go home. They wanted us to know what we are. They've known it for ... for eons. And they want us to go home and tell our people. The fools!' he spat suddenly. 'Gryce surprised them. They didn't know we had advanced as far as capsule-flight. Gryce did it, and I followed, and they judge all humanity by Gryce. They don't know, they just don't know—"

"Hawton said he only partly understood. 'I mean, I know that when we contact them, there is an insane violence; but why? Why?'

" 'They're contraterrene,' said Falu.

"Hawton grunted in surprise. 'I thought that was simply an idle amusement for theoretical physicists.'

"Falu waved at the screens. 'You saw.'

" 'Contraterrene,' Hawton mused. 'Matter with the signs transposed—atoms with negative nuclei, and positive satellite-shells. And when terrene matter comes close, the whole thing becomes unstable and turns to energy. *Falu!* Were they telling us that the whole universe, except Sol and a few other outer-edge stars are contraterrene?' I think that only at that moment had Hawton received the full impact of what he had seen with his own eyes.

"Falu simply nodded tiredly.

"And they have commerce—galaxy-wide commerce, and civilizations on every habitable planet, while we—"

" 'We're in the corner. Excommunicado. Left to our own devices, as long as those devices don't bring us to contact them,' Falu finished."

With the bland *non sequitur* quality of his writing, Gudge here departs from the narrative, in a welter of thoughts of his own. He looked on Englehart and Horton—(Hawton?)—with new eyes; indeed, he seemed to regard all of humanity in a new way. He himself had always lived "in Coventry"—out of contact with those around him; and he seemed to take a certain pleasure in the chance to regard all mankind as in the same position. These long and gleeful passages contain nothing of the events which followed, except for one brief and important scene:

"Falu had told him and told him not to say it again, but he did. He shrieked at Falu. He said, 'You must tell the world, Falu! You'll be great, don't you see? Terrene beings can rule the galaxy. What science would the Contraterrene peoples share with us, to appease us? What man could fail to see the advantage of his unique position, when every stone he throws can be an atomic bomb? Let us build a fleet of Gryce-drive capsule ships, and go out and demand equality in the universe!'

"Falu said, 'Hawton, for the last time—for really and truly the last time—the Earth isn't ready for this yet. What you suggest would have one of two results; if we succeeded, which isn't likely, we would only bring terror and destruction into a highly organized, peaceful universe—just as we have brought it on ourselves repeatedly. The other and more likely result is that before we could launch our ships, the Contraterrenes would wipe us out. There will be no more picture-shows. We have already killed a planet; in return they gave us some information about ourselves which we had not known. The next time we make a move toward them, they will destroy us with a clear conscience. I don't doubt for a moment their ability to hurl a planet the size of Earth into Sol, and then you know what would happen. You've studied supernovae.'

" 'You're an idealistic child,' Hawton screamed. 'And if you won't tell the world, I will.'

"Falu squinted up at him through his heavy glasses. He saw, I think, the beginnings of fanatic purpose in the man. 'Gudge,' he said.

"I went to him. He pointed his finger at Hawton, and said, 'Gudge, kill him.'

"So I did, with my hands, very quickly, and put him into the disposal lock and turned the valve.

"When I came back Falu looked at me strangely. 'I suppose I should kill you, monster,' he said. 'Can I rely on your not talking?'

"I said nothing. Suddenly he shrugged. 'I'd give a whole lot to know what goes on in that ugly head of yours. If I wanted to kill you, I don't believe you'd try to stop me. Right?'

"I nodded, pitying him a little, for he was thinking about loyalty and wondering why I had given him mine; he did not know that one goes on doing what one is doing, and never stops."

And that is how, according to the sheets found in a carven spaceship model, Samuel Falu Englehart made his journey, and how he saved us from certain doom at the hands of those who are perfectly willing to leave us alone. Now we can know the story, for we are grown and no longer acquisitive, and have our farms and our minds, and can bridge space telepathically, wherein there is no valence.

Prodigy

MAYB, CHIEF GUARDIAN for the Third Sector of the Crèche, writhed in her sleep. She pressed her grizzled head into the mattress, and her face twisted. She was deep in slumber, but slumber could not keep out the niggling, soundless, insistent pressure that had slipped into her mind. Sleep was as futile a guard as the sheet which she instinctively pulled up about her ears.

"*Mayb!*"

She rolled over, facing the wall, her mind refusing to distinguish between the sound of her name in the annunciator and this other, silent, imperative, thing.

"*Mayb!*"

She opened her eyes, saw on the wall the ruby radiance from the annunciator light, grunted and sat up, wincing as she recognized consciously both summonses. Swinging her legs out of the bed, she leaned forward and threw the toggle on the annunciator. "Yes, Examiner."

The voice was resonant but plaintive. "Can't you do something with that little br—with that Andi child? I need my sleep."

"I'll see what he wants," she said resignedly, "although I *do* think, Examiner, that these midnight attentions are doing him more harm than good. One simply does not cater to children this way."

"This is not an ordinary child," said the speaker unnecessarily. "And I still need my sleep. Do what you can, Mayb. And thank you." The light went out.

There was a time, thought Mayb grumpily, as she pulled on her robe, when I thought I could shield the little demon. I thought I could do something for him. That was before he began to know his own power.

She let herself out into the hall. "Subtle," she muttered bitterly. Sector One, where children entered the Crèche at the age of nine

257

months, and Sector Two, into which went those who had not fallen by the wayside in eighteen months of examinations—they were simple. The mutants and the aberrants were easy to detect. The subtlety came in Sector Three, where abnormal metabolisms, undeveloped or non-developing limbs or organs, and high-threshold reactive mentalities were weeded out by the time they got there and behavior, almost alone, was the key to normality.

Mayb loved children, all children—which was one of the most important parts of being a Guardian. When it became necessary for her to recommend a child for Disposal, she sometimes stalled a little, sometimes, after it was done, cried a great deal. But she did it when it had to be done, which was the other part of being a good Guardian. She hadn't been so good with Andi, though. Perhaps the little demon had crawled farther into her affections—at first, anyway—with his unpretty, puckish face and his extraordinary coloring, his toasted-gold hair and the eyes that should have belonged to a true redhead. She remembered—though at present it was difficult to recall a tenderness—how she had put aside the first suspicions that he was an Irregular, how she had tried to imagine signs that his infuriating demands were temporary, that some normal behavior might emerge to replace the wild talent for nuisance that he possessed.

On the other hand, she thought as she shuffled down the hall, it may seem hard-hearted of me, but things like this justify the Code of the Norm. Things like this can be remembered when we have to send some completely endearing little moppet into the Quiet Room, to await the soft hiss of gas and the chute to the incinerator.

Mayb reacted violently to the thought, and wondered, shaking, whether she was getting calloused in her old age, whether she was turning a personal resentment on the child because of this personal inconvenience. She shook off the thought, and for a moment tried not to think at all. Then came the shadow of a wish for the early days of the Normalcy program, two centuries before. That must have been wonderful. Normalcy came first. The children went into the crèches for observation, and were normal or were disposed of. Homo superior could wait. It was humanity's only choice; restore itself to what it had been before the Fourth War—a mammal which could predictably breed true—or face a future of battles between mutations which, singly and in groups, would fight holy wars on the basis of "What I am is normal."

And now, though the idea behind the program was still the same, and the organizations of the crèches were still the same, a new idea was gaining weight daily—to examine Irregulars always more meticulously, with a view, perhaps, to letting one live—one which might benefit all of humanity by his very difference; one who might be a genius, a great artist in some field, or who might have a phenomenal talent for organizing or some form of engineering. It was the thin end of the wedge for Homo superior, who would, by definition, be an Irregular. Irregulars, however, were not necessarily Homo superior, and the winnowing process could be most trying. As with Andi, for example.

Holding her breath, she opened the door of his cubicle. As she did so the light came on and the ravening emanation from the child stopped. He rose up from his bed like a little pink seal and knelt, blinking at her, in the middle of the bed.

"Now, what do you want?"

"I want a drink of water and a plastibubble and go swimmin'" said the four-year-old.

"Now Andi," Mayb said, not unkindly, "there's water right here in your room. The plastibubbles have all been put away and it isn't *time* for swimming. Why can't you be a good boy and sleep like all the other children?"

"I am NOT like the uvver children," he said emphatically. "I want a plastibubble."

Mayb sighed and pulled out an old, old psychological trick. "Which would you like—a drink of water or a plastibubble?" As she spoke she slid her foot onto the pedal of the drinking fountain in the corner of the tiny room. The water gurgled enticingly. Before he was well aware of what he was doing. Andi was out of bed and slurping up the water, with the cancellation of his want for the plastibubble taking root in his mind.

"It tas—tuz better when you push the pedal," he said charmingly.

"Well, that's sweet of you, Andi. But did you know I was fast asleep and had to get up and come here to do it?"

"Thass all right," said Andi blandly.

She turned to the door as he climbed back on the bed. "I wanna go swimmin'."

"No one goes swimming at night!"

"Fishes do."

"You're not a fish."

"Well, ducks, then."

"You're not—" No; this could go on all night. "You go to sleep, young fellow."

"Tell me a story."

"Now Andi, this isn't story telling time. I told you a story before bedtime."

"You tol' it to everybody. Now tell it to *me*."

"I'm sorry, Andi, this isn't the time," she said firmly. She touched the stud which would switch the light off when she closed the door. "Shut your eyes, now, and have a nice dream. Good night, Andi."

She closed the door, shaking her head and yawning. And instantly that soundless, pressurized command began yammering out, unstoppable, unanswerable. Telepathy was not a novelty nowadays, with the welter of mutations which had reared their strange, unviable heads since the Fourth War; but this kind of thing was beyond belief. It was unbearable. Mayb could sense the Examiner rearing up on his bed, clapping his hands uselessly over his ears, and swearing volubly. She opened the door. "Andi!"

"Well, tell me a story."

"No, Andi!"

He rolled over with his face to the wall. She could see him tensing his body. At the first wave of fury from him she cried out and struck herself on the temples. "All right, all right! What story do you want to hear?"

"Tell me about the bear and the liger."

She sat down wearily on the bed. He hunkered up with his back to the wall, his strange auburn eyes round and completely, unmercifully, awake.

"Lie down and I'll tell you."

"I do-wanna."

"Andi," she said sternly. For once it worked. He lay down. She covered up his smooth pink body, tucking the sheet-blanket carefully around him in the way she sometimes did for the others at bedtime. It was a deft operation, soothing, suggesting warmth and quiet and, above all, sleep. It did nothing of the kind for Andi.

"Once upon a time there was a bear who was bare because his mother was radioactive," she began, "and one day he was walking along beside a neon mine, when a liger jumped out. Now a liger is half lion and half tiger. And *he* said,

"'Hey, you, bear; you have no hair;
You're not normal; get away there!'

"And the bear said,

'You chase me, liger, at your peril
You're not normal because you're sterile.'

"So they began to fight. The liger fought the bear because he thought it was right to be natural-born, even if he couldn't have babies. And the bear fought the liger because he thought it was right to be what he was as long as he could have babies, even if his mother was radioactive. So they fought and they fought until they killed each other dead. And *that* was because they were both wrong.

"And then from out of the rocks around the neon mine came a whole hundred lemmings. And they frisked and played around the dead bear and the dead liger, and they bred, and pretty soon they had their babies, a thousand of them, and they all lived and grew fat. And do you know why?"

"What was they?"

"Lemmings. Well, they—"

"I want some lemonade," said Andi.

Mayb threw up her hands in exasperation. You can't cure an Irregular by indoctrination, she thought. She said, "I haven't finished. You see, the lemmings lived because their babies were the same as *they* were. That's called breeding true. They were Nor—"

"You know what I'd do if I was a bear without any hair?" Andi shouted, popping up from under the covers. "I'd rear back at that old liger and I'd say don't touch me, you. I hate you and you can't touch me." A wave of emotion from the child nearly knocked Mayb off the bed. "If you come near me, I'll make your brains FRY!" and with the last syllable he loosed a flood of psychic force that made Mayb grunt as if she had walked into the end of an I-beam in the dark.

Andi lay down again and gave her a sweet smile. "Thass what I'd do," he said gently.

"My!" said Mayb. She rose and backed off from him as if he were loaded with high explosive. The movement was quite involuntary.

"You can go away now," said Andi.

"All right. Good night, Andi."

"You better hurry, you ol' liger you," he said, raising himself on one elbow.

She hurried. Outside, she leaned against the door jamb, sweating profusely. She waited tensely for some further sign from within the cubicle, and when there was none after minutes, she heaved a vast sigh of relief and started back to her bed. This was the third time this week, and the unscheduled nightwork made her feel every one of her twenty-eight years of service to the Crèche. Fuming and yawning, she composed herself for what was left of her night's sleep.

"Mayb!"

She twitched in her sleep. *Not again,* said her subconscious. *Oh, not again. Send him to the Quiet Room and have done with it.* Again she made the futile, unconscious gesture of pulling the covers over her head.

"Mayb! Mayb!"

The annunciator light seemed fainter now, like the slight blush of a pale person. Mayb lowered the covers from her face and looked at the wall, blinked, and sat upright with a squeal. Her eye fell on the clock; she had to look three times to believe what it told her. "Oh no, oh no," she said, and threw the toggle. "Yes Examiner. Oh, I'm so *sorry!* I overslept and it's three whole hours. Oh, what shall I do?"

"That part's all right," said the speaker. "I had your gong

disconnected. You needed the sleep. But you'd better come to my office. Andi's gone."

"Gone? He can't be gone. He was just about to go to sl—oh. *Oh!* The door! I was so distraught when I left him; I must have left the door unl ... oh-h, Examiner, how awful!"

"It isn't good," said the speaker. "Essie took over for you and she's new and doesn't know all the children. So he wasn't missed until the Free Time when Observation 2 missed him. Well, come on in. We'll see what we can do." The light went out, and the toggle clicked back.

Mayb muttered a little while she dressed. Up the corridor she flew, down a resilient ramp and round to the right, where she burst into the door over which the letters EXAMINER drifted in midair. "Oh dear," she said as she huddled to a stop in the middle of a room which was more lounge than office. "*Dear* oh, dear—"

"Poor Mayb." The Examiner was a beaming, tight-skinned pink man with cotton hair. "You've had the worst of this case all along. Don't blame yourself so!"

"What shall we do?"

"Do you know Andi's mother?"

"Yes. Library-Beth."

"Oh, yes," the Examiner nodded. "I was going to look her up and vize her, but I thought perhaps you'd rather."

"Anything, Examiner, anything I can do. Why, that poor little tyke wandering around loose—"

The Examiner laughed shortly. "Think of the poor little people he wanders against.. Uh—call her home first."

Mayb went to the corner and wheeled the index to the Library designations, found the number and spoke it into the screen, which lit up. A moment later its blankness dissolved away like windblown fog, to show a young woman's face. She was the true redhead from whom Andi had his eyes, that was certain.

"You remember me," said Mayb. "Crèche-Mayb; I'm Andi's Sector-Guardian."

"Uh-huh," said the woman positively.

"Is ... is Andi there?"

"Uh-uh," said the woman negatively.

"Now Beth—are you sure?"

The woman wet her lips. "Sure I'm sure. Isn't he locked up in your old crèche? What are you trying to do; trick me again into signing that paper to have him put in the Quiet Room?"

"Why, Beth! No one ever tried to trick you! We just sent you a report and our recommendation."

"I know, I know," said the woman sullenly. "And if I sign it you'll put him away, and if I don't sign it you'll appeal it and the Examining Board'll back you up. They always do."

"That's because we're very careful. Guardians—"

"Guardians!" snarled Beth. "What kind of Guardians let a four-year-old child wander out of the Crèche?"

"We are not guardians of the children," said Mayb with sudden dignity, "we are Guardians of the Norm."

"Well, you'll never get him back!" screamed Beth. "Never, you hear?" The screen went black.

"Is Andi there?" The Examiner's eyes twinkled.

"My goodness," murmured Mayb. "My, my goodness!"

"I wish the predisposal examinations had never passed the Board. If it weren't for them, this would never have happened. Why, ten years ago, we'd have quietly put the little fellow out of the way when we found he was an Irregular. Now we have to wait three weeks, and poke and prod and pry to see if the irregularity can possibly turn into a talent. I tell you, it'll break the crèches. The mother of every last freak on earth is going to cry that her little monster is a genius."

"Oh, if only I hadn't been careless with that silly old door!" She wrung her hands.

"Mayb, don't get worked up. It'll be all right. I'm sure it will."

"You're so nice!" Her voice was shockingly loud in the still room. "Oh dear! Suppose that woman really does hide him? I mean, suppose she takes him away? Do you realize what it will be like if that child is allowed to grow up?"

"Now that is a terrifying thought."

"Think of it! He already knows what he can do, and he's only four years old. Think of those radiations of his grown up man-sized!

Suppose he suddenly appeared, grown up, in the middle of a city. Why, when he wanted anything, he'd get it. He'd *have* to get it. And he couldn't be stopped! He can't be reached at all when he does that!"

The Examiner took her arms and gently led her to a mirror on the wall. "Look at yourself, Mayb. You know, you don't look at all like the fine, reliable Guardian you are. Suppose Essie saw you now; you'd never be able to teach her a thing. I'm head of the Crèche. That's a privilege and there's a certain amount of worrying I have to do to earn it. So let me do the worrying."

"You're so good," she sobbed. "But—I'm *afraid!*"

"I'm afraid, too," he agreed soberly. "It's a bad business. But—don't worry. Tell you what. You just go and lie down for a while. Cry yourself out if you want to—it'll do you good. And then go on with your work." He patted her on the shoulder. "This isn't the end of the world."

"It might be," she gasped, "with creatures like that loose in it, forcing and pressing and pushing and not to be stopped until they had what they wanted."

"Go on now."

She went, wringing her hands.

It was almost exactly the same time the next morning when Mayb was summoned from the Assembly Room where she was teaching her children to sing

> "There was a young fellow called Smitti
> Who lived in an abnormal city.
> His children were bugs
> And two-headed slugs,
> Oh, dear! What a terrible pity!"

and in the midst of the children's shrill merriment at Smitti's comic predicament, she got the Examiner's call.

The thin veil of laughter fell from her face and she rose. "Free time!" she called. The children took the signal as a permission to play; the hidden watchers behind one-way glass in Observation 1 and 2 bent toward their panes, Normalcy Reaction charts at their elbows.

Mayb hurried to the Examiner's office. She found him alone rubbing his hands. "Well, Mayb! I knew it would be all right."

"It's about Andi? You've found him? Did you get the police?"

"She got them." He laughed. "She got them, herself. She just couldn't take it—his own mother."

"Where is he?"

"She's bringing him ... and I'll bet that's her, right now."

The door swung open. An Under-Guardian said, "Library-Beth, Examiner."

Pushing past the underling, Library-Beth entered. Her flaming hair was unkempt; her face was white and her eyes wild. In her arms she carried the limp form of Andi.

"Here he is ... *here!* Take him; I can't stand it! I thought I could, but I can't. I didn't know what I was doing. I'm a good citizen; I want to do my duty; I care about the law, and the Norm, and the race. I was crazy, I guess. I had a thing all made up to tell you, about Andi, about him surviving, that was it—he can survive better than anyone else on earth, he can; he can get anything he wants just by wanting it, and no one can say no to him, not so it makes any difference to him." It poured from her in a torrent. She put the limp form down on the settee. "But I didn't know it was like this. And he badgered me all night and I couldn't sleep, and he ran away in the morning and I couldn't find him, and he hated me and when I saw him and ran to him he hated me with his mind, more and more and more the nearer I got, so that I couldn't touch him, and people gathered round and looked at him as if he was a monster, and he is, and he hated them all, every one of them. And somebody got a policeman and he threw sleep-dust, and Andi made a hate then that made everyone cry out and run away, and he hated everyone until he fell asleep. Now take him. Where is that paper? Where is it?"

"Beth, Beth, don't. Please don't. You'll flurry everyone in the place, and all the children."

"Where's the paper?" she screamed, joltingly. It made Mayb's ears ring.

The Examiner went for the form, handed two copies and a stylus to Beth. She signed them, and then collapsed weeping into a chair.

"M-mayb?" The voice was faint.

"He's waking up. Quick, Mayb. Take him to the Quiet Room!"

Mayb scooped up the child and ran, kicking the door open. Two doors down the hall was a cubicle exactly like all the other cubicles, except that it had a black door. And certain concealed equipment. This time she did not forget to press the door until it was locked. Gray with tension, she went back to the office. "All right, Examiner."

The Examiner nodded and stepped swiftly to his button-board. He pressed a certain button firmly, and a red light appeared.

"Andi!" Beth moaned.

Mayb went to her and put her arms around her. "There now. It's for the best. This doesn't happen much any more. We used to have to do it all the time. Soon we'll never have to do it again."

The Examiner's expression was bitter, and sad, too. Minority victims don't give a damn for statistics, he thought.

Mayb changed her approach. "Beth, we're getting our norm back. Think—really think what that means. Humans used to live in complete confidence that they would be real, hundred per cent humans, with all the senses and talents and abilities that humans can have. And we're getting that back! It's a pity, a thousand times a pity, but it has to be done like this. There is no other way!"

Her carefully chosen thoughts could not override the mental pressure which began to squeeze at them from somewhere—from the Quiet Room.

The light on the board turned yellow.

"Andi—"

"And it's a good norm," thought Mayb desperately, "chosen in a congress of the most wonderful, objective minds we have ever had on earth. Why, some of them weren't normal according to the Code they drew up! Think how brave—"

The agonizing, yammering call blared up, dwindled, flickered a moment, surged again and was suddenly gone. Through Mayb's mind trickled the phrase "in at the death." She knew it came from the Examiner, who was standing stiffly, his face registering a harrowing repulsion. He turned abruptly and threw a lever. The incinerator was fed.

"Don't cry. It's better this way," Mayb radiated to the weeping woman. "It's better for him. He never could have been happy, even if men left him alone. Poor, poor unfinished little thing—imagine the life he'd have, always able to speak, never to know when he shouted or screamed, and never being able to hear except with his ears—the only nontelepath in the whole world!"

Farewell to Eden

THERE WAS NOTHING in his mind but a warm blackness, or perhaps a very dark redness. There was a field of it in which he was lying, a sheet of it over him; the field reached from his back into infinity and the sheet was as thick as the universe. The darkness was in his eyes and in his lungs, in his bones. He was part of the darkness, inside and out, through and through.

He could never know how long it was that he stared at the spot of light before he realized that it was there. There was no way of telling how large it was—or how small—how near or how distant. It was vague; it had no discernible limits, no edges. It grew until it was an oval patch of clear yellow light in the surrounding darkness.

And at last it was more than a patch of light; it was a hole in the darkness through which he could see. He saw a mechanical elbow, a housing from the ends of which two metal arms extended down and into the impenetrable darkness beside him. The arms were moving rhythmically.

Something was fraying the edges of the oval hole. A translucent border ate away at the darkness, continuously feeding the patch of clear light, slowly pushing back the darkness.

And then he began to feel—a surge of sensation, a tickling, prickling wash of feeling. It had the rhythm of the moving metal arms. It was pins-and-needles, "my foot's asleep," the seed of unconsciousness in the lungs of a man being gassed. It was comfort and agony; as it grew and as it faded he wanted to laugh, but when it was at its peak he wanted to scream.

When at last he could see everything around him he did not know when it was that the widening hole had become the real world, spreading to his horizons and beyond, having eaten and eaten at the dark until the last round speck of black had ceased to exist somewhere behind him, far, far out in infinity.

The housing above him with its pair of moving arms was only one of many, one of eight. The sixteen arms reached down to his body. At their ends were padded packages of something—something which pulsed and tingled—and the arms were making these packages massage his skin, back and forth, down and back, over and over, with the same firm pressure, the constant rhythm. This rhythm paralleled the washes of prickling agony, of tickling pleasure.

He was lying on his back, naked. His body was free. Either he could not move it or he did not think of trying. His head was clamped; he felt a padded band on each side. Suddenly this seemed an affront, an insult. He moved his head—and was rewarded by a stab of anguish which came, not from within him, a protest of disused muscles, but from outside, from the head-clamp.

He did not try to fight it. Lying quite still he felt four thick needles being withdrawn from the back of his neck, easing a pressure he had not known was there. When they were gone he began to suffocate.

The light dimmed. The spot of red-blackness reappeared and grew, spreading fast—much faster than it had left him. Now it was his horizon—now its edges were an oval before him—now they had enclosed the housing above his head. With the growth of the darkness a pressure that became a pain grew into a tearing agony, unbearable. All the pain and all the fear that had ever been, since the beginning of time, sat on his chest.

To move it, to get away from it, to stop that deadly agony, he breathed.

When he drew in the first breath the darkness stopped growing. When he breathed again the oval of light widened and the pain lessened. With yet another breath, the oval widened again and stopped, and the pain became even less. With each breath he drove back the darkness. So he breathed more deeply, a little faster. It became easier to do as the darkness and the pain fled away from him, to his horizons, back and around behind him somewhere, dwindled to a patch, a spot, a speck—and ceased to exist.

He laughed then, and moved his head confidently against the clamps. They broke and fell away—

The inside of his mouth, his tongue and his teeth, were ice-cold. The rest of his body was warm—too warm on the outside, around a core of cold. Having laughed and moved his head, he fell asleep, still on his back, but with his head turned sidewise and a smile on his lips. The arms, with their pulsing, tingling pads, kept working while he slept.

The veil of sleep had thinned about him and was easily torn by the breath of laughter which awoke him. He opened his eyes and lay looking, seeing nothing but the laughter—it was gone, but he could see it: a rushing of golden steps; veined gold, the veins full of wind-whispers, for it was not a completely voiced laugh, but partly an alive, joyful expulsion of unwanted pressure.

At first he thought it was the memory of his own laugh, but on looking, as it were, at the fingerprints of the laugh—on the particular sensory impressions the sound had made he found them not in his throat, as if he himself had made it, but in his ears.

He sat up. Blood roared in his head. Blackness closed, filmed, and cleared away. He raised his head and saw that the metal arms were folded up out of the way now, motionless. He was on a complicated bed, over which was a great transparent hood. This had separated at his right and a second had slid downward—a section the full length of the bed. It was an invitation, and though he was conscious of no desire to move, he reacted to the fact of the open door. He swung his legs out and sat on the edge, and began to tremble with weakness. He looked around.

There were three lights, two of which he could see, the third one under a deep shade. One was over his head, one on the wall, the shaded one between him and the wall, flooding another bed like his with light. On it the eight pairs of metal arms were moving rhythmically, the pads at their ends pressing and caressing a woman. It seemed that the pressure of them went down into the body, coating itself like a paint on the bones, layer on layer, and he knew, somehow, that these layers were life, and that when they were thick enough to include the skin the whole woman would be alive. It must be, he

271

thought (in a way which was not thought at all) that a part of her must have been alive before the pads started moving, so that they would have something on which to lay their paint. She must have been—the alive part—only a wire woman, a line drawing of living threads, one for each arm, one for each leg, one for the torso, and a knot for the head.

She was naked. Her body was young and firm. It interested him only as part of the moving unit, with its padded arms stroking and pressing. He slid off his bed to the floor, cushioning his fall with knees and hands. His elbows refused to hold him up and his chin went almost to the floor. He stayed there for a moment in an equilibrium like that of his first breath, when he had stopped the darkness but had not yet driven it back. Then, as he had done before, he threw off the discomfort and straightened his elbows, his back straining to help. He dragged himself across the floor and squatted back on his haunches to watch.

To watch, he had to hold his head up higher than normal. It hurt to do this and he began to tremble again, but for a long, tense period—three minutes, four perhaps—he watched. The pads moved on her feet, pressing and stroking; at every third stroke one would sweep around and run up the sole of her foot, from heel to toe. Another pair tended her calves, one inside, one outside. The flesh beneath them swelled and hollowed, swelled and hollowed into complete quiescence while the inside pad made its special trip—one in every fifth movement—over her kneecap. There was a pair of pads for each thigh, running from the knee to the hollow of her groin, and a pair which danced around each other to alternate with them on the groin then to follow upward to the lower ribs and back. Another pair swept between her breasts and downward, around to the back and up to the ribs, where the others had finished; every twelfth stroke pressed downward from her collarbones to her solar plexus, ignoring the route around to her back.

He watched in wonder. After a short while his head sagged. He turned it, and fell asleep again, squatting his cheekbone on his knee and the top of his head against the side of the woman's bed.

It was another sound that awoke him the next time. Again he

opened his eyes and looked for it, found it and examined it, though it was gone. Again he failed to find the imprint of it in him anywhere, and he understood, too, that it was not from the woman. The laugh— the second one—had been hers; he knew that. This new sound came from neither of them.

He raised his head and, doing so, swayed forward. He put out an arm to keep from falling, and the act further awakened him.

The woman was lying beside him, sprawled brokenly on the floor. She looked at him and away, looked around her—and back to him again. She lay as if she had done what he had done—as if she had left her bed and slid to the floor. But she had not crawled; she lay there beside him, taking in the room, his bed, herself, and him.

"*Gowry*"

That was the sound, coming again. It did a strange thing to him. He looked for the source of the sound. He could not find it, but inside he—recognized something: those syllables meant something of surpassing importance, but he could not determine what it was—

"*Gowry!*"

He looked for the source of sound and could not find it. He saw that the woman was looking at him.

"*Gowry!*"

He looked again—and saw it. It was a cone, its wide mouth pointing at him, its throat a smooth, bland disc of metal. He turned to the woman, and she was looking at him.

There was a silence. He thought, *When it says "Gowry" I look for the sound and she looks at me.*

"*Gowry*"

He looked at the cone quickly, and then at the girl. The thing had spoken and he had looked at it, but she had looked at him.

He said, "Gowry." His mind reached out, comprehension close—

"Gowry—" the woman faltered.

He nodded. He understood now—he was Gowry.

"Gowry?"

His breath hissed out in response; he drew in more and tried again: 'Yes-s-s," he said. "Yes." Then: "Yes, s-s-silf—Tilsa—Tilsa."

"Tilsa," said the woman.

They were quiet for a moment, looking at each other. The cone said, *"Tilsa!"*

She looked at the cone, and he looked at her. He understood immediately that she was Tilsa. She was Tilsa; he was Gowry.

He put out his hand, and she looked at it. He was not yet strong enough to hold it up; it fell to the floor beside her, and she stared at it. Then, swiftly, unexpectedly, sleep overcame her.

For a long while he squatted there, looking at her; then he slept too.

He awoke with an awareness of something within himself. He lay with his eyes closed, relaxed and receptive. He knew, somehow, that he was strong now, that if he moved he would not tremble—knew it so well that he did not have to try to move.

There was a skin full of knowledge within him—a thin skin, stretched tight by the knowledge it held. The knowledge swirled and swelled, stretching the skin tighter and more transparent every second. He saw things inside the skin—

A bearded face. A clutter of rusty, crumbled ruin. A flight of dart-shaped aircraft, with a sound to them like a blow-torch in a barrel. The sun shining on rolling green lawns, and, repeatedly, black, star-spangled space in which a cloudy planet floated. The tones of a voice were there too, circling and weaving amid the swirling knowledge. The voice meant something to him. Suddenly he knew what it was; it was the voice which had said, *"Gowry!"* and *"Tilsa!"*—the voice from the cone. It was not his voice; it belonged to a thing—a person, someone who knew him, knew Tilsa, too—everything about them.

"Gowry—"

He opened his eyes. Tilsa was awake, still lying on the floor, looking at him and smiling. He was on his bed; he must have dragged himself back to it in the beginnings of sleep.

Suddenly, harshly, he said, "Be quiet." He hardly realized he had used the words. Her call had punctured the skin of knowledge within him; it burst and flooded his mind, a bewildering deluge. He shut Tilsa out with his voice and eyelids, to be alone with the knowledge again.

The bearded face was—Alan. Alan was Tilsa's father. He was dead. The ruined cities were dead. The flights of dart-like aircraft had killed them. The rolling green lawns were outside his room— was it a room? Wasn't it more a machine, some kind of equipment?

The room, or machine, was by itself, away from all the world, carved out of a forest on the floor of a deep ravine in mesa country. The ravine was deep, wider at the bottom than at the top, most secret. He remembered sunlight on the lawns because they used to snatch at it, he and Tilsa, as it whisked by day after day, for their hurried half hour of basking as the stripe of sunlight swept finger-like over their hidden buildings.

The world was mad. The world was an insane worm, toothed and hating itself. It broke itself in two, in four, in eight, and each part was toothed and hating itself and all the other parts. Each part fought, biting and tearing at itself and the parts of itself in a fury of immolation. The worm was man, a species destroying itself, a race destroying itself; a culture, a nation, a city—a single human being snapping and snarling at his internal selves.

"But you'll be saved," Alan had said. "The radioactive dusts will soon be filtering down to us, even out here. You can imagine what it must be in the cities. Most of them will die, most of those who don't will be sterile, and probably the few who can breed won't breed true. But you will, you and Tilsa; you'll do it—*there.*"

"There" was the cloudy planet, afloat in space. Its clouds were not like the ones here, its atmosphere held different elements, poisonous to the animals of Earth. They would have been to Gowry and Tilsa too, then—before their long sleep, the longest sleep any humans had ever slept; before the tireless, meticulous workings of their bed-machines. Their bodies had "stopped" completely, through and through, and then the cells had been altered, each a little, to rest awhile, and then to be altered a little more.

Now they were—and were not—Gowry and Tilsa, even as any human, in seven years has completely replaced every cell of his body and is—and is not—the same. But the replacement in Gowry and Tilsa was an adjustment to another environment, even to a slightly different gravity. They were aliens on Earth now, as a ship is an alien—a manufactured alien—when it lies completed and as yet dry in the launching ways.

Gowry sat up, swung his legs to the floor, and stood up, stretching. He felt the good muscles of his back and thighs. He flexed and watched his fingers. "I remember," he said simply.

Tilsa shaped her mouth around words: "I—remember—too."

"Alan, and—the ship, Tilsa—the ship!"

"Yes, it's up there." She pointed at the ceiling.

He laughed. "He did it—Alan did it!"

Tilsa rose, feeling air—the new kind of air—in her lungs, feeling the new way her body obeyed. "Wasn't there a—something we had to do first?"

"I don't remember," he said. "Where's the ship?"

He cast about him; there was a door with a great stainless-steel bar across it. He lifted against the bar, and immediately the flat-throated cone spoke:

"Have you read the book?"

"That was it—the thing I couldn't remember!" Tilsa cried.

The book was on a shelf under the wall light. They pounced on it. Its opening words were in very simple language, as if written for the benefit of young children: *You, man, are Gowry. You, woman, are Tilsa. Read this book. Do not go out of this room until you have read this book.*

There were tests to be made on themselves, and on the air. There were solutions to be mixed from the racks of stores they found. There was much to be learned, but they learned it with increasing ease; they had learned it all once before, prior to their long sleep. It was an engrossing study, and they slept twice before they finished it. And then they opened the door.

Outside was a corridor to another closed door. On the wall hung two heavy suits, with transparent spherical helmets. Eagerly they climbed into them, inspected each other's fastenings. Then they closed the door behind them and opened the one ahead.

The Earth's air swirled in. They could see the water vapor in it with their new eyes; the air seemed turgid, misty. It frightened them a little, for they knew it was choking poison to them now.

They crossed a narrow gully to a place where two low mounds, rounded and covered with brush, stood against a rock wall. They looked at the mounds, appalled.

"They were pylons," Gowry breathed. "Tall, square pylons—"

"How many years?" asked Tilsa, expecting no answer.

Shrugging off his sudden sadness, Gowry took a tool from his belt and pressed a stud on the side of it. Blue flame licked out and washed over the cliff between what was left of the pylons. The deposits of years crumbled away under the lash of flame, and suddenly a great square section cracked and toppled toward them. They jumped back as it crashed and broke. Gowry put away the tool.

Before them was still another door. Gowry pressed it with his gloved hands, kicked it once with a heavy boot, and it swung open, admitting them to a shaft. They switched on the lights built into their suits, their beams shooting forward and upward.

A stainless-steel ladder took them up perhaps fifty feet to a room built off the side of the shaft. At this point the shaft was roofed by the banked tubes of the ship, and the room gave access to the ship's side. The ship seemed to fit in the shaft like a piston in its cylinder.

They entered the open port and, by means of the controls inside, swung it shut. There was the distant hum of machinery as the air in the lock was replaced with the atmosphere they had been readied for. Gowry's gloved hand touched Tilsa's and, suddenly overawed, he grasped it. It was such a long way they had come—and yet the journey was only beginning—

A green light flashed on, and the inner door swung open. They stepped into the ship. "It's all right," said Gowry, nodding toward the green light, and began to remove his suit.

They hung the suits carefully on the clips which had been built for them. For a moment they clung together, trembling. Then they mounted to the control room in the ship's nose, and found another book, a thick one.

"Remember?"

"Yes," she nodded. "Fuel, food, water, air; jet tests, star sights, course computations— We are going to be busy."

Gowry looked around the compact control room with learning, re-learning eyes. "Let's get to it," he said.

Two days later they had learned their ship and themselves, and had tested themselves and their ship. With every small step of progress they felt an increasing awe of Alan, and of the thing he had built. They remembered his words: *"Mankind is accursed everywhere. It must start anew, in a place which it has not burned over and ruined."*

His words awed them, but even more the nature of his work awed them, for he did it knowing that he would never see the result, for a purpose transcending the two lives he was saving—saving and re-creating. He had done it as an act of faith in a creature which had violated every faith ever put in it. . . .

A rock-fall had damaged the great winch designed to raise the ship up through its tunnel until it could break through the surface of the mesa above them. They worked shoulder to shoulder to repair it, and at last had their craft with its nose to the outer air. They took their star sights, and found that in just four days they could blast off, hurl themselves free of Earth's gravity, and run out to intersect the orbit of their new world.

They used the time to examine a tired planet and its graves, and the horrors that were worse than graves—mankind's living dead. With a tight-beam scanner they ranged the surface, throwing on a screen pictures of places near them, and of places far away.

"It's a sunny place," Tilsa observed, watching the screen. It seemed they had seen so little of the sun; they had been very young when they first came to the mesa.

"Look!" tore from Gowry's throat.

They saw a cliff, cave openings. Creatures squatted around a fire at the foot of the cliff. They were short and broad, their torsos as long and thick as Gowry's, but their legs seeming to have no thighs— short, stiff, thick, ending in enormous, flat, toeless feet. Some of them moved about slowly, their feet in a grotesque, shuffling dance; one or two, approaching faster from a distance, vaulted along on their knuckles, making crutches of their arms.

Burning and sputtering on the coals of the fire was—one of their own. They tore off handfuls of the hot, half-raw meat, gnawing at it with yellow fangs.

Gowry's throat was thick with nausea. "Humanity's children," he whispered, and spun the control to blank the screen. "What the world must have gone through while we slept," he mused, "to have such things fit to survive here."

"Look some more," said Tilsa. Her face was rapt, half-hypnotized with revulsion. "We should know—we should find out everything we can—"

Reluctantly Gowry turned to the controls again, scanning the Earth. He stopped briefly here and there. A ruined, grave-quiet city. A road, beautiful in its narrowing course, but with its surface crumbled and overgrown. Deserts where crawling giant weeds had choked out all life, including their own. Then came the picture they were never to forget.

"Tilsa—a different kind!"

They saw a house, seemingly of metal, in rolling country near wooded mountains. It was hexagonal, quite low, with a shining, peaked roof. There were creatures near it—two of them.

They were tall, slender, blue-hued, with long heads and curved, muscular tails. They ran out into the sun in great, graceful leaps. They stopped, hand in hand, brought their free hands to touch too, and their tails curved up over their heads until they touched each other. They stood there in this curious contact for a long moment.

"Why—how beautiful!" cried Tilsa.

Then, from the foot of the meadow in which they stood, like a spilling over of some foul container, came a mass of the short-legged humanoids. The crutch-like sweep of their long arms advanced them with terrifying speed as they crowded up the slope—

"Look out! Run!" Gowry shouted at the screen, uselessly.

The blue creatures stood, oblivious of their danger, until the leaders of the horde were on them. They did not appear to resist. There was a swirl of motion, a piling up of the ravening humanoids, and it was over. One by one, they crept away from the snarling mob, bearing grisly blue fragments which they tore to bits with their teeth—and spat out.

"No more," Tilsa said faintly. "No more—"

Gowry turned off the set and sank down beside her. "What for?" he said, as if to himself. "What did they do it for?"

"They saw a difference," she said, her eyes agonized. "Mankind has always pulled down and destroyed anything that is different. Even if the differences are slight, they will be sought out. Alan used to say that if there was just one human left on earth he would kill himself because of the differences he would find in his own thought."

"It won't be that way with us," he said quietly.

"No, it can't be—it can't."

Their time came. The automatic machinery clicked and hummed and purred about its many tasks. Gowry fed a punched card into the course integrator and switched it on; the ship would blast off at the precise instant for which it was set.

They strapped themselves into the acceleration chairs, side by side. Moving his hand spiderwise against the restraining fabric, Gowry edged it over until it touched Tilsa's. To his surprise, she pulled away.

"Don't," she said. "You make me think of those blue ones—"

The jets thundered and they hurtled away; the great shaft fell in on itself under the battering thrust of the flames.

They both blacked out. When Gowry came to he was aware first of his laboring heart and the great pressure which lay upon him. At seven gravities, his limbs weighed hundreds of pounds; his eyeballs ached and his heart all but groaned its protest. He forced his eyelids open and looked ahead, and his heart began to beat more strongly, exultantly—before him was the majesty of interstellar space, a bejeweled purple curtain.

Eight and a half hours later the acceleration cut down to a more comfortable two and a third gravities. Breathing was easier, and they could talk. But they said little, instead lying in the chairs, drinking in the wonder before them.

The days fled, marked only by the clock, by hunger and sleep. Once Tilsa spoke of the blue beings: "I wish I had never seen them. I wish I didn't know about the part of humanity that kills for nothing."

"Think of this ship," he told her, "of that part of humanity that made Alan do this work."

"Waste," she murmured. "That's the sin of it—the waste. Oh, the songs men have sung, the fine and beautiful things written and painted and built—all come to ruination—" She wept. "Oh, the waste—"

"Humanity's trademark," he said bitterly. "Stamped, sooner or later, on all of man's works."

She stroked the edge of the instrument panel. "Not all," she pleaded; "not all—"

They made their planetfall with Gowry at the manual controls. Round and round the cloudy globe they went, the braking rockets roaring, until at last the outer skin of the ship trembled to a high screaming—atmosphere. They plunged through it and out again, letting it check their speed but not taking enough to burn them, meteor-like. He threw out blast after blast from the forward jets and they entered the atmosphere again, lost it, took it, held it—and began to spiral in.

He kicked in the six gyro-controlled supporting jets, which blasted down and outward. They settled, until they were in the white sea of cloud around the planet. Blinded by it, they turned on the scanner and coupled the supporting jets to the radar altimeter. They passed a mountain range, and another, and a long series of foothills, and a great sea. And at last, in the radarscope, they saw a coast.

Gowry slid the ship in toward it. He touched the water; the ship porpoised with a grinding wrench, settled and skipped again, rode the surface until it slowed enough to displace some of its weight. Huge sheets of spray whipped out, and the ship floated. Gowry kicked it forward with the jets, driving it confidently up onto the beach, where it stopped and rolled a little to the right, to lie still like some great sea animal.

"Beautifully done, darling!"

"Thanks," he said proudly. "It wasn't anything you could work up to—had to be done right the first time. Are you running the atmosphere tests?"

"All done, while you were piloting in." She held up a phial of purple fluid. "It reacts perfectly—and Alan's gravity, magnetic-density, and radio-active indices all check. Let's go out!" she caroled.

"The suits—"

"Damn the suits, darling—we're *home!*"

Laughing, they ran to the airlock, waited impatiently for the outside door to open. As it rolled back, Gowry caught her wrist.

"No, you don't," he said, checking her as she was about to leap. "We go into Our House like this," and he swept her into his arms and stepped through the port, dropping easily to the ground beneath.

"Put me down!" she commanded. "I want to run!"

He let her go and she was off like a deer, into the mist. Shouting delightedly, he sprinted after her. He caught her on a knoll, a little hummocky island of ground in the surrounding mist. He pressed her to him, capturing her laughing mouth with his lips. . . .

There was something near them in the fog. He raised his head, holding her tight, and saw it settle down through the air a little way off—something big, angular, metallic—

A house—a hexagonal house, he wondered mutely; *like the blue people's house—but this is a ship—and* their *house was a ship, then; and they—*

Out of the hexagonal ship tumbled scores of them: blue people—but blue people dwarfed and transformed, with knotty little tails and shambling limbs, without the leaping grace, their beauty warped and gone—

It was over in seconds. One by one the blue mutants crawled away, spitting out the torn, bloody fragments.

One Foot and the Grave

I was out in Fulgey Wood trying to find out what had happened to my foot, and I all but walked on her. Claire, I mean. Not Luana. You wouldn't catch Luana rolled up in a nylon sleeping bag, a moonbeam bright on her face.

Her face gleamed up like a jewel sunk deep in a crystal spring. I stood looking at it, not moving, not even breathing, hoping that she would not wake. I'd found that horror of a skull ten minutes ago and I'd much rather she didn't see it.

She stirred. I stepped back and sideward into a bear-trap. The steel jaws were cushioned by my heavy boot; they sliced through from instep to heel, but did not quite meet. All the same, it was a noise in the soughing silences of the wood, and Claire's eyes opened. She studied the moon wonderingly for a moment because, I presume, her face was turned to it. Then she seemed to recall where she was. She sat up and glanced about. Her gaze swept over me twice as I stood there stiff and straight, trying to look like a beech. Or a birch. I must be of the wrong family. She saw me.

"Thad ..." She sat up and knuckled her eyes. Claire has a deep voice, and meticulous. She peered. "It—*is* Thad?"

"Most of me. Hi."

"Hi." She moved her mouth, chewing, apparently, the end of sleepiness. She swallowed it and said. "You've been looking for me."

"For years," I said gallantly. That might have been true. At the moment, however, I was in pursuit of my foot, and possibly some peace and quiet. I hadn't counted on this at all.

"Well, Lochinvar, why don't you sweep me into your arms?"

"I've told you before. You're everything in the world I need, but you don't strike sparks. Go on back to bed."

She shook her hair, forward, out and down, and then breathtak-ingly back. She had masses of it. In the moonlight it was blue-gray, an obedient cloud. "You don't seem surprised to find me out here."

"I'm not. The last thing I said to you in town was to sit tight, stay where you were, and let me handle this. The fact that you are here therefore does not surprise me."

"You know," she said, putting one elbow on one knee, one chin in one palm, and twinkling, "you say 'therefore' prettier than any-one else I ever met. Why don't you come over here and talk to me? Are you standing in a bear-trap?"

She was wearing a one-piece sunsuit. It was backless and side-less and the summer flying suit, hanging on the bush at her head, plus the light nylon sleeping bag, were obviously everything in the world she had with her. About the bear-trap I said, "Well, yes."

She laughed gaily, and lay back. Her hair spread and spilled; she burrowed into it with the back of her head. She pulled the sleeping bag tight up around her throat and said, "All right, silly. Stand there if you want to. It's a big boudoir."

I said nothing. I tugged cautiously at the trap, moving just my leg. The boot all but parted; the moon gleamed on the steel jaws, now only an inch apart and closing slowly. I stopped pulling. I hoped she would go back to sleep. I hoped the trap wouldn't clank together when it finally went all the way through. I stood still. There was sweat on my mouth.

"You still there?"

"Yup," I said.

She sat up again. "Thad, this is stupid! *Do* something! Go away, or talk to me or something, but don't just *stand* there!"

"Why don't you just go on to sleep and let me worry about what I do? I'm not in your way. I won't touch you."

"That I don't doubt," she said acidly. "Go away." She thumped down, turned away, turned back and sat up, peering. "I just thought ... maybe you *can't* ..." She flung out of the bag and stood up, slim in the moonlight. I could see her toenails gleam as she stepped on the fabric. Her right toenails, I mean. Her left foot wasn't a foot. It was a cloven hoof, hairy-fetlocked, sharp and heavy. She was as unselfconscious about it as she was of the casual coverage her sun-suit afforded her. She came to me, limping slightly.

"Go on back to—let me al—oh for Pete's sake, Claire, I'm perfectly—"

She breathed a wordless, sighing syllable, all horror and pity. "Thad," she cried. "Your—your *foot!*"

"I didn't want you to know."

"How could you just *stand* there with that—that— Oh!" She knelt, reached toward my trapped foot, recoiled before she touched it and stayed there looking up at me with her eyes bright in the silver light, silver tear-streaks on her face like lode-veinings. "What shall I *do?*"

I sighed. "Keep your fingers away from the trap." I leaned back and pulled. The macerated leather of my high-laced hunting boot held, gave, held—and then the jaws whanged together, close-meshed. I fell back against a birch-trunk, banging my head painfully. Claire, seeing almost the entire foot dangling under the arch of the trap's jaws, started a shriek, then jammed it back into her mouth with her whole hand. I grunted.

"Oh," she said, " you poor *darling!* Does it hurt?" she added inanely.

"No," I said, rubbing my skull. "It was just my head . . ."

"But your foot! Your poor foot!"

I began unlacing what was left of the boot. "Don't bother your pretty little head about it," I said. I pulled the boot-wings aside and slipped my leg out of boot and woolen stocking together. She looked, and sat down plump! before me, her jaw swinging slackly. "Shut it," I said conversationally. "You really looked beautiful a while back. Now you look silly."

She pointed to my hoof. It was larger than hers, and shaggier. "Oh, Thad! I didn't know . . . how long?"

"About three weeks. Damn it, Claire, I didn't want you to know."

"You should have told me. You should have told me the second it started."

"Why? You had enough on your mind. You'd already been through all the treatment that anyone could figure out, and I was in on all of it. So when it happened to me, I didn't see the sense in making a federal case out of it." I shrugged. "If Dr. Ponder can't cure this no one can. And he can't. Therefore—"

Through her shock, she giggled.

"Therefore," I continued, "there was nothing left for me to do but try to find out what had happened, by myself." I saw her lower lip push out before she dropped her face and hid it. "What's the matter?" I asked.

"I—kind of thought you were trying to help just me."

Claire can switch from giggles to tears, from shock to laughter to horror to fright, faster than anyone I ever met. It goes all the way down too. I said, "Don't kid yourself. I don't do things for people."

"Well," she said in a very small voice, "that's what I thought, for a while anyway."

"You better get back in that sleeping bag. You'll catch cold," I said.

She rose and crept obediently back to the sleeping bag. Once into it, she said, "Well, you'll care if I catch cold."

I went and hunkered down beside her. "Well sure. I might catch it."

"You wouldn't get that close!"

"Oh, I don't know. I read somewhere that a sneeze can travel thirty feet."

"I hate you."

"Because I sneaked out behind your back and got a fancy foot just like yours?"

"Oh, Thad! How can you joke about it?"

I sat back and lifted my hoof, regarding it thoughtfully. I had found it possible to spread the two halves and relax suddenly. They made a nice loud click. I did this a couple of times. "I'd rather joke about it. How frantic can you get?"

"Thad, Thad ... It's my fault, it is, it is!"

"Uh-huh. That's what I get for playing footsie with you in roadhouses. You're contagious, that's what."

"You're no comfort."

"I don't comfort stupid people. This isn't your fault, and you're being stupid when you talk like that. Does yours itch?"

"Not any more."

"Mine does." I clicked my hoof some more. It felt good. "What gave you the idea of coming out here?"

"Well," she said shyly, "after you said you'd track this thing down for me, but wouldn't say how, I thought it all out from the very beginning. This crazy trouble, whatever it is, started out here; I mean, it developed after I came out here that time. So I figured that this is where you'd be."

"But why come?"

"I didn't know what you'd get into here. I thought you might—might need me."

"Like a hole in the head," I said bluntly.

"And I thought you were doing it just for me. I didn't know you had a foot like that too." Her voice was very small.

"So now you know. And you're sorry you came. And first thing in the morning you'll hightail it straight back to town where you belong."

"Oh no! Not now. Not when I know we're in this together. I like being in something together with you, Thad."

I sighed. "Why does my luck run like this? If I got all hog-wild and feverish about you, you'd turn around and get short of breath over some other joker. Everybody loves somebody—else."

"You're thinking about Luana," she said with accuracy. Luana was Dr. Ponder's typist. She had taut coral pneumatic lips, a cleft chin, and a tear-stained voice like that of an English horn in the lower register. She had other assets and I was quite taken with both of them.

"If I were as honest about my feelings as you are about yours," I said, "and as loud-mouthed, I'd only hurt your feelings. Let's talk about our feet."

"All right," she said submissively. "Thad . . ."

"Mm?"

"What did you mean when you said you'd seen me be beautiful?"

"Oh, for Pete's sake! Skip it, will you? What has that to do with feet?"

"Well. . . Nothing, I guess." She sounded so forlorn that, before I could check myself, I reached out and patted her shoulder. "I'm

287

sorry, Claire. I shouldn't brutalize you, I guess. But it's better than stringing you along."

She held my hand for a moment against her cheek. "I s'pose it is," she said softly. "You're so good ... so good, and—so sensible."

"So tired. Give me back my hand. Now; let's put all this fantastic business together and see what comes out. You start. Right from the beginning, now; somewhere, somehow, there's got to be an answer to all this. I know we've been over it and over it, but maybe this time something will make sense. You start."

She lay back, put her hands behind her head, and looked at the moon. She had to turn her head for this, because the moon was sinking, and there were knife-edges of light among the cords of her throat. "I still say it was the night I met you. Oh, don't worry; I won't get off on that again ... but it was. You were just a face among faces to me then. A nice face, but—anyway, it was the Medusa Club meeting, the night we got talking about magic"

"I'll never forget that night," I said. "What a collection of neurotics! Saving your presence, ma'am."

"That's the only purpose of the club—to find those things which frighten neurotics and stare them down, and to keep on doing it until somebody drops dead. Score to date: umpteen-odd dead boogiemen, no dead people. Hence the discussion of magic that night."

"That makes sense. And I remember Ponder's point that we are not as far removed from the days of the witches and wizards as we like to think. We knock on wood; we slip bits of wedding-cake under our pillows; we hook fingers with each other when we suddenly say the same thing together, and so on and on. And he said that perhaps this subconscious clinging to ritual was not because of a lingering childishness but because the original magic forces were still in operation!"

"That was it," said Claire. "And a fine flurry of snorts he got for that!"

"Yup. Especially from you. I still don't understand why you got so steamed up."

"I *hate* that kind of talk!" she said vociferously. "But I hated it especially hearing it from Dr. Ponder. Ever since I've known him he's been so reasonable, so logical, so—well, so wonderful—"

I grinned. "I'm jealous"

"Are you, Thad? Are you really?" she said eagerly; then, "No. You're laughing at me, you heel ... anyway, I couldn't stand hearing that kind of poppycock from him."

I put out my cloven hoof and snapped it in front of her nose. "What do you think now?"

"I don't know what to think ..." she whispered, and then, with one of her startling switches of mood, continued in a normal voice, "so the next day I decided to track down some of the old superstitions for myself. Heaven knows this part of the country is full of them. The Indians left a lot, and then the Dutch and the French and the Spanish. There's something about these hills that breeds such things."

I laughed. "Sounds like Lovecraft."

"Sounds like Charles Fort, too!" she snapped. "Some day you'll learn that you can't laugh at one and admire the other. Where was I?"

"In the woods."

"Oh. Well, the most persistent superstition in these parts is the old legend of the Camel's Grave. I came out here to find it."

I scrabbled up some of the soft earth to make a pit for my elbow and a hummock for my armpit. I lay on my side, propped up my head with my hand, and was comfortable. "Just run off that legend again, once over lightly."

She closed her eyes. "Somewhere in this no-good country—no one's ever been able to farm it, and there's too much jimson weed and nightshade for grazing—there's supposed to be a little hollow called Forbidden Valley. At the north end of it they say there's a grave with something funny about it. There's no headstone. Just a skull. Some say a man was buried there up to his neck and left to die."

"The Amazon Indians have a stunt like that. But they pick an anthill for the job. Cut off the feller's eyelids first. After that, the potato race, ducking for apples and ice cream is served in the main tent."

"A picnic," she agreed, shuddering. "But there was never anything like that among the local Indians here. Besides, we don't run to that kind of ant either. Anyway, this skull is chained, so the story goes, with a link through the edge of the eye-socket. It's supposed to be a magician buried there. Thing is, the legend is that he isn't dead. He'll live forever and be chained forever. Nothing can help him. But he doesn't know it. So if anyone wanders too close, he'll capture whoever it is and put' em to work trying to dig him out. The old tales keep coming out—kids who had wandered out here and disappeared, the old woman who went out of her head after she got back to town, the half-witted boy who mumbled something about the skull that talked to him out of the ground. You know."

"Why do they call it the Camel's Grave?"

"*I* don't know. Some say the magician was an Egyptian who used to ride a camel around. Some say it comes from some Indian name. The nearest I can find in the library to 'Camel' is 'ko-mai' which means the green stick they used to spit meat over a fire. But that's Winnebago, and there were no Winnebagos around here."

"Wait. You mean there were Indian legends about this?"

"Oh, sure. I dug those out. There are all sorts of stories. Some of them are shocking—I mean in a nice way." She giggled. "But they all have one thing in common—the imprisoned magician, who, by the way, was old, old as the hills. He wasn't an Indian either. They made that quite clear. And always Camel, or 'Grave of the Camel.' Just to mix that up even more for you, I looked up 'camel' in the dictionary and found out that the word is derived from 'Djemal,' which is Arabic, or 'Gamal,' which is Hebrew."

"Fine," I said bitterly. "Much progress. So go on with your little trip out here."

"That first time? Oh, nothing happened. I brought some chow and stayed out here about four days at the full moon, which is supposed to be the time when the Forbidden Valley can be found. I didn't see a soul but old Goo-goo running his traps. No one pays attention to Goo-goo."

"Not even people who step into one of his bear-traps? You're lucky you didn't bed down in it."

"Oh, don't blame him, Thad! He's a sweet old man, really. He's deaf and dumb, you know. He keeps out of people's way as much as he can. Comes in with a few skins every now and then and lives off the land. He could tell us a thing or two about Forbidden Valley if he could talk. But he can't even write. They say he doesn't mind the haunted hills because no one ever found a way to tell him about them. What he doesn't know can't hurt him. As for the trap, he put it where he thought it might do him some good, among the birches where bears sometimes come to hunt for bugs under the bark. Practically no one ever comes out here. When they do, it's their lookout, not Goo-goo's."

"Hey." I straightened up. "How can you be so casual about bunking out here with a wildcat or two and an occasional bear wandering around? There are copperheads too, to say nothing of a trapper who must be lonesome, to put it mildly."

"Why I—" She paused, wonderingly. "I never thought about it, I guess. Thad—nothing ever hurt me. I mean it. No dog ever bit me, no cat ever scratched me. I don't seem to be very tempting to mosquitoes. Once when I was a little girl a bull gored a hired man who was walking across a field with me. The bull bellowed and jumped and capered all around me, but he didn't touch me. I've never even been stung by a bee."

"You don't say." I considered her thoughtfully. "I begin to see why I asked you out for a beer the night of the meeting."

"Why, Thad?"

"Now don't get ideas. I just pegged you as being—different, that's all. Not better—different. You puzzled me. I've been a lot of places, Claire. Tropics. At sea. Construction jobs. I've met a lot of people, but no one like you."

"That again," she snorted. "People are always telling me that, one way or another. And what's it get me? The very first time I fall for a big dead-pan stranger, he doesn't know I'm alive. All large muscles and bad taste."

"What do you mean bad taste?"

"Luana."

"Now look. I won't bandy her about. Stay off the subject, see?"

Surprisingly, she laughed. "Temper—temper," she cautioned. "My, you roar purty. But back to the subject at hand. I was out here

four days and nights, wandering around, trying to find the Forbidden Valley. Once I thought I had it. It was about midnight. The moon
was bright, like tonight. I was near here somewhere. There was a
little swag in the ground with a high bluff at one end. I went up to
it. I tripped over something. I don't know what it was. I almost *never*
fall over things but I sure did that time. I fell right on top of some
little animal. I hope I didn't hurt it. I don't know what it was. It wrig-
gled out from under me and whizzed away fast as a deer-fly. I never
saw anything move so fast; a blur and it was gone. It was about as
big as a chipmunk, but longer—oh, three times as long. I got a vague
impression of pointed ears and the funniest broad, flat tail. It was
like nothing I've ever seen."

"I thought nothing happened in those four days."

"Well—that couldn't be important. Oh; I see what you mean.
Anything might be important. All right. Now—what else?"

"Goo-goo."

"Oh. I saw him once. Twice. The first time he was setting a whip-
snare in a clearing in the woods. I waved at him and smiled and he
nodded and gurgled the way he does and smiled back. The second
time I don't think he saw me. He was out in the open. Early morning. He was tramping round and round in a circle in the grass. Then
he stopped and faced the sun. He did something with his knife. Held
it out, sort of, and touched himself on the shoulders and chin with
it. I don't remember very clearly. It didn't last long. And that's all."

"Hmp." I plucked some grass and skinned it with my front teeth,
to get the juice. "Then you came back to town and your foot went
haywire."

"Yes. It only took about six days to get the way it is. It was awful
at first. The toes gathered, and the whole foot began to get pointed.
It was longer at first. I mean, my foot straightened out like a ballet
dancer's and I couldn't get my heel down. Then the whole thing
thickened up and grew shorter, and the tip turned black and hard-
ened and—"

I interrupted, "I know, I know. Had one once myself. Now, how
many people did you tell about it?"

"Oh, nobody. I mean, Dr. Ponder, of course, and then you. Dr. Ponder was so—so—"

"Wonderful," I submitted.

"Shut up. So *understanding*, I mean."

"That's an odd word to use."

"Is it? Anyway, he said I had a—a—"

"Chitinous podomorphia."

"Yes. How did you know?"

"You told me, right after he told you. Only *I* remembered it. Mine began shortly afterward, and I remembered it again." I spit out my grass and selected another stem. "A brilliant diagnosis."

"Thad ... you—sometimes you say things in a way I don't understand."

"Do I?" In the growing predawn darkness, I could feel her sharp swift gaze on me. I said, "Go on. He treated the foot?"

"He bound it. It was very clever. As the foot changed shape from day to day he changed the bandages, so that it never looked any worse than a slightly sprained ankle. He seemed to know all about the trouble. He predicted the course of the trouble as it developed, and told me that it would go just so far and stop, and he kept me from getting frightened, and explained why I should keep it a secret."

"What did he say?

"He harked back to the meeting, and the things that had been said. Especially about the readiness of people to believe in so-called mystical events. He said there was enough residual superstition in town to make life miserable for a girl with a cloven hoof. Especially for me."

"Why you especially?"

"Didn't I ever tell you? I thought I had... See, my mother and father ... they were engaged. I mean, they were each engaged to someone else. Dad came from Scoville way. That's eight miles or more on the other side of these woods. He didn't know Mother at all. He took to coming out here at night. He didn't know why. He couldn't help it. And Mother—she was about eighteen at the time— Mother jumped up from the dinner table one night and ran. She just *ran* out here. It's a long way. Granddad tried to follow her, but she ran like a deer. When he finally came huffing and puffing into the wood—it was a white night like tonight—and stopped to get his breath back, he heard a man calling, 'Jessica! Jessica!' That was Mother's name. Granddad followed the sound. It was out here in the open somewhere. Granddad climbed a rise and looked down and saw this young man standing with his arms out, calling and calling, turning every which way as he called. Granddad was going to yell at him but then he saw Mother. She was going down the slope ahead of him, walking slowly—he used to say 'as if the meadow was a grand marble stair, and she in a gold dress, for all she was tattered with thorns.'

"The two of them stopped two yards apart and stood there staring at one another for longer than it took Granddad to get to them. He had to yell twice or three times before she even knew he was there. She kept her eyes on the young man's face and just said, 'Yes, Father.' And Granddad bellowed at her to come home. She stepped to the young man—that was my dad—and she put a hand on his arm and said, 'He'll come too.' Granddad said, 'The hell he will!' He wouldn't talk to my dad, he was so upset and angry. 'I don't even know his name!' and Mother said quietly, 'No more do I. You'd better ask him, Father.' And that was how it was."

I sat up and crossed my legs, entranced. "You mean that was the first time they saw each other?"

She nodded, though by now I could barely see her, for the moon was gone and only its cold loom stood in the sky over the western hills. "The very first time," she said. "And they were together every minute they could be after that. They were married right away."

"How?"

She shifted uncomfortably as I asked it, and said, "By a judge. It wasn't a church wedding. It was quicker. People talked. They still talk. They have lots of ideas about what went on out here, but what I'm telling you is the truth. Anyway, Granddad got used to the idea very soon, though he was against it at first. Even the talk didn't bother him; those two lived in a world of their own. Nothing touched them. Dad made wood-carvings—clock cases and newel-figurines and so on, and Mother was with him almost every minute. Grand-dad used to say if you pinched the one, the other'd say 'Ouch.' He said nobody could stay mad in that house; he knew because he tried. So . . . it didn't matter what people said." She paused, and I just waited. Later, questions.

Presently she said sleepily, "And it *doesn't* matter. My mother and dad are like that now. They always will be. Nothing can change what you remember."

I waited again. This was a long time. Finally I asked, gently, "Where are they?"

"They died."

She slept. Somehow the moon had moved around to the east again. No: it wasn't the moon. It was a cloudless dawn, a dilution; light staining the hem of the sky. I sank back with my elbow in the hole I had dug and my armpit on the me-shaped hummock, and looked at the sleeping girl. I knew now what the single thing was that made her different. She was as changeable as bubble-colors; she felt, immediately and noticeably, all the emotions except one. And that was her difference. She was absolutely fearless.

That story . . . so simply told, and then, "They died."

Cloven hooves.

"They died." People like that . . . for a time I was angrier at such a death than I was, even, at the ugly excrescence that was once a foot. Dr. Ponder seemed to know a lot about these things. "Chitinous podomorphia." Oh, fine. That meant, "change of a foot into chitin—hoof, horn, and fingernail material." I hadn't gone to Ponder. I couldn't really say why. Maybe Luana was the reason for that. Somehow I couldn't take the idea of Luana writing up my case history on her neat file-cards. And there was no other doctor in town. Here was Claire with the same trouble, and I'd been in on that from the word go. I just did for my foot what Ponder had done for Claire's, and hoped that Luana would never hear about it. What girl would give a tumble to a man with a cloven hoof?

The sun poked a flaming forehead over the wall of hills. By its light I studied Claire's relaxed face. She was not beautiful, by any means. She had a round, pleasant face. When she laughed, a transverse crease appeared under her nose; she was the only human being with that particular upper lip that I had ever liked. Her lashes were thick but not long, and now, with her eyes closed, half the beauty she had was cloaked, for she had the most brilliant eyes I had ever seen. Her jaw was round and small, slightly cleft. She missed being square and stocky by fractional proportions.

"I must be out of my mind," I muttered. Claire was a wonderful person . . . a wonderful person. Genuine, honest, full of high humor, and, for me, no fireworks.

But Luana, the beautiful secretary of Dr. Ponder, now, that was a different story. She had an odd, triangular face and a skin that seemed lit softly from underneath. Her cheeks were a brighter rose than the sides of her neck but you couldn't tell just where the gradations began. Her hair was the extremely dark but vivid red of black-iron in a forge just beginning to heat. Her hands were so delicate and smooth you'd think they'd break on a typewriter, and her canine teeth were a shade too long, so that her head looked like a flower with fangs. She had one expression—complete composure. Her unshakable poise made me grind my teeth; some way, somehow, I wanted it broken. I don't think she had brain-one and I didn't care; it wasn't her brains I was after. Her face floated before me on the flames of the fireworks she generated in me, and there wasn't a thing in the world I could do about it. When I was in town I'd date her, when I could. On the dates we didn't talk. She danced sedately and watched movies attentively and ate pineapple frappés with delicacy and thoroughness, and I'd just sit there and bask, and count the seconds until, after I walked her to her gate, she closed it between us and leaned across for a demure kiss. Her lips were cool, smooth, and taut. Pneumatic. Then I'd stride away snarling at myself. "You're a bumpkin," I'd say. "You're all feet and Adam's apple." I'd tell myself I had a hole in the head. I called myself forty kinds of a fool. "There's no future in it," I'd say. I'd tell myself, "You know that ten years from now, when the bloom is off, she'll look like something the cat dragged in, her and her teeth." And thinking about the teeth would make me visualize those lips again, and—so cool!

Often, those nights, I'd run into Claire, who just happened to be in Callow's Friendly Drug and Meat Market buying a whodunit, and we'd get a soda or something and talk. Those were the talks where everything came out. I never got so thick with anyone so fast. Talking to Claire is like talking to yourself. And she told me, somehow or other, about the foot, right from the first. She didn't tell anyone else. Except Dr. Ponder, of course....

What a strange person she was! It was inconceivable that she should not have questioned Dr. Ponder more about her foot—yet she had not. His prognosis was that the condition would stop at her ankle, and may or may not be permanent, and, for her, that was that. In the same situation anyone else on Earth would be scrambling around from specialist to specialist between trips to a wailing wall. Not Claire. She accepted it and was not afraid.

A patch of sun the size of a kitten crept up the edge of her sleeping bag and nestled in her hair. After a pause to warm and brighten itself, it thrust a golden pseudopod around the curve of her cheek and touched her eyelid. She stirred, smiled briefly at what must have been a most tender dream, and woke.

"Good morning."

She looked at me mistily, and smiled a different smile. "I fell asleep."

"You did. Come on—stir your stumps. I want to show you something that I've discovered."

She stretched and yawned. "I was talking to you and I fell asleep right in the middle of it. I'm sorry."

"I'm glad. You got your beauty sleep." Her face softened, so I added, "You need it."

"You're so sweet, Thad," she said. "Much sweeter than gall. 'Bout like vinegar, when you try hard." She slid out of the sleeping bag and idly scratched her hairy ankle. "If I had to choose between this thing with you, and my ordinary old foot without you, I think I'd keep the hoof. How do you make that noise with it?"

I showed her. She tried it. All she could get was a muffled pop, like fingers snapping with gloves on. She laughed and said I was a genius, and rose and climbed into her flying suit. She had half-length

297

boots, padded inside to support her hoof. Once they were on, no one could have guessed. While she was about these small chores, and others concerning folding and stowing the sleeping bag and breaking out some C and K rations, I rescued my amputated shoe from the bear-trap and, by cutting and piecing the leather straps, made a sort of stirrup that would hold it together once it was on.

When that was done, Claire, looking shapeless and tousled in the loose-fitting coverall, handed me one of the sticky-rich candy bars from the rations. "Thad," she said with her mouth full, "you just *wouldn't* go to see Dr. Ponder. Why not? Don't you trust him?"

"Sure I trust him," I said shortly. Why mention that I was keeping away from him because of Luana? "Come on," I said.

We crossed through a neck of the forest to the rolling scrub-meadow on the other side, and down and across the first little valley.

"This is where I was last night. There's something just over the next rise that I want you to see. Last night I was afraid you'd see it."

"What's so different about today, then?"

"I found out last night you're not afraid of anything."

She did not answer. I looked back at her. She was grinning. "You said something nice about me," she half-sang.

"Not necessarily. Sometimes fearlessness is nothing more than rank stupidity."

She swallowed that silently. As we climbed the rise she asked, "Will you tell me about the time you saw me be beautiful?"

"Later," I said.

Abruptly she clutched my arm. *"Look!"*

"Where? What?"

"There!" She pointed. "No—there—there, see?" She pointed rapidly to the ground, to a rock, to a spot in midair to our left. "See?"

"What is it, Claire? A deer-fly? Or spots in the eyes?"

"Just watch," she said with exaggerated patience. "The little animal I fell on that time—remember? It's all around here, and moving so *fast!*"

There are certain optical illusions where a missing object becomes vividly clear as soon as you know what to look for. I focused my mind's eye on what she had described as a tapering, fan-tailed monstrosity with two front legs and a blue-black hide, and suddenly, fleetingly, there it was, crouching against the sheer side of the bluff. It blinked at me, and then disappeared, only to pop into sight for a fraction of a second right in front of us. We moved back with alacrity as if pulled by the same string.

"I want out!" I gasped. "That's the thing that gave you the fancy boot!"

Somehow we were twenty feet back and still backing. Claire laughed. "I thought that was your specialty."

"You pick the dog-gonnedest times ... get back, Claire! Heaven knows what will happen to you if it gets to you again!"

She stood still, peering. The thing, whatever it was, appeared twice, once a little to the right, once—and this time, for a full two or three seconds—over against the side-hill. It balanced on two forelegs, its head thrust out, its wide fluked tail curled up over its back, and it blinked rapidly. Its eyes were the same color as its skin, but shiny. It disappeared. Claire said, "It can't hurt us. Dr. Ponder said the condition would be arrested where it is."

I snorted. "That's like saying you're immunized against being bumped by a truck because one ran over you once. Let's get out of here."

She laughed at me again. "Why, Thad! I've never seen you like this! You're pale as milk!"

"You have so seen me like this," I quavered. "The last time you called me sensible. Remember?"

The blue-black thing appeared again almost under my feet. I squeaked and jumped. Then it was by Claire, inches away. She bent toward it, hand outstretched, but it vanished.

"Thad, it seems terribly excited. I think it wants something."

"That I don't doubt," I said through clenched teeth. "Claire. Listen to me. Either you will hightail with me out of this imp-ridden corner of hell, or you and that monstrosity can stay here and watch me dwindle."

"Oh, *Thad!* stop blithering. The poor little thing is probably ten times as frightened as you are."

"Oh no it isn't," I said with authority. "It's alive, isn't it?"

299

She snorted and squatted down in the grass, her hands out and close together. Simultaneously with my warning cry, the creature appeared between her hands. Very slowly she moved them together. I stood petrified, babbling. "Claire, don't, please don't, just this once how do you know what that thing might do, Claire ... Okay—it's small, Claire. So is a *fer de lance*. So is a forty-five slug. Please, Claire ..."

"*Will* you stop that infernal chattering!" she snapped. And just before her closing hands could touch the beast it was gone, to reappear six inches to the left.

She rose and stepped forward gently, stooping. The poised animal—if it was an animal—waited until she was a fraction of an inch away and again bounded out of visibility and in again, this time a yard away, where it waited, blinking violently.

"I think it wants us to follow it," said Claire. "Come on, Thad!"

It moved again, farther away, and bounced up and down.

"Oh, Claire," I said at last, "I give up. We're in this together and we've got to depend on each other. Maybe you're right after all."

Surprisingly, there were tears in her eyes as she said, "I feel as if you had been away a long time and just got back."

I thumped her shoulder, and we went on. We followed the strange creature up the slope to its crest, where the creature disappeared again, this time, apparently, for good.

Claire had been right, we found a moment later. Distantly, sunlight flashed on the windshield of Ponder's parked convertible, which was parked where the Wood road skirted the desolate flatland. Nearing the foothills where we stood were two plodding figures, and it was easy to spot Ponder, for no one else in the area had his stooped height and breadth. He was so perfectly in proportion that he made normal people look underdone. The other, I noticed with a gulp, was Luana, with her contained, erect posture, and the sunlight, after its cold journey through space, reveling in the heat of her hair.

We went to meet them. I looked once at Claire, catching her at the woman's trick of swift comparative appraisal of Luana's trim plaid skirt and snug windbreaker, and I smiled. Claire's coverall was not a company garment.

"Thad!" the doctor boomed. He had an organ voice; in conversation it always seemed to be throttled down, and his shout was a relaxation rather an effort. "And Claire ... we were worried."

"Why?" asked Claire. We reached them. I buzzed right on past the doctor—"Hi, Doc,"—and took both Luana's hands. "Lu."

She looked up at me and smiled. Those lips, so taut, so filled with what strange honey ... when they smiled they grew still fuller. She said Hello, and I thought, what's language for? what's poetry for? when two small syllables can mean so much ... I held her hands so hard and so long that it may have been embarrassing. It was for me, anyway, when Claire's voice broke into my ardent scansion of Luana's eyes with "Hey! Svengali! Got her hypnotized yet?"

I released Luana, who looked Claire's rumpled flying suit up and down. "Hello, Claire," she purred. "Hunting?"

"Just walking the dog," said Claire through her teeth.

I met the doctor's eyes and he grinned. "Good of you to take all this trouble over Claire's trouble," he said. "She just told me you knew about it. Does anyone else?"

I shook my head, but said, "Why all the mystery, Doctor?"

"I certainly don't have to tell you that this is not an ordinary medical matter."

Claire said, "Let's go on up to the Wood and sit down and talk. It's getting hot."

"I'll tote that if it's heavy," I offered, indicating Ponder's black bag.

"Oh no. Just a couple of things I brought with me, just in case."

He and Claire started back up toward the Wood. I put my hand on Luana's forearm and checked her.

"What is it, Thad?"

"I just want them to get a little way ahead. Luana, this is wonderful. What on earth made him come out here? And with you?"

"I don't know. He's a strange man, Thad. Sometimes I think he knows everything. Nothing surprises him." We began to walk. "We were working this morning—he was dictating some letters—and he all of a sudden stopped as if he was listening to something. Next thing I knew we were on our way."

"Does he really know what's the matter with Claire's foot?"

She looked at me. Her eyes were auburn and most disturbing. "I'm not supposed to talk about it."

"She told me. It turned into a cloven hoof. I've seen it."

"Oh. Then why ask?"

I hadn't expected this kind of resistance. "I mean, does he know *why* it happened?"

"Of course he does."

"Well, why?" I asked impatiently.

"Why not ask him?" She shrugged. "He's the doctor. I'm not."

"Sorry I asked," I said glumly. I was annoyed—I think at myself. I don't know why, subconsciously, I always expected this vision to melt into my arms, and was always sticking my neck out. But that's the way it is when you get fireworks

We walked on in silence. Claire and the doctor had disappeared into the Wood when we entered the edge of it. We stopped for a moment to look about. There was, of course, no path, and the windless growth muffled and absorbed sounds, so it was difficult to know which way they had gone. I started in, but Luana held me back. "I don't think they're that way."

"I'll yell," I said, but she put a hand to her mouth. "Oh, *no!*"

"Why not, Lu?"

"I'm—I don't know. You shouldn't, in here." She looked about the silent halls of the forest. "Please, Thad. Go look for them. I'll wait. But don't shout, please."

Completely puzzled, I said, "Well, sure, honey. But I don't get it. Is something the matter?"

"No. Nothing." Her arched nostrils twitched. "Go look for them, Thad. I'll wait here, in case they come back for us."

"You're sure you'll be all right?"

"Go on. Go on," she said urgently. I suddenly thought that for certain reasons I might be behaving tactlessly. I must have blushed like a schoolgirl. "Well, sure. I'll be right back. I mean, I'll find 'em and call you." I flapped a good-bye self-consciously and blundered off through the woods. That girl really threw me for a loss.

I followed the level ground until I emerged from the Wood at the other side of its narrow neck—just what I should have done in the first place. Doctor Ponder and Claire were out in the open fifty yards away, apparently waiting for us. I went to them. "We lost you," I said. "Luana's waiting back there. She didn't want to thrash around in the woods hunting for you. Hold on and I'll get her."

Ponder's big head went up, and his eyes seemed to focus on something I couldn't see for a moment. Then, "Don't bother," he said. "She's all right. I wanted to talk to you two anyway. Let's go in the shade and sit down."

"But—will she be all right?"

"She'll be all right," he grinned. He had good teeth.

I shrugged. "Everybody seems to know what's right around here but me," I said petulantly. "All right." I led the way to a thicket at the edge of the wood and plumped down with my back against a tree. Claire and the doctor joined me, Ponder setting his bag carefully within his reach.

"Now for heaven's sake tell us," said Claire, who had kept an amused silence during my jitterings about Luana. She turned to me. "He wouldn't say a thing until you got here."

"Tell us about what? Who knows anything?" I said resignedly.

"You know about her foot," said Dr. Ponder. He looked down. "What, speaking of feet, has happened to your boot?"

I happened to be looking at Claire, and microscopically shook my head. "Oh," I said casually, "I left it on a railroad track while I was frog hunting in a culvert. Go on about Claire." Claire's eyes widened in astonishment at this continued deception, but she said nothing. I was pleased.

Ponder leaned back. He had a long head and a big jaw. The touch of gray at his temples and the stretched smoothness of his skin told lies about each other. He said, "First, I want to thank you both—you, Claire, because you have trusted me in this matter, when I had every reason to expect nothing but hysteria from you, and you, Thad, for having kept your own counsel. Now I'll tell you what I know. Please don't mind if I seem to wander a bit. I want you to get this straight in your minds." He closed his eyes for a moment, his brow furrowed. Then he wet his lips and continued.

"Imagine a man walking up to a door which stands firmly locked. He raises his hand and makes a certain motion. The door opens. He enters, picks up a wand. He waves it; it suddenly glows with light. He says two words, and a fire appears in the fireplace. Now: could you duplicate that?"

"I've seen doors open for people in a railroad station," said Claire. "They had a beam of light in front of them. When you walked into it, a photoelectric cell made the door open."

"About that wand," I put in. "If it was made of glass, it could have been a fluorescent tube. If there was a radio frequency generator in the room, it could make a tube glow, even without wire connections."

"I once saw a gadget connected to a toy electric train," Claire said. "You say 'Go!' into a speaker and the train would go. You say 'Now back up' and it would back up. It worked by the number of syllables you spoke. One would make the train go forward; three would make it stop and back up. That fire you mentioned, that could be controlled by a gadget like that."

"Right. Quite right," said the doctor. "Now, suppose you fixed up all that gadgetry and took it back in time a couple of centuries. What would the performance look like to a person of the time— even an intelligent, reasonable one?"

I said, "Witchcraft." Claire said, "Why, magic."

Ponder nodded. "But they'd understand a kitchen match. But take a kitchen match back a couple more centuries, and you'd get burned at the stake. What I'm driving at is that given the equipment, you can get the results, whether those results can be understood by the observer or not. The only sane attitude to take about such things is to conclude that they are caused by some natural, logically explained agency—and that we haven't the knowledge to explain it any more than the most erudite scholar could have explained radar two centuries ago."

"I follow that," I said, and Claire nodded.

"However," said Ponder, "most people don't seem to accept such things that easily. Something happens that you can't understand, and either you refuse to believe it happened at all—even if you saw it with your own eyes—or you attribute it to supernatural forces, with all their associated claptrap of good and evil, rituals and exorcisms. What I'm putting to you is that everything that's happened to you is perfectly logical and believable in its own terms—but it's much larger than you think. I'm asking you to accept something much more mysterious than an r-f generator would be to a Puritan settler. You just have to take my word for it that it's as reasonable a thing as an r-f generator."

"I don't understand an r-f generator, as it is," smiled Claire. I heard the soft sound of her hoof clicking. "Go ahead, Doctor. At this point I'm ready to believe anything."

"Fine," applauded the doctor. "It's a pleasure to talk to you. Now, I'm going to use 'good' and 'evil' in this explanation because they're handy. Bear in mind that they are loose terms, partial ones: external evidences of forces that extend forward and back and to either side in time and space." He laughed. "Don't try to follow that. Just listen.

"A long time ago there were two opposed forces—call them intelligences. One was good and one was evil. It turned out to be quite a battle, and it went on for some time. There were gains and losses on each side, until one was captured by the other. Now, these intelligences were not living creatures in the ordinary sense, and in the ordinary sense they could not be killed. There are legends of such captures—the bound Prometheus, for example, and the monster under Yggdrasil. The only way to keep such forces imprisoned is to lock them up and set a watch over them. But, just as in our civilization, it may take profound intelligence and a great deal of hard work to capture a criminal, but far less intelligence and effort to keep him in jail.

"And that's the situation we have here. Not far from where we sit, one of those things is imprisoned, and he—I say 'he' for convenience—has his jailer.

"That's the thing known as 'The Camel's Grave.' The Camel is a living intelligence, captured and held here and, if right has its way, doomed to spend the rest of eternity here."

"That's a long time," I put in. "The Earth won't last that long."

"He'll be moved in time," said Ponder complacently; and that was when I began to realize how big this thing was. There was that about Doctor Ponder which made it impossible to disbelieve him. I stared at Claire, who stared back. Finally she turned to him and asked in a small voice, "And—what about my foot?"

"That was a piece of tough luck," said Ponder. "You are a sort of—uh—innocent bystander. You see, the Camel is surrounded by ... damn it, it's hard to find words that make sense! Fields. Look: if I call them 'spells,' will you understand that I'm not talking mumbo-jumbo? If I call them 'fields,' it presupposes coils and generators and circuits and so on. In this way 'spells' is more accurate."

"I'm with you so far," I said. Claire nodded.

"Well, the Camel is conscious. He wants out. Like any other prisoner, he looks through the bars from time to time and talks with his jailer—and with anyone else he can reach. What you stumbled into, though, wasn't the Camel: he's pretty well sealed away from that. You hit one of the spells—one of the small warning devices set there in case he should begin to escape. If it had hit him, it would have stung him a little, perhaps like an electric fence. But when you walked into it, you got that hoof. Why the result was exactly that I can't say. It's the nature of the thing. It's happened before, as mythology will tell you."

"I've thought of that," I said. "Pan and the satyrs, and so on. They all had cloven hooves. And isn't the Devil supposed to have one too?"

"One of the marks of the beast." Ponder nodded. "Now, as to what can be done about it, I'm here to do the best I can. Claire, exactly where was it that you walked into—whatever it was, and fell down on that little animal?"

"I don't know," she said calmly. "I haven't been able to locate it. I should be able to—ever since I was a child I've had dream compulsions to come out here, and I know this country like my own house."

"I wish you could find it. It would help." Ponder twiddled the catch on his black bag thoughtfully. "We have to try to get through to the Camel and let him know what has happened to you. He could counteract it. Well, anyway, we might be able to do something. We'll see."

"Doc," I said, "about that hoof. You're sure it was from contact with something out here. I mean, couldn't it have been something in town that caused it?"

"Positively not," he said. And I said to myself, now that is damned interesting, because I have a hoof too and I was never out here before last night.

Ponder turned to Claire. "Exactly why did you come out here that time you saw the little animal?"

"In a way it was your doing, Doctor. It was that Medusa Club meeting. You made me so mad with your intimations that there were still magical forces at work, and that superstitions served to guard humanity against them." She laughed diffidently. "I don't feel the same way now, so much . . . Anyway, I know this part of the country well. I made up my mind to go to the most magical part of it at the most magical time—the full moon—and stick my neck out. Well, I did."

"Uh-huh," said the doctor. "And why did you come out yesterday?"

"To find Thad."

"Well, Thad? What were you after?"

"I wanted to see what is was Claire had walked into."

"Didn't trust my diagnosis?"

"Oh, it wasn't that. If I'd found anything at all, I probably would have told you about it. I was just curious about the cause and cure of cloven hooves."

"Well, I could have told you that you wouldn't find anything. Claire might, but you wouldn't."

"How so?"

"Hasn't it dawned on you yet that Claire is something special? In a sense she's a product of this very ground. Her parents—"

"I told him that story," said Claire.

"Oh. Well, that was the Camel at work. The only conceivable way for him to break out of his prison is through a human agency; for there is that in human nature that not even forces such as the one which imprisoned him can predict. They can be controlled, but not predicted. And if the Camel should ever be freed—"

"Well?" I asked, after a pause.

"I can't tell you. Not 'won't.' 'Can't.' It's big, though. Bigger than you can dream. But as I was saying, Claire's very presence on Earth is his doing."

"My parents were murdered," said Claire.

I turned to her, shocked. She nodded soberly. "When I was six."

"I think you're right," said Ponder. "Their marriage was a thing that could cancel many of the—the devices that imprison the Camel. The very existence of a union like that threatened the—what we can call the prison walls. It had to be stopped."

"What happened?"

"They died," said Claire. "No one knew why. They were found sitting on a rock by the road. He had his arm around her and her head was on his shoulder and they were dead. I always felt that they were killed on purpose, but I never knew why."

"The Camel's fault," said Ponder, shrugging.

I asked. "But why didn't they—he—kill Claire too while he was about it?"

"She was no menace. The thing that was dangerous was the— the radiation from the union that her parents had. It was an unusual marriage."

"My God!" I cried. "You mean to say that Camel creature, what-ever it is, can sit out here and push people's lives around like that?"

"That's small fry, Thad. What he could do it he were free is inconceivable."

I rubbed my head. "I dunno, Doc. This is getting to be too much. Can I ask some questions now?"

"Certainly."

"How come you know so much about all this?"

"I am a student of such things. I stumbled on this whole story in some old documents. As a matter of fact, I took the medical prac-tice out here just so I could be near it. It's the biggest thing of its kind I've ever run across."

"Hm. Yet you don't know where the Camel's Grave is, exactly."

"Wrong," said the doctor. "I do. I wanted to know if Claire had been able to find it. If she had been able to, it would mean that the

Camel had established some sort of contact with her. Since he hasn't, I'll have to do what I can."

"Oh. Anyone who can find the Grave is in contact with the Camel, then."

"That's right. It takes a special kind of person."

I very consciously did not meet Claire's gaze. There was something very fishy going on here, and I began to feel frightened. This thing that could shrivel a foot into a hoof, it could kill too. I asked, "What about this 'jailer' you mentioned. Sort of a low-grade variety of the Camel himself?"

"Something like that."

"That little animal—would that be it?"

A peculiar expression crossed the doctor's face, as if he had remembered something, dragged it out, glanced at it, found it satisfactory, and put it away again. "No," he said. "Did you ever hear of a familiar?"

"A familiar?" asked Claire. "Isn't that the sort of pet that a witch or a wizard has—black cats and so on?"

"Yes. Depending on the degree of 'wizard' we're dealing with, the familiar may be a real animal or something more—the concretion, perhaps, of a certain kind of thought-matrix. That little animal you described to me is undoubtedly the Camel's familiar."

"Then where's the jailer?" And as I asked, I snapped my fingers. "Goo-goo!"

"Not Goo-goo!" Claire cried. "Why, he's perfectly harmless. Besides—he isn't all there, Thad."

"He wouldn't have to be," said the doctor, and smiled. "It doesn't take much brains to be a turnkey."

"I'll be darned," I said. "Well, now, what have we got? A cloven hoof and an imprisoned *something* that must stay imprisoned or else. A couple of nice people murdered, and their pixilated daughter. All right, Doctor—how do you go about curing cloven hooves?"

"Locate the Camel's Grave," said Doctor Ponder, "and then make a rather simple incantation. Sound foolish?" He looked at both of us. "Well, it isn't. It's as simple and foolish as pressing a button—or pulling a trigger. The important thing is who does it to which

THE PERFECT HOST

control on what equipment. In this case Claire is the one indicated, because she's—what was it Thad said?—pixilated. That's it. Because of the nature of her parents' meeting, because of what they had together, because she is of such a character as to have been affected by the Camel to the extent of the thing that happened to her foot—it all adds up. She's the one to do it."

"Then anyone who's subject to this particular kind of falling arches could do it?" I asked innocently.

" 'Anyone'—yes. But that can't happen to just anyone."

I asked another question, quickly, to cover up what I was thinking. "About familiars," I said. "Don't I recall something about their feeding on blood?"

"Traditionally, yes. They do."

"Uh-huh. The blood of the witch, as I recall. Well how in time can the Camel character supply any blood to his familiar if he's been buried here for—how long is it?"

"Longer than you think ... Well, in a case like that the familiar gets along on whatever blood it can find. It isn't as good, but it serves. Unless, of course, the familiar makes a side trip just for variety. Occasionally one does. That's where the vampire legends come from."

"How to you like that?" I breathed. "I'll bet a cookie that the animals Goo-goo traps are supplying blood to the Camel's familiar—and Goo-goo supposed to be guarding the jail!"

"It's very likely—and not very important. The familiar can do very little by itself," said the doctor. He turned to Claire. "Did you ever see anything like a familiar taking blood? Think, now."

Claire considered. "No. Should I have?"

"Not necessarily. You could though," he indicated her foot, "being what you are."

She shuddered slightly. "So I'm privileged. I'd as soon not, thank you."

I sprang to my feet. "I just thought ... Luana. What could have happened to her?"

"Oh, she's all right. Sit down, Thad."

"No," I said. "I'd better go look for her."

Claire leaned back, caught her knee in her hands, and made a soft and surprisingly accurate replica of a wolf-howl. "Drop desperately ill," I said to her, and to Doctor Ponder, "That's for people you like too well to tell 'em to drop dead." And I strode off.

It took only a few minutes to regain the spot where I had left Luana. She was not there.

I stood still, my brain racing. Witches, wizards, familiars ... people who could see familiars sucking blood, and people who could not ... one more cloven hoof than the good doctor bargained for, and a theory that such a thing came from contact with Something out here, when I knew darned well I had acquired mine in town ... a girl who did what her dreams told her to do and another with hair like hot metal and lips bursting with some cool sweetness. And where was she?

I moved into the Wood, walking quietly more because of caution for my torn boot than for any other reason, and peering into the mottled shadows. Once, with my eyes fixed on a distant clearing, I blundered into a nest of paper-wasps with my neck and shoulder. I started violently and moved back. The angry creatures swarmed out and around the damaged nest, and came after me as I sidled away, batting at them. They bumbled against my mouth and hair and forearms, but not one stung me. I remember thinking, when at last I was clear of them, that Claire had said something about bees ... but before I could dredge up the thought I saw Luana.

If it had not been for the plaid skirt I couldn't possibly have seen her. She was as still as a tree-trunk in a little glade, her head bent, watching something which struggled on the ground. Moving closer, silently, I could see her face; and, seeing it, I checked any impulse I might have to call out to her. For her face was a mask, smooth, round-eyed, with curling lips and sharp white teeth, and it was completely motionless except for the irregular flickering of her nostrils, which quivered in a way reminiscent of a snake's swift, seeking tongue. Slowly she began to bend down. When I could no longer see her face I came closer.

Then I could see. I shall never forget it. That was when the fireworks went out ... and a terrible truth took their place.

At the foot of a little bush was a bare spot, brushed clean now of loose leaves, doubtless by the struggles of the rabbit. It was a large brown-brindle rabbit caught in a whip-snare which had fouled in the bush. The snare had caught the animal around the barrel, just behind the forelegs, probably having been set in a runway. The rabbit was very much alive and frightened.

Luana knelt slowly and put out her hands. She picked the rabbit up. I said to myself, the darling! She's going to help it! . . . and I said, down deeper, but a woman looks tenderly at the thing she is about to help, and Luana's face, now, whatever it was, it wasn't tender.

She lifted the rabbit and bit into it as if it were an apple.

I don't know what I did. Not exactly. I remember a blur of trunks, and a dim green. I think I heard Luana make a sound, a sign, perhaps—even a low laugh. I don't know. And I must have run. Once I hit something with my shoulder. Anyway, when I reached Claire and the doctor I was panting hoarsely. They looked up at me as I stood panting, not speaking. Then without a word, Ponder got up and ran back the way I had come.

"Thad! Oh, Thad—what is it?"

I sank down beside her and shook my head.

"Luana? Did something happen to Luana, Thad?"

"I'll tell you," I whispered. Something trickled down the outside of my nose. Sweat, I suppose. "I'll tell you, but not now."

She pushed my hair back. "All right, Thad," she said. And that was all, until I got my breath back.

She began to talk then, softly and in a matter-of-fact tone, so that I had to follow what she said; and the sharp crooked edges of horror blunted themselves on new thoughts. She said, "I'm beginning to understand it now, Thad. Some of it is hard to believe, and some of it I just don't *like* to believe. Doctor Ponder knows a lot, Thad, a whole lot . . . Look." She reached into the doctor's bag, now open, and brought out a limp black book. On its cover, glittering boldly in a sunbeam, was a gilt cross. "You see, Thad? Good and evil . . . Doctor Ponder's using this. Could that be evil? And look. Here—read it yourself." She opened the book at a mark and give it to me.

I wiped my eyes with my knuckles and took the book. It was the Bible, the New Testament, open to the sixth chapter of Matthew. The thirteenth verse was circled: It was the familiar formula of praise:

"Thine is the Kingdom, the Power, and the Glory for ever and ever. Amen."

"Look at the bottom margin," she urged.

I looked at the neat block lettering penciled there. *"Ah-tay mahlkuth vé-G'boorah vé-Gédula lé o'lam, om,"* I read haltingly. "What on earth is that?"

"It's the Hebrew translation of the thirteenth verse. And—it's the trigger, the incantation Doctor Ponder told us about."

"Just that? That little bit?"

"Yes. And I'm supposed to go to the Camel's Grave and face the east and say it. Then the Camel will know that I have been affected and will fix the trouble. Doctor Ponder says that although he is evil—a 'black' magician—he can have no reason to leave me in this state." She leaned forward and lowered her voice. "Nor you either. You'll go with me and we'll both be cured."

"Claire—why haven't you told him I've got a hoof too?"

She looked frightened. "I—can't," she whispered. "I tried, and I can't. There's something that stops me."

I looked at the book, reading over the strange, musical sounds of the formula. They had a rhythm, a lilt. Claire said, "Doctor Ponder said I must recite that in a slow monotone, all the while thinking 'Camel, be buried forever, and never show yourself to mankind.'"

"Be buried forever? What about your foot? Aren't you supposed to say something about your foot?"

"Well, didn't I?"

"You did not." I leaned forward and looked close into her eyes. "Say it again."

"'Camel, be buried forever, and never show yourself to mankind.'"

"Where's the part about the foot?"

She looked at me, puzzled. "Thad—didn't you hear me? I distinctly said that the Camel was to restore my foot and yours and then lie down and rest."

"Did you, now? Say it again, just once more, the way you're supposed to."

Obediently she said, " 'Camel, be buried forever, and never show yourself to mankind.' There. Was that clear enough? About the foot, and all?"

Suddenly I understood. She didn't know what she was saying! I patted her knee. "That was fine," I said. I stood up.

"Where are you going?"

"I have to think," I said. "Mind, Claire? I think better when I walk. Doctor Ponder'll be back soon. Wait here, will you?"

She called to me, but I went on into the Wood. Once out of her sight, I circled back and downgrade, emerging on the rim of what I now knew was the Forbidden Valley. From this point I could easily see the bluff at the far end. There was no sign of the skull. I began to walk down to where it should be. I knew now that it was there, whether it could be seen or not. I wished I could be sure of a few dozen other things. Inside, I was still deeply shaken by what I had seen Luana doing, and by what it meant—by what it made of me, of Claire, of Ponder. . . .

Behind me there was a horrible gargling sound. It was not a growl or a gurgle; it was exactly the hollow, fluid sound that emerges from bathrooms in the laryngitis season. I spun, stared.

Staring back at me was one of the most unprepossessing human beings I have ever seen. He had matted hair and a scraggly beard. His eyes were out of line horizontally, and in disagreement with each other as to what they wanted to look at. One ear was pointed and the other was a mere clump of serrated flesh.

I backed off a pace. "You're Goo-goo."

He gabbled at me, waving his arms. It was a disgusting sound. I said, "Don't try to stop me, Mister America. I know what I'm doing and I mean to do it. If you get too near me I'll butter these rocks with you."

He gargled and bubbled away like mad, but kept his distance. Warily I turned and went on down the slope. I thought I heard Claire calling. I strode on, my mind awhirl. Luana. Ponder. Claire. Goo-goo. The chained skull, and the blue beast. The rabbit. Luana, Luana and those lips ... *Ah-tay mahlkuth* ... and a cloven hoof. I shook my head to clear my brain ... *vé-G'boorah*....

I was on level ground, approaching the bluff. "Get up, Camel!" I barked hoarsely. "Here I come, ready or not!"

Shocking, the skull, the famous mark of the Camel's Grave, appeared on the ground. It was a worn, weather-beaten skull, worn far past the brilliant bleaching of bones merely desiccated and clean. It was yellowed, paper-brittle. The eyebrow ridges were not very prominent, and the lower jaw, what I could see of it, was long, firm. Its most shocking feature was part of it, but not naturally part of it. It was a chain of some black metal, its lower link disappearing into the ground, its upper one entering the eye socket and coming out through the temple. The chain had a hand-wrought appearance, and although it was probably as thick as the day it was made, unrusted and strong, I knew instinctively that it was old, old. It seemed to be—it *must* be—watching me through its empty sockets. I thought I heard the chain clink once. The bleached horror seemed to be waiting.

There was a small scuffling sound right at my heels. It was Goo-goo. I wheeled, snarling at him. He retreated, mouthing. I ground out, "Keep out of my reach, rosebud, or I'll flatten you!" and moved around to the left of the skull where I could face the east.

"*Ah-tay mahlkuth vé—*" I began; and something ran across my foot. It was the blue beast, the familiar. It balanced by the skull, blinking, and disappeared. I looked up to see Goo-goo approaching again. His face was working; he was babbling and drooling.

"Keep clear," I warned him.

He stopped. His clawlike hand went to his belt. He drew a horn-handled sheath knife. It was blue and keen. I had some difficulty in separating my tongue from the roof of my mouth. I stood stiffly, trying to brace myself the way an alerted cat does, ready to leap in any direction, or up, or flat down.

Goo-goo watched me. He was terrifying because he did not seem particularly tense, and I did not know what he was going to do. What was he, anyway? Surely more than a crazy deaf-mute, mad with loneliness. Was he really the jailer of a great Power? Or was he, in some way, in league with that disappearing bad-dream of a familiar?

I began again: *"At-tay mahlkuth vé-G'boor—"* and again was distracted by the madman. For instead of threatening me with his glittering blade, he was performing some strange manual of arms with it, moving it from shoulder to shoulder as I spoke, extending it outward, upward ... and he stopped when I stopped, looking at me anxiously.

At last there seemed to be some pattern, some purpose, to what he was trying to do. When I spoke a certain phrase, he made a certain motion with the knife. *"Ah-tay ..."* I said experimentally. He touched his forehead with the knife. I tried it again; he did it again. Slowly, then, without chanting, I recited the whole rigmarole. Following me attentively, he touched his forehead, his chest, his right shoulder, his left, and on the final *"om"* he clasped his hands together with the point of the knife upward.

"Okay, chum," I said. "Now what?"

He immediately extended the knife to me, hilt first. Amazed, I took it. He nodded encouragingly and babbled. He also smiled, though the same grimace a few minutes earlier, before I was convinced of his honest intentions, would have looked like a yellow-fanged snarl to me. And upon me descended the weight of my appalling ignorance. How much difference did the knife make to the ritual? Was it the difference between blanks and slugs in a gun? Or was it the difference between pointing it at myself or up in the air?

Ponder would know. Ponder, it developed, did, and he told me, and I think he did it in spite of himself. As I stood there staring from the steel to the gibbering Goo-goo, Ponder's great voice rolled down to me from the Wood end of the vale. *"Thad! Not with the knife!"*

I glanced up. Ponder was coming down as fast as he could, helping Claire with one hand and all but dragging Luana with the other. Goo-goo began to dance with impatience, guggling away like an excited ape, pointing at me, at his mouth, at the knife, the staring skull. The blue beast flickered into sight between his legs, beside him, on his shoulder, and for a brief moment on his head, teetering there like some surrealistic plume. I took all this in and felt nothing but utter confusion.

Claire called, "Put down the knife, Thad!"

Something—some strange impulse from deep inside me, made me turn and grin at them as they scurried down toward me. I bellowed, "Why, Doc! I don't qualify, do I?"

Ponder's face purpled. "Come out of there!" he roared. "Let Claire do it!"

I reached down and yanked the makeshift stirrup from my boot, laughing like a maniac. I kicked off the toe of the boot with its padding, and hauled the rest up my leg. "What's she got that I haven't got?" I yelled.

Ponder, still urging the girls forward, turned on Luana. "You see? He saw you feeding! He could *see* you! You should have known!" and he released her and backhanded her viciously. She rolled with the blow deftly, but a lot of it connected. It was not she, however, but Claire who gasped. Luana's face was as impassive as ever. I grunted and turned to face the skull, raising the knife. "How's it go, little man?" I asked Goo-goo. I put the point of the knife on my forehead. "That it?"

He nodded vociferously, and I began to chant.

"*Ay-tay* . . ." I shifted the knife downward to my chest. Ponder was bellowing something. Claire screamed my name.

"*Mahlkuth* . . ." With part of my mind I heard, now, what Ponder was yelling. "You'll free him! Stop it, you fool, you'll free him!" And Claire's voice again: "A gun . . ." I thought, down deep inside, *Free him!* I put the knife-point on my right shoulder.

"*Vé-G'boorah!*" There was a sharp bark of a shot. Something hit the small of my back. The blue beast stumbled from between my feet, and as I shifted the knife to my left shoulder, I saw it bow down and, with its mouth, lay something at my feet. It teetered there for a split second, its eyes winking like fan-blades in bright light, and I'll swear the little devil grinned at me. Then it was gone, leaving behind a bullet on the grass.

"*Vé-Gédula* . . ." I chanted, conscious that so far I had not broken the compelling rhythm of the ancient syllables, not missed a motion with the knife. Twice more the gun yapped, and with each explosion I was struck, once in the face, once on the neck. Not by bullets, however, but by the cold rubbery hide of the swift familiar, which dropped in front of me with its little cheeks bulging out like those of a chipmunk at acorn time. It put the two bullets down by the first and vanished. I clasped my hands on the knife-hilt, pressing it to my chest, point upward the way Goo-goo had done.

"*Lé o'lam* ..." From the corner of my eye I saw Ponder hurling himself at me, and the ragged figure of little Goo-goo rising up between us. Ponder struck the little man aside with one bear-like clubbing of his forearm, and was suddenly assaulted either by fifty of the blue familiars or by one moving fifty times as fast as a living thing ought to. It was in his ears, fluttering on his face, nipping the back of his neck, clawing at his nostrils, all at once. Ponder lost one precious second in trying to bat the thing away, and then apparently decided to ignore it. He launched himself at me with a roar, just as I came out with the final syllable of the incantation: "*OM!*"

It isn't easy to tell what happened then. They say The Egg hit Hiroshima with "a soundless flash." It was like that. I stood where I was, my head turned away from the place where the skull had been, my eyes all but closed against that terrible cold radiance. Filtering my vision through my lashes, I saw Ponder still in midair, still coming toward me. But as he moved, he—changed. For a second he must have been hot, for his clothes charred. But he was cold when he hit me, cold as death. His clothes were a flurry of chilled soot; his skin was a brittle, frigid eggshell through which his bones burst and powdered. I stood, braced for a solid impact that never came, showered with the scorched and frozen detritus of what had been a man.

Still I stood, holding the knife, for hardly a full second had passed; and my vision went out with that blinding light. I saw Claire thirty yards away on her knees, her face in her hands; and whether she had fallen or was praying I could not know. Goo-goo was on the ground where Ponder had stretched him and near his body was the familiar, still at last. Beyond stood Luana, still on her feet, her auburn eyes blindly open to the great light, her face composed. She stepped forward slowly, hanging her arms, but with her head erect, her heated hair flung back. The cruel, steady light made sharp-edged shadows on the hinges of her jaw, for all they were sunlit. For a brief moment she was beautiful, and then she seemed to be walking down a stair-case, for she grew shorter as she walked. Her taut skin billowed suddenly like a pillow-slip on a clothesline, and her hair slipped down and drifted off in a writhing cloud. She opened her mouth, and it made a triangle, and she began to bleat.

They were wordless sounds, each one higher in pitch than the one before. Up and up they went, growing fainter as they grew higher, turning to rat-squeaks, mouse-squeaks, bat-squeaks, and at last a high thin whistle that was not a sound at all but a pressure on the eardrums. Suddenly there was nothing moving there at all; there was only a plaid skirt and a windbreaker tumbled together with blood on them. And a naked, lizard-like thing nosed out of the pathetic pile, raised itself up on skinny forelimbs, sniffed with its pointed snout at the light, and fell dead.

Claire drew a long, gasping breath. The sound said nothing for Claire, but much for the vale. It said how utterly quiet it was. I looked again at the plaid skirt lying tumbled on the grass, and I felt a deep pain. I did not mourn Luana, for Luana was never a woman; and I knew now that had I never seen her again after our last kiss over the gate, I would not have remembered her as a woman. But she had been beauty; she had been cool lips and infernal hair, and skin of many subtle sorts of rose; I mourned these things, in the face of which her lack of humanity was completely unimportant.

The light dimmed. I dropped the knife and went to Claire. I sank down beside her and put my arms around her. She let her hands slide off her face and turned it into my shoulder. She was not crying. I patted her hair, and we rested there until I was moved to say, "We can look at him now," and for a moment longer while we enjoyed the awe of knowing that all the while he had been standing there, released.

Then, together, we turned our heads and looked at him.

He had dimmed his pent-up light, but still he blazed. I will not say what he looked like, because he looked like only himself. I will not say he looked like a man, because no man could look like him. He said, "Claire, take off your boot."

She bent to do it, and when she had, something flowed from him to us. I had my hoof under me. I felt it writhe and swell. There was an instant of pain. I grasped the hairy ankle as the coarse hair fell out, and then my foot was whole again. Claire laughed, patting and stroking her restored foot. I had never seen her face like that before.

Then *he* laughed. I will not say what that was like either. "Thad, Thad, you've done it. You've bungled and stumbled, but you've done it." I'll say how he spoke, though. He spoke like a man.

"What have I done?" I asked. "I have been pushed and pulled; I've thought some things out, and I've been both right and wrong—what have I done?"

"You have done right—finally," he chuckled. "You have set me free. You have broken walls and melted bars that are inconceivable to you ... I'll tell you as much as I can, though.

"You see, for some hundreds of thousands of years I have had a—call it a jailer. He did not capture me: that was done by a far greater one than he. But the jailer's name was Korm. And sometimes he lived as a bird and sometimes as an animal or a man. You knew him as Ponder. He was a minor wizard, and Luana was his familiar. I too have a familiar—Tiltol there." He indicated the blue beast, stretched quietly out at his feet.

"Imprisoned, I could do very little. Korm used to amuse himself by watching my struggles, and occasionally he would set up a spell to block me even further. Sometimes he would leave me alone, to get my hopes up, to let me begin to free myself, so that he could step in and check me again, and laugh ...

"One thing I managed to do during one of those periods was to bring Claire's parents together. Korm thought that the magic thing they had between them was the tool I was developing, and when it began to look like a strong magic, he killed them. He did not know until much later that Claire was my magic; and when he found it out, he made a new and irritating spell around me, and induced Claire to come out here and walk into it. It was supposed to kill her, but she was protected; all it did was to touch her with the mark of the beast—a cloven hoof. And it immobilized me completely for some hours.

"When I could, I sent Tiltol after her with a new protection; without it she would be in real danger from Korm, for he was bound to find out how very special she was. Tiltol tried to weave the new protection around her—and found that he could not. Her aura was no longer completely her own. She had fallen in love; she had given part of herself away to you, Thad. Now, since the new spell would work only on one in Claire's particular condition, and since he could not change that, Tiltol found a very logical solution: He gave you a cloven hoof too, and then cast the protection over both of you. That's why the bear-trap did not hurt you, and why the wasps couldn't sting you."

"I'm beginning to see," I said. "But—what's this about the ritual? How did it set you free?"

"I can't explain that. Roughly, though, I might say that if you regard my prison as locked, and your presence as the key in the lock, then the ritual was the turning of the key, and use of the knife was the direction in which the key was turned. If you—or Claire, which was Korm's intention—had used the ritual without the knife, I would have been more firmly imprisoned than ever, and you two would have lived out your lives with those hooves."

"What about Goo-goo? I thought for a while that he was the jailer."

He chuckled. "Bless you, no. He is what he seems to be—a harmless, half-demented old man, keeping himself out of people's way. He isn't dead, by the way. When he wakes, he'll have no recollection of all this. I practiced on him, to see if I could get a human being to perform the ritual, and he has been a good friend. He won't lose by it. Speaking of the ritual, though, I'd like you to know that, spectacular as it might have been, it wasn't the biggest part of the battle. That happened before—when you and Claire were talking to Ponder. Remember when Claire recited the spell and didn't know what she was saying?"

"I certainly do. That was when I suddenly decided there was something funny about Ponder's story. He had hypnotized her, hadn't he?"

"Something very like it . . . he was in her mind and I, by the way, was in yours. That's what made you leap up and go to Luana."

I shuddered. "That was bad . . . evil. What about this 'good and evil' theory of Ponder's, incidentally? How could he have worked evil on you with a spell from the Bible?"

There was a trace of irritation in his voice. "You'll have to get rid of this 'black and white magic' misconception," he said. "Is a force like electricity 'white' or 'black'? You use it for the iron lung. You use it also for the electric chair. You can't define magic by its methods and its materials, but only in terms of its purpose. Regard it, not as 'black' and 'white,' but as High and Low magic. As to the Testament, why, that ritual is older than the Bible or it couldn't have been recorded there. Believe me, Ponder was using it well out of its context. Ah well, it's all over with now. You two are blessed—do you realize that? You both will keep your special immunity, and Claire shall have what she most wants, besides."

"What about you?"

"I must go. I have work to do. The world was not ordained to be without me.

"For there is reason in the world, and all the world is free to use it. But there has been no will to use it. There's wilfulness aplenty, in individuals and in groups, but no great encompassing will to work with reason. Almost no one reads a Communist newspaper but Communists, and only prohibitionists attend a dry convention. Humanity is split up into tiny groups, each clinging to some single segment of Truth, and earnestly keeping itself unaware of the other Truths that make up the great mosaic. And even when humans are aware of the fact that others share the same truth, they allow themselves to be kept apart from each other. The farmer here knows that the farmer there does not want to fight a war against him, yet they fight. I am that Will. I am the brother of Reason, who came here with me. My brother has done well, but he needs me, and you have set me free."

"Who are you?" I asked.

"The earliest men called me Kamäel."

"The Camel . . . in every language," murmured Claire. Suddenly her eyes widened. "You are—an . . . an *archangel,* Kamäel! I've read . . ."

He smiled, and we looked down, blinded.

"Tiltol!"

The tiny familiar twitched and was suddenly balancing on its two legs. It moved abruptly, impossibly fast, zoomed up to Kamäel, where it nestled in the crook of his arm. And suddenly it began to grow and change. Great golden feathers sprouted from its naked hide, and a noble crest. It spread wide wings. Its plumage was an incredible purple under its golden crest and gold-tipped wings. We stared, filling our minds with a sight no human being alive had seen—of all birds, the noblest.

"Good-bye," said Kamäel. "Perhaps one day you will know the size of the thing you have done. The One who imprisoned me will come back, one day, and we will be ready for him."

"Satan?"

"Some call him that."

"Did he leave Earth?"

"Bless you, yes! Mankind has had no devil but himself these last twenty thousand years! But we'll be ready for the Old One, now."

There was more sun, there were more colors in the world as we walked back to town.

"It was the Phoenix!" breathed Claire for the twentieth time. "What a thing to tell our children."

"Whose children?"

"Ours."

"Now look," I said, but she interrupted me. "Didn't he say I was to have what I wanted most?"

I looked down at her, trying hard not to smile. "Oh, all right," I said.

What Dead Men Tell

HE HAD TALKED with two dead men and one dead girl, and now he lay in lightlessness. He was conscious, but there was nothing anywhere to which to bring consciousness. This was a black that was darker than any other blackness. A smear of this would make a black hole in precipitated carbon.

His philosophy urged him to take an inventory. This couldn't be just *nothing*. Consciousness itself cannot exist with nothing; they are mutually exclusive. Inventory, then:

Item: A blackness.

Item: Body. Breath warmly moistening the inside edges of his nostrils, coolly drying them. A sluggish heart. Barely resilient pressure on shoulders, buttocks, calves, heels. So the body lay on its back. Fingers on chest. Fingers on fingers. Hands together, then, on the breast. Therefore: Item, body laid out. Well, of course. This was the place where death was. This was the place to discover whether death was death, or life everlasting.

Item: The philosophy itself. The important thing. The thing that all this was about. The philosophy was ... was— Later he could think of that. He had to find death first. So—

Item: Death. Just as surely as there was breath in his nostrils, as surely as he was lying there, death was here. If death found him, death was death. But if he found death, he would find his immortality. Death was here. Here; so—

Item: *Here.* There was nothing to conclude about *here. Here* was the place where he lay. It was not a place he had ever been before. There was something he had to find out about it. What? But how could he know?

Look and see, he told himself, and opened his eyes.

A blue-green radiance pressed itself between his lids. He lay with his eyes stupidly unfocused, seeing as little in the light as he had in its absence, until the straight band of lesser brightness directly above him commanded his lenses, and he saw.

He was in a tent. No—not a tent. The walls slanted up to meet overhead, but the juncture of the walls ran forward into blackness and back into blackness. It was a corridor with a triangular cross section, and he was lying on the floor. He sat up. The conscious muscular effort completed his inventory:

Item: Identity. I am me. I am Hulon—I am here.

He knelt, and automatically pulled at his single, simple garment. It was a belted tunic, sleeveless, with wide shoulder straps, and it fell to mid-thigh. He wore nothing else. He pulled at the skirt self-consciously, and examined the belt. It was a half-belt, sewn to the fabric on each side above his hips. It had no buckle; the two ends of material, when laid together, stayed together. He separated them—easily when they were peeled apart, impossible when they were pulled straight—and put them together again.

He looked about him. The floor was about thirty feet wide, and the walls seemed about the same; the cross section was an equilateral triangle. The quiet blue-green radiance flooded the floor around him and, less brilliantly, the walls and the pointed overhead. Before him and behind him, however, was utter blackness, a thick, absorbent dark that coaxed and sucked and beckoned to the light.

There was a death waiting here for him—behind him or ahead—he did not know which, but he knew it was there. He had to find out what death was, before it found him. And he had to find out one other thing, and that had to do with the corridor. He peered into the darkness before him. Was the floor tilted the slightest bit to the right?

He glanced over his shoulder at the other blackness, and steeled himself. *You know you will feel fear behind you. That's natural. It may come up behind you—but be sure. Be quite sure, or you'll have fear to fear, as well as death.*

He rose to his feet, really noticing for the first time that they were bare. The floor was resilient, cool—not cold; and there was a feeling so odd about the floor that he bent quickly and put his hand to it.

It was smooth, solid, for all its slight yielding; but in addition there was a sensation of movement in it, as if its surface were composed of myriads of microscopic eddies in violent, tiny motion.

He stood erect. The sensation was very slight under his feet, and so constant that he knew he would ignore it soon. He stepped forward, peering ahead at the floor, which seemed to be not quite canted.

He was mistaken, he found when he had moved ten or twelve paces. *Trick of the light.* The floor ahead still seemed to tilt a little, but it was certainly level under his feet. The light—it moved with him!

He stared around him, and saw only the same featureless floor and two walls, It was as if he were lighted by a spotlight which was concealed from him.

He looked behind him, and just as he turned his head, caught a movement in the corner of his eye. He gasped and leaped to the wall, pressing his back against it, staring into the blackness. There was something—there *was!* A ... a thing, an *eye!*

It was low down, almost on the floor, and it was moving toward him. Toward him, and then away, and then it stopped, and swayed, and came toward him again, and emerged into the light.

It was a bubble. A big bubble, perhaps fourteen inches in diameter, loosely filled, and apparently it derived its motion from the strange mosaic of miniature maelstroms in the floor. It danced and swayed erratically on them, sometimes turning one way, sometimes another, occasionally rolling a little.

Hulon stepped toward it. If it was alive, it paid him no attention. It moved, but quite aimlessly. As Hulon moved, the light moved with him, brightly illuminating the bubble. He watched it cautiously for a moment, and finally went down on one knee near it. He saw his distorted, dancing reflection in its side. It seemed to be filled with a clear, pale-brown fluid. He put out his hand, screwed up his courage, and touched it. It quivered like jelly but made no effort to escape. He waited until it began to roll again and quickly put his hand on the floor in front of it. It bumped off his fingers like a toy balloon, and bounced sluggishly up and down until it rested, waiting for the next capricious movement of the floor under it.

Hulon impulsively reached out and picked it up. It sagged in his hands. He pressed it gently—and it burst, leaving him staring ludicrously at his empty hands. There was a great gush of liquid which disappeared immediately when it reached the floor. There was no sign of a skin or bladder of any kind; the thing was simply gone.

Hulon wiped his hands on his tunic and shrugged. The thing was obviously inanimate. It reminded him that he was a little thirsty, but that was all. Thirsty? Perhaps a thing like this would come in handy. He had no idea how long he might be here before— He shrugged again and sniffed at his fingers. The bubble had left a faint, stimulating tang on them. Hulon nodded. If things got bad—

But couldn't this be the death? Poison?

Wait and see, he told himself. *First find out what's at the end of the corridor.* And in a flash he knew that that was what he had been hunting for in the back of his mind—the thing about *here* that he must find out. With the knowledge came the realization that only now did he have all his faculties—that from the moment he had found himself stretched out in the corridor, he had been only gradually regaining them.

How had he got here? What place was this? What was that thought about the two dead men and the dead girl he had talked with? What was the meaning of this fantastic, skimpy garment he was wearing? Where were his clothes? How did the light follow him?

His heart began to thump. He looked at the darknesses, the one which led, the one which followed. Cumulative shock began to take its toll. He turned, turned again, and then stood stock-still, his jaw muscles standing out, his eyes narrowed.

His nerves screamed *"run!"*

He stood still, trembling with the effort. Slowly, then, he went to the right wall and sat at its foot, his back comfortingly against it, his eyes shifting from darkness to darkness; and he began to sort out his thoughts.

"There are thoughts for here," he muttered, " and thoughts for outside—for before I came here." He wet his lips, and consciously relaxed his shoulders, which had begun to ache. "I am Hulon. I work at the Empire Theater, projectionist on the day shift."

327

He fixed this in his mind, refusing to think of anything else until the thought stood clear and alone.

"Now," he said, speaking softly because the absorbent walls—they seemed to be of the same static-mobile material as the floor—seemed to drink sound the way those darknesses lapped up light. "I will think of *here* first because I am here. Whatever is to happen to me will happen here, and not at the Empire Theater." Again he waited, fixing the thought on the sturdy walls of his mind until it stopped quivering.

"I don't know where this place is nor who built it. I do know that I'm here to meet death, and to find out what is at the end of the corridor. I know that if I can find out what kind of death I am to meet here, and if I can discover what is at the end of the corridor, I will live forever. If I do not find out these things, I will die here. I agreed to this, and I came of my own accord."

He looked up the corridor, and down. He saw no death. He saw in-leaning walls and a floor illuminated by the pool of light in which he was centered. He saw two bottomless mouths of darkness. And with a start he saw another bubble, wandering aimlessly out of the dark to his left. He grinned at himself, and automatically wiped his hands again on his tunic. As he did so, there was a swift movement on the wall opposite. He tensed, stared. There was nothing there. Trick of the light?

What of the light?

He moved his hands over the brief tunic again, and again saw the blurred motion on the wall.

A shadow!

He lifted the hem of the tunic, turned it up. The light was not coming to the material, but *from* it! It was luminous, through and through. No wonder the light followed him!

Conclusion made and filed. He waited, but nothing followed it in his mind, so he turned his attention to the events *outside* this place. This compartmentation of ideas was the *modus* of his philosophy, and he needed it now as never before. He completely displaced his attention from his current situation and studied the events which had led to it.

The real beginning was when he wrote "Where is Security?" for *Coswell's Magazine,* an obscure quarterly review. But his first knowledge of these strange events was the dead man he saw in the Empire Theater.

Remembering it, he was surprised that he had noticed the man at all. There are, at the best of times, three degrees of work for a theater projectionist—attentive, busy, and frantic. All three are intensified when the theater is running revivals, if it happens that the brittle old film is used, rather than remakes. And that particular night he was stuck with three of them—two features and a short, fresh from a theater where the projectionist apparently didn't believe in splicing film straight across like everybody else, and who cued only two frames instead of four, so that the little flicker of light up at the corner of the screen, which indicated when to change over projectors, was so brief that a man had to have eyes like photocells to see them at all. He missed two of them at one performance, getting a white screen and a gargle from the sound track, and the second time Mr. Shenkman, the manager, came up to the booth and was nice about it. Hulon hadn't done that in months, and he would have felt very much better about it if Mr. Shenkman had stamped and cussed, but that wasn't the manager's way, and Hulon had no one to be sore at but himself.

He had three viewing windows through which to see the screen—one by each of the big IPC Simplex projectors with their hissing Magnarcs, and one in the splicing room where the film was stored in a steel, asbestos-chimneyed locker. As he moved about the booth, his attention was almost constantly on these windows and the screen. As each reel approached its end he found himself in a near-ecstasy of concentration, trying to determine which, if any, of these spots and speckles was a scratch on the old film or a cue.

It was unthinkable, then, that his attention should have been drawn to anything else through those windows but the screen. But it was. Perhaps the picture itself—an old War I epic starring Conrad Veidt—had something to do with it. Whatever it was, as he leaned close to the glass, his foot ready to stamp the change-over switch by B projector, his eye caught the side-loom of the tobacco-filtered light over the loges directly in front of the booth.

A man sat there, his spine stiff and straight—not unnaturally, but as if this were a characteristic. The light edged a strong cheekbone, a gleaming forehead, and a monocle. There was a slender cigarette-holder—and then the cue-sign winked on the screen, and Hulon's foot came down. Projector A clattered and Projector B's arc began to hiss, the sprockets began to feed, the shields flipped down for A, up for B, and the change was made. Hulon made a slight adjustment for centering, increased the gain by the duplicated volume control directly under the viewing window. Glancing once again at the screen, he walked around the projector and stared at the line of light which was periscoped up from the arc-case and projected between two black lines on a white card, to show the size of the arc-gap. Satisfied, he opened the lower reel-housing of Projector A and unclipped the used reel. As he did so he glanced again at the screen, and again found himself staring at the man in the loges. He knew that man—he was sure of it. And if that was who he thought it was, that man was dead.

He went into the splicing room and put the reel into the rewinding machine, which started automatically as he closed its cover. Again he glanced out the window, and to his annoyance found that he was not looking at the screen at all, but at the man.

He could have sworn it was Conrad Veidt himself, the famous captain of a score of cinematic U-boats and raiders, the archetype of villainous *Oberleutnant,* the personification of the Prussian martinet.

But Veidt died years ago.

Something touched his shoulder and he grunted and jumped violently.

"Hey," said Frank, the second-shift man, "what's the matter, Hulon? Seein' ghosts?"

"Revivals are full of 'em," said Hulon. He looked at Frank's grinning, easy-going face and decided not to bother him with his hallucinations. "You'll have your hands full tonight, Frank. Here's the schedule. We're eight minutes behind. I blew two changeovers. You'll have to trim the Coming Attractions rushes a couple feet each, and Mr. Shenkman says it'll be O.K. to leave out the Merchant's Association announcement in the second show. Watch the cues. Whoever marked them has a hole in his head. And you ought to see some of the splicing! I've recut and fixed up a few of 'em and"—he opened the fire-proof locker— "I stuck slips of paper in the reels as some of that sloppy work came through. If you want to make it easier for the next guy, you can go on fixing 'em up."

"Gotcha," said Frank. "What do you keep peering out there for? See a chick in the loges you like?"

"Huh?' said Hulon. "Oh . . . thought I saw someone I knew. You all ready to take over?" The man in the loges was rising.

"That's why I'm here."

Hulon took down his coat. "O.K., chum. Don't let Hollywood go to your head." Conscious of Frank's surprise—for he usually stayed for ten or fifteen minutes to bat the breeze—he whipped open the door and went down the ladder two rungs at a time.

The man who looked like Conrad Veidt was silhouetted against the screen as he stalked down the center aisle. Hulon hurried after him, following him to and through the lobby. He breezed past Mr. Shenkman with a bare nod and was beside the monocled man as they went through the wide doors to the street.

I don't want to do this, Hulon thought to himself, *but I'll kick myself for the rest of my life if I don't.* He drew up beside the man at the corner and touched his elbow. "I beg your pardon—"

"Yess?" It was the same voice, too—full and precise.

Hulon said: "You're Conrad Veidt." He had meant to say: "You *look* like—" but the way the man turned, the way his eyebrow arched, were too like what he had seen on the screen to allow any doubt.

"Am I?" said the man, and smiled. "And do you believe in immortality?"

Hulon shuffled his feet. "Well, I . . . I guess not. No, of course not."

The man shrugged. "You know Conrad Veidt is dead. Obviously you are mistaken. Good day."

" 'Bye," said Hulon miserably. He watched the man walk away, and stood there feeling very, very foolish.

That was the first dead man, Hulon thought as he crouched against the wall of the strange corridor. Another bubble circled and danced clumsily near him. He kicked at it; it burst and its fluid disappeared into the floor. Now—who was the second?

Leslie Howard—two days later, under exactly similar circumstances: a Leslie Howard picture, a familiar profile in the loges just before Frank relieved him. He remembered wondering, as he hurried after the figure from the past, down the aisle and through the lobby, whether his attention had been drawn purposely this way, by some mysterious means, or whether it was purely accidental. If it was on purpose, what could be the purpose? What was he, that he should receive such attentions from— He lost the thought in the moment of panic in which he stood in front of the theater, peering, thinking he had lost his man. He saw him, then, at the magazine stand, buying a copy of *Coswell's Magazine.* Hulon stepped up to him. "May I have a word with you?"

The man looked at him, his head very slightly held to one side in Howard's well-remembered way. "Certainly, old man."

Hulon wet his lips. He was going to be more cautious this time. "I think you're Leslie Howard."

"The devil you do! Wasn't he killed during the war?"

"So they say."

"Then how could I possibly be?"

"I don't know. I'm not even trying to find that out. Look, whoever you are; please don't think I'm a crackpot. I'm just sort of clutching at straws, I suppose. I've got some—ideas. I do what I can with them, but as far as I can see, it'll take me more than a lifetime to work them all out. When I see someone alive who ought to be dead, something happens to me. I know it must be a resemblance, but in the zillion to one chance that a man might live longer than an average lifetime—much longer, I mean—why, I go hog-wild on it, hunt it out, track it down, just like"—the torrent of words slowed, stopped, and Hulon stood flushing while the other waited politely— "I'm doing with you right now." He laughed uncertainly. "I don't know why I feel I can sound off like this to you."

"I'll take it as a compliment," smiled the other, and clapped him on the shoulder. "But—Leslie Howard was killed, all right. Sorry." And he walked off.

Hulon thought. *No one can know a person's face like a projectionist.*

Day after day, hour after hour these faces are drilled into him; nuances of voice and expression emerge that the public never sees, any more than the public sees the flicker of a starting-cue.

The Leslie Howard man paused and said a word to a girl who stood in the doorway of the haberdashery two doors down from the Empire. She nodded and the man went away. She stood still; Hulon went toward her. *I can just walk by and look at her. There's something—*

As he neared her, she turned, and he gasped. That strange, full-lipped face and spun-aluminum hair ... they used to call her "The Blonde Bombshell." She was dead too. "Jean Harlow," he choked.

She smiled and put out her hand. "How do you do?" she said astonishingly.

He took the hand, his own self-animated to do so. He looked down at the clasped hands as if, at the job, he had found film with triangular sprocket-holes. He looked at her face and blinked. "My name's Hulon—"

"And it's your first name," said the blonde. "I know. Can we go somewhere to talk?"

He noticed under her arm the familiar orange cover of *Coswell's Magazine*—the issue in which his article had appeared. He said: "The Empire Bar has booths."

They went there. *I'll wait,* he thought. *This is crazy; there are too many questions to ask. I'll wait. She knows what she's doing.*

She asked: "How much education have you had, Hulon?"

He helped her with her coat and sat opposite. "Not much. High school. I read some."

"What made you submit to *Coswell's?*"

"They use things like that. I thought I had an important idea. It's part of a … call it a philosophy, if that doesn't sound too high-falutin'," he said.

"It's a philosophy," she said. "We can call things by their names. What a funny, shy sort of person, you are, Hulon!"

There was nothing to say to this, so he waited. A waiter came and went. Drinks arrived. "What got you interested in the idea of security enough to provoke an article like this?"

"I'm a theater projectionist. I don't follow pictures too closely, but a lot of what they're about sinks in. Seems to me a lot of real-life people are worried about security, too. I began to listen to people I know talk. A lot of them are worried about it. I began to wonder where it was. Everybody thinks it's somewhere else, never where a man can lay his hand to it and say, 'Here it is. I have it.' So I figured out where it was, and wrote it down, and *Coswell's* printed it. That's all."

"I read the article. But tell me again—where is security?"

"Behind us." He looked at her expectant face, and expanded the statement. "No use looking into the future for security because the future doesn't belong to us—it's a dream, a bunch of maybes. No use looking in the present for it because the present is, in time, like a mathematical point—a position, without any area. So the only thing a man has is behind him—his memories. The only thing a man can look forward to is looking back at where he's been. What he has means nothing. What he *has had* is the only thing he can hold on to—the only thing that no power on Earth can touch. And anybody who tries to run security down will come up against that—possessions that nothing can touch, things that really belong to a man. So"—he shrugged—"security is not in the future, a sort of mountaintop that people are climbing to. And it isn't in the present, because 'now' covers such a small area in time that it's nonexistent; you can't have security or a cigarette or an automobile in a portion of time so small it can't be measured. It's behind us. It lies only in what we've had and in what we've done."

"That's a startling idea," she said. "It sort of takes away any possibility of self-determination, though, doesn't it? According to your idea, a man can act only in his present, and the present is too short a time to do anything with."

"No it isn't," said Hulon positively. "You can do this much with your present—you can shape the nature of things to form the best possible memory for yourself. You can form the cross section of the passing time-stream as if you were a diamond die, and give it just the cross section that will suit your memory the best."

"And that means that there can be no security for *now,* for this minute?"

"No," Hulon said again. "Security for this minute is a kind of self-confidence that comes from a sort of radar; impulses sent from now, reflecting from things we have been and had and done."

"Good," said the girl. "I'm sorry to be catechizing you like this. I had to know whether you retain what you set down or whether you were amusing yourself with a passing idea. Now tell me; is this security business your philosophy?"

"Oh no," said Hulon. "It's just part of it. It comes from it."

"Ah. And have you reduced that philosophy to its essentials? Can you say what it is in a few words?"

"Not yet. Not few enough." He pondered for a moment. "I can say this much. And mind you, it isn't as rock bottom as it will be, but it's as far as I've gone, from watching people, and machines, and from reading and listening to music. It's this:

"What is basic is important.

"What is basic is simple.

"So what is complicated isn't important. It might be interesting or exciting—it might even be necessary to something else that's complicated— but it isn't important."

She nodded. "That's good. That's very good. And—what would you do with an idea like that? Turn the whole world into a gigantic Walden?"

Hulon had not read Thoreau. He missed the reference, and said so. When she explained, he said: "Gosh no. I'm no fanatic, wanting to get everybody back to hunting, fishing and building their own log cabins. All I want to do is to think everything out according to that idea of mine. I mean everything: art and engineering and business and politics. I think I could work it all out, if I had time."

"And then what would you do with it?"

"I'd try to teach it to people—to more and more people, until it got to be a natural way of thinking. The way people let themselves think now just makes trouble. People think if it's bigger it's better. They think if a little is good, a lot has just got to be wonderful. They can see the sense of balance in a diet or in a bridge, but they stop too easily at things like that, and don't try to balance enough other things. Or enough other *kinds* of things," he added, after a pause. "But all that's 'way ahead of me. What bothers me now is that I don't have time to think all this out. I know how big it is, and what a little moment a life is. I could do more with an idea like this if I knew, somehow, that all my thinking wasn't going to get cut off one fine day by the old man with the scythe."

"And that's really important to you?"

"Really important. Basic," he added, grinning shyly. "So much that if I see someone on the street who ought to be dead, I'll stop and ask him who he is, just in case—just on the crazy chance that someone might've found out how to live longer."

"How do you know anyone could?"

Hulon spread his hands. "I don't. But it could happen. Old age is some kind of a biological mistake. Maybe someone has figured out where the mistake was made. Maybe that was done a long time ago. If it had been done, it wouldn't be the sort of thing you'd advertise in the daily papers. Too many people are afraid of dying. Too many more people want to live so that they can get more and more things, more and more power. People would mob whoever had a treatment like that to sell, and either the wrong people would live long, or the treatment would overpopulate the Earth, and the human race would war itself out of existence for food and space to live."

"You're so right. You have a startling kind of simplicity, Hulon. You drive and drive right to the root of a thing. Suppose there were such a treatment; can you say anything else about the person or persons who might control it?"

Hulon thought for a moment. "I think so. They would be very careful people. They would have to be able to consider the greatest good for humanity above any race or religious or national lines. They would have to be able to think ahead—years, centuries ahead. They would have to be able to hold their hands, keep from interfering, even when interfering might save thousands of lives. They would have to put pressure here and nudge a little there in quiet ways, so that they would never be found out, and so that humanity would always think it was learning from its own mistakes and nothing else."

"Do you think you are such a person?"

"No!" Hulon said immediately. "But I know I could be if I lived long enough. I think the right way to be that kind of person." The statement was simple and sincere, without braggadocio.

The girl considered him for a long, pensive moment. At last she asked him softly: "If there were immortals on Earth, and if they were all you say, what would be their most urgent need?"

Twice, captured by her eyes, he opened his mouth to speak and closed it again. Finally he said: "Recruits."

She held her gaze on him, unmoving; then she nodded, as if to herself. "How much would you give for a chance to join them?"

"How much have I got? I'd give anything."

"Your life? Would you undertake a test that would kill you if you failed?"

"Of course."

She swirled her drink, "Hulon. Nothing is unique about that philosophy of yours. There is something unusual about your method. You've come a long way on very little material. You think clearly and your motives are clean. That's not much to go on. If you took such a test, the odds would be very much against you."

"Tell me," he asked, wrinkling his brow. "Why would I have to die if I failed?"

"Because you'd know too much."

"I know a great deal now."

"You are having a barroom conversation with a girl you picked up," she said bluntly. "No one would believe a word you might say even if I confirmed it, which of course I wouldn't. But if—and mind you, I'm still talking ifs—if such a situation did exist, and if you did take such a test, fail it, and emerge from it, you might cause trouble. Such a risk cannot be taken."

"That makes sense. Well, when do I start?"

She opened her handbag and took out a lipstick. Unscrewing the cap, she slipped a nail file from under the flap of the purse and inserted it into the cap. She worked it deftly forward and back; it fell into two parts, and a small blue pill rolled into the hollow of her hand. She took Hulon's glass and dropped the tablet in. The liquid began to effervesce violently. She handed it back. "When the effervescence stops, drink it immediately. All of it."

He took it, held it, waiting, and said gravely: "Are you Jean Harlow?"

She laughed. "Of course not. You had to seek us out, and you had to do it because you might find one case of extended life, and not for any other reason. You passed that part of it, Hulon. We did it this way because you are a projectionist; you could be expected to notice us particularly. We have other ways, too."

It was the first time she had said "we." His heart began to pound. Abruptly the activity in the glass ceased, completely. "May you live forever," he said, and drank it down.

He could not remember very clearly what happened after that. He saw clearly, he walked steadily, he spoke coherently. There is a linkage between the conscious mind and the memory, through which flows each impression, as noticed, to be stored. And in Hulon, this link was broken, or at least compressed, pinched off, so that any impression, once received, was lost in seconds. He remembered walking, and then a ride—it was a car, but whether a taxi or a private automobile he could not recall—and, after riding for a time which may have been minutes or hours, there was a room with several people in it. The girl was lost somewhere en route; there were other women, but how many or what they looked like was lost to him. There was a man with a stern gray face who talked with him for a long time, and a room with a wheeled table and pale-green cornerless walls. And there was a time when he repeated and repeated two questions:

Where is the end of the corridor?
What death will I meet there?

And the gray-faced man, kindly now, wishing him well, xreassuring

338

him, making him certain that he would have his reward if he could answer these questions.

And the next thing had been his awakening here in the green-lit dark.

Hulon rose and stepped to the center of the corridor. He paused and listened. Nothing. He drew a deep breath, turned to the right and began to march down the corridor. The skin on his back crawled occasionally, away from the following darkness, and he did what he could to ignore it. He began to count his paces, looking back as he counted each fifteen. Surely nothing would overtake him in the time it took him to walk fifteen paces.

After a few minutes the counting and turning became automatic, and his senses became quite soothed—almost dulled—by the sameness of his surroundings. Occasionally, he passed one or two of the bubbles doing their purposeless gavotte on the floor. Once he saw two collide, fuse, burst and disappear.

Where was death?

It would have to be a death from outside himself, he reasoned. Aside from the fact that the featureless walls and floor gave him nothing to hang himself on, and the complete absence of anything which he might turn on himself, the idea of self-destruction was contrary to the very nature of the test. So, he realized suddenly, was any idea that he might die of hunger or thirst. There was no time limit to his test. Death must present itself to him, or he to it, and that might take days. He must sleep. Would death come to him in his sleep? He shrugged. He could only put off sleep as long as possible and then hope that he would sleep lightly enough to be warned of its approach.

He began to be thirsty. The next bubble he approached took his attention. He stopped and watched it for a moment, then drew a deep breath and picked it up gently. He remembered a story he had read once, called "Goldfish Bowl," in which two men were trapped by super-intelligences, and got their water in globules which were apparently made of just water: when they bit into one they could drink what didn't spill. Hulon was in a mood to forget everything he had ever learned and simply to use what he saw. Accordingly he pressed his face into the bubble and drew it into his mouth. The surface let go and the bubble ceased to be a bubble, pouring down through his fingers. He cupped his hands and managed to gulp heartily, twice, before all the liquid was gone. It had a flavor something like beef extract and something like the water in which asparagus has been cooked, and he found it delicious. If the fluid had any ill effects, he could not feel them. He wondered for an instant at his own foolhardiness, and then concluded that he must have been told, before he came here, that the bubbles were safe for him.

He began to walk, and the resumption of his attention to the corridor brought sharply to him that something was different. It had happened gradually, and only his transient concentration on his thirst made it possible for him to notice the difference. It was in the light. It had lost its greenish cast and was now pure yellow.

"—Thirteen, fourteen, fifteen," he muttered, and looked behind him. Nothing but advancing darkness. "One, two, three—

"*Uh!*"

The wordless syllable was wrenched from him by the glimmer ahead. It was utterly shocking. It was a feature in the featureless triangle. It was a new color in the dichromatic yellow and black. It was a new factor in the lulling sameness of the corridor. And it was a dead man.

He could tell that the man was dead. It was the sparseness of the flesh about the nostrils, the waxen quality of the wrinkled hands folded so meticulously, the statuesque stillness, and, ever so faintly, the smell.

It was the body of an old, old man. It was laid out stiffly, ankles together, hands folded on the thin chest. It wore a garment like Hulon's but without the luminescence. It glowed, but obviously by reflection, and the color of that reflection made his eyes ache. It was red.

Hulon approached the corpse slowly and looked down at it. Was this the death he was to meet?

No. Death was here, all right, but there was no question in his mind that the death he sought was his own, not that of anyone else.

This was someone else who had found it. This was, if he chose to make it so, evidence that death visited this corridor from time to time.

He knelt and put the back of his hand against the still forehead. It was cold. Hulon stood up, stood back. Who had laid out the corpse?

Well, who had put Hulon there? These were pointless questions. He hesitated a moment longer, and then resolutely turned his back on the corpse and strode on. Before him was the same open blackness. Behind him the glimmer of reflected light dwindled, and blackness paced him. "—Twelve, thirteen, fourteen, look back. One, two, three—"

The light was changing again. When had the pure yellow taken on that orange cast?

He determined not to think. He would watch ahead and behind. He would notice the light. He would drink when he was thirsty and, if he must, he would sleep. If he were to deduce the nature of the death that was here, he wanted more evidence. If he were to find what was at the end of the corridor, he must walk to it. Meanwhile he would not think.

The orange color was deepening, somehow—reddening. He watched as he walked, walked, turned, walked, walked, turned. And at about the moment he recognized it as a yellowless red, a true red, he saw another gleam of light ahead. He was not sure how much later this was—two hours, three—he knew only that he had been walking a long time

He slowed his pace and approached the glimmer cautiously. Last time it had been a corpse. This time—

He grunted. This time it was a corpse, too. An old man, and again he sensed death. This one was worse to look on than the other. It, too, wore a short tunic, glowing with reflected light which, insanely, was not the same color as the light which struck it. It was pure blue. That was not the horrible thing, though. What horrified Hulon was the pose of the corpse.

It was not neatly laid out like the other. It was tumbled rudely on the floor, not quite in the middle of the corridor, as if it had been thrown there. The tunic was up around its chest and one arm was crumpled underneath in a way impossible unless it had been broken.

For years Hulon had felt that the flesh, once dead, was of little importance, and had regarded the rituals of burial and the somber traditions of *de mortuis nil nisi bonum* mere carry-overs of barbarism. In spite of this he found himself filled with horror and pity at the sight of this poor tumbled thing. He knelt by it, turned it on its back. An eye stared. He closed it gently, gently folded the hands and straightened the legs, and smoothed the tunic.

He stood up, feeling, somehow, better than he had. "You take it easy now, feller," he said. "'Bye now." He began to walk, walk, turn again. At the first look back the corpse was a corpse; at the second, a dim blue. At the third there was only the respectful, persistent, stalking darkness. After that, only the unchanging, hypnotic triangle in which he walked between shadows.

In due time his tunic was violet, and when he saw the third dead man, the one in yellow, his tunic had turned blue.

The yellow-clad corpse was harder for him to see, somehow. Perhaps it was weariness, perhaps it was the undefining blue which streamed around him, but it took him some moments to discover, as he rolled and pulled the corpse, straightening it out, that it, too, had a broken arm. This one was heaped and tossed, worse even than the last one had been.

He stood over the body, after he had finished, and tried to think. A bubble wandered drunkenly over to him and began to nudge the dead man. Hulon kicked it so hard he hurt his knee. It splashed its liquid all over the corpse's face and neck.

"Sorry," said Hulon abjectly. He turned away and began plodding down the corridor, counting aloud "—Nine, ten, eleven—" By the third time he got to "fifteen" and looked back, the darkness had swallowed up the third corpse.

It was a long time later when he came on the next rumpled, disordered corpse. He did not touch this one. He moved close enough so that his light—yellow now, after an interminable shift through the greens—would immediately fall on the fourth corpse. It was dressed in red, and had an unnatural arm. Hulon breathed slowly, deeply, through flared nostrils. His eyes were dull and he ached with weariness, and the soles of his feet tingled infuriatingly from their constant contact with the strange irresolute surface of the floor.

If I could sleep for a while, he thought desperately.

A bubble pirouetted into the wall and bounced. He went to it and picked it up in widespread hands. This time he was careful and drank deeply of it. He shook his hands and wiped them on his tunic, and sat down by the wall to rest, and to think if he could. The taste of the bubble liquid was good in his throat. He could feel strength pouring back into his abused tissues. The light seemed to grow brighter, though he knew that it was his clearing eyes that caused it. He pulled his feet in and rested his chin on his knees, and at last thought returned to him.

Four old dead men. He fixed his mind on this and let everything else disappear from his mind. Then he took them in order.

The first was dressed in red, the second in blue, the third, yellow—and the fourth was red again. There was something about these colors that niggled at him. It wasn't the specific colors; it was the order in which they appeared. There was some sort of regimentation to the colors he had seen.

He put the thought of the dead men's clothes aside, because, at the moment, he could go no further with it. He closed his eyes and concentrated. The color of his own garment—yellow-green when he awoke here; pure yellow when he found the first corpse; then yellow-orange; orange; orange-red; pure red. The word "primaries" occurred to him. He caught it and held it. *Yellow is to red as red is to blue as—* He shook himself violently. Either he was near something important or he was delirious.

He looked at the corpse. An unremarkable old man, except for his age, which was extreme. What mad system was behind this business of corpses with broken arms? What point was proved, what evidence given, by a collection of ancient and similar cadavers which were somehow associated with the primary colors and broken arms and—and what else was it? Oh yes; they were huddled, dumped out on the floor. Except for the first one, of course.

Colors. A luminous garment—he racked his brains now—which changed from yellow-green to yellow, orange, red, violet, blue, green and yellow again. Spectral.

The light had been yellow when he saw the corpse in red; red when he saw the corpse in blue; and—yes, and blue when he saw the corpse in yellow. And the one he looked at now was the same as the first; the light was yellow and the corpse was dressed in red.

Same as the first! The idea smote him—and he immediately discarded it. There are some things one may not doubt. If this were the same corpse over again, then one of two things was happening; the corpse was being shifted—snatched from the corridor behind him and rushed up and dumped ahead, and being changed in the meantime, to boot—or this corridor was circular. The first hypothesis was ridiculous in terms of the test he was undergoing; the people who controlled it were certainly not going to indulge in fantastic and harmless complications just to annoy him pointlessly. The second—that the corridor was circular—could be believed only if he disbelieved everything his sense of balance and direction and orientation told him. He *knew* he had been walking on a level surface, and in a straight line. Every sense involved told him he had.

And, yet—

He crawled to the corpse and knelt beside it. It *was* very like the one before. And the broken arm, and—suddenly he remembered the vicious kick he had given that bubble, and how it had splashed on the last corpse—or was it the last but one? He couldn't remember, and it wasn't important. He sniffed at his fingers. The refreshing, meaty odor of the bubble-liquid was still on his hands from the last time he had drunk. He bent low over the corpse's still, twisted face.

Unmistakably, the odor was there.

He scrambled back to the wall and huddled there. He clung to a single conviction, that whatever was there, whether he could understand it or not, was here by design, for a specific purpose which involved him. And he knew now, beyond the slightest doubt, that the colors had confused him utterly. It had taken him four encounters to realize it, and he was almost certain that he could expect no more "evidence." Now, of all times, was the occasion for him to apply the philosophical analysis of which he had been so proud. It seemed a paltry tool indeed.

Could this corridor be circular?

It seemed impossible. Even though he had walked a long way between corpses, he was sure he would have been conscious of the arc. One or another of the walls would have continually crowded him.

With a conscious effort he opened his imaginative faculty. He had read fantasies in which antigravity and gravity-controlling devices had been used. Suppose his corridor really was circular—but vertically, like an automobile tire? And suppose, at its hub, was an artificial gravity device. Would he not then walk in a straight line, turning neither to right nor left, and then come back to his starting point? Such a fantastic device would have to compensate for the Earth constant, of course, but if he could imagine a gravity generator, a gravity insulator was no problem.

He opened his mouth to shout his conclusion—and checked himself. *Wait*. This was only a hypothesis, and it did not answer the two questions. It made ridiculous the first one: "What is at the end of the corridor?" and did not answer the second at all: "What death will you meet there?"

No: He must think of something which covered everything—the shape and size of the corridor, the changing colors, the nutrient bubbles, the corpses. The *corpse*.

He stared at the body of the old, old man. "You could tell me—" he muttered. "Think—*think!*"

The corridor couldn't be circular; it just *couldn't*. And yet, if there were some way— If he could only ... only— He snapped his fingers. All he had to do was mark the wall or the floor, and walk! If he could come back upon the mark again—

"Mark it how?" he asked himself aloud. This crazy surface wouldn't take a mark. Moisture disappeared on it. The corpse stayed on it; he himself stayed on it, but the resilient surface couldn't be scratched, wouldn't stain.

Use the corpse as a mark, then. But—he couldn't trust it. He found it tumbled about, and wearing a different tunic each time.

The answer occurred to him. It had undoubtedly been in his mind for minutes, but he could not face it. For a time he crouched there not thinking at all. Gradually, then, he let the terrifying thought emerge. He began to tremble.

He looked at the beckoning blacknesses. He clenched his fists and made a sobbing sound. He rose then, and carefully bent to the corpse, straightening the light old limbs, crossing the hands on the chest, smoothing the scarlet tunic. "Don't go away," he murmured.

He peeled his own belt apart and slipped the shining yellow garment off. Kneeling, he tucked it under the belt the corpse wore, tightening it down until there could be no chance of its coming free by itself. Then naked and terribly alone, he strode into the darkness.

The shadows folded themselves happily about him. He looked back. The golden radiance from his tunic poured upward from the red-clad corpse. And there was something wrong about the floor on which it lay.

He moved closer to the right wall, trailing his fingers lightly along it to guide him as he walked into deeper blackness. He looked back again. What he saw made him clutch convulsively at the leaning wall, in a sudden attack of vertigo.

The corpse, as clear and distant as something spotlighted on a stage, was just as he had left it. But between him and the corpse, the floor seemed to have bellied downward, and twisted as well, so that the dead man lay as if on a slanted deck. The slant seemed almost enough to make the body roll, though it did not.

Hulon moved sidewise along the wall, away from the dimming light. The floor where the corpse was seemed to be canting more and more as he moved, and the floor between him and the body seemed to fall downward away from the corpse and up again to him. And in a few minutes the distant picture apparently rotated up and out of sight, and he moved steadily forward into an unthinkable dark.

It must have been a half hour later when he began to whimper. He was hardly aware of it at first. He ground his teeth and walked. His inner conviction was that he had analyzed his situation correctly, and that there was, therefore, nothing to fear. But if he were wrong—

what might be lurking in this blackness? What horror might spring at him to rip and tear his soft unprotected flesh, or slide slimily over him, throwing fold after fold of cold wet coils about him?

He heard his own soft whimpering and stopped it abruptly. *You are alone here,* he told himself fervently. *There is nothing to fear.* He stopped, slid down to the floor, huddled up in a foetal posture, to rest. In the quiet, in a blackness so complete that he could see the ruddy flashes of his own pulse, he forced his mind to be still.

Something cold touched his bare hip. He writhed away and screamed, knowing in the same instant that it was one of the bubbles. His heart thumped so hard that he was panicked, suddenly, lest it make so much noise that he could not hear the approach of . . . of— *But I'm alone here,* he scoffed.

He fumbled for the bubble, touched it, lifted it and drank quickly. The highly nutrient solution soothed him in and out as he drank and spilled. He rested a moment more and then rose, stretched. *Soon I should see light,* he thought as he walked. *And if I am right, the light should be red, and the old man will be dressed in . . . in—* Aloud he began to chant softly as he walked, "Violet, blue, green, yellow, orange, red, violet, blue, green—"

Before him, so dimly that it could easily have been a trick over his hypersensitive, straining eyes, he began to see a loom of light. He quickened his pace. Soon, now, he would know.

His whole body strained toward the light, and he became increasingly conscious of the deeper darkness behind him. Almost hysterically he blanked out the ancestral fears which crowded at his bare back and shoulders, which increased as he increased his speed.

And now it was unmistakably light, and the light was red. Hulon laughed, and began to run. He could see the walls now, and again could know the shape of the corridor. Again he saw the floor sweeping down and away from him and then up to the hidden light-source. When the source finally burst upon his vision, he grunted and threw his arm over his eyes. He slowed to a panting walk, slitted his lids, until he could see again.

He saw a tumbled corpse, and it was dressed in blue. Red light and a blue tunic, and he was right! He was right!

347

He sprinted toward the spraddled, dead figure which, distantly, seemed to be clinging to the wall—a wall which leaned and twisted and joined the leaning and twisting floor under his feet. This gave him no more vertigo, for now he understood it, and his vision was no longer in conflict with the sense of balance and orientation which told him with all the authority of thirty years of refined experience that the floor was level and flat.

He pounded up to the corpse, which was, when he reached it, lying on the level floor on which he stood. He grinned at it. "Thanks, fella," he chuckled. He took the luminous red tunic and slipped it out of the blue belt of the garment the corpse wore. He slipped it over his head and fastened it. Then he filled his lungs and shouted.

"Come get me! I have the answers!"

His voice was lapped up greedily in the echoless place. Stiffly he waited. Then, shockingly, the light went out.

Hulon stood stiffly in the total dark. *I've shot my bolt,* he thought defiantly. *There can't be any other answer.*

Barely to be heard over his tense breathing, there was a small, steady hiss. An acrid mist swirled into his nostrils. He tried not to breathe, but it made him gasp, and when he did that there was a loud singing in his ears and he fell heavily, quite conscious, quite unable to move.

The hiss ceased. Silence. Then the hum of a suction fan. The acrid smell disappeared. He lay limply, half on his side, for minutes.

A blaze of yellow light hurt his eyes. Somewhere the wall had opened. There were people around him. A girl—the same one he had spoken with first, but her hair was chestnut now. And the gray-faced man, who asked "Can you hear me, Hulon?"

"Yes," said Hulon clearly.

"You're ready to give the answers?"

"Yes."

The man knelt beside him. "The vapor you just breathed will kill you in two minutes," he said calmly. "I have a hypodermic here which can keep that from happening. After I give you that—if I do—you will die within two hours. There is further treatment, of course. It's the one you came here for. It will kill you within ... oh, say twelve

348

or fourteen hundred years if it isn't renewed. Now: give me the answers, and if they are correct, you'll get the hypo. Give me your reasoning and if that's acceptable you get the final treatment. Do you understand? You will die now, or in two hours, or not at all."

"I understand," said Hulon steadily. It was odd, being able to speak but not to move.

"What is at the end of the corridor?"

"I am," said Hulon. It—has no end."

"What death was waiting for you?"

Hulon said carefully, "Aside from anything you might do to me, there was only one kind of death here, as long as it was warm and I was fed. Old age."

The hypodermic bit into his shoulder. "Oh, good boy, good boy!" said the girl.

They helped him up when he said his legs were beginning to tingle, and turned him toward an irregular opening in one wall. He noticed that the surface of the wall seemed violently agitated at the edges of the doorway. He was half carried into a short tunnel with a steel door at the other end. This door swung open at their approach, and they stepped down into what appeared to be a comfortably furnished doctor's office. Hulon was put into an easy-chair near the desk. The gray-faced man sat on the swivel-chair and the girl perched on the edge of the desk. She smiled at him, and he smiled back.

"Look," said the man, pointing to a box on his desk. It looked like a small speaker. He flipped a switch on its side. "This is a microphone. There are a lot of people listening. If they like what they hear, you're in. There's a green light and a red light—see? I don't have to explain that much further, eh? Except to tell you that all votes are integrated and it'll take a two-thirds majority to make either light come on. Shall we go ahead?"

"I have something less than two hours," said Hulon wryly. "P'raps we'd better."

The doctor grinned. "Right. Just tell it in your own way; what you figured out about that corridor, and how."

"Well," said Hulon carefully, "the easiest thing to figure out was that it was endless—that is, it turned back on itself in some way. I figured that it has some sort of gravity mechanism under the floor. That right?"

The girl nodded. "How did you think of that?"

"That was the only way it could have worked. It didn't appear to curve to right or left. And at first I guessed that it was a vertical circle, like an automobile tire. But that idea fell down after I tied my tunic to the dead man and walked away from it, and saw the way the corridor twisted. The color of the light was the real tip-off. As I moved through the corridor, it went right around the spectrum. Every time I ran into the corpse, I found that his clothes were a different color—and his colors changed around the spectrum, too. When I was a kid in school we learned the colors by their initials: V, B, G, Y, O, R. Well, if you consider those as six 'points' on the band, you'll see that the color of the dead man's clothes were always two 'points' behind. On top of that, I saw that every time I bumped into the dead man I was one third of the way through the spectrum. So I had three 'thirds' to put together: I met the corpse a third of the way through the spectrum—the corpse's clothes were a third of the spectrum behind the color of mine—and the triangular cross section of the corridor. There's only one explanation that fits all these things, along with the fact that that poor old fellow was tumbled all over himself each time I came on him. And it's sort of . . . hard to describe.

"Try," said the doctor.

"Well," said Hulon, "a while back my relief at the theater, Frank, showed me something that kept me tickled for hours. He'd read about it in a magazine or somewhere. He took a strip of scrap film about eighteen inches long and put the ends together. He turned one end over and spliced 'em. Now, if you trace that strip, or mark it with a grease pencil, right up the center, you find that the doggone thing only has one side!"

The doctor nodded, and the girl said: "A Möbius strip."

"That what they call it?" said Hulon. "Well, I figured this corridor must be something like that. On that strip, a single continuous line touched both sides. All I had to do was figure out an object built so that a continuous line would cover all three of three sides, and I'd have it. So I sat down and thought it out.

"If you take a piece of clay and make a long ... uh ... sausage out of it, and then form it so it has a triangular cross section; and then if you bring the ends together and rotate one one hundred twenty degrees and stick 'em together, you'd have a figure like that. It would have only one side, like the ... what was it? ... Möbius strip."

"Nice reasoning," said the doctor. "You're quite right. Incidentally, it would have only one edge, too."

"It would? I never thought of that. Anyway, I visualized a figure like that, and then imagined one that was hollow, and myself inside it. Now, as for the light, my guess is that it moved through the spectrum one third of the way each time I went around the circle, and all the way through the spectrum when I'd been around three times—that is, when I reached the place where the same 'wall' was a floor again. I think the walls of the corridor were a floor, one after the other, I mean."

"That's pretty clear. The corridor is what a topologist calls a non-simply-connected continuous trifacial. Now, what's your guess about gravity?"

"I can only say *what* was done," said Hulon, frowning. "Not *how*. But it seems to me that the whole corridor was somehow insulated from Earth's gravity, and that my feet in some way controlled an artificial gravity in the place. In other words, wherever I walked was 'down'. And that effect only worked lengthwise along any side that was a 'floor' at the moment. I mean, if I had turned and tried walking up the wall, it wouldn't have worked, even though that wall did become a floor later, when I came on it endwise. That's what tumbled the dead man around like that every time I got him laid out. He'd lie nice and still until a wall beside him became a floor, and the floor on which he lay became a wall. Then he'd simply fall away onto what was now a floor."

"Good!" said the doctor heartily. "And have you any idea why you always found him dressed in a different color?"

"Not really. Unless it was just a characteristic of the material to reflect yellow in blue light, red in yellow light, and blue in red light. I don't know how that could be, but I don't know how controlled gravity could be either."

"All right! You're doing fine. One more question, and we'll have the vote. Why do you suppose we set up the test just the way we did?"

"Why I . . . I imagine so you could test about everything there is to test in a man," said Hulon. "To see if he can analyze things he observes—even things that are against all his previous experience."

"That's right," smiled the doctor. "Including how badly he can be scared, and still think straight." He bent to the speaker. "Vote," he said shortly.

There was a tense pause, and then the green light flickered, went out, lit—and stayed alight.

The doctor clapped his hands together delightedly, and the girl skipped down from the desk and kissed Hulon's cheek.

"You're in, boy," said the doctor. "You are right all down the line. Antigravity is something we've had for a long time. The surfaces in the corridor are coated with a substance that is in superficial molecular motion; we used it because it can't be marked. Your tunic is treated with a substance that fluoresces right through the spectrum, excited by ultra-high-frequency radio waves. And the dead man—not a real one, by the way—had a tunic treated to do just what you guessed—it reflects light a third of the spectrum away from the color of the light-source. You'll learn all about these things in time." He rose. "Let's get to it."

Hulon rose with him. He felt wonderful. "And then what?"

"Then you'll go right back to your job, like the rest of us. You'll spend a lot of time with your new 'steady,' of course, and once in a while you'll attend a meeting. But by and large, things will be the same."

" 'Steady'?" asked Hulon.

The girl said, "Me," and gave him a smile that made his head swim.

"Now this," said Hulon, "I am going to like!"

The Hurkle Is a Happy Beast

THIS ALL HAPPENED quite a long time ago. . . .

Lirht is either in a different universal plane or in another island galaxy. Perhaps these terms mean the same thing. The fact remains that Lirht is a planet with three moons, one of which is unknown, and a sun, which is as important in its universe as is ours.

Lirht is inhabited by gwik, its dominant race, and by several less highly developed species which, for purposes of this narrative, can be ignored. Except, of course, for the hurkle. The hurkle are highly regarded by the gwik as pets, in spite of the fact that a hurkle is so affectionate that it can have no loyalty.

The prettiest of the hurkle are blue.

Now, on Lirht, in its greatest city, there was trouble, the nature of which does not matter to us, and a gwik named Hvov, whom you may immediately forget, blew up a building which was important for reasons we cannot understand. This event caused great excitement, and gwik left their homes and factories and strubles and streamed toward the center of town, which is how a certain laboratory door was left open.

In times of such huge confusion, the little things go on. During the "Ten Days That Shook the World" the cafes and theaters of Moscow and Petrograd remained open, people fell in love, sued each other, died, shed sweat and tears; and some of these were tears of laughter. So on Lirht, while the decisions on the fate of the miserable Hvov were being formulated, gwik still fardled, funted, and fupped. The great central hewton still beat out its mighty pulse, and in the anams the corsons grew. . . .

Into the above-mentioned laboratory, which had been left open through the circumstances described, wandered a hurkle kitten. It was very happy to find itself there; but then, the hurkle is a happy

353

beast. It prowled about fearlessly—it could become invisible if frightened—and it glowed at the legs of the tables and at the glittering, racked walls. It moved sinuously, humping its back and arching along on the floor. Its front and rear legs were as stiff and straight as the legs of a chair; the middle pair had two sets of knees, one bending forward; one back. It was engineered as ingeniously as a scorpion, and it was exceedingly blue.

Occupying almost a quarter of the laboratory was a huge and intricate machine, unhoused, showing the signs of development projects the galaxies over—temporary hook-ups from one component to another, cables terminating in spring clips, measuring devices standing about on small tables near the main work. The kitten regarded the machine with curiosity and friendly intent, sending a wave of radiations outward which were its glow, or purr. It arched daintily around to the other side, stepping delicately but firmly on a floor switch.

Immediately there was a rushing, humming sound, like small birds chasing large mosquitoes, and parts of the machine began to get warm. The kitten watched curiously, and saw, high up inside the clutter of coils and wires, the most entrancing muzziness it had ever seen. It was like heat flicker over a fallow field; it was like a smoke vortex; it was like red neon lights on a wet pavement. To the hurkle kitten's senses, that red-orange flicker was also like the smell of catnip to a cat, or anise to a terrestrial terrier.

It reared up toward the glow, hooked its forelegs over a bus bar—fortunately there was no ground potential—and drew itself upward. It climbed from transformer to power pack, skittered up a variable condenser—the setting of which was changed thereby—disappeared momentarily as it felt the bite of a hot tube, and finally teetered on the edge of the glow.

The glow hovered in mid-air in a sort of cabinet, which was surrounded by heavy coils embodying tens of thousands of turns of small wire and great loops of bus. One side, the front, of the cabinet was open, and the kitten hung there fascinated, rocking back and forth to the rhythm of some unheard music it made to contrast this sourceless flame. Back and forth, back and forth it rocked and wove, riding a wave of delicious, compelling sensation. And once, just once, it moved its center of gravity too far from its point of support. Too far—far enough. It tumbled into the cabinet, into the flame.

One muggy mid-June a teacher, whose name was Stott and whose duties were to teach seven subjects to forty moppets in a very small town, was writing on a blackboard. He was writing the word Madagascar, and the air was so sticky and warm that he could feel his undershirt pasting and unpasting itself on his shoulderblade with each round "a" he wrote.

Behind him there was a sudden rustle from the moist seventh-graders. His schooled reflexes kept him from turning from the board until he had finished what he was doing, by which time the room was in a young uproar. Stott about-faced, opened his mouth, closed it again. A thing like this would require more than a routine reprimand.

His forty-odd charges were writhing and squirming in an extraordinary fashion, and the sound they made, a sort of whimpering giggle, was unique. He look at one pupil after another. Here a hand was busily scratching a nape; there a boy was digging guiltily under his shirt; yonder a scrubbed and shining damsel violently worried her scalp.

Knowing the value of individual attack, Stott intoned; "Hubert, what seems to be the trouble?"

The room immediately quieted, though diminished scrabblings continued. "Nothin', Mister Stott," quavered Hubert.

Stott flicked his gaze from side to side. Wherever it rested, the scratching stopped and was replaced by agonized control. In its wake was rubbing and twitching. Stott glared, and idly thumbed a lower left rib. Someone snickered. Before he could identify the source, Stott was suddenly aware of an intense itching. He checked the impulse to go after it, knotted his jaw, and swore to himself that he wouldn't scratch as long as he was out there, front and center. "The class will—" he began tautly, and then stopped.

There was a—a *something* on the sill of an open window. He blinked and looked again. It was a translucent, bluish cloud which was almost nothing at all. It was less than a something should be, but it was indeed more than a nothing. If he stretched his imagination just a little, he might make out the outlines of an arched creature with too many legs, but of course that was ridiculous.

He looked away from it and scowled at his class. He had had two unfortunate experiences with stink bombs, and in the back of his mind was the thought of having seen once, in a trick-store window, a product called "itching powder." Could this be it, this terrible itch? He knew better, however, than to accuse anyone yet; if he was wrong, there was no point in giving the little geniuses any extracurricular notions.

He tried again. "The cl—" He swallowed. This itch was ... "The class will—" He noticed that one head, then another and another, was turning toward the window. He realized that if the class got too interested in what he thought he saw on the window sill, he'd have a panic on his hands. He fumbled for his ruler and rapped twice on the desk. His control was not what it should have been at the moment; he struck far too hard, and the reports were like gunshots. The class turned to him as one, and behind them the thing on the window sill appeared with great distinctness.

It was blue—a truly beautiful blue. It has a small spherical head and an almost identical knob at the other end. There were four stiff, straight legs, a long, sinuous body, and two central limbs with a boneless look about them. On the side of the head were four pairs of eyes, of graduated sizes. It teetered there for perhaps ten seconds, and then, without a sound, leaped through the window and was gone.

Mr. Stott, pale and shaking, closed his eyes. His knees trembled and weakened, and a delicate, dewy mustache of perspiration appeared on his upper lip. He clutched at the desk and forced his eyes open; and then, flooding him with relief, pealing into his terror, swinging his control back to him, the bell rang to end the class and the school day.

"Dismissed," he mumbled, and sat down. The class picked up and left, changing itself from a twittering pattern of rows to a rowdy kaleidoscope around the bottleneck doorway. Mr. Stott slumped down in his chair, noticing that the dreadful itch was gone, had been gone since he had made that thunderclap with the ruler.

Now, Mr. Stott was a man of method. Mr. Stott prided himself on his ability to teach his charges to use their powers of observation and all the machinery of logic at their command. Perhaps, then, he had more of both at his command—after he recovered himself— than could be expected of an ordinary man.

He sat and stared at the open window, not seeing the sun-swept lawns outside. And after going over these events a half-dozen times, he fixed on two important facts:

First, the animal he had seen, or thought he had seen, had six legs.

Second, that the animal was of such a nature as to make anyone who had not seen it believe he was out of his mind.

These two thoughts had their corollaries:

First, that every animal he had ever seen which had six legs was an insect.

Second, that if anything was to be done about this fantastic creature, he had better do it by himself. And whatever action he took must be taken immediately. He imagined the windows being kept shut to keep the thing out—in this heat—and he cowered away from the thought. He imagined the effect of such a monstrosity if it bounded into the midst of a classroom full of children in their early teens, and he recoiled. No, there could be no delay in this matter.

He went to the window and examined the sill. Nothing. There was nothing to be seen outside, either. He stood thoughtfully for a moment, pulling on his lower lip and thinking hard. Then he went downstairs to borrow five pounds of DDT powder from the janitor for an "experiment." He got a wide, flat wooden box and an electric fan, and set them on a table he pushed close to the window. Then he sat down to wait, in case, just in case the blue beast returned.

When the hurkle kitten fell into the flame, it braced itself for a fall at least as far as the floor of the cabinet. Its shock was tremendous, then, when it found itself so braced and already resting on a surface. It looked around, panting with fright, its invisibility reflex in full operation.

The cabinet was gone. The flame was gone. The laboratory with its windows, lit by the orange Lirhtian sky, its ranks of shining equipment, its hulking, complex machine—all were gone.

The hurkle kitten sprawled in an open area, a sort of lawn. No colors were right; everything seemed half-lit, filmy, out of focus. There we trees, but they were not low and flat and bushy like honest Lirhtian trees; these had straight naked trunks and leaves like a portle's tooth. The different atmospheric gases had colors; clouds of fading, changing faint colors obscured and revealed everything. The kitten twitched its cafmors and ruddled its kump, right there where it stood, for no amount of early training could overcome a shock like this.

It gathered itself together and tried to move, and then it got its second shock. Instead of arching over inchworm-wise, it floated into the air and came down three times as far as it had ever jumped in its life.

It cowered on the dreamlike grass, darting glances all about, under, and up. It was lonely and terrified and felt very much put upon. It saw its shadow through the shifting haze, and the sight terrified it even more, for it had no shadow when it was frightened on Lirht. Everything here was all backwards and wrong way up; it got more visible, instead of less, when it was frightened; its legs didn't work right, it couldn't see properly, and there wasn't a single, solitary malapek to be throdded anywhere. It thought some music; happily, that sounded all right inside its round head, though somehow it didn't resonate as well as it had.

It tried, with extreme caution, to move again. This time its trajectory was shorter and more controlled. It tried a small, grounded pace, and was quite successful. Then it bobbed for a moment, seesawing on its flexing middle pair of legs, and, with utter abandon, flung itself skyward. It went up perhaps fifteen feet, turning end over end, and landed with its stiff forefeet in the turf.

It was completely delighted with this sensation. It gathered itself together, gryting with joy, and leapt up again. This time it made more distance than altitude, and bounced two long, happy bounces as it landed.

Its fears were gone in the exploration of this delicious new freedom of motion. The hurkle, as has been said before, is a happy beast.

It curveted and sailed, soared and somersaulted, and at last brought up against a brick wall with stunning and unpleasant results. It was learning, the hard way, a distinction between weight and mass. The effect was slight but painful. It drew back and stared forlornly at the bricks. Just when it was beginning to feel friendly again ...

It looked upward, and saw what appeared to be an opening in the wall some eight feet above the ground. Overcome by a spirit of high adventure, it sprang upward and came to rest on a window sill—a feat of which it was very proud. It crouched there, preening itself, and looked inside.

It saw a most pleasing vista. More than forty amusingly ugly animals, apparently imprisoned by their lower extremities in individual stalls, bowed and nodded and mumbled. At the far end of the room stood a taller, more slender monster with a naked head—naked compared with those of the trapped ones, which were covered with hair like a mawson's egg. A few moments' study showed the kitten that in reality only one side of the heads was hairy; the tall one turned around and began making tracks in the end wall, and its head proved to be hairy on the other side too.

The hurkle kitten found this vastly entertaining. It began to radiate what was, on Lirht, a purr, or glow. In this fantastic place it was not visible; instead, the trapped animals began to respond with most curious writhings and squirmings and sussurant rubbings of their hides with their claws. This pleased the kitten even more, for it loved to be noticed and it redoubled the glow. The receptive motions of the animals became almost frantic.

Then the tall one turned around again. It made a curious sound or two. Then it picked up a stick from the platform before it and brought it down with a horrible crash.

The sudden noise frightened the hurkle kitten half out of its wits. It went invisible; but its visibility system was reversed here, and it was suddenly outstandingly evident. It turned and leaped outside, and before it reached the ground, a loud metallic shrilling pursued it. There were gabblings and shufflings from the room which added force to the kitten's consuming terror. It scrambled to a low growth of shrubbery and concealed itself among the leaves.

Very soon, however, its irrepressible good nature returned. It lay relaxed, watching the slight movement of the stems and leaves—some of them may have been flowers—in a slight breeze. A winged creature came humming and dancing about one of the blossoms. The kitten rested on one of its middle legs, shot the other out, and caught the creature in flight. The thing promptly jabbed the kitten's foot with a sharp black probe. This the kitten ignored. It ate the thing, and belched. It lay still for a few minutes, savoring the sensation of the bee in its clarfel. The experiment was suddenly not a success. It ate the bee twice more and then gave it up as a bad job.

It turned its attention again to the window, wondering what those racks of animals might be up to now. It seemed very quiet up there. . . . Boldly the kitten came from hiding and launched itself at the window again. It was pleased with itself; it was getting quite proficient at precision leaps in this mad place. Preening itself, it balanced on the window sill and looked inside.

Surprisingly, all the smaller animals were gone. The larger one was huddled behind the shelf at the end of the room. The kitten and the animal watched each other for a long moment. The animal leaned down and stuck something into the wall.

Immediately there was a mechanical humming sound and something on the platform near the window began to revolve. The next thing the kitten knew it was enveloped in a cloud of pungent dust.

It choked and became as visible as it was frightened, which was very. For a long moment it was incapable of motion; gradually, however, it became conscious of a poignant, painfully penetrating sensation which thrilled it to the core. It gave itself up to the feeling. Wave after wave of agonized ecstasy rolled over it, and it began to dance to the waves. It glowed brilliantly, though the emanation served only to make the animal in the room scratch hysterically.

The hurkle felt strange, transported. It turned and leaped high into the air, out from the building.

Mr. Stott stopped scratching. Disheveled indeed, he went to the window and watched the odd sight of the blue beast, quite invisible now, but coated with dust, so that it was like a bubble in a fog. It bounced across the lawn in huge floating leaps, leaving behind it diminishing patches of white powder in the grass. He smacked his hands one on the other and, smirking, withdrew to straighten up. He had saved the Earth from battle, murder, and bloodshed forever, but he did not know that. No one ever found out what he had done. So he lived a long and happy life.

And the hurkle kitten?

It bounded off through the long shadows, and vanished in a copse of bushes. There it dug itself a shallow pit, working drowsily, more and more slowly. And at last it sank down and lay motionless, thinking strange thoughts, making strange music, and racked by strange sensations. Soon even its slightest movements ceased, and it stretched out stiffly, motionless. . . .

For about two weeks. At the end of that time, the hurkle, no longer a kitten, was possessed of a fine, healthy litter of just under two hundred young. Perhaps it was the DDT, and perhaps it was the new variety of radiation that the hurkle received from the terrestrial sky, but they were all parthenogenetic females, even as you and I.

And the humans? Oh, we *bred* so! And how happy we were!

But the humans had the slidy itch, and the scratchy itch, and the prickly or tingly or titillative paresthetic formication. And there wasn't a thing they could do about it.

So they left.

Isn't this a lovely place?

Story Notes

by Paul Williams

"Quietly": unpublished until now. Probably written in late 1947. Recently discovered amidst the author's papers in storage at the home of his estate's trustee. This was intended as the beginning of a novel; as far as we know it was Theodore Sturgeon's first start on a piece of writing that he conceived of as a book-length novel. It is included in this collection on the editor's judgment that it can in fact be read as a short story (and despite the puzzling or intriguing circumstance that there is no evidence of Sturgeon ever having offered this unfinished novel-start to any magazine or other possible market as a story). One year later (late 1948) he did begin writing what became his first completed and published novel, *The Dreaming Jewels*.

It is quite surprising, and perhaps a sufficient explanation as to why Sturgeon did not find the inspiration or motivation/energy to complete *Quietly,* that this first conscious effort at writing a book-length work of fiction was not in the fantasy or science fiction genres, but was quite unambiguously a "mainstream" (i.e., non-genre) story or novel.

The manuscript I found is untitled, and consists of 23 double-spaced typewritten pages, with the author's family name in the upper left corner (indicating he was writing and typing with the idea that this draft might someday be submitted for publication). The last page ends at the normal page-bottom and the last paragraph ends in the middle of a line of type, indicating that the paragraph is complete. There are no apparently related manuscript pages among Sturgeon's papers, and it seems very likely that the bottom of page 23 is where Sturgeon paused in this attempt sometime before writing the following comments to his mother in a letter dated January 2, 1948:

[after a page and a half describing stories he has sold or failed to sell to various markets and telling of recent sales to anthologies and of his effort to sell his magazine short novel "Killdozer!" to a mainstream publisher (Simon and Schuster) and of his forthcoming first book (from a small specialty press, his first collection of stories, *Without Sorcery*)...] *And then there's my novel, if I can only get it done. It's called QUIETLY, and it's about a girl who is also called Quietly. Her father was a hermit who brought her up to be truly self-sufficient. Just as THE FOUNTAINHEAD (Ayn Rand) deals with the discovery of Ego as the important individual factor, rather than the ever-popular Alter (heroes are always kind and good) so QUIETLY will bring out the importance of We— not altruistic We; altruism is essentially a third-person motivation; but a first-person-plural, utterly subjective We. Quietly, at the age of eighteen, finds herself locked out of her father's house, naked, and eighteen years of age, and [with] the certain knowledge that she must leave, live among people, and stay away for a year. Her thinking is simple and functional; her success is as complete as her unhappiness; her enlightenment comes with her full evaluation of that We. With it comes the terrible realization that her deified father is a twisted, sick old escapist.*

I really don't know if I'll finish it this year; I intend to let it write itself.

It's clear from Sturgeon's comments elsewhere that he regarded some of his finest and most-acclaimed stories—i.e. "Bianca's Hands," "It," "Killdozer!"—as having "written themselves" in the sense that the story flowed from him very easily as soon as he wrote the first sentence or passed another turning point in the narrative or in the writing experience. Evidently he had hopes that one day he would sit down to write page 24 of *Quietly* and the flood-gates would open. But this was not to happen. Instead, at the end of the year, he found himself writing a different and more specifically fantastic novel about the journey-into-the-world of a young person who'd been raised by a difficult father. Different sort of difficult, and a different sort of novel. I will describe the somewhat strained circumstances of the birth of that novel, *The Dreaming Jewels*, at the conclusion of these story notes.

But what is most striking about "Quietly" is not its remote thematic connection to *The Dreaming Jewels* but the unmistakable parallels between it and the opening scenes of Theodore Sturgeon's most acclaimed and most beloved and influential piece of writing, his 1953 novel *More than Human*.

In light of Sturgeon's comments to his mother (above) about "the importance of We," it is not unreasonable to suggest that *More than Human* may indeed be the novel Sturgeon had the scent of when he started *Quietly* sometime in late 1947. It just took a long gestation (five years) before it was ready to write itself.

The text of "Quietly" does not in any way foreshadow the *homo gestalt* theme of *More than Human*. Only Sturgeon's announcement to his mother that his intention is to explore what "We" means (subjectively) to humans, hints at the extraordinarily powerful theme and vision that the 1953 novel *More than Human* would explore and express.

The text of "Quietly" does bear considerable resemblance to vital (and very powerful in establishing the reader's relationship to the characters of the novel and to its narrative conceit and voice) elements of the opening scenes of "The Fabulous Idiot," the first section of *More than Human*. "Baby Is Three," the middle section of the novel, was written well before "The Fabulous Idiot," which was written when Ballantine Books asked Sturgeon to make a novel out of the very well-received magazine novella "Baby Is Three." Looking (in himself perhaps) for the part of the story that could believably and effectively lead up to and lay the emotional groundwork for the situation in "Baby Is Three," Sturgeon evidently (and either consciously or unconsciously) found himself back in the world of "Quietly"—the young woman (in the case of *More than Human*, women) raised by the insane, obsessive hermit father, and her very unusual interaction with and perspective on humanity and civilization as a result.

The nature of the two fathers' obsessions is quite different in the two stories; yet the similarity in the situations is remarkable, particularly that in each case the father focuses on extreme "home schooling" techniques—on education as well as isolation—to try to create in his daughter or daughters his own ideal or wished-for perfect state. (He wants to reclaim the Garden of Eden by reprogramming or reeducating Eve, one might say.) A few noteworthy parallels between the texts of "Quietly" and of the first section of *More than Human*:

1) Quietly's mother and Alicia and Evelyn's mother both die in childbirth. *Alicia was four when little Evelyn had been born and their mother had died cursing* [their father], *her indignation at last awake and greater than her agony and her fear.* When Quietly was born, *Her father was lost in his studies.... Her mother lay still by the light of a candle. The peak of her suffering came to her swiftly.... The breath whistled out of her delicate, quivering nostrils; and then she decided to draw no more, and in silence she trembled and died.*

2) Quietly is eighteen when her father locks her out of their house in the woods and the action of the novel begins. Alicia is celebrating her nineteenth birthday when the idiot, Lone, crawls under the picket fence surrounding their house in the woods and her father kills her sister and the action of the novel begins.

3) Each father is described as living in a large, isolated house and spending a lot of time in his study with his very old books.

4) Each daughter is successfully isolated from contact with the entire human world outside her house throughout her childhood.

5) In both texts the father's education of his daughter specifically includes him teaching her his definition of "evil."

6) Sturgeon describes to his mother an intended climax of the novel as [Quietly's] *terrible realization that her deified father is a twisted, sick old escapist.* This scene is actually included in *More than Human* (ironically on pages 23–24 of most paperback editions), when Alicia Kew realizes her father was mad, and curses him as her mother did before her.

A number of themes that are important in Sturgeon's later work surface in this fragment called "Quietly." The idea that "civilized" people may be driven by their fear of being alone plays an important part in Sturgeon's 1953 response to/portrait of McCarthyism, "Mr. Costello, Hero."

In his 1/2/48 letter quoted above, Sturgeon indicates that one model or stimulus for this non-sf polemical novel of ideas that he wants to write is Ayn Rand's *The Fountainhead*. In another letter to his mother (who was living in Scotland at the time) on July 4, 1947, he tells her he is planning to marry the singer he's living with, Mary Mair, and writes, *Jay Stanton, on hearing that our first child will be called Ayn (after the remarkable author of the remarkable FOUNTAINHEAD) Mair Sturgeon, said "Ayn Mair is e'en enow..."*

When Sturgeon in the 1/2/48 letter speaks of *The Fountainhead* and says his novel *Quietly* will bring out the importance of an "utterly subjective 'We'" this can be understood as a distinction to Rand's widely-discussed (her novel was published in 1943) philosophy of "objectivism."

The word "function" turns up several times in "Quietly": *Fear is a functional thing, and she was happy to yield to it when it had a function.* In still another letter to "Mum," dated 9/25/47, Sturgeon says in relation to his wish to get married: *I also want to make more children, and this time do it right ... they will be tall children and graceful, with good brains and good profiles and good bodies, and by God they'll have a sense of values. Keynote: Functionalism. Function is a thing which can find its place among large artificial values, as well as the verities ... hey, I'd like to tell you a codification which I have learned from Mary Mair. This sounds easy to say, but believe me, it has taken me nearly thirty years of reasonably intensive living to realize fully what it means. It can be stated as an axiom and a couple of corollaries:*

What is important is basic.

What is basic is by definition simple.

What is complicated is therefore not important.

See the note to "What Dead Men Tell" for more on this "codification," which can be found almost verbatim on the third page of "Quietly." Possibly Sturgeon's difficulties in his relationship with Mair throughout 1948 (they eventually married, briefly, in 1949) had an impact on his ability to go on writing this novel that year.

Regarding Quietly's efforts, when she first encounters other humans (the girls in the lake), to recall what she had learned from her father about "the clothing convention": Sturgeon when he wrote this was already a practicing nudist. TS to A. Bertram Chandler, 5/16/48: *When TAN (The American Nudist—Phil Klass dreamed up that cute acrostic) comes out this year I'll do a colyum for it, the purpose of which will be to inject the light touch as far as possible...will call it THE NAKED EYE... If organized nudism could speak with the high-hearted idiom of its full membership, the outsider's view of 'crackpot' and 'fetishist' would be quickly and forcibly revised. These are real people—a higher percentage of true values than in any other resort group I ever ran into. What else can you expect when people are forced to stand or fall on their merits as people, and not because of wealth or position or origin?*

"The Music": written in 1947 or early 1948; first published in Sturgeon's story collection *E Pluribus Unicorn* in 1953.

In a letter to his Lower East Side neighbor Armand Winfield, April 12, 1948, Sturgeon wrote: *Have you made the NEUROTICA connection yet? I have a couple more suitable yarns for them, but won't show them any more unless they evince some real interest. I have a pretty good potential spot for THE MUSIC, by the way; would appreciate NEUROTICA's prompt report. It really is good of you to try this contact for me.*

Neurotica was a New-York-based literary magazine, described by Ann Charters as "an early counterculture magazine." In 1950 it printed one of Allen Ginsberg's first published poems. This is the only instance I know of of Sturgeon attempting to be published in a literary magazine.

The original manuscript of this story is among Sturgeon's papers and its text is identical to the 1953 book version, suggesting that when Sturgeon decided to include this unpublished piece in his second short story collection, he made no changes in what he'd written years earlier.

This story has also been published under the title "In the Hospital," in a mystery magazine in 1962.

"Unite and Conquer": first published in *Astounding Science-Fiction*, October 1948. Purchased (and presumably written) in early 1948.

In the previous volume I quoted TS in 1949 saying his story "Thunder and Roses" *was written in 1947 out of a black depression caused by the uncaring reception of books like* One World or None *by a public happy to goad the United Nations into a state of yapping uselessness.* The plot/theme of "Unite and Conquer" presumably has similar origins. But to understand the historical context in which readers of *Astounding* read this novelette in 1948, it is useful to know that *One World or None,* a 1946 book by atomic scientists trying to awaken humanity to its post-Hiroshima circumstances, derived its title from a 1943 bestseller by former presidential candidate Wendell Willkie called *One World.* In Doris Kearns Goodwin's book *No Ordinary Time,* she speaks of President Roosevelt's "change of heart" regarding the political acceptability of discussing, while war still raged in 1943, the sort of cooperation between nations that a meaningful peace would require. "His change of heart," writes Goodwin, "could be traced to the phenomenal success of Wendell Willkie's book, *One World.* No book in American publishing history had ever sold so fast. Within two months of its publication, sales had reached a million copies. Based on Willkie's travels through Russia, China, and the Middle East, the book was an eloquent plea for international cooperation to preserve the peace." So Sturgeon in 1947 and 1948 was disappointed that an American public that had briefly shown great interest in the idea of world cooperation seemed to have lost interest only a few years after the founding of the United Nations and the dropping of the first atomic bomb. We can imagine him asking himself, What would it take for us to overcome our emotional attachment to nationalism?

"Unite and Conquer" is one of a number of Theodore Sturgeon stories ("Memorial," 1946; "Brownshoes," 1969; "Occam's Scalpel," 1971) that explore the circumstances in which one person, acting alone, might have the power to save or awaken the world. It is reasonable to assume the author identified with these protagonists. On April 22nd, 1939 he wrote to his fiancee: *Here's another feeling I have had for years, my darling, that I may now tell you; from the bottom of my soul I have a deep conviction that some day the consequences of something I will do or say or write are going to have a profound effect on the entire world. In what way I do not know; with what effect to me and mu* [me and you] *I do not know; but I do know that it will happen. Odd, too, since I am not generically a revolutionist...*

He goes on to speak of the power of love: *What have you done to me, princess consort? Look at me now! Look at what you have given me! Look at that in which I exult! Because of you I am a Messiah. Is that too unbelievable? But what is a Messiah? He who changes a world ... no? He who brings a great and gentle influence to bear on things about him. And why can I say this? Because I know that I love you as you love me, and that you have brought such a change into my world, and that therefore I have done the same for you...*

When Sturgeon was asked in 1969 what authors had influenced him the most, H. G. Wells was the first name he mentioned. *Wells had something to do with it,* as Dr. Simmons tells his brother in "Unite and Conquer."

Editor's "blurb" atop the first page of the story in *Astounding*: OLD AS HUMAN GOVERNMENT IS THE FACT THAT A DISUNITED POPULATION WILL UNITE TO REPEL THE ALIEN INVADER. BUT THAT WAS SOMETHING THE ALIEN INVADER HADN'T COUNTED ON, PERHAPS! This story was voted best-in-the-issue in the readers' poll, even though its competition was the first installment of one of A.E. van Vogt's popular "Null-A" novels.

"The Love of Heaven": first published in *Astounding Science-Fiction,* November 1948.

In an undated letter to Judith Merril, probably mid-1949, Sturgeon talks of stories already written. One is called "Blight," presumably his original title for this story. He refers to it as *the new mystical Sturgeon.*

A 1949 letter to TS from his young friend (and fellow sf writer) Chan Davis says, "It's easy for me to understand why you didn't get charged by 'The Love of Heaven.' Some of the things that are best about it are things you do automatically, tho not usually so well: The correctness of the characters' attitudes & reactions; the justeness of the mots (particularly the alien's groping for words, which is something most writers can't do convincingly); the careful plot completely in accord with the logic of the situation. On this last point, the most impressively correct angle was the fact that the alien clearly didn't realize himself when he left that his people wd come back to Earth, yet the reader can see that they'll have to, & why, & how. Some of the things that aren't so good you did automatically too: The episode of the dog, which *sounded* automatic; & the excessive superness of the alien. I wonder how the story wd have turned out if you'd been in love with it the way you've been with some of your good stories (& some of your bad ones)."

The word "Dalinese" in the description of the stranger departing in his matter transmitter is a reference to the surrealist painter Salvador Dali. Dali was a hero of Sturgeon's, a kind of role-model. In July 1944, TS wrote to his mother, about Dali's illustrated autobiography, *The Secret Life of Salvador Dali: It is totally unlike anything I have ever read, and the illustrations are really out of this world. It is full of the strangest kind of bragging, the most incredible sexual motivations, and glimpses of sane, cool beauty that make you gasp for breath. Some of it is riotous. He tells on himself—I might say he kisses and tells on himself, with more accuracy—and throughout he dares you to call him crazy, or a braggart, or anything else. In every instance he's beaten you to it, particularly when you finally find out just how much salt to use and admit to yourself that he is a genius.*

Magazine blurb: FOR THEM, THE LOVE OF THE WORLDLY THINGS AND THE LOVE OF HEAVEN WERE MUCH ALIKE— AND IN THAT THEY WERE FOREVER UNTOUCHABLE!

"Till Death Do Us Join": first published in *Shock*, July 1948. Written early 1948. Sturgeon's original title was "The Rivals."

TS to his mother, 7/6/48: *Sold a story to new magazine recently which was a honey; the magazine was just what I've been looking for for years, ever since UNKNOWN folded. This one did too... A* letter to TS from Erik Fennel, who apparently had also been writing for the magazine, says, "That's tough about SHOCK. Damn it, that was a good pulp with a novel slant, and was actually beginning to pull away from a few of the usual taboos and make something of itself. It must have been rough on you, having it blow in your face that way." July 1948 was the final issue of the magazine.

In his 1953 essay "Why So Much Syzygy?" Sturgeon lists some of the different "investigations" into "this matter of love, sexual and asexual" that he has attempted in stories over the years, and says: *In "Until Death Do Us Join" [sic] it was the murderous jealousy between two personalities in a schizophrenic, both in love with the same girl.* He notes that: *"Bianca's Hands" and "The World Well Lost" cause the violently extreme reactions they do because of the simple fact that the protagonist was happy with the situation. No one was churned up (in these areas) by "Until Death Do Us Join" because the crazy mixed-up little guy was killed in the end.*

Magazine blurb: SANDRA WAS HAUNTED BY THE CHAMELEON MAN WHO STOLE A MARCH ON PAUL—AND TOOK THEM TO A MIDNIGHT FUNERAL.

"The Perfect Host": first published in *Weird Tales*, November 1948.

In a letter to his mother in the fall of 1948, TS wrote, *Something very nice happened to me yesterday. I have an outlet for the literary forms of my catharses, the doughty WEIRD TALES, which doesn't pay much but leaves its gates open to such mouthings as I put out from time to time when I feel that way. I had the lead in the November issue this year, a yarn called THE PERFECT HOST. In one sequence a man grieved for his wife, and I got a letter yesterday from South Africa containing a poem, an epitaph for the girl. It was a bit crude, but nicely put together; at the third reading I realized that the poet, one Desmond Bagley, had put the whole thing together, almost without alteration, with lines from the story. It is good to feel that something of one's own can have not only reflective, but creative and recreative effects.*

So we may thank the open gates of *Weird Tales* for giving Theodore Sturgeon the freedom to experiment with form and style—

to start with, "The Perfect Host" is a narrative told powerfully and effectively from eight different points of view, in eight very different voices—in ways that would have enormous impact on almost every writer of science fiction and fantasy during the next five decades.

"Because of Sturgeon other writers have been freer to write what they wished to write and able to find a market for it." —James Gunn, in *Alternate Worlds, The Illustrated History of Science Fiction* (1975).

"The most important science fiction writer of the forties was probably Theodore Sturgeon.... What Sturgeon did was to keep open the possibility for a kind of science fiction that eventually many others came to do.... In his use of style, internalization and quirky characterization he was keeping the door open for everything that happened after 1950. If Sturgeon had not established that the literature could be style-oriented ... no basis would have existed upon which writers within the field could build." —Barry Malzberg, in *The Engines of the Night* (1982).

Commenting on Sturgeon's 1952 story "The Sex Opposite," James Blish complained that Sturgeon was writing too many stories about "syzygy" (defined in that story as *a non-sexual interflow between the nuclei of two animals*) and said Sturgeon had already handled the subject "definitively" in "The Perfect Host." In a 1953 letter to the editor of the magazine Blish's comments appeared in, Sturgeon quoted the editor as having said, "without sexual pleasure there would be no passionate attachments between humans," and then wrote: *I think that in "Bianca's Hands" and "The Perfect Host" and in "The World Well Lost," and in the remarks just quoted, we have sufficient material for the tentative establishment of a lowest common denominator* [in Sturgeon's fiction].

"Sturgeon's failures, some of them, are as triumphant as his successes; they made the successes. Sturgeon is the most accomplished technician this field has produced,bar nobody, not even Bradbury; and part of the reason is that he never stops working at it. He tried writing about each character in a story in a different meter once— iambs for one, trochees for another—a trick, not viable, but it taught him something about rhythm in prose." —Damon Knight, in *In Search of Wonder, Essays on Modern Science Fiction*.

Like such related stories as "Blabbermouth" and "Ghost of a Chance" (see Volume III of *The Complete Stories of Theodore Sturgeon*), "The Perfect Host" blurs the line between fantasy and science fiction by firmly portraying the parasitic entity referred to in the title as a real (i.e., "scientific") energy creature which cohabits our physical as well as psychological universe. This is the basic Sturgeon theme: what is love? what is guilt? what is jealousy? what is curiosity? what is the gestalt "we" that empowers and oppresses humans? His answers always conjecture a science fictional universe in which these forces are living entities subject to physical laws, and even capable of interacting with the story's characters or even, in this case, with the story's readers. Not only does Sturgeon break the "fifth wall" between playwright and audience in section 7 of this story (becoming a sort of character in the story himself), he goes further in section 8, breaking a sixth wall by warning the reader that he or she may already have become infected by the parasite just by reading this far. Of course he had already made a similar radical leap and warning in the opening lines of "It Wasn't Syzygy" (1947). Sturgeon like Philip K. Dick doesn't just entertain the reader with fantastic tales, but actually corrupts/invades his or her reality. Metafiction indeed.

"The Martian and the Moron": first published in *Weird Tales*, March 1949.

Sturgeon's introduction to this story in his collection *Alien Cargo* (1984): *This is one of the first writings after that long period of silence* [1941-46; but there is reason to believe it was witten in 1948]. *Oddly enough it comes out as comedy—sheer joyous comedy for itself, with no effort to be metaphor or anything else but itself. The events concerning the cessation of all broadcasts during the near approach of Mars in the 'twenties, did indeed happen; and back in those days of newspaper articles about guys who built crystal sets into peanuts, of 100-foot braided copper antennas enabling you to pick up Chicago all the way from Philadelphia, late at night, of cats-whiskers and variocouplers (anybody out there know what a variocouple is? I mean, was?) back in those days, there was surely more than one*

THE PERFECT HOST

radio buff with flanged-up equipment like that "dad" built in his basement. As for that girl—I think I met that girl one time at a party. Nov shmoz ka pop!

In his 1965 childhood memoir (published in 1993 as *Argyll*), TS describes at some length his youthful passion for building and operating crystal radios. Certain very specific details used in "The Martian and the Moron"—the UX-11 tube and picking up WLS all the way from Chicago and learning later *that I probably yanked it off someone else's receiver by antenna induction*—also turn up in the autobiographical account. But unlike the Dad in the story, Sturgeon's stepfather was not a radio bug; in fact in *Argyll* TS tells the story of *getting in bad trouble over one of my radios.* This occurred because he told a local radio station about his clever rig that allowed him to keep his hobby a secret, and the announcer broadcast *the whole story, horsehair antenna and all. Few orgasms in my life have so transported me.* But his joy turned to terror when he realized his parents were listening to the broadcast in the next room. His radio and antenna system and workbench were all taken away from him. The gruff but loving father in "The Martian and the Moron" is strikingly different from the cruel stepfather portrayed in *The Dreaming Jewels,* written later in 1948.

In the David Hartwell interview in 1972 Sturgeon says Cordelia *was drawn largely from life.* The paragraph in this story where the disillusioned narrator says, *I remember wondering smokily whether anyone ever loves another person. People seem to love dreams instead,* reveals that this is another in the long series of stories in which TS tried to *investigate this matter of love.* Indeed, Sturgeon overtly draws a parallel here between the son's love for the Cordelia he thinks he sees and the father's love for his amateur science project. In various interviews and speeches Sturgeon has insisted that his study of "love" is not confined to sexual love but includes, for example, a man's love for a bulldozer.

"Die, Maestro, Die!": first published in *Dime Detective*, May 1949. Author's original title was "Fluke." We know this because that's how the story is listed on a handwritten list of "1948 Income" that survives

374

in Sturgeon's papers. (This list also provides a basis for guessing at the sequence in which his 1948 stories were written.) The copyright page of *E Pluribus Unicorn* suggests that TS intended to use the original title when the story was included in this collection; one imagines the publisher then talked him out of it (and forgot to correct the copyright page).

Since I have noted that 1947's "Quietly" foreshadows significant aspects of *More than Human* but not its "homo gestalt" theme, it is noteworthy that "Die, Maestro, Die!" is explicitly focused on the idea (Fluke's idea) that Lutch Crawford did not die when Fluke drowned his body, because he lived on stubbornly in the musical "unit" of his band. Fluke's problem is to find out what he can change in order to destroy that seemingly immortal *gestalt*. This is as far as I know the most specific exploration of the "homo gestalt" theme in Sturgeon's work before he wrote *More than Human*. It is particularly interesting that Sturgeon's interest in the concept evidently began with his observation of the nature of jazz bands he encountered in the 1940s ... because members of the Grateful Dead and the Byrds and other important 1960s rock groups have stated in interviews that the novel *More than Human* and its description of "bleshing" was to them the best and perhaps only description they encountered anywhere of what they were experiencing by working as a musical/creative/social group or unit or entity. "Phil Lesh had read *More than Human* by the time he joined the band that became the Grateful Dead. The book didn't exactly provide a blueprint for group consciousness, but it suggested to him that the possibility existed. Still, like the characters in the novel, the Grateful Dead didn't see the extent of their collective potential at first. 'We didn't declare it,' said Lesh in 1983, 'It declared us.' " —David Gans, in *Playing in the Band* (1985)

Among a pile of what Sturgeon called "maunderings" (ruminations on paper in an effort to come up with story ideas) Noël Sturgeon and I found in a cache of her father's papers in his former home in Woodstock, was a sheet of paper that evidently immediately preceded the writing of "Fluke." Atop the page is TS's address (*one seventy three monroe street new york two*) and the date (*April*

20, 1948). Then a heading: *THE BENEKE STORY.* Under that is the following text, broken up into paragraphs as you see here:

Hutch is dead. Shorty Glincka, alto man, picks it up. He had been arranging for Hutch. Hutch's wife, Fawn, is the thrush. She just soaks in the music from this band, which is kept as close as possible as it always was. Hutch has disappeared; she hangs on to the idea that he might walk in again. and the band has the same idea ... there's one guy who is a great comfort to her—Twill.

Glincka gets killed by a hit-and-run driver. The orchestra continues to play; hires an arranger. The guy quickly learns to style like Hutch; it becomes obvious that the distinctive tone of the orchestra comes from the instrumentalists. The guitarist gets attacked. That almost kills the orchestra; they get a filler for the spot, though, and go on. Then the trombone loses his lip, literally.

All through this Twill is holding Fawn's head.

Windup: Twill killed Hutch, psychopathically thinks Hutch isn't dead until he can kill the distinctiveness of the band.

Mech gimmick: final orchestra performance where Stan's guitar is standing on his chair. Orchestra plays around his part; on the second chorus the guitar comes in srong and Twill's reaction gives him away. Recording of selection has been made, and engineer has wiped out all but git part; plays recording thru guitar amplifier.

Under this is the beginning of another maundering, headed *CAT SKINNER STORY.* So Sturgeon was still in the process of trying to find a story that would "write itself" and be marketable, when he wrote the above. I am certain that what we know as "Die, Maestro, Die!" did indeed write itself once TS decided to use Twill/Fluke as the viewpoint character/narrator, and wrote the opening paragraph.

Sturgeon's keen interest in progressive jazz orchestras is further demonstrated in a letter he wrote on May 11, 1948, to Stan Kenton (c/o Capitol Records):

Dear Stan Kenton,

Can you admit honestly that you have made a mistake?

If you can't, then resign. Resign from your place in my estimation as a phenomenon, as a free man among men chained, as a synonym for the progressive, the experimental, the singular exponent of new directions.

In the name of quality, in the name of aesthetic consistency, of truth at its artistic truest—admit that you have been wrong. And then in the name of all the verities, correct your terrible error!

THIS IS MY THEME is a remarkable work. Lyric like that is thirstily needed now, and the music—you know about the music, and why you do music like that. These lyrics suit that music—an astonishing feat in itself. I know of two works which match it—the extraordinary FACADE SUITE of Sitwell and Walton, and THE MEDIUM of Gion-Carlo Menotti.

The thing that makes murder in THIS IS MY THEME is the rendition of the lyrics by June Christy. Let this not be read as a personal criticism of June Christy or of any of her other work; she has always justified your judgment. But she is completely unsuited to a work of this kind. Had she been confined to a monotone, even, she might have done the trick—that may even have been effective, letting the words, not the diction, carry the message, even as these black and white letters carry my message to you. But the emotion she pretends to put into her recitatif is nothing real; if she feels it, she lacks the ability to transmit or even to transmute harmonically the deep beauty of those flexing, fluxing words. What you have here, then, is an artistic offense far worse than, for example, Freddy Martin's treatment of Tschaikovsky; for at least Tschaikovsky's work has fine renditions extant for reference, while your masterpiece has none.

You will not always be where you are. You will be greater or less great, but only at this period can you reproduce the mood, the music, the instrumentals of your curent organization. You will change, your outfit will change—and suddenly it will be impossible to duplicate the greatness of the almost-great thing you have done.

Please, then, while you can—re-record THIS IS MY THEME with someone else doing the vocal. There are a thousand known people who could do it adequately—and probably a hundred thousand unknowns, to whom the assignment would be a great chance. That is a side issue, however; the important thing is to put this astounding work on the plane it deserves. It is being laughed at and ignored—not as were Satie and Ravel and Honegger, for sheer difference, but for its one gaping flaw, a ridiculous incompetence in one component part.

Do it at any cost, and quickly: "It is later than you think!" and remember—THIS IS MY THEME is greater, far greater, than Stan Kenton, and deserves his best.

I ardently wish to keep myself from intruding at all in this matter, but I am compelled to say that this is written for no reason at all except my high regard for the high roads of esthetic expression, and my complete disgust with any "almost." I have no nominations for this new vocal job, and ask only that you talk this thing over with yourself within the framework set forth here.

Sincerely,

Theodore Sturgeon

Kenton's reply to TS begins, "First of all I want you to know that out of all the mail I have received, either praising us or otherwise, I don't think I have ever received one more sincere than yours. This I appreciate.

"I realize fully and completely my mistake and wish there was some way to un-do it, but it is just not possible. The current recording ban makes recording music of any kind completely out of the question..."

Although it has often been said, by Sturgeon and others, that most of his stories are about love, he has also written a number of major stories that explore the nature of hatred. "Die, Maestro, Die!" is a prime example, as noted by Betty Ballantine (his editor on *More than Human* and several other books) in her appreciation of TS published in *Locus* after his death: "Someone has said, and many have made their own discovery, that Ted always wrote of love. I think also that there was a perverse element in him, drawn to the scarlet thread of tragedy in the human condition, from the haunting quality of 'Bianca's Hands' to the pitiless cruelty of 'Die, Maestro, Die!' to the grand symphony of human idiocy that he put together to create *More than Human*." And by Samuel R. Delany, in his Foreword to the second volume of this series: "Dealing with such an awesome communion [his ongoing 'syzygy' theme], Sturgeon might well want to keep himself oriented toward love. It would be rather heady, if not horrifying, to explore that communion without such a fixed point to home on—though a few times Sturgeon has given us a portrait of this communion with the orientation toward hate ('Die, Maestro, Die!' and 'Mr. Costello, Hero'), and these are among his most powerful stories."

Later in 1948, when Sturgeon began his novel *The Dreaming Jewels*, he would return to the theme of hatred and the graphic image of the chopping off of a person's fingers.

"The Dark Goddess": unpublished until now. This manuscript was among Sturgeon's papers with a letter dated June 18, 1948 from the Fiction Editor of *Cosmopolitan* Magazine, who says, "Dear Mr. Sturgeon: I very much regret that your manuscript was not one of the twelve winners in the *Cosmopolitan* Dark Goddess short story contest. However, I think you will be pleased to know that it was among the final hundred seriously considered out of almost six thousand which were submitted. We shall be glad to consider any stories which you may write in the future, and want to thank you very much for this excellent attempt." Together with the ms. and this letter is a photo of the dark goddess figurine as described in the story, so evidently the contest was to write a story inspired by this picture/object.

On the title page, Sturgeon typed: "THE DARK GODDESS by Theodore Sturgeon." Under this is typed: "Subtitle: ... MORE TO A MARRIAGE..."

The author's own unconventional ideas about marriage are hinted at in a letter he wrote to a lady-friend named Marcia on Dec. 29, 1946: *My wife is with me always, and yet she is known to me by different names. For a long time she wore a garment called Dorothe. My wife, who is always with me, could be touched and spoken with through the garment called Dorothe. My wife was with me in this form for several years, and just as there is change in all things that are truly alive, so there was change in my wife and in Dorothe. For three years or more they changed together, and my wife wore the garment called Dorothe with grace and distinction. But then Dorothe changed, while my wife followed her own growing, and the garment began to fit badly. Not badly—differently. Dorothe was good and my wife was good but they grew increasingly apart. As a result my wife took off the garment called Dorothe and became invisible. She has been a strange wife to live with since then...*

"**Scars**": first published in *Zane Grey's Western Magazine*, May 1949. Written in mid-1948. Sturgeon's working title for this story was "Chivalry."

Lucy Menger in her study *Theodore Sturgeon* (1981) says: " 'Scars' beautifully illustrates Sturgeon's growing sympathy for people, his developing psychological insight, and his increasing technical skill... His approach to sex in this story is typical of his approach to sex in later stories: frank but without sensationalism... Many of Sturgeon's technical skills as a writer come together in his portrait stories. In these, the protagonist's subjective experience provides the framework and tone for the narrative. 'Scars' is probably the prototype of this genre."

Theodore Sturgeon from a recorded conversation with Paul Williams, April 5, 1978: *Yeah. Sometimes not knowing is a great advantage. I sometimes think of one of the best stories I've ever written—it's called "Scars," a western story, remember? And years later I got ahold of a copy of the journal of the Western Writers of America, and in there someone had witten an article about the clichés that one does not do in writing a western story. And virtually at the head of the list was, "A cowboy is riding along, comes around a rock and some girl is bathing naked in a stream. If that story occurs to you, don't write it!" And I didn't know that, when I wrote one of the best stories I've ever written in my life. If I had known that, as soon as the thing occurred to me I'd have said, "No, I can't do that." I wouldn't have had a story. So sometimes it pays to be ignorant.*

"**Messenger**": first published in *Thrilling Wonder Stories*, February 1949.

Magazine blurb: THERE IS MORE THAN ONE WAY TO SKIN A RAT—AS THE OLD SCIENTIST DISCOVERS

"Minority Report": first published in *Astounding Science-Fiction,* June 1949.

In a rubric written in 1980 for an unpublished collection called *Slow Sculpture,* TS said of "Minority Report": *A very early story. It has nice hardcore s-f content, but the one thing that interests me most is the hulking wordless character on the space-ship, who looks like an ape and thinks like a poet/philosopher. He appears again in another story (not here) called "The World Well Lost" [1953] and in another costume in a story called "Need" [1960]. This guy is very real to me—more so than many I have met in the flesh; yet to my most intense recollection, I have never met or seen anyone like him. I can report a blinding shock of recognition when I read (years after "Minority") Richard McKenna's unforgettable "Casey Agonistes" [1958].*

There is a strong parallel between the themes of "The Love of Heaven" and "Minority Report." In the former early humanoids are separated from their beloved homeland (our Earth) because their biochemistry is somehow poisonous to current Earth life forms. "Minority Report" recounts humanity's experience of discovering in 2700 AD that it is similarly alienated from most of the inhabited universe because we turn out to be misfits in the cosmos, made out of antimatter. And thus forced to accept and live with a vast aloneness.

Magazine blurb: A FASCINATING BASIC IDEA; MANKIND FACED WITH THE HOPELESS PROBLEM OF BEING ALL DRESSED UP WITH INTERSTELLAR SPACESHIPS, AND NO PLACE TO GO!

"Prodigy" first published in *Astounding Science-Fiction,* April 1949. Written in fall 1948.

Magazine blurb: HE WAS A VERY STRANGE CHILD—AND A STRANGE CHILD WAS SOMETHING THAT WORLD COULDN'T STAND. PARTICULARLY, THAT KIND OF STRANGENESS—

"Farewell to Eden" first published in *Invasion from Mars: Inter-planetary Stories,* edited by Orson Welles, a paperback book published in 1949 (Sturgeon's appearance in this collection may have been arranged by his friend Don Ward, who edited *Zane Grey's Western Magazine* and did some work for Dell paperbacks; the "1948 Income" page indicates that TS was paid $116. for this story at the end of '48 by "Dell—Ward").

"One Foot and the Grave": first published in *Weird Tales,* September 1949. Written in early 1949.

William F. Nolan, in his introduction to this story in his 1968 anthology *3 to the Highest Power,* says, "One Foot and the Grave" is full of Sturgeon's particular magic, his humor, his poetic images, his elfin girls, his ability to shock and delight; it is a story of fantasy and fear, beauty and suspense. And it takes place in deep woods . . . the woods of "It," the woods of New York, the dark, surprising mystery-brimming woods of Ted Sturgeon's childhood." *More than Human* and *Some of Your Blood* and "Quietly" are also partly set in those woods. (See note to "It" in Vol. I of *The Complete Short Stories of Theodore Sturgeon* for more on the location of the woods TS experienced as a child.) Nolan quotes Sturgeon as telling him, in a telephone interview, that he remembers Staten Island, where he spent the first eleven years of his life, as *a place of dark woods and mystery.*

"What Dead Men Tell": first published in *Astounding Science-Fiction,* November 1949. Written in early 1949. The title of this story was suggested by Richard Hoen, a reader of *Astounding* who wrote a letter to the editor published in the 11/48 issue, praising the stories in the 11/49 issue and naming those stories and their authors. The editor, John W. Campbell, Jr., decided to make the letter come true, and asked those writers (Heinlein, Asimov, van Vogt, del Rey, de Camp, Sturgeon) to write those stories. *Time* Magazine made mention of this stunt when the 11/49 issue hit the newstands; it was thereafter known to fans as "the predicted issue of *ASF.*"

Mary Mair's "codification" showing that "what is complicated is not important" (see notes to "Quietly") shows up again in "What Dead Men Tell," where it is cited as being at the heart of the young philosopher/protagonist's philosophy. Lucy Menger, in her critical study *Theodore Sturgeon*, is greatly provoked by this statement ("so what is complicated isn't important"). She calls it "an arrow aimed at the heart of intellectualism" and says, "With that one sentence, Sturgeon sweeps aside as of no importance all the intricacies and complexities the human intellect can uncover." She believes " 'What Dead Men Tell' was probably the peak of Sturgeon's anti-intellectualism."

"What Dead Men Tell" is one of the stories TS could be referring to in his 1983 Science Fiction Radio Show interview when he says, *I have been accused of inventing Velcro, which was in one of my stories about 15 years before it appeared on the market.*

One wonders if poet Michael McClure might have been influenced by this story when he wrote his play *The Beard*, a dialogue in eternity between Jean Harlow and Billy the Kid.

Magazine blurb: IT'S A CURIOUS THING THAT A CORPSE—A REMARKABLY NOTICEABLE OBJECT—CAN BE OVERLOOKED SO EASILY. ONE TENDS TO SHY AWAY, EVEN WHEN IT HAS A MESSAGE TO DELIVER—

"The Hurkle Is a Happy Beast": first published in the first issue of *The Magazine of Fantasy and Science Fiction*, fall 1949. Written at the end of April, 1949.

This was the last piece of fiction Sturgeon wrote until the beginning of 1950; in the second half of 1949 he was preoccupied with his new job in the promotion department of Time, Inc. and writing scripts for a television program that apparently never found a sponsor.

Anthony Boucher, coeditor of the new magazine, wrote to TS care of Prime Press on April 14, 1949 asking if he could write (on a short deadline) a short science fiction story "with human values, literacy and humor" for what would be called at first *The Magazine of Fantasy*. TS received the letter on April 23, and immediately wrote back, *It sounds like what I've been looking for for years. I started to write at the time* Unknown *was born, and became a stf writer by default. I'd rather write fantasy than anything else, and I can't because*

I can't market it and I have to eat... I'd much rather be known as a fantasist than a stf writer. But since Boucher's letter explained the publisher felt they should have "one pure stf [scientifiction] item" amongst the fantasy, TS did write this science fiction story and mailed it to Boucher on April 25, with this note:

Here's the HURKLE and I hope you like it.

I have another story in mind about Lirht and its gwiks and hurkles. This one concerns the gwik Hvov, who was an anti-religionist fanatic, dedicated to the destruction of the symbol of a certain sect. This symbol was two hollow cylinders joined at the top, and the destruction was always confined to the symbol, never to anything it might contain. When Hvov was exiled from Lirht through space-time, he arrived on earth and found himself surrounded by people wearing the detested symbol on their nether limbs. He built a radiating incunabulator coupled to a defriction lens and proceeded to dissolve the hated things wherever he found them.

In the mid-1950s, TS began one of his maundering sheets (efforts to talk himself into a story idea) with the following lines:

Oh, ye Shottle Bop!

Where is the light-hearted, character-filled, surprising and make-you-feel-good attitude of the Hurkle and the Brat? ... much of that stuff, like The Green-Eyed Monster ["Ghost of a Chance"], I wrote when I was in deep trouble and worried to death. There has to be more like it somewhere...

"The Hurkle Is a Happy Beast" has been included in at least ten different anthologies of science fiction stories published in the United States between 1950 and 1989. Theodore Sturgeon was in fact, during his lifetime, one of the most-anthologized living short story writers in the English language.

An additional note on the circumstances of the writing of *The Dreaming Jewels:*

Theodore Sturgeon's first novel, *The Dreaming Jewels* (also published as *The Synthetic Man*), was first published in the February 1950 issue of *Fantastic Adventures* magazine and as a hardcover book in August of 1950. When I interviewed TS for my introduction to the 1978 Gregg Press edition of the novel, he thought he had written it on assignment to go with an already painted cover—but when I showed him the *Fantastic Adventures* cover, which is inconsistent with the novel in various details, he agreed it couldn't have been that cover. New information has since become available to me which clarifies the actual circumstances of the writing of the novel (evidently not remembered by TS when we spoke in '78). In a letter to his mother dated July 5, 1949, Sturgeon says:

Last October Mary Mair and I broke up [later they got together again and eventually got married], *and I went into a tailspin. I tried to ship out and couldn't, and spent five or six weeks doing nothing because I was sure the phone would ring at any moment calling me to a ship. Things began to get desperate so I got to work on a magazine novel, working in close cahoots with the editor. I worked on it for nearly three no-income months and it was fine with him all the way; I felt I was justified in working on spec. It took a whole month for it to be read at his office and it got seven "pro" votes. Then the editorial director mysteriously and without precedent changed the policy of the magazine and rejected it out of hand, leaving me with dispossess notices, the gas and electricity shut off, my hospitalization and insurance policies lapsed, a demand note and threat of suit, doctor's and dentist's bills, and holes in my shoes in exchange for three months' work. A short while later...I was hired as Assistant Circulation Manager of the fabulous FORTUNE Magazine, a thing that had been in the works for 15 months... About three days after I went to work the accursed novel sold to another magazine, and then I got a television show to do which is going on the air towards the fall, DV* [Deo volente—God willing].

So *The Dreaming Jewels* was evidently written 11/48–2/49, probably between "Farewell to Eden" and "One Foot and the Grave."

Corrections and addenda:

Because the character Robin English in Sturgeon's story "Maturity" (revised in 1948) is so central to Sturgeon's body of work and such a primary influence on Robert Heinlein's magnum opus *Stranger in a Strange Land*, and because these notes might be the only biography this fine twentieth century storyteller receives, I think it is worthwhile to append here (one volume late) two paragraphs from a letter TS wrote to his parents at age 20, April 27, 1938, which speak eloquently of the extent to which Robin English and Michael Valentine Smith are modeled after the real Theodore Sturgeon:

While I am here I spend hours on Times Square. I can't understand the fools who blindly plow through it looking for somewhere to spend money most of them can't afford, when there is so much free entertainment going on all around them. There is a new Wilson Whiskey ad that—in a square of lights closely set like the band around the Times Building which gives news flashes, that presents a whole animated cartoon. I would dearly like to see the mechanism of that thing. That tremendous Wrigley sign is still there, with its brilliant bubbling fishes. The Salvation Army has procured a portable mike and amplifier and are there every night distributing paperback copies of Matthew. I have taken about fourteen of them because I get such a huge kick out of the little brunette who gives them out; she most obsequiously and humbly thanks me for her generosity. The last five or six times she has shown growing suspicion; I'm going to keep it up until she says something. Don't disapprove; the gospels aren't going to waste, as I leave them on the subway. Everyone leaves tracts in the subway; I am only doing my duty.

Then there is the popular grand opera at the Hip. I make it a point to meet someone interesting every time I go. I have stopped my very bad habit of following up such acquaintances; I find it either a nuisance or a disappointment or genuine trouble afterwards; hence I never mention my name or my place in the world, but just try to contribute by listening. It is of real value; since I have been doing all Pearl Zeid's English themes (she's in U. of P.) I often have some knotty problem in dramatics or dialectics or philosophy to clear up. I spot my victim: "Pardon me, sir, but what is the difference between urbanity and sophistication?" or "I beg your pardon, but I was wondering if censorship is good for movies and the moviegoer." You would be surprised at how few blank stares and cold shoulders I get, and how many people will bunch their brows and screw up their shoulders and attack the problem.